I0751920

AIDS TO THE STUDY OF DANTE

BY

CHARLES ALLEN DINSMORE

DANTE

Considered by a commission of the Italian government the most authentic likeness of Dante. See p. 159.

AIDS TO THE STUDY OF DANTE

BY

CHARLES ALLEN DINSMORE

BOSTON AND NEW YORK
HOUGHTON, MIFFLIN AND COMPANY
The Riverside Press, Cambridge
1903

Published September, 1903

Dedicated

TO

CHARLES ELIOT NORTON

WHOSE LOVE FOR DANTE
BEGINNING IN EARLY YEARS AND CONTINUING THROUGH
A LONG LIFE HAS BORNE FRUIT IN INVALUABLE
STUDIES AND TRANSLATIONS AND IN AN
UNFAILING COURTESY TOWARD
THOSE HAVING A LIKE
ENTHUSIASM

PREFACE

Dante lived in an age so different from our own that in order thoroughly to appreciate him much supplementary reading is necessary. One must know the time in which he lived, its fierce political contentions, its glowing religious ideals, and its conceptions of the structure of the universe. Yet one does not progress far in his reading without meeting constant references to certain original documents, such as the early lives of Dante and the letter to Can Grande. He will also learn that while he can profitably pass by the bulk of what has been written interpretative of Dante, there are essays so comprehensive and of such rare insight that they have become classics. These no lover of the poet should fail to read. Much of this indispensable collateral reading is inaccessible to those not living near large Dante collections. It is the threefold purpose of this book to present in a serviceable form the knowledge essential to the understanding of the poet as stated by the best authorities, the original documents most commonly quoted, and those interpretations which most clearly reveal the significance and greatness of Dante's work. It thus occupies a field of its own and in no way competes with the many excellent handbooks already at the disposal of the reader. Many will fail to find here what may seem to them indispensable. Dante presents so many interesting points of approach that only an ambitious encyclopædia could contain all that every reader might wish to find. Many Dante scholars have been consulted, and no two have agreed on what should go into the book. What one considered of great value another thought unimportant. The editor also begs to remind his reader that this volume makes no pretense of entering upon the details of Dante criticism. It offers "Aids" to the study of the poet; it does not pass upon all the questions which such a study may raise.

To those whose privilege it is to study Dante under an instructor no suggestions need be made. But for those less fortunate ones who enter alone into the labyrinth of mediæval thought a few hints on making this volume most helpful may not be out of place. The proper way to begin the study of Dante would be to take first the Vita Nuova and in connection with it to read chapter iv. of this book. Many, however, will begin with the more famous work. After one has read so far in the Comedy that he feels the need of a guide to make the poem understandable, it will be of advantage to get a clear idea of Dante's universe by studying the diagrams found on pages 254, 288, 304, 338. In connection with these it is well to read Dante's Cosmography, p. 231. One naturally turns after this to the Moral Topography of Hell, p. 287, and Table III. The Times of Dante and the Sources of our Knowledge of him will early claim attention. The reader of the Inferno will not proceed far before its revolting horrors will drive him to seek Dante's own explanation of his purpose as contained in the letter to Can Grande, and he will often turn to the "Interpretations" of Gaspary, Church, and Lowell to learn how they vindicate the poet for much that seems barbarous. The articles on Purgatory and Paradise will follow in due course. Every reader should carefully peruse chapter iv. in order to appreciate the significance of the Vita Nuova and its vital connection with the Divina Commedia. Chapter v. is the least satisfactory of all to the editor, as the limits of space have allowed him merely to quote statements of the contents of the minor works of Dante and have forbidden an adequate treatment of them. Especial attention is called to the illustrations of the book. The frontispiece is taken from a copy of the water color found in Codex 1040 in the Riccardi Library and pronounced by a commission of the Italian government to be the most authentic likeness of Dante extant. The

Bargello portrait is from the Arundel lithograph of Kirkup's drawing, while the two photographs of the death mask are from a monograph Professor Norton contributed to the sixth centenary of Dante's birth. It is a satisfaction to embody copies of the original portraits not improved by well-meaning artists and engravers.

I wish to express my indebtedness to Professor Norton for generously allowing me to draw largely from his writings; to James Robinson Smith for giving me cordial permission to use freely his valuable translations of Boccaccio's and Bruni's lives of Dante; to Dr. Edward Moore, P. H. Wicksteed, H. Oelsner, and James Bryce for granting me the privilege of quoting from their writings; to E. G. Gardner, from whose handbook on Dante I have taken several short paragraphs; to Mrs. H. F. Dwight for the right to insert Mr. Latham's translation of the letter to Can Grande; to Macmillan and Company for the liberty of printing extended extracts from Dean Church's essays; to Geo. Bell & Sons, J. M. Dent & Co., Manresa Press, Houghton, Mifflin & Co., Little, Brown & Co., Ginn & Co., Swan Sonnenschein & Co., for the use of articles of which they are publishers.

I owe much to the interest and valuable suggestions of Professors A. S. Cook and Kenneth McKenzie of Yale, Professors J. Geddes and F. M. Josselyn of Boston University, and Professor C. H. Grandgent of Harvard. Especially have I availed myself of the courtesy and exact scholarship of Professor Oscar Kuhns of Wesleyan University, who to my great gratification read the proofs of the book.

I do not endorse all the statements which have been made by the writers whose opinions have been inserted; but for the selection of the articles, for the introductory matter printed in small type, and for the footnotes signed (D.) I am responsible.

CHARLES ALLEN DINSMORE.

BOSTON, August 12, 1903.

CONTENTS

CHAPTER I

THE TIMES OF DANTE

CHAPTER II

SOURCES OF OUR KNOWLEDGE OF DANTE

CHAPTER III

DANTE'S PERSONAL APPEARANCE

CHAPTER IV

THE VITA NUOVA

CHAPTER V

MINOR WORKS

CHAPTER VI

THE DIVINA COMMEDIA

CHAPTER VII

INTERPRETATIONS

ILLUSTRATIONS

CHAPTER I

THE TIMES OF DANTE

I

FLORENTINE POLITICAL FEUDS AND THEIR INFLUENCE UPON DANTE

By Dean Church.[1]

The Divina Commedia is one of the landmarks of history. More than a magnificent poem, more than the beginning of a language aud the opening of a national literature, more than the inspirer of art, and the glory of a great people, it is one of those rare and solemn monuments of the miud's power, which measure and test what it can reach to, which rise up ineffaceably aud forever as time goes on, marking out its advance by grander divisions than its centuries, and adopted as epochs by the consent of all who come after. It stands with the Iliad and Shakespeare's Plays, with the writings of Aristotle and Plato, with the Novum Organon and the Principia, with Justinian's Code, with the Parthenon and St. Peter's. It is the first Christian poem; and it opens European literature, as the Iliad did that of Greece and Rome. And, like the Iliad, it has never become out of date; it accompanies in undiminished freshness the literature which it began.

We approach the history of such works, in which

[1] *Dante*. R. W. Church. Published in 1850. Now published by Macmillan & Co., Ltd., London, in a volume entitled *Dante and Other Essays*. Reproduced by permission.

genius seems to have pushed its achievements to a new limit, with a kind of awe. The beginnings of all things, their bursting out from nothing, and gradual evolution into substance and shape, cast on the mind a solemn influence. They come too near the fount of being to be followed up without our feeling the shadows which surround it. We cannot but fear, cannot but feel ourselves cut off from this visible and familiar world — as we enter into the cloud. And as with the processes of nature, so it is with those offsprings of man's mind, by which he has added permanently one more great feature to the world, and created a new power which is to act on mankind to the end. The mystery of the inventive and creative faculty, the subtle and incalculable combinations by which it was led to its work, and carried through it, are out of the reach of investigating thought. Often the idea recurs of the precariousness of the result, — by how little the world might have lost one of its ornaments — by one sharp pang, or one chance meeting, or any other among the countless accidents among which man runs his course. And then the solemn recollection supervenes, that powers were formed, and life preserved, and circumstances arranged, and actions controlled, that thus it should be: and the work which man has brooded over, and at last created, is the foster-child too of that "Wisdom which reaches from end to end, strongly and sweetly disposing all things."

It does not abate these feelings that we can follow in some cases, and to a certain extent, the progress of a work. Indeed, the sight of the particular accidents among which it was developed — which belong perhaps to a heterogeneous and widely discordant order of things, which are out of proportion and out of harmony with it, which do not explain it, which have, as it may seem to us, no natural right to be connected with it, to bear on its character, or contribute to its accomplishment, to which we feel, as it were, ashamed to owe what we can least spare, yet on which its forming mind and purpose were dependent, and with which they had to conspire — affects the imagination even more than cases where we see nothing. We are tempted less to musing and wonder by the Iliad, a work without a history, cut off from its past, the sole relic and vestige of its age, unexplained in its origin and perfection, than by the Divina Commedia, destined for the highest ends and most universal sympathy, yet the reflection of a personal history, and issuing seemingly from its chance incidents.

The Divina Commedia is singular among the great works with which it ranks, for its strong stamp of personal character and history. In general we associate little more than the name — not the life — of a great poet with his works; personal interest belongs more usually to greatness in its active than its creative forms. But the whole idea and purpose of the Commedia, as well as its filling up and coloring, are determined by Dante's peculiar history. The loftiest, perhaps, in its aim and flight of all poems, it is also the most individual; the writer's own life is chronicled in it, as well as the issues and upshot of all things. It is at once the mirror to all time of the sins and perfections of men, of the judgments and grace of God, and the record, often the only one, of the transient names, and local factions, and obscure ambitions, and forgotten crimes, of the poet's own day; and in that awful company to which he leads us, in the most unearthly of his scenes, we never lose sight of himself. And when this peculiarity sends us to history, it seems as if the poem which was to hold such a place in Christian literature hung upon and grew out of chance events, rather than the deliberate design of its author. History indeed here, as generally, is but a feeble exponent of the course of growth in a great mind and great ideas. It shows us early a bent and purpose — the man conscious of power and intending to use it — and then the accidents among which he worked: but how that current of purpose threaded its way among them, how it was thrown back, deflected, deepened, by them, we cannot learn from history. It presents but a broken and mysterious picture. A boy of quick and enthusiastic temper grows up into youth in a dream of love. The lady of his mystic passion dies early. He dreams of her still, not as a wonder of earth, but as a Saint in Paradise, and relieves his heart in an autobiography, a strange and perplexing work of fiction — quaint and subtle enough for a metaphysical conceit; but, on the other hand, with far too much of genuine and deep feeling. It is a first essay; he closes it abruptly as if dissatisfied with his work, but with the resolution of raising at a future day a worthy monument to the memory of her whom he has lost. It is the promise and purpose of a great work. But a prosaic change seems to come over this half-ideal character. The lover becomes the student — the student of the thirteenth century — struggling painfully against difficulties, eager and hot after knowledge, wasting eyesight and stinting sleep, subtle, inquisitive, active-minded and sanguine, but omnivorous, overflowing with dialectical forms, loose in premise and ostentatiously rigid in syllogism, fettered by the refinements of half-awakened taste, and the mannerisms of the Provençals. Boethius and Cicero, and the mass of mixed learning within his reach, are accepted as the consolation of his human griefs; he is filled with the passion of universal knowledge, and the desire to communicate it. Philosophy has become the lady of his soul — to write allegorical poems in her honor, and to comment on them with all the apparatus of his learning in prose, his mode of celebrating her. Further, he marries; it is said, not happily. The antiquaries, too, have disturbed romance by discovering that Beatrice also was married some years before her death. He appears, as time goes on, as a burgher of Florence, the father of a family, a politician, an envoy, a magistrate, a partisan, taking his full share in the quarrels of the day. At length we see him, at once an exile, and the poet of the Commedia. Beatrice reappears — shadowy, melting at times into symbol and figure — but far too living and real, addressed with too intense and natural feeling, to be the mere personification of anything. The lady of the philosophical Canzoni has vanished. The student's dream has been broken, as the boy's had been; and the earnestness of the man, enlightened by sorrow, overleaping the student's formalities and abstractions, reverted in sympathy to the earnestness of the boy, and brooded once more on that Saint in Paradise, whose presence and memory had once been so soothing, and who now seemed a real link between him and that stable country, "where the angels are in peace." Round her image, the reflection of purity, and truth, and forbearing love, was grouped that confused scene of trouble and effort, of failure and success, which the poet saw round him; round her image it arranged itself in awful order — and that image, not a metaphysical abstraction, but the living memory, freshened by sorrow, and seen through the softening and hallowing vista of years, of Beatrice Portinari — no figment of imagination, but God's creature and servant. A childish love, dissipated by study and business, and revived in memory by heavy sorrow — a boyish resolution, made in a moment of feeling, interrupted, though it would be hazardous to say in Dante's case, laid aside, for apparently more manly studies, gave the idea and suggested the form of the "sacred poem of earth and heaven."

And the occasion of this startling unfolding of the poetic gift, of this passage of a soft and dreamy boy into the keenest, boldest, sternest of poets, the free and mighty leader of European song, was, what is not ordinarily held to be a source of poetical inspiration, — the political life. The boy had sensibility, high aspirations, and a versatile and passionate nature; the student added to this energy, various learning, gifts of language, and noble ideas on the capacities and ends of man. But it was the factions of Florence which made Dante a great poet. But for them, he might have been a modern critic and essayist born before his time, and have held a high place among the writers of fugitive verses; in Italy, a graceful but trifling and idle tribe, often casting a deep and beautiful thought into a mould of expressive diction, but oftener toying with a foolish and glittering conceit, and whose languid genius was exhausted by a sonnet. He might have thrown into the shade the Guidos and Cinos of his day, to be eclipsed by Petrarch. But he learned in the bitter feuds of Italy not to trifle; they opened to his view, and he had an eye to see, the true springs and abysses of this mortal life — motives and passions stronger than lovers' sentiments, evils beyond the consolations of Boethius and Cicero; and from that fiery trial which without searing his heart, annealed his strength and purpose, he drew that great gift and power by which he stands preëminent even among his high compeers, the gift of being real. And the idea of the Commedia took shape, and expanded into its endless forms of terror and beauty, not under the roof-tree of the literary citizen, but when the exile had been driven out to the highways of the world, to study nature on the sea or by the river or on the mountain track, and to study men in the courts of Verona and Ravenna, and in the schools of Bologna and Paris — perhaps of Oxford.

The connection of these feuds with Dante's poem has given to the middle age history of Italy an interest of which it is not undeserving in itself, full as it is of curious exhibitions of character and contrivance, but to which politically it cannot lay claim, amid the social phenomena, so far grander in scale and purpose and more felicitous in issue, of the other western nations. It is remarkable for keeping up an antique phase, which, in spite of modern arrangements, it has not yet lost. It is a history of cities. In ancient history all that is most memorable and instructive gathers round cities — civilization and empire were concentrated within walls; and it baffled the ancient mind to conceive how power should be possessed and wielded, by numbers larger than might be collected in a single market-place. The Roman Empire indeed aimed at being one in its administration and law; but it was not a nation, nor were its provinces nations. Yet everywhere but in Italy it prepared them for becoming nations. And while everywhere else parts were uniting and union was becoming organization — and neither geographical remoteness, nor unwieldiness of numbers, nor local interests and differences, were untractable obstacles to that spirit of fusion which was at once the ambition of the few and the instinct of the many; and cities, even where most powerful, had become the centres of the attracting and joining forces, knots in the political network — while this was going on more or less happily throughout the rest of Europe, in Italy the ancient classic idea liugered in its simplicity, its narrowness and jealousy, wherever there was any political activity. The history of Southern Italy indeed is mainly a foreign one, the history of modern Rome merges in that of the Papacy; but Northern Italy has a history of its own, and that is a history of separate and independent cities — points of reciprocal and indestructible repulsion, and within, theatres of action where the blind tendencies and traditions of classes and parties weighed little on the freedom of individual character, and citizens could watch and measure and study one another with the minuteness of private life.

Two cities were the centres of ancient history in its most interesting time. And two cities of modern Italy represent, with entirely undesigned but curiously exact coincidence, the parts of Athens and Rome. Venice, superficially so unlike, is yet in many of its accidental features, and still more in its spirit, the counterpart of Rome, in its obscure and mixed origin, in its steady growth, in its quick sense of order and early settlement of its polity, in its grand and serious public spirit, in its subordination of the individual to the family, and the family to the state, in its combination of remote dominion with the liberty of a solitary and sovereign city. And though the associations and the scale of the two were so different — though Rome had its hills and its legions, and Venice its lagunes and galleys — the long empire of Venice, the heir of Carthage and predecessor of England on the seas, the great aristocratic republic of a thousand years, is the only empire that has yet matched Rome in length and steadiness of tenure. Brennus and Hannibal were not resisted with greater constancy than Doria and Louis XII.; and that great aristocracy, long so proud, so high-spirited, so intelligent, so practical, who combined the enterprise and wealth of merchants, the self-devotion of soldiers and gravity of senators, with the uniformity and obedience of a religious order, may compare without shame its Giustiniani, and Zenos, and Morosini, with Roman Fabii and Claudii. And Rome could not be more contrasted with Athens than Venice with Italian and contemporary Florence — stability with fitfulness, independence impregnable and secure, with a short-lived and troubled liberty, empire meditated and achieved, with a course of barren intrigues and quarrels. Florence, gay, capricious, turbulent, the city of party, the head and busy patroness of democracy in the cities round her — Florence, where popular government was inaugurated with its utmost exclusiveness and most pompous ceremonial; waging her little summer wars against Ghibelline tyrants, revolted democracies, and her own exiles; and further, so rich in intellectual gifts, in variety of individual character, in poets, artists, wits, historians — Florence in its brilliant days recalled the image of ancient Athens, and did not depart from its prototype in the beauty of its natural site, in its noble public buildings, in the size and nature of its territory. And the course of its history is similar and the result of similar causes — a traditional spirit of freedom, with its accesses of fitful energy, its periods of grand display and moments of glorious achievement, but producing nothing politically great or durable, and sinking at length into a resigned servitude. It had its Peisistratidæ more successful than those of Athens; it had, too, its Harmodius and Aristogeiton; it had its great orator of liberty, as potent and as unfortunate as the antagonist of Philip. And finally, like Athens, it became content with the remembrance of its former glory, with being the fashionable and acknowledged seat of refinement and taste, with being a favored dependency on the modern heir of the Cæsars. But if to Venice belongs a grander public history, Florentine names and works, like Athenian, will be living among men, when the Brenta shall have been left unchecked to turn the lagunes into ploughland, and when Rome herself may no longer be the seat of the popes.

The year of Dante's birth was a memorable one in the annals of Florence, of Italy, and of Christendom.[1]

[1] May, 1265. (Pelli.) *Battle of Benevento:* Feb. 26, $126\frac{5}{6}$. The Florentine year began March 25.

The year 1265 was the year of that great victory of Benevento, where Charles of Anjou overthrew Manfred of Naples, and destroyed at one blow the power of the house of Swabia. From that time till the time of Charles V., the emperors had no footing in Italy. Further, that victory set up the French influence in Italy, which, transient in itself, produced such strange and momentous consequences, by the intimate connection to which it led between the French kings and the popes. The protection of France was dearly bought by the captivity of Avignon, the great western schism, and the consequent secularization of the Papacy, which lasted on uninterrupted until the Council of Trent. Nearly three centuries of degradation and scandal, unrelieved by one heroic effort among the successors of Gregory VII., connected the Reformation with the triumph of Charles and the Pope at Benevento. Finally, by it the Guelf party was restored for good in Florence; the Guelf democracy, which had been trampled down by the Uberti and Manfred's chivalry at Monteaperti, once more raised its head; and fortune, which had long wavered between the rival lilies, finally turned against the white one, till the name of Ghibelline became a proscribed one in Florence, as Jacobite was once in Scotland, or Papist in England, or Royalist in France.

The names of Guelf and Ghibelline were the inheritance of a contest which, in its original meaning, had been long over. The old struggle between the priesthood and the empire was still kept up traditionally, but its ideas and interests were changed: they were still great and important ones, but not those of Gregory VII. It had passed over from the mixed region of the spiritual and temporal into the purely political. The cause of the popes was that of the independence of Italy — the freedom and alliance of the great cities of the north, and the dependence of the centre and south on the Roman See. To keep the Emperor out of Italy — to create a barrier of powerful cities against him south of the Alps — to form behind themselves a compact territory, rich, removed from the first burst of invasion, and maintaining a strong body of interested feudatories, had now become the great object of the popes. It may have been a wise policy on their part, for the maintenance of their spiritual influence, to attempt to connect their own independence with the political freedom of the Italian communities; but certain it is that the ideas and the characters which gave a religious interest and grandeur to the earlier part of the contest, appear but sparingly, if at all, in its later forms.

The two parties did not care to keep in view principles which their chiefs had lost sight of. The Emperor and the Pope were both real powers, able to protect and assist; and they divided between them those who required protection and assistance. Geographical position, the rivalry of neighborhood, family tradition, private feuds, and above all private interest, were the main causes which assigned cities, families, and individuals to the Ghibelline or Guelf party. One party called themselves the Emperor's liegemen, and their watchword was authority and law; the other side were the liegemen of Holy Church, and their cry was liberty; and the distinction as a broad one is true. But a democracy would become Ghibelline, without scruple, if its neighbor town was Guelf; and among the Guelf liegemen of the Church and liberty, the pride of blood and love of power were not a whit inferior to that of their opponents. Yet, though the original principle of the contest was lost, and the political distinctions of parties were often interfered with by interest or accident, it is not impossible to trace in the two factions differences of temper, of moral and political inclinations, which, though visible only on a large scale and in the mass, were quite sufficient to give meaning and reality to their mutual opposition. These differences had come down, greatly altered of course, from the quarrel in which the parties took their rise. The Ghibellines as a body reflected the worldliness, the license, the irreligion, the reckless selfishness, the daring insolence, and at the same time the gayety and pomp, the princely magnificence and generosity and largeness of mind of the house of Swabia; they were the men of the court and camp, imperious and haughty from ancient lineage or the Imperial cause, yet not wanting in the frankness and courtesy of nobility; careless of public opinion and public rights, but not dead to the grandeur of public objects and public services. Among them were found, or to them inclined, all who, whether from a base or a lofty ambition, desired to place their will above law — the lord of the feudal castle, the robber-knight of the Apennine pass, the magnificent but terrible tyrants of the cities, the pride and shame of Italy, the Visconti and Scaligers. That renowned Ghibelline chief, whom the poet finds in the fiery sepulchres of the unbelievers with the great Ghibelline emperor and the princely Ghibelline cardinal — the disdainful and bitter but lofty spirit of Farinata degli Uberti, the conqueror, and then singly and at his own risk, the saviour of his country which had wronged him — represents the good as well as the bad side of his party.

The Guelfs, on the other hand, were the party of the middle classes; they rose out of and held to the people: they were strong by their compactness, their organization in cities, their commercial relations and interests, their command of money. Further, they were professedly the party of strictness and religion, a profession which fettered them as little as their opponents were fettered by the respect they claimed for imperial law. But though by personal unscrupulousness and selfishness, and in instances of public vengeance, they sinned as deeply as the Ghibellines, they stood far more committed as a party to a public meaning and purpose — to improvement in law and the condition of the poor, to a protest against the insolence of the strong, to the encouragement of industry. The genuine Guelf spirit was austere, frugal, independent, earnest, religious, fond of its home and Church, and of those celebrations which bound together Church and home; but withal very proud, very intolerant; in its higher form intolerant of evil, but intolerant always to whatever displeased it. Yet there was a grave and noble manliness about it which long kept it alive in Florence. It had not as yet turned itself against the practical corruptions of the Church, which was its ally; but this also it was to do, when the popes had forsaken the cause of liberty, and leagued themselves with the brilliant tyranny of the Medici. Then Savonarola invoked, and not in vain, the stern old Guelf spirit of resistance, of domestic purity and severity, and of domestic religion, against unbelief and licentiousness even in the Church; and the Guelf "Piagnoni" presented, in a more simple and generous shape, a resemblance to our own Puritans, as the Ghibellines often recall the coarser and worse features of our own Cavaliers.

In Florence, these distinctions had become mere nominal ones, confined to the great families who carried on their private feuds under the old party names, when Frederick II. once more gave them their meaning. "Although the accursed Guelf and Ghibelline factions lasted amongst the nobles of Florence, and they often waged war among themselves out of private grudges, and took sides for the said factions, and held one with another, and those who called themselves Guelfs desired the establishment of the Pope and Holy Church, and those who called themselves Ghibellines favored the Emperor and his adherents, yet withal the people and commonalty of Florence maintained itself in unity, to the well-being and honor and establishment of the commonwealth."[1] But the appearance on the scene of an emperor of such talent and bold designs revived the languid contest, and gave to party a cause, and to individual passions and ambition an impulse and pretext. The division between Guelf and Ghibelline again became serious, involved all Florence, armed house against house, and neighborhood against neighborhood, issued in merciless and vindictive warfare, grew on into a hopeless and deadly breach, and finally lost to Florence, without remedy or repair, half her noble houses and the love of the greatest of her sons. The old badge of their common country became to

[1] G. Villani, vi. 33.

the two factions the sign of their implacable hatred; the white lily of Florence, borne by the Ghibellines, was turned to red by the Guelfs, and the flower of two colors marked a civil strife as cruel and as fatal, if on a smaller scale, as that of the English roses.[1]

It was waged with the peculiar characteristics of Italian civil war. There the city itself was the scene of battle. A thirteenth-century city in Italy bore on its face the evidence that it was built and arranged for such emergencies. Its crowded and narrow streets were a collection of rival castles, whose tall towers, rising thick and close over its roofs, or hanging perilously over its close courts, attested the emulous pride and the insecurity of Italian civic life. There, within a separate precinct, flanked and faced by jealous friends or deadly enemies, were clustered together the dwellings of the various members of each great house — their common home and the monument of their magnificence and pride, and capable of being, as was so often necessary, their common refuge. In these fortresses of the leading families, scattered about the city, were the various points of onset and recovery in civic battle; in the streets barricades were raised, mangonels and crossbows were plied from the towers, a series of separate combats raged through the city, till chance at length connected the attacks of one side, or some panic paralyzed the resistance of the other, or a conflagration interposed itself between the combatants, burning out at once Guelf and Ghibelline, and laying half Florence in ashes. Each party had their turn of victory; each, when vanquished, went into exile, and carried on

[1] G. Vill. vi. 33, 43; *Parad.* 19.

the war outside the walls; each had their opportunity of remodeling the orders and framework of government, and each did so relentlessly at the cost of their opponents. They excluded classes, they proscribed families, they confiscated property, they sacked and burned warehouses, they leveled the palaces, and outraged the pride of their antagonists. To destroy was not enough, without adding to it the keenest and newest refinement of insult. Two buildings in Florence were peculiarly dear — among their *cari luoghi* — to the popular feeling and the Guelf party: the Baptistery of St. John, "il mio bel San Giovanni," "to which all the good people resorted on Sundays,"[1] where they had all received baptism, where they had been married, where families were solemnly reconciled; and a tall and beautiful tower close by it, called the "Torre del Guardamorto," where the bodies of the "good people," who of old were all buried at San Giovanni, rested on their way to the grave. The victorious Ghibellines, when they leveled the Guelf towers, overthrew this one, and endeavored to make it crush in its fall the sacred church, "which," says the old chronicler, "was prevented by a miracle." The Guelfs, when their day came, built the walls of Florence with the stones of Ghibelline palaces.[2] One great family stands out preëminent in this fierce conflict as the victim and monument of party war. The head of the Ghibellines was the proud and powerful house of the Uberti, who shared with another great Ghibelline family, the Pazzi, the valley of the upper Arno. They lighted

[1] G. Vill. iv. 10, vi. 33; *Inf.* 19; *Parad.* 25.
[2] G. Vill. vi. 39, 65.

up the war in the Emperor's cause. They supported its weight and guided it. In time of peace they were foremost and unrestrained in defiance of law and in scorn of the people — in war, the people's fiercest and most active enemies. Heavy sufferers, in their property, and by the sword and axe, yet untamed and incorrigible, they led the van in that battle, so long remembered to their cost by the Guelfs, the battle of Monteaperti (1260) —

> Lo strazio, e 'l gran scempio
> Che fece l' Arbia colorata in rossa (*Inf.* 10).[1]

That the head of their house, Farinata, saved Florence from the vengeance of his meaner associates, was not enough to atone for the unpardonable wrongs which they had done to the Guelfs and the democracy. When the red lily of the Guelfs finally supplanted the white one as the arms of Florence, and the badge of Guelf triumph, they were proscribed forever, like the Peisistratidæ and the Tarquins. In every amnesty their names were excepted. The site on which their houses had stood was never again to be built upon, and remains the Great Square of Florence; the architect of the Palace of the People was obliged to sacrifice its symmetry, and to place it awry, that its walls might not encroach on the accursed ground.[2] "They had been," says a writer, contemporary with Dante, speaking of the time when he also became an exile; "they had been for more than forty years outlaws from their country, nor ever found mercy or pity, remain-

[1] The slaughter and great havoc, I replied,
That colored Arbia's flood with crimson stain.

[2] G. Vill. vi. 33, viii. 26; Vasari, *Arnolfo di Lapo*, i. 255 (Fir. 1846).

ing always abroad in great state, nor ever abased their honor, seeing that they ever abode with kings and lords, and to great things applied themselves."[1] They were loved as they were hated. When, under the protection of a cardinal, one of them visited the city, and the checkered blue and gold blazon of their house was, after an interval of half a century, again seen in the streets of Florence; "many ancient Ghibelline men and women pressed to kiss the arms,"[2] and even the common people did him honor.

But the fortunes of Florentine factions depended on other causes than merely the address or vigor of their leaders. From the year of Dante's birth and Charles's victory, Florence, as far as we shall have to do with it, became irrevocably Guelf. Not that the whole commonalty of Florence formally called itself Guelf, or that the Guelf party was coextensive with it; but the city was controlled by Guelf councils, devoted to the objects of the great Guelf party, and received in return the support of that party in curbing the pride of the nobles and maintaining democratic forms. The Guelf party of Florence, though it was the life and soul of the republic, and irresistible in its disposal of the influence and arms of Florence, and though it embraced a large number of the most powerful families, is always spoken of as something distinct from, and external to, the governing powers and the whole body of the people. It was a body with a separate and self-constituted existence; — in the state and allied to it, but an independent element, holding on to a large and comprehensive union without the state. Its organization in Florence is one of the most curious

[1] Dino Compagni, p. 88. [2] *Ibid.* p. 107.

among the many curious combinations which meet us in Italian history. After the final expulsion of the Ghibellines the Guelf party took form as an institution, with definite powers, and a local existence. It appears with as distinct a shape as the Jacobin Club or the Orange Lodges, side by side with the government. It was a corporate body with a common seal, common property, not only in funds but lands — officers, archives, a common palace,[1] a great council, a secret committee, and last of all, a public accuser of the Ghibellines; of the confiscated Ghibelline estates one third went to the republic, another third to compensate individual Guelfs, the rest was assigned to the Guelf party.[2] A pope (Clement IV., 1265–68) had granted them his own arms;[3] and their device, a red eagle clutching a serpent, may be yet seen, with the red lily and the party-colored banner of the commonalty, on the battlements of the Palazzo Vecchio.

But the expulsion of the Ghibellines did but little to restore peace. The great Guelf families, as old as many of the Ghibellines, had as little reverence as they for law or civic rights. Below these the acknowledged nobility of Florence, were the leading families of the "people," houses created by successful industry or commerce, and pushing up into that privileged order, which, however ignored and even discredited by the laws, was fully recognized by feeling and opinion in the most democratic times of the republic. Rivalries and feuds, street broils and conspiracies, high-handed insolence from the great men, rough ven-

[1] Giotto painted in it: Vasari, *Vit. di Giotto*, p. 314.

[2] G. Vill. vii. 2, 17.

[3] *Ibid*. vii. 2.

geance from the populace, still continued to vex jealous and changeful Florence. The popes sought in vain to keep in order their quarrelsome liegemen; to reconcile Guelf with Guelf, and even Guelf with Ghibelline. Embassies went and came, to ask for mediation and to proffer it; to apply the healing paternal hand; to present an obsequious and ostentatious submission. Cardinal legates came in state, and were received with reverential pomp; they formed private committees, and held assemblies, and made marriages; they harangued in honeyed words, and gained the largest promises; on one occasion the Great Square was turned into a vast theatre, and on this stage one hundred and fifty dissidents on each side came forward, and in the presence and with the benediction of the cardinal kissed each other on the mouth.[1] And if persuasion failed, the Pope's representative hesitated not to excommunicate and interdict the faithful but obdurate city. But whether excommunicated or blessed, Florence could not be at peace; however wise and subtle had been the peacemaker's arrangements, his departing cortège was hardly out of sight of the city before they were blown to the winds. Not more successful were the efforts of the sensible and moderate citizens who sighed for tranquillity within its walls. Dino Compagni's interesting though not very orderly narrative describes with great frankness, and with the perplexity of a simple-hearted man puzzled by the continual triumph of clever wickedness, the variety and the fruitlessness of the expedients devised by him and other good citizens against the resolute and incorrigible selfishness of the great Guelfs — ever, when

[1] G. Vill. vii. 56.

checked in one form, breaking out in another; proof against all persuasion, all benefits; not to be bound by law, or compact, or oath; eluding or turning to its own account the deepest and sagest contrivances of constitutional wisdom.

A great battle won against Ghibelline Arezzo[1] raised the renown and the military spirit of the Guelf party, for the fame of the battle was very great; the hosts contained the choicest chivalry of either side, armed and appointed with emulous splendor. The fighting was hard, there was brilliant and conspicuous gallantry, and the victory was complete. It sealed Guelf ascendency. The Ghibelline warrior-bishop of Arezzo fell, with three of the Uberti, and other Ghibelline chiefs. It was a day of trial. "Many that day who had been thought of great prowess were found dastards, and many who had never been spoken of were held in high esteem." It repaired the honor of Florence, and the citizens showed their feeling of its importance by mixing up the marvelous with its story. Its tidings came to Florence — so runs the tale in Villani, who declares what he "heard and saw" himself — at the very hour in which it was won. The Priors of the Republic were resting in their palace during the noonday heat; suddenly the chamber door was shaken, and the cry heard, "Rise up! the Aretini are defeated." The door was opened, but there was no one; their servants had seen no one enter the palace, and no one came from the army till the hour of vespers, on a long summer's day. In this battle the Guelf leaders had won great glory. The hero of the day was the

1 Campaldino, in 1289. G. Vill. vii. 131; Dino Comp. p. 14.

proudest, handsomest, craftiest, most winning, most ambitious, most unscrupulous Guelf noble in Florence — one of a family who inherited the spirit and recklessness of the proscribed Uberti, and did not refuse the popular epithet of *Malefami* — Corso Donati. He did not come back from the field of Campaldino, where he had won the battle by disobeying orders, with any increased disposition to yield to rivals, or court the populace, or respect other men's rights. Those rivals, too — and they also had fought gallantly in the post of honor at Campaldino — were such as he hated from his soul — rivals whom he despised, and who yet were too strong for him. His blood was ancient, they were upstarts; he was a soldier, they were traders; he was poor, they the richest men in Florence. They had come to live close to the Donati, they had bought the palace of an old Ghibelline family, they had enlarged, adorned, and fortified it, and kept great state there. They had crossed him in marriages, bargains, inheritances. They had won popularity, honor, influence; and yet they were but men of business, while he had a part in all the political movements of the day. He was the friend and intimate of lords and noblemen, with great connections and famous through all Italy; they were the favorites of the common people for their kindness and good nature; they even showed consideration for Ghibellines. He was an accomplished man of the world, keen and subtle, "full of malicious thoughts, mischievous, and crafty;" they were inexperienced in intrigue, and had the reputation of being clumsy and stupid. He was the most graceful and engaging of courtiers; they were not even gentlemen. Lastly, in the debates of that excitable republic he was the most eloquent speaker, and they were tongue-tied.[1]

"There was a family," writes Dino Compagni, "who called themselves the Cerchi, men of low estate, but good merchants and very rich; and they dressed richly, and maintained many servants and horses, and made a brave show; and some of them bought the palace of the Conti Guidi, which was near the houses of the Pazzi and Donati, who were more ancient of blood, but not so rich; therefore, seeing the Cerchi rise to great dignity, and that they had walled and enlarged the palace, and kept great state, the Donati began to have a great hatred against them." Villani gives the same account of the feud.[2] "It began in that quarter of scandal the Sesto of Porta St. Piero, between the Cerchi and Donati, on the one side through jealousy, on the other through churlish rudeness. Of the house of the Cerchi was head Messer Vieri de' Cerchi, and he and those of his house were people of great business, and powerful, and of great relationships, and most wealthy traders, so that their company was one of the greatest in the world; men they were of soft life, and who meant no harm; boorish and ill-mannered, like people who had come in a short time to great state and power. The Donati were gentlemen and warriors, and of no excessive wealth. . . . They were neighbors in Florence and in the country, and by the conversation of their jealousy with the peevish boorishness of the others, arose the proud scorn that there was between them." The glories of Campaldino were not as oil on these troubled waters. The conquerors flouted

[1] Dino Comp. pp. 32, 75, 94, 133.

[2] G. Vill. viii. 39.

each other all the more fiercely in the streets on their return, and ill-treated the lower people with less scruple. No gathering for festive or serious purposes could be held without tempting strife. A marriage, a funeral, a ball, a gay procession of cavaliers and ladies — any meeting where one stood while another sat, where horse or man might jostle another, where pride might be nettled or temper shown, was in danger of ending in blood. The lesser quarrels meanwhile ranged themselves under the greater ones; and these, especially that between the Cerchi and Donati, took more and more a political character. The Cerchi inclined more and more to the trading classes and the lower people; they threw themselves on their popularity, and began to hold aloof from the meetings of the "Parte Guelfa," while this organized body became an instrument in the hands of their opponents, a club of the nobles. Corso Donati, besides mischief of a more substantial kind, turned his ridicule on their solemn dullness and awkward speech, and his friends the jesters, one Scampolino in particular, carried his jibes and nicknames all over Florence. The Cerchi received all in sullen and dogged indifference. They were satisfied with repelling attacks, and nursed their hatred.[1]

Thus the city was divided, and the attempts to check the factions only exasperated them. It was in vain that, when at times the government and the populace lost patience, severe measures were taken. It was in vain that the reformer, Gian della Bella, carried for a time his harsh "orders of justice" against the nobles, and invested popular vengeance

[1] Dino Comp. pp. 32, 34, 38.

with the solemnity of law and with the pomp and ceremony of a public act — that when a noble had been convicted of killing a citizen, the great officer, "Standard-bearer," as he was called, "of justice," issued forth in state and procession, with the banner of justice borne before him, with all his train, and at the head of the armed citizens, to the house of the criminal, and razed it to the ground. An eye-witness describes the effect of such chastisement: "I, Dino Compagni, being Gonfalonier of Justice in 1293, went to their houses, and to those of their relations, and these I caused to be pulled down according to the laws. This beginning in the case of the other Gonfaloniers came to an evil effect; because, if they demolished the houses according to the laws, the people said that they were cruel; and if they did not demolish them completely, they said that they were cowards; and many distorted justice for fear of the people." Gian della Bella was overthrown with few regrets even on the part of the people. Equally vain was the attempt to keep the peace by separating the leaders of the disturbances. They were banished by a kind of ostracism; they departed in ostentatious meekness, Corso Donati to plot at Rome, Vieri de' Cerchi to return immediately to Florence. Anarchy had got too fast a hold on the city, and it required a stronger hand than that of the pope, or the signory of the Republic, to keep it down.

Yet Florence prospered. Every year it grew richer, more intellectual, more refined, more beautiful, more gay. With its anarchy there was no stagnation. Torn and divided as it was, its energy did not slacken, its busy and creative spirit was not deadened, its hopefulness not abated. The factions, fierce and personal as they were, did not hinder that interest in political ideas, that active and subtle study of the questions of civil government, that passion and ingenuity displayed in political contrivance, which now pervaded Northern Italy, everywhere marvelously patient and hopeful, though far from being equally successful. In Venice at the close of the thirteenth century, that polity was finally settled and consolidated by which she was great as long as cities could be imperial, and which even in its decay survived the monarchy of Louis XIV. and existed within the memory of living men.[1] In Florence the constructive spirit of law and order only resisted, but never triumphed. Yet it was resolute and sanguine, and not yet dispirited by continual failure. Political interest, however, and party contests were not sufficient to absorb and employ the citizens of Florence. Their genial and versatile spirit, so keen, so inventive, so elastic, which made them such hot and impetuous partisans, kept them from being only this. The time was one of growth; new knowledge, new powers, new tastes were opening to men — new pursuits attracted them. There was commerce, there was the school of philosophy, there was the science of nature, there was ancient learning, there was the civil law, there were the arts, there was poetry, all rude as yet, and unformed, but full of hope — the living parents of mightier offspring. Frederick II. had once more opened Aristotle to the Latin world; he had given an impulse to the study of the great monuments of Roman legislation which was responded to through

[1] [This was written in 1850.]

Italy; himself a poet, his example and his splendid court had made poetry fashionable. In the end of the thirteenth century a great stride was made at Florence. While her great poet was growing up to manhood, as rapid a change went on in her streets, her social customs, the wealth of her citizens, their ideas of magnificence and beauty, their appreciation of literature. It was the age of growing commerce and travel; Franciscan missionaries had reached China, and settled there;[1] in 1294 Marco Polo returned to Venice, the first successful explorer of the East. The merchants of Florence lagged not; their field of operation was Italy and the West; they had their correspondents in London, Paris, and Bruges; they were the bankers of popes and kings.[2] And their city shows to this day the wealth and magnificence of the last years of the thirteenth century. The ancient buildings, consecrated in the memory of the Florentine people, were repaired, enlarged, adorned with marble and bronze — Or San Michele, the Badia, the Baptistery; and new buildings rose on a grander scale. In 1294 was begun the mausoleum of the great Florentine dead, the Church of St. Croce. In the same year, a few months later, Arnolfo laid the deep foundations which were afterwards to bear up Brunelleschi's dome, and traced the plan of the magnificent cathedral. In 1298 he began to raise a town hall worthy of the Republic, and of being the habitation of its magistrates, the frowning

[1] See the curious *Letters of John de Monte Corvino* abont his mission in Cathay, 1289–1305, in Wadding, vi. 69.

[2] *E. g.* the Mozzi, of Gregory X.; Peruzzi, of Philip le Bel; Spini, of Boniface VIII.; Cerchi del Garbo, of Benedict XI. G. Vill. vii. 42, viii. 63, 71; Dino Comp. p. 35.

mass of the Palazzo Vecchio. In 1299 the third circle of the walls was commenced with the benediction of bishops and the concourse of all the "lords and orders" of Florence. And Giotto was now beginning to throw Cimabue into the shade — Giotto, the shepherd's boy, painter, sculptor, architect, and engineer at once, who a few years later was to complete and crown the architectural glories of Florence by that masterpiece of grace, his marble Campanile.

Fifty years made then all that striking difference in domestic habits, in the materials of dress, in the value of money, which they have usually made in later centuries. The poet of the fourteenth century describes the proudest nobleman of a hundred years before, "with his leathern girdle and clasp of bone;" and in one of the most beautiful of all poetic celebrations of the good old time, draws the domestic life of ancient Florence in the household where his ancestor was born.[1] There high-born dames, he says, still plied the distaff and the loom; still rocked the cradle with the words which their own mothers had used; or working with their maidens, told them old tales of the forefathers of the city, "of the Trojans, of Fiesole, and of Rome." Villani still finds this rudeness within forty years of the end of the century, almost within the limits of his own and Dante's life; and speaks of that "old first people," *il primo Popolo Vecchio*, with their coarse food and expenditure, their leather jerkins, and plain close gowns, their small dowries and late marriages, as if they were the first founders of the city, and not a generation which had lasted on into his own.[2] Twenty years later his story is of the

[1] *Parad.* xv. 47–133. [2] G. Vill. vi. 69 (1259).

gayety, the riches, the profuse munificence, the brilliant festivities, the careless and joyous life which attracted foreigners to Florence as the city of pleasure; of companies of a thousand or more, all clad in white robes, under a lord, styled "of Love," passing their time in sports and dances; of ladies and knights, "going through the city with trumpets and other instruments, with joy and gladness," and meeting together in banquets evening and morning; entertaining illustrious strangers, and honorably escorting them on horseback in their passage through the city; tempting by their liberality courtiers and wits, and minstrels and jesters, to add to the amusements of Florence.[1] Nor were these the boisterous triumphs of unrefined and coarse merriment. How variety of character was drawn out, how its more delicate elements were elicited and tempered, how nicely it was observed, and how finely drawn, let the racy and open-eyed story-tellers of Florence testify.

Not perhaps in these troops of revelers, but amid music and song, and in the pleasant places of social and private life, belonging to the Florence of arts and poetry, not to the Florence of factions and strife, should we expect to find the friend of the sweet singer, Casella, and of the reserved aud bold speculator, Guido Cavalcanti; the mystic poet of the Vita Nuova, so sensitive and delicate, trembling at a gaze or a touch, recording visions, painting angels, composing Canzoni and commenting on them; finally devoting himself to the austere consolations of deep study. To superadd to such a character that of a democratic politician of the Middle Ages, seems an incongruous

[1] *Ibid.* vii. 89 (1283).

and harsh combination. Yet it was a real one in this instance. The scholar's life is, in our idea of it, far separated from the practical and the political; we have been taught by our experience to disjoin enthusiasm in love, in art, in what is abstract or imaginative, from keen interest and successful interference in the affairs and conflicts of life. The practical man may sometimes be also a dilettante; but the dreamer or the thinker wisely or indolently keeps out of the rough ways where real passions and characters meet and jostle, or if he ventures, seldom gains honor there. The separation, though a natural one, grows wider as society becomes more vast and manifold, as its ends, functions, and pursuits are disentangled, while they multiply. But in Dante's time, and in an Italian city, it was not such a strange thing that the most refined and tender interpreter of feeling, the popular poet, whose verses touched all hearts, and were in every mouth, should be also at once the ardent follower of all abstruse and difficult learning, and a prominent character among those who administered the state. In that narrow sphere of action, in that period of dawning powers and circumscribed knowledge, it seemed no unreasonable hope or unwise ambition to attempt the compassing of all science, and to make it subserve and illustrate the praise of active citizenship.[1] Dante, like other literary celebrities of the time, was not less from the custom of the day than from his own purpose a public man. He took his place among his fellow-citizens; he went out to war with them; he fought, it is said, among the skirmishers at the great Guelf victory of Campaldino;

[1] *Vide* the opening of the *De Monarchia*.

to qualify himself for office in the democracy, he enrolled himself in one of the Guilds of the people, and was matriculated in the "Art" of the Apothecaries; he served the state as its agent abroad; he went on important missions to the cities and courts of Italy — according to a Florentine tradition, which enumerates fourteen distinct embassies, even to Hungary and France. In the memorable year of Jubilee, 1300, he was one of the Priors of the Republic. There is no shrinking from fellowship and coöperation and conflict with the keen or bold men of the market-place and council-hall in that mind of exquisite and, as drawn by itself, exaggerated sensibility. The doings and characters of men, the workings of society, the fortunes of Italy, were watched and thought of with as deep an interest as the courses of the stars, and read in the real spectacle of life with as profound emotion as in the miraculous page of Virgil; and no scholar ever read Virgil with such feeling — no astronomer ever watched the stars with more eager inquisitiveness. The whole man opens to the world around him; all affections and powers, soul and sense, diligently and thoughtfully directed and trained, with free and concurrent and equal energy, with distinct yet harmonious purposes, seek out their respective and appropriate objects, moral, intellectual, natural, spiritual, in that admirable scene and hard field where man is placed to labor and love, to be exercised, proved, and judged.

In a fresco in the chapel of the old palace of the Podestà[1] at Florence is a portrait of Dante, said to be

[1] The Bargello, a prison (1850); a museum (1878). *Vide* Vasari, p. 311.

by the hand of his contemporary Giotto.[1] It was discovered in 1841 under the whitewash, and a tracing made by Mr. Seymour Kirkup has been reproduced in facsimile by the Arundel Society. The fresco was afterwards restored or repainted with no happy success. He is represented as he might have been in the year of Campaldino (1289). The couutenance is youthful yet manly, more manly than it appears in the engravings of the picture; but it only suggests the strong, deep features of the well-known traditional face. He is drawn with much of the softness and melancholy, pensive sweetness, and with something also of the quaint stiffness of the Vita Nuova, — with his flower and his book. With him is drawn his master, Brunetto Latini, [2] and Corso Donati. We do not know what occasion led Giotto thus to associate him with the great "Baron." Dante was, indeed, closely connected with the Donati. The dwelling of his family was near theirs, in the "Quarter of Scandal," the ward of the Porta St. Piero. He married a daughter of their house, Madonna Gemma. None of his friends are commemorated with more affection than the companion of his light and wayward days, remembered not without a shade of anxious sadness, yet with love and hope, Corso's brother, Forese.[3] No sweeter spirit sings and smiles in the illumined spheres of Paradise than she whom Forese remembers as on earth one —

> Che tra bella e buona
> Non so qual fosse più (*Purg.* c. 24),[4]

[1] See p. 151, n.

[2] He died in 1294. G. Vill. viii. 10. That the two figures are Latini and Donati lacks proof. (D.)

[3] *Purg.* c. 23.

[4] My sister, good and beautiful — which most I know not. (Wright.)

and who, from the depth of her heavenly joy, teaches the poet that in the lowest place among the blessed there can be no envy[1] — the sister of Forese and Corso, Piccarda. The Commedia, though it speaks, as if in prophecy, of Corso's miserable death, avoids the mention of his name.[2] Its silence is so remarkable as to seem significant. But though history does not group together Corso and Dante, the picture represents the truth — their fortunes were linked together. They were actors in the same scene — at this distance of time two of the most prominent; though a scene very different from that calm and grave assembly which Giotto's placid pencil has drawn on the old chapel wall.

The outlines of this part of Dante's history are so well known that it is not necessary to dwell on them; and more than the outlines we know not. The family quarrels came to a head, issued in parties, and the parties took names; they borrowed them from two rival factions in a neighboring town, Pistoia, whose feud was imported into Florence; and the Guelfs became divided into the Black Guelfs, who were led by the Donati, and the White Guelfs, who sided with the Cerchi.[3] It still professed to be but a family feud, confined to the great houses; but they were too powerful and Florence too small for it not to affect the whole Republic. The middle classes and the artisans looked on, and for a time not without satisfaction, at the strife of the great men; but it grew evident that one party must crush the other, and become dominant in Florence; and of the two, the

[1] *Parad.* c. 3. [2] *Purg.* c. 24, 82–87.
[3] In 1300. G. Vill. viii. 38, 39.

Cerchi and their White adherents were less formidable to the democracy than the unscrupulous and overbearing Donati, with their military renown and lordly tastes; proud not merely of being nobles, but Guelf nobles; always loyal champions, once the martyrs and now the hereditary assertors of the great Guelf cause. The Cerchi, with less character and less zeal, but rich, liberal, and showy, and with more of rough kindness and vulgar good-nature for the common people, were more popular in Guelf Florence than the "Parte Guelfa;" and, of course, the Ghibellines wished them well. Both the contemporary historians of Florence lead us to think that they might have been the governors and guides of the Republic — if they had chosen, and had known how; and both, though condemning the two parties equally, seem to have thought that this would have been the best result for the state. But the accounts of both, though they are very different writers, agree in their scorn of the leaders of the White Guelfs. They were upstarts, purse-proud, vain, and coarse-minded; and they dared to aspire to an ambition which they were too dull and too cowardly to pursue, when the game was in their hands. They wished to rule; but when they might, they were afraid. The commons were on their side, the moderate men, the party of law, the lovers of republican government, and for the most part the magistrates; but they shrank from their fortune, "more from cowardice than from goodness, because they exceedingly feared their adversaries."[1] Boniface VIII. had no prepossessions in Florence, except for energy and an open hand; the side which was most popular he

[1] Dino Comp. p. 45.

would have accepted and backed; but "he would not lose," he said, "the men for the women." "Io non voglio perdere gli uomini per le femminelle."[1] If the Black party furnished types for the grosser or fiercer forms of wickedness in the poet's Hell, the White party surely were the originals of that picture of stupid and cowardly selfishness, in the miserable crowd who moan and are buffeted in the vestibule of the Pit, mingled with the angels who dared neither to rebel nor be faithful, but "were for themselves;" and whoever it may be who is singled out in the *setta dei cattivi* for deeper and special scorn, he —

> Che fece per viltà il gran rifiuto (*Inf.* c. 3, 60),[2]

the idea was derived from the Cerchi in Florence.

A French prince was sent by the Pope to mediate and make peace in Florence. The Black Guelfs and Corso Donati came with him. The magistrates were overawed and perplexed. The White party were step by step amused, entrapped, led blindly into false plots, entangled in the elaborate subtleties, and exposed with all the zest and mockery of Italian intrigue — finally chased out of their houses and from the city, condemned unheard, outlawed, ruined in name and property, by the Pope's French mediator. With them fell many citizens who had tried to hold the balance between the two parties; for the leaders of the Black Guelfs were guilty of no errors of weakness. In two extant lists of the proscribed — condemned by default, for corruption and various crimes, especially for hindering the entrance into Florence of Charles de Valois, to a heavy fine and banishment;

[1] I am not going to lose the men for the old women. *Ibid.* p. 62.

[2] The coward who the great refusal made.

then, two months after, for contumacy, to be burned alive if he ever fell into the hands of the Republic; appears the name of Dante Alighieri; and more than this, concerning the history of his expulsion, we know not.

Of his subsequent life, history tells us little more than the general character. He acted for a time in concert with the expelled party, when they attempted to force their way back to Florence; he gave them up at last in scorn and despair; but he never returned to Florence. And he found no new home for the rest of his days. Nineteen years, from his exile to his death, he was a wanderer. The character is stamped on his writings. History, tradition, documents, all scanty or dim, do but disclose him to us at different points, appearing here and there, we are not told how or why. One old record, discovered by antiquarian industry, shows him in a village church near Florence, planning, with the Cerchi and the White party, an attack on the Black Guelfs. In another, he appears in the Val di Magra, making peace between its small potentates: in another, as the inhabitant of a certain street in Padua. The traditions of some remote spots about Italy still connect his name with a ruined tower, a mountain glen, a cell in a convent. In the recollections of the following generation, his solemn and melancholy form mingled reluctantly, and for a while, in the brilliant court of the Scaligers; and scared the women, as a visitant of the other world, as he passed by their doors in the streets of Verona. Rumor brings him to the West — with probability to Paris, more doubtfully to Oxford. But little certain can be made out about the places where he was an honored and admired, but it may be not always a welcome guest, till we find him sheltered, cherished, and then laid at last to rest, by the Lords of Ravenna. There he still rests, in a small, solitary chapel, built, not by a Florentine, but a Venetian. Florence, "that mother of little love," asked for his bones; but rightly asked in vain. His place of repose is better in those remote and forsaken streets "by the shore of the Adrian Sea," hard by the last relics of the Roman Empire — the mausoleum of the children of Theodosius, and the mosaics of Justinian — than among the assembled dead of St. Croce, or amid the magnificence of Santa Maria del Fiore.

II

THE INTELLECTUAL AND MORAL AWAKENING OF ITALY.

By Charles Eliot Norton[1]

To acquire a love for the best poetry, and a just understanding of it, is the chief end of the study of literature; for it is by means of poetry that the imagination is quickened, nurtured, and invigorated, and it is only through the exercise of his imagination that man can live a life that is in a true sense worth living. For it is the imagination which lifts him from the petty, transient, and physical interests that engross the greater part of his time and thoughts in self-regarding pursuits, to the large, permanent, and spiritual interests that ennoble his nature, and transform him from a solitary individual into a member of the brotherhood of the human race.

In the poet the imagination works more powerfully and consistently than in other men, and thus qualifies him to become the teacher and inspirer of his fellows. He sees men, by its means, more clearly than they see themselves; he discloses them to themselves, and reveals to them their own dim ideals. He becomes the interpreter of his age to itself; and not merely of his

[1] *The Library of the World's Best Literature.* Essay on Dante. (By permission.)

own age is he the interpreter, but of man to man in all ages. For change as the world may in outward aspect, with the rise and fall of empires, — change as men may, from generation to generation, in knowledge, belief, and manners, — human nature remains unalterable in its elements, unchanged from age to age; and it is human nature, under its various guises, with which the great poets deal.

The Iliad and the Odyssey do not become antiquated to us. The characters of Shakespeare are perpetually modern. Homer, Dante, Shakespeare stand alone in the closeness of their relation to nature. Each after his own manner gives us a view of life, as seen by the poetic imagination, such as no other poet has given to us. Homer, first of all poets, shows us individual personages sharply defined, but iu the early stages of intellectual and moral development, — the first representatives of the race at its conscious entrance upon the path of progress, with simple motives, simple theories of existence, simple and limited experience. He is plain and direct in the presentation of life, and in the substance no less than in the expression of his thought.

In Shakespeare's work the individual man is no less sharply defined, no less true to nature, but the long procession of his personages is wholly different in effect from that of the Iliad and the Odyssey. They have lost the simplicity of the older race; they are the products of a longer and more varied experience; they have become more complex. And Shakespeare is plain and direct neither in the substance of his thought nor in the expression of it. The world has grown older, and in the evolution of his nature man has become conscious of the irreconcilable paradoxes of life, and more or less aware that while he is infinite in faculty, he is also the quintessence of dust. But there is one essential characteristic in which Shakespeare and Homer resemble each other as poets, — that they both show to us the scene of life without the interference of their own personality. Each simply holds the mirror up to nature, and lets us see the reflection, without making comment on the show. If there be a lesson in it we must learn it for ourselves.

Dante comes between the two, and differs more widely from each of them than they from one another. They are primarily poets. He is primarily a moralist who is also a poet. Of Homer the man, and of Shakespeare the man, we know, and need to know, nothing; it is only with them as poets that we are concerned. But it is needful to know Dante as man in order fully to appreciate him as poet. He gives us his world not as reflection from an unconscious and indifferent mirror, but as from a mirror that shapes and orders its reflections for a definite end beyond that of art, and extraneous to it. And in this lies the secret of Dante's hold upon so many and so various minds. He is the chief poet of man as a moral being.

To understand aright the work of any great poet we must know the conditions of his times; but this is not enough in the case of Dante. We must know not only the conditions of the generation to which he belonged, we must also know the specific conditions which shaped him into the man he was, and differentiated him from his fellows. How came he, endowed with a poetic imagination which puts him in the same class with Homer and Shakespeare, not to be content, like them, to give us a simple view of the phantasmagoria of life, but eager to use the fleeting images as instruments by which to enforce the lesson of righteousness, to set forth a theory of existence and a scheme of the universe?

The question cannot be answered without a consideration of the change wrought in the life and thoughts of men in Europe by the Christian doctrine as expounded and enforced by the Roman Church, and of the simultaneous changes in outward conditions resulting from the destruction of the ancient civilization, and the slow evolution of the modern world as it rose from the ruins of the old. The period which immediately preceded and followed the fall of the Roman Empire was too disorderly, confused, and broken for men during its course to be conscious of the directions in which they were treading. Century after century passed without settled institutions, without orderly language, without literature, without art. But institutions, languages, literature, and art were germinating, and before the end of the eleventh century clear signs of a new civilization were manifest in Western Europe. The nations, distinguished by differences of race and history, were settling down within definite geographical limits; the various languages were shaping themselves for the uses of intercourse and of literature; institutions accommodated to actual needs were growing strong; here and there the social order was becoming comparatively tranquil and secure. Progress once begun became rapid, and the twelfth century is one of the most splendid periods of the intellectual life of man expressing itself in an infinite variety of noble and attractive forms. These new conditions were most strongly marked in France; in Provence at the South, and in and around the Ile de France at the North; and from both these regions a quickening influence diffused itself eastward into Italy.

The conditions of Italy throughout the Dark and Middle Ages were widely different from those of other parts of Europe. Through all the ruin and confusion of these centuries a tradition of ancient culture and ancient power was handed down from generation to generation, strongly affecting the imagination of the Italian people, whether recent invaders or descendants of the old population. Italy had never had a national unity and life, and the divisions of her different regions remained as wide in the later as in the earlier times; but there was one sentiment which bound all her various and conflicting elements in a common bond, which touched every Italian heart and roused every Italian imagination, — the sentiment of the imperial grandeur and authority of Rome. Shrunken, feeble, fallen, as the city was, the thought of what she had once been still occupied the fancy of the Italian people, determined their conceptions of the government of the world, and quickened within them a glow of patriotic pride. Her laws were still the main fount of whatsoever law existed for the maintenance of public and private right; the imperial dignity, however interrupted in transmission, however often assumed by foreign and barbarian conquerors, was still, to the imagination, supreme above all other earthly titles; the story of Roman deeds was known of all men; the legends of Roman heroes were the familiar tales of infancy and age. Cities that had risen since Rome fell claimed, with pardonable falsehood, to have had their origin from her, and their rulers adopted the designations of their consuls and her senators. The fragments of her literature that had survived the destruction of her culture were the models for the rude writers of ignorant centuries, and her language formed the basis for the new language which was gradually shaping itself in accordance with the slowly growing needs of expression. The traces of her material dominion, the ruins of her wide arch of empire, were still to be found from the far West to the farther East, and were but the types and emblems of her moral dominion in the law, the language, the customs, the traditions of the different lands. Nothing in the whole course of profane history has so affected the imaginations of men, or so influenced their destinies, as the achievements and authority of Rome.

The Roman Church inherited, together with the city, the tradition of Roman dominion over the world. Ancient Rome largely shaped modern Christianity,—by the transmission of the idea of the authority which the Empire once exerted to the Church which grew up upon its ruins. The tremendous drama of Roman history displayed itself to the imagination from scene to scene, from act to act, with completeness of poetic progress and climax,—first the growth, the extension, the absoluteness of material supremacy, the heathen being made the instruments of Divine power for preparing the world for the revelation of the true God; then the tragedy of Christ's death wrought by Roman hands, and the expiation of it in the fall of the Roman imperial power; followed by the new era in which

Rome again was asserting herself as mistress of the world, but now with spiritual instead of material supremacy, and with a dominion against which the gates of hell itself should not prevail.

It was, indeed, not at once that this conception of the Church as the inheritor of the rights of Rome to the obedience of mankind took form. It grew slowly and against opposition. But at the end of the eleventh century, through the genius of Pope Gregory VII., the ideas hitherto disputed, of the supreme authority of the pope within the Church and of the supremacy of the Church over the State, were established as the accepted ecclesiastical theory, and adopted as the basis of the definitely organized ecclesiastical system. Little more than a hundred years later, at the beginning of the thirteenth century, Innocent III. enforced the claims of the Church with a vigor and ability hardly less than that of his great predecessor, maintaining openly that the pope — Pontifex Maximus — was the vicar of God upon earth.

This theory was the logical conclusion from a long series of historic premises; and resting upon a firm foundation of dogma, it was supported by the genuine belief, no less than by the worldly interests and ambitions, of those who profited by it. The ideal it presented was at once a simple and a noble conception,— narrow indeed, for the ignorance of men was such that only narrow conceptions, in matters relating to the nature and destiny of man and the order of the universe, were possible. But it was a theory that offered an apparently sufficient solution of the mysteries of religion, of the relation between God and man, between the visible creation and the unseen world. It was a theory of a material rather than a spiritual order: it reduced the things of the spirit into terms of the things of the flesh. It was crude, it was easily comprehensible, it was fitted to the mental conditions of the age.

The power which the Church claimed, and which to a large degree it exercised over the imagination and over the conduct of the Middle Ages, was the power which belonged to its head as the earthly representative and vicegerent of God. No wonder that such power was often abused, and that the corruption among the ministers of the Church was widespread. Yet in spite of abuse, in spite of corruption, the Church was the ark of civilization.

The religious — no less than the intellectual — life of Europe had revived in the eleventh and twelfth centuries, and had displayed its fervor in the marvels of Crusades and of church-building,— external modes of manifesting zeal for the glory of God, and ardor for personal salvation. But with the progress of intelligence the spirit which had found its expression in these modes of service, now in the thirteenth century in Italy, fired the hearts of men with an even more intense and far more vital flame, quickening within them sympathies which had long lain dormant, aud which now at last burst into activity in efforts and sacrifices for the relief of misery, and for the bringing of all men within the fold of Christian brotherhood. St. Francis and St. Dominic, in founding their orders, and in setting an example to their brethren, only gave measure and direction to a common impulse.[1]

[1] By the middle of the thirteenth century the Franciscan order had 8,000 monasteries and 200,000 monks. St. Francis also established

Yet such were the general hardness of heart and cruelty of temper which had resulted from the centuries of violence, oppression, and suffering out of which Italy with the rest of Europe was slowly emerging, that the strivings of religious emotion and the efforts of humane sympathy were less powerful to bring about an improvement in social order than influences which had their root in material conditions. Chief among these was the increasing strength of the civic communities, through the development of industry and of commerce. The people of the cities, united for the protection of their common interests, were gaining a sense of power. The little people, as they were called, — mechanics, tradesmen, and the like, — were organizing themselves, and growing strong enough to compel the great to submit to the restrictions of a more or less orderly and peaceful life. In spite of the violent contentions of the great, in spite of frequent civic uproar, of war with neighbors, of impassioned party disputes, in spite of incessant interruptions of their tranquillity, many of the cities of Italy were advancing in prosperity and wealth. No one of them made more rapid and steady progress than Florence.

The history of Florence during the thirteenth cen-

the order of the *Tertiaries*, composed of those who, while remaining in the ordinary paths of life, pledged themselves to cherish a loving spirit, to live as simply as possible, to minister to the poor, and not to take up arms except in defense of their country. The effect of this order was immediate. Hundreds of thousands were enrolled in it. Refusing to engage in the petty feuds of their lords, they broke the power of the feudal system in Italy. In 1233 a wave of religious enthusiasm swept over Italy, and again in 1260 with the rise of the *Flagellants*. *Vide* Gaspary, *Hist. of Early Italian Literature*, p. 141 ff. (D.)

tury is a splendid tale of civic energy and resolute self-confidence.[1] The little city was full of eager and vigorous life. Her story abounds in picturesque incident. She had her experience of the turn of the wheel of Fortune, being now at the summit of power in Tuscany, now in the depths of defeat and humiliation.

The spiritual emotion, the improvement in the conditions of society, the increase of wealth, the growth in power of the cities of Italy, were naturally accompanied by a corresponding intellectual development, and the thirteenth century became for Italy what the twelfth had been for France, a period of splendid activity in the expression of her new life. Every mode of expression in literature and in the arts was sought and practiced, at first with feeble and ignorant hands, but with steady gain of mastery. At the beginning of the century the language was a mere spoken tongue, not yet shaped for literary use. But the example of Provence was strongly felt at the court of the Emperor Frederick II. in Sicily, and the first half of the century was not ended before many poets were imitating in the Italian tongue the poems of the troubadours. Form and substance were alike copied; there is scarcely a single original note; but the practice was of service in giving suppleness to the language, in forming it for nobler uses, and in opening the way for poetry which should be Italian in sentiment as well as in words. At the north of Italy the influence of the trouvères was felt in like manner. Everywhere the desire for expression was manifest. The spring had come, the young birds had begun to twitter, but no full song was yet heard. Love was

[1] *Vide* pp. 28 ff.

the main theme of the poets, but it had few accents of sincerity; the common tone was artificial, was unreal.

In the second half of the century new voices are heard, with accents of genuine and natural feeling; the poets begin to treat the old themes with more freshness, and to deal with religion, politics, and morals, as well as with love. The language still possesses, indeed, the quality of youth; it is still pliant, its forms have not become stiffened by age, it is fit for larger use than has yet been made of it, and lies ready and waiting, like a noble instrument, for the hand of the master which shall draw from it its full harmonies and reveal its latent power in the service he exacts from it.

But it was not in poetry alone that the life of Italy found expression. Before the invention of printing, — which gave to the literary arts such an advantage as secured their preëminence,— architecture, sculpture, and painting were hardly less important means for the expression of the ideals of the imagination and the creative energy of man. The practice of them had never wholly ceased in Italy; but her native artists had lost the traditions of technical skill; their work was rude and childish. The conventional and lifeless forms of Byzantine art in its decline were adopted by workmen who no longer felt the impulse, and no longer possessed the capacity, of original design. Venice and Pisa, early enriched by Eastern commerce, and with citizens both instructed and inspired by knowledge of foreign lands, had begun great works of building even in the eleventh century; but these works had been designed, and mainly executed, by masters from abroad. But now the awakened soul of

Italy breathed new life into all the arts in its efforts at self-expression. A splendid revival began. The inspiring influence of France was felt in the arts of construction and design as it had been felt in poetry. The magnificent display of the highest powers of the imagination and the intelligence in France, the creation during the twelfth and early thirteenth centuries of the unrivaled productions of Gothic art, stimulated and quickened the growth of the native art of Italy. But the French forms were seldom adopted for direct imitation, as the forms of Provençal poetry had been. The power of classic tradition was strong enough to resist their attraction. The taste of Italy rejected the marvels of Gothic design in favor of modes of expression inherited from her own past, but vivified with fresh spirit, and adapted to her new requirements. The inland cities, as they grew rich through native industry, and powerful through the organization of their citizens, were stirred with rivalry to make themselves beautiful, and the motives of religion no less than those of civic pride contributed to their adornment. The Church was the object of interest common to all. Piety, superstition, pride, emulation, all alike called for art in which their spirit should be embodied. The imagination answered to the call. The eyes of the artist were once more opened to see the beauty of life, and his hand sought to reproduce it. The bonds of tradition were broken. The Greek marble vase on the platform of the Duomo at Pisa taught Niccola Pisano the right methods of sculpture, and directed him to the source of his art in the study of nature. His work was a new wonder and delight, and showed the way along which many followed him. Painting took her lesson from sculpture, and before the end of the century both arts had become responsive to the demand of the time, and had entered upon that course of triumph which was not to end till, three centuries later, chisel and brush dropped from hands enfeebled in the general decline of national vigor, and incapable of resistance to the tyrannous and exclusive autocracy of the printed page.

But it was not only the new birth of sentiment and emotion which quickened these arts: it was also the aroused curiosity of men concerning themselves, their history, and the earth. They felt their own ignorance. The vast region of the unknown, which encircled with its immeasurable spaces the little tract of the known world, appealed to their fancy and their spirit of enterprise, with its boundless promise and its innumerable allurements to adventure. Learning, long confined and starved in the cell of the monk, was coming out into the open world, and was gathering fresh stores alike from the past and the present. The treasure of the wisdom and knowledge of the Greeks was eagerly sought, especially in translations of Aristotle, — translations which, though imperfect indeed, and disfigured by numberless misinterpretations and mistakes, nevertheless contain a body of instruction invaluable as a guide and stimulant to the awakened intelligence. Encyclopædic compends of knowledge put at the disposition of students all that was known or fancied in the various fields of science. The division between knowledge and belief was not sharply drawn, and the wonders of legend and of fable were accepted with as ready a faith as the actual facts of observation and of experience. Travelers for gain or for adventure, and missionaries for the sake of religion, were venturing to lands hitherto unvisited. The growth of knowledge, small as it was compared with later increase, widened thought and deepened life. The increase of thought strengthened the faculties of the mind. Man becomes more truly man in proportion to what he knows, and one of the most striking and characteristic features of this great century is the advance of man through increase of knowledge out of childishness towards maturity. The insoluble problems which had been discussed with astonishing acuteness by the schoolmen of the preceding generation were giving place to a philosophy of more immediate application to the conduct and discipline of life. The Summa Theologica of St. Thomas Aquinas not only treated with incomparable logic the vexed questions of scholastic philosophy, but brought all the resources of a noble and well-trained intelligence and of a fine moral sense to the study and determination of the order and government of the universe, and of the nature and destiny of man.

The scope of learning remained, indeed, at the end of the century, narrow in its range. The little tract of truth which men had acquired lay encompassed by ignorance, like a scant garden-plot surrounded by a high wall. But here and there the wall was broken through, and paths were leading out into wider fields to be won for culture, or into deserts wider still, in which the wanderers should perish.

But as yet there was no comprehensive and philosophic grasp of the new conditions in their total significance; no harmonizing of their various elements into one consistent scheme of human life; no criticism of the new life as a whole. For this task was required not only acquaintance with the whole range of existing knowledge, by which the conceptions of men in regard to themselves and the universe were determined, but also a profound view of the meaning of life itself, and an imaginative insight into the nature of man. A mere image of the drama of life as presented to the eye would not suffice. The meaning of it would be lost in the confusion and multiplicity of the scene. The only possible explanation and reconcilement of its aspects lay in the universal application to them of the moral law, and in the exhibition of man as a spiritual and immortal being for whom this world was but the first stage of existence. This was the task undertaken and accomplished by Dante.

CHAPTER II

SOURCES OF OUR KNOWLEDGE OF DANTE

SOURCES OF OUR KNOWLEDGE OF DANTE

OUR best knowledge of Dante we gain from his published works. Beginning with the quaint sonnet which he wrote when a youth of eighteen, after Beatrice had saluted him with such ineffable courtesy, and closing with the *visio Dei*, we have a marvelous self-revelation of the mind of the great Florentine. We must remember, however, that Dante is fashioning his works after poetical ideals, and we reach reliable historical data only by the patient stripping off of symbol and allegory. The historical and poetical are so intermingled that the creations of the imagination must not be mistaken for accurate statements of fact.

Next in importance to Dante's self-disclosure in his works is our knowledge of him derived from his early biographers. We are exceedingly fortunate in possessing a reliable account of the impression the poet made upon his contemporaries. Pope Boniface VIII. proclaimed a jubilee lasting through the year 1300. Among the throngs which went to Rome was a young man whose mind was stirred to its depths by the sights and associations of the sacred city. "And I," writes Giovanni Villani,[1] "finding myself on that blessed pilgrimage in the holy city of Rome, beholding the great and ancient things therein, and reading the stories and the great doings of the Romans, written by Virgil, and by Sallust, and by Lucan, and Titus Livius, and Valerius, and Paulus Orosius, and other masters of history, which wrote alike of small things as of great, of the deeds and actions of the Romans, and also of foreign nations throughout the

[1] Selections from the *Croniche Fiorentine* of Villani, trans. by Selfe and Wicksteed, p. 321.

world — considering that our city of Florence, the daughter and creature of Rome, was rising, whilst Rome was declining, it seemed to me fitting to collect in this volume and chronicle all the deeds and beginnings of the city of Florence, in so far as it has been possible for me to find and gather them together, and to follow the doings of the Florentines in detail, and the other notable things of the universe in brief, as long as it shall be God's pleasure; in hope of whose grace rather than in my own poor learning, I have undertaken the said enterprise; and thus in the year 1300, having returned from Rome, I began to compile this book, in reverence to God and the blessed John, and in commendation of our city of Florence." Having a clear mind, and being accustomed to business and the observation of mankind, in his Cronica Fiorentina, which extends from Biblical times down to 1346, he has given us a vivid description of the intellectual, political, and economic life of his native city. Being a contemporary of Dante, the description of him is of incomparable value.

I

GIOVANNI VILLANI'S ACCOUNT OF DANTE[1]

In the month of July, 1321, died the poet Dante Alighieri of Florence, in the city of Ravenna in Romagna, after his return from an embassy to Venice for the Lords of Polenta, with whom he resided; and in Ravenna before the door of the principal church he was interred with high honor, in the habit of a poet and great philosopher. He died in banishment from the community of Florence, at the age of about fifty-six. This Dante was an honorable and ancient citizen of Porta San Piero at Florence, and our neighbor; and his exile from Florence was on the occasion of Charles of Valois, of the house of France, coming to Florence in 1301, and the expulsion of the White party, as has already in its place been mentioned. The said Dante was of the supreme governors of our city, and of that party although a Guelf; and therefore without any other crime was with the said White party expelled and banished from Florence; and he went to the University of Bologna, and into many ts of the world. This was a great and learned son in almost every science, although a layman; he s a consummate poet and philosopher, and rhetori-

Cronica, lib. ix. cap. 136. Tr. in Napier's *Florentine History*, k i. ch. 16.

cian; as perfect in prose and verse a he was in public speaking a most noble orator; in rhyming excellent, with the most polished and beautiful style that ever appeared in our language up to this time or since. He wrote in his youth the book of The Early Life of Love, and afterwards when in exile made twenty moral and amorous canzonets very excellent, and among other things three noble epistles: one he sent to the Florentine government, complaining of his undeserved exile; another to the Emperor Henry when he was at the siege of Brescia, reprehending him for his delay, and almost prophesying; the third to the Italian cardinals during the vacancy after the death of Pope Clement, urging them to agree in electing an Italian Pope; all in Latin, with noble precepts and excellent sentences and authorities, which were much commended by the wise and learned. And he wrote the Commedia, where, in polished verse and with great and subtile arguments, moral, natural, astrological, philosophical, and theological, with new and beautiful figures, similes, and poetical graces, he composed and treated in a hundred chapters or cantos of the existence of hell, purgatory, and paradise; so loftily as may be said of it, that whoever is of subtile intellect may by his said treatise perceive and understand. He was well pleased in this poem to blame and cry out, in the manner of poets, in some places perhaps more than he ought to have done; but it may be that his exile made him do so. He also wrote the Monarch where he treats of the office of popes and emperor And he began a comment on fourteen of the abov named moral canzonets in the vulgar tongue, which consequence of his death is found imperfect except three, which, to judge from what is seen, would have proved a lofty, beautiful, subtile, and most important work; because it is equally ornamented with noble opinions and fine philosophical and astrological reasoning. Besides these he composed a little book which he entitled De Vulgari Eloquentia, of which he promised to make four books, but only two are to be found, perhaps in consequence of his early death; where, in powerful and elegant Latin and good reasoning, he rejects all the vulgar tongues of Italy. This Dante, from his knowledge, was somewhat presumptuous, harsh, and disdainful, like an ungracious philosopher; he scarcely deigned to converse with laymen; but for his other virtues, science, and worth as a citizen, it seems but reasonable to give him perpetual remembrance in this our chronicle; nevertheless, his noble works, left to us in writing, bear true testimony of him, and honorable fame to our city.[1]

[1] *Vide* pp. 95 ff.

II

BOCCACCIO'S VITA DI DANTE

Dr. Edward Moore,[1] than whom there is not a more careful and judicious Dante scholar, discusses as follows the reliability of Boccaccio's account of Dante: —

"It is needless to point out the peculiar advantages possessed by Boccaccio as a biographer of the poet. He was born during Dante's lifetime, —

ancorche fosse tardi,

too late indeed for personal knowledge of him, though not too late to have intercourse and acquaintance with those who knew him familiarly; at a time consequently when in living memories there existed a store of anecdotes and personal reminiscences of the man as he lived and moved among his fellows, of the aspect he wore to them, of the impression he made upon them. Boccaccio had also another qualification, that of —

lungo studio e grande amore,

in respect of the poet and his works. When the Florentines in 1373 determined to establish a public Lectureship on Dante, Boccaccio was appointed to the office, and delivered his first lecture on October 12th in that year, in the Church of San Stefano, near the Ponte Vecchio. His Lectures took the form of a minute and elaborate Commentary, which is preserved to us as a fragment only, since his work was unhappily interrupted by death in December, 1375, when his Commentary had reached the 17th line of the 17th Canto of the Inferno. The language of this Commentary

[1] *Dante and His Early Biographers.* Edward Moore, D. D. Rivingtons, London, 1890. (By permission.)

is (as one might say) saturated with Dantesque phraseology; the frequency of apparently unconscious quotations of phrases and expressions indicates a very thorough acquaintance with all parts of the Divina Commedia. We know him to have had personal communication with one at least of the children of Dante, his daughter Beatrice, a nun in the convent of San Stefano dell' Uliva at Ravenna, for he was commissioned by a decree of the citizens of Florence (or, to speak more precisely, the company of Or San Michelo), in the year 1350, to convey to her a subsidy of ten florins of gold. Other personal sources of information will be mentioned later."

Having exhaustively considered the two works, each claiming to be Boccaccio's Life of Dante, which have come down to us, and having concluded that the one usually received is the genuine one, Dr. Moore proceeds: —

"Now the credibility of such a work depends on two things: (1) the opportunities for information possessed by its author; and (2) the character of the author himself. We will take them in order, and as to the first we further note that the opportunities for information are of two kinds, general and special.

"In a general sense, any one whatever living either as a contemporary with, or very soon after, the events or persons about which or whom he writes, has obviously opportunities both for gathering, and also for testing, information such as no later author can possess. This qualification of course Boccaccio, as we have already observed, possessed in a preeminent degree. But he had also special qualifications from his actual intercourse with friends and relations of the poet himself. Not only was he brought into contact, as we have seen, with Dante's own daughter Beatrice, but there are *three* other persons mentioned by Boccaccio by name, either relations or intimate friends of Dante himself, from whom he expressly says that he received definite information. First we have Pier Giardino of Ravenna, who, as we read near the beginning of Boccaccio's Commentary, was one of the most intimate and devoted friends whom Dante had in Ravenna. Now Pier Giardino himself informed Boccaccio of Dante's age as it was stated to him by Dante when he lay upon his deathbed. Pier is again mentioned in the Vita (c. xlv.), where he is described as *lungamente stato discepolo di Dante*, as the authority for Boccaccio's statement of the strange loss and recovery of the last thirteen cantos of the Paradiso. Pier Giardino had no doubt the incident well impressed on his memory —

> chiavata in mezzo della testa
> Con maggior chiovi, che d' altrui sermone,

by the fact that he was knocked up out of his bed one night before daybreak by Dante's son Jacopo, who came to tell him of the mysterious vision which he had had during the night in reference to the lost cantos. Now recent researches have discovered abundant contemporary documents proving the presence of Pier Giardino at Ravenna early in the fourteenth century, and notably in the years 1320, 1328, 1346, etc. (See Guerrini e Ricci, Studi e Polemiche Dantesche.) Further, beside other documentary evidence of the presence of Boccaccio also at Ravenna, we have an extract from the Storie Ravennati of Rossi, given by Guerrini, etc., pp. 38, 39: Joannes Boccatius . . . frequenter consueverat urbem hanc, ubi Boccatiorum familia Ravennas erat.

"Next we have Dante's nephew, son of his sister, by name Andrea Poggi. In the Commentary on Inf. viii. 1, he is mentioned as having narrated to Boccaccio, with whom he was intimate (*dimestico divenuto*), the story of the loss and recovery of Inf. cantos i.-vii., claiming to have been himself the person who discovered them. Boccaccio there describes this Andrea Poggi as marvelously resembling Dante in face and stature, and moreover that he walked as though he were slightly humpbacked, as Dante himself is said to have done (*come Dante si dice che faceva*). After testifying to his straightforward and honest character, Boccaccio states that he knew him intimately, and that he derived much information from him respecting Dante's ways and habits (*costumi e modi*).

"We have yet a third person mentioned by name with whom Boccaccio had communications on the subject of Dante, viz. Dino Perini, the rival claimant for the discovery of the missing cantos. He narrated the story himself to Boccaccio, and he had enjoyed (as Boccaccio adds), according to his own statement, the greatest possible intimacy and friendship with Dante (*stato quanto più esser si potesse familiare ed amico di Dante*).

"Again, in his Commentary on Inf. ii. 57, Lez. 8 (vol. i. p. 224), Boccaccio says that his information about Beatrice Portinari (and this is important, as our knowledge of her rests on his statement alone) was derived by him from the mouth of a person worthy of trust, who not only knew her, but was very closely connected with her (*fu per consanguinta strettissima a lei*).

"Here, then, we have five or six distinct sources of direct and special information both accessible to and actually employed by Boccaccio, besides the opportunities for general information possessed by any intelligent person living at a time so very nearly contemporary with the subject of his narratives.

"This being so, let us pass on to the other and last point. Seeing that the writer could give us trustworthy information, is there any reason to doubt that he did do so? Have we any ground for suspecting in the author himself, either deliberate perversion of the truth, or the incapacity, from want of sober judgment or the critical faculty, to keep himself within its limits?

"It has often been maintained that this was the case with Boccaccio. Lionardo (whose life we shall consider later) regards that of Boccaccio as a tissue of fables and gossip. And quite recently so sober a critic as Scartazzini declares, with much emphasis, that in this work Boccaccio has 'written a poem or a romance, not a history.'

"Now such criticism as this appears to me to proceed on a very false and superficial notion of the conditions and limits of trustworthiness in any author, and especially in one living in a different age, and trained in different habits of thought from our own. No doubt the author of the Decameron is to be credited with a lively imagination, and a keen sense of dramatic effect; but are these conditions, which naturally have full play when the author is professedly composing fiction or poetry, entirely incompatible with veracity (subject of course to the different conceptions of accuracy, and of the value of evidence in the fourteenth and nineteenth centuries), when he undertakes to write history?

"Is it quite impossible to suppose, that, as the 'spirits of the prophets are subject to the prophets,' so even a poet may exercise some control over his imagination when he sets himself to deal with facts? Doubtless these qualities in Boccaccio may have colored and heightened some of his pictures, but we have no reason therefore to suppose that he entirely falsified or invented them. We may well give up, for example, such mythical elements as the dream of Dante's mother, and also perhaps that of his son Jacopo, as due to the superstition or facile credulity of the age. But this is no reason for denying that some portions of the poem were probably lost, and strangely and unexpectedly recovered. We may well believe this without necessarily accepting the element of the marvelous with which fancy has surrounded the surprising fact of their recovery. That such facts should be thus clothed with accessories of mystery is as much a result of the age in which they were recorded, as that the movements of the heavenly bodies should be described in the language of the cycles and epi-cycles of the Ptolemaic system. Or to take another point. We need not accept Boccaccio's offhand and positive assertion as to the dates of Dante's several works, since, as we have seen, the superficial reasons for some of his statements are not difficult to guess, and the actual determination of this complicated question is one depending on minute and careful criticism, which is certainly not to be looked for in the age when he wrote, and assuredly is not found even in Dante himself. But the rejection of such portions of the work as these, and perhaps even much else, is no reason whatever for casting doubt upon those others in which Boccaccio had unique and copious opportunities for securing knowledge, and as to which there is simply no reason whatever for saying what is false rather than what is true; I mean such details — and most interesting they are — as the features, gait, habits, manners, and other personal traits of the poet. Here there is simply no motive for invention or falsification, for it is by no means an ideal picture, and these details were still fresh and lively in the minds and memories of many with whom Boccaccio had familiar intercourse. As Dr. Witte very well remarks, 'Though we find much that we reject as fabulous in the history of Livy, and that even in the later periods of his narrative as well as the earlier, we do not therefore feel any suspicion as to the truthfulness of his account of the Second Punic War.' Even so, I feel no doubt that in the Life of Boccaccio, though we may not commit ourselves to the accuracy of every fact and detail, we certainly have a generally trustworthy and truthful picture of Dante as he appeared to his contemporaries, and as he lived in the memories of his fellow-men.

"Most grateful should we be to Boccaccio for this precious heritage; for not only is it recorded in his own delicious and inimitable prose, not only is the portrait traced with loving and skilful hand, but without it we should not have possessed any such portraiture at all."

It is interesting to compare Scartazzini's [1] estimate of the value of the Vita with that of Dr. Moore. "Different and divergent have been, are, and will be, the judgments of different and divergent writers with regard to the historic value of Boccaccio's Life of Dante. Some have praised it as a work of unique merit, and as a perfectly trustworthy source for the history of Dante's life; others have decried it as a mere historical romance, the work rather of a declaimer and a rhetorician than of a careful biographer. If we study it seriously in the light of a sane criticism, we shall find ourselves, how-

[1] *Dante Handbook*, Scartazzini and Davidson, Ginn & Co., pp. 5, 6.

ever reluctantly, compelled, in the main, to take part with the latter, and this too in spite of the fact that we owe to Messer Giovanni not a little information, some of which is precious. Indeed we should have willfully to close our eyes, if we were not to see that the garrulous Certaldese has nothing in the world of the conscientious accuracy of the serious historian, and that, if he did not invent the facts which he relates, in order to add weight to his declamations, as certain too rigorous critics have not hesitated to accuse him of having done, he certainly took no manner of care to verify the historical truth and accuracy of the facts related by him. Whatever view others may take of this work, all serious critics have, for some time, agreed that it must be used with great caution, that nothing must be adopted from it without criticism, and that the assertions of the Certaldese must not be accepted as historic facts, without the fullest and freest criticism and the utmost reserve."

VITA DI DANTE.[1]

§ 1. PROEM.

Inasmuch as we should not only flee evil deeds, albeit they seem to go unpunished, but also by right action should strive to amend them, I, although not fitted for so great a task, will try to do according to my little talent what the city should have done with magnificence, but has not. For I recognize that I am a part, though a small one, of that same city whereof Dante Alighieri, if his merits, his nobleness, and his virtue be considered, was a very great part, and that

[1] This excellent translation is by James Robinson Smith, and was first published in *Yale Studies in English*, Professor A. S. Cook, editor. By the kind permission of Mr. Smith practically the whole of Boccaccio's *Vita* is inserted, only irrelevant portions being omitted.

for this reason I, like every other citizen, am personally responsible for the honors due him. Not with a statue shall I honor him, nor with splendid obsequies — which customs no longer hold among us, nor would my powers suffice therefor — but with words I shall honor him, feeble though they be for so great an undertaking. Of these I have, and of these will I give, that other nations may not say that his native land, both as a whole and in part, has been equally ungrateful to so great a poet.

And I shall write in a style full light and humble, for higher my art does not permit me; and in the Florentine idiom, that it may not differ from that which Dante used in the greater part of his writings. I shall first record those things about which he himself preserved a modest silence, namely, the nobleness of his birth, his life, his studies, and his habits. Afterwards I shall gather under one head the works he composed, whereby he has rendered himself so evident to posterity that perchance my words will throw as much darkness upon him as light, albeit this is neither my intention nor wish. For I am content always to be set right, here and elsewhere, by those wiser than I, in all that I have spoken mistakingly. And that I may not err, I humbly pray that He who, as we know, drew Dante to his vision by a stair so lofty, will now aid and guide my spirit and my feeble hand.

§ 2. DANTE'S BIRTH AND STUDIES.

Florence, the noblest of Italian cities, had her beginning, as ancient history and the general opinion of the present time seem to declare, from the Romans. Increasing in size as years went on, and filled with people and famous men, she began to appear to all her neighbors not only as a city but a power. What the cause of change was from these great beginnings — whether adverse fortune, or unfavorable skies, or the deserts of her citizens — we cannot be sure. But certain it is that, not many centuries later, Attila, that most cruel King of the Vandals and general spoiler of nearly all Italy, after he had slain or dispersed all or the greater part of the citizens that were known for their noble blood or for some other distinction, reduced the city to ashes and ruins.

In this condition it is thought to have remained for more than three hundred years. At the end of that period the Roman Empire having been transferred, and not without cause, from Greece to Gaul, Charles the Great, then the most clement King of the French, was raised to the imperial throne. At the close of many labors, moved, as I believe, by the Divine Spirit, he turned his imperial mind to the rebuilding of the desolated city. He it was who caused it to be rebuilt and inhabited by members of the same families from which the original founders were drawn, making it as far as possible like to Rome. And although he reduced the circumference of the walls, he nevertheless gathered within them the few descendants of the ancient fugitives.

Now among the new inhabitants (perhaps, as fame attests, the director of the rebuilding, allotter of the houses and streets, and giver of wise laws to the new people) was one who came from Rome, a most noble youth of the house of the Frangipani, whom everybody called Eliseo. When he had finished the main work for which he had come, he became either from love of the city newly laid out by him, or from the pleasantness of the site, to which he perceived perhaps that the skies were in the future to be propitious, or drawn on by whatever other cause, a permanent citizen there. And the family of children and descendants, not small, nor little to be praised, which he left behind him, abandoned the ancient surname of their ancestors, and took in its stead the name of their founder in Florence, and all called themselves the Elisei.

Among the other members of this family, as time went on and son descended from father, there was born and there lived a knight by the name of Cacciaguida, in arms and in judgment excellent and brave. In his youth his elders gave him for a bride a maiden born of the Aldighieri of Ferrara, prized for her beauty and her character, no less than for her noble blood. They lived together many years, and had several children. Whatever the others may have been called, in one of the children it pleased the mother to renew the name of her ancestors — as women often are fond of doing — and so she called him Aldighieri, although the word later, corrupted by the dropping of the "d," survived as Alighieri. The excellence of this man caused his descendants to relinquish the title Elisei, and take as their patronymic Alighieri; which name holds to this day. From him were descended many children, grandchildren, and great-grandchildren; and, during the reign of Emperor Frederick II., an Alighieri was born who was destined more through his son than of himself, to become famous. His wife in her pregnancy, and near the time of her delivery, saw in a dream what the fruit of her womb was to be; although the matter was not then understood by her nor by any other, and only from that which followed is to-day manifest to all.

This gentle lady seemed in her dream to be beneath

a lofty laurel tree, in a green meadow, beside a clear spring, and there she felt herself delivered of a son. And he, partaking merely of the berries that fell from the laurel and of the waters of the clear spring, seemed almost immediately to become a shepherd that strove with all his power to secure some leaves of the tree whose fruit had nourished him. And as he strove she thought he fell, and when he rose again she perceived that he was no longer a man but a peacock; whereat so great wonder seized her that her sleep broke. Not long after it befell that the due time for her labor arrived, and she brought forth a son whom she and his father by common consent named Dante; and rightly so, for as will be seen as we proceed, the issue corresponded exactly to the name.

This was that Dante of whom the present discourse treats. This was that Dante given to our age by the special grace of God. This was that Dante who was the first to open the way for the return of the Muses, banished from Italy. By him the glory of the Florentine idiom has been made manifest; by him all the beauties of the vulgar tongue have been set to fitting numbers; by him dead poesy may truly be said to have been revived. A due consideration of these things will show that he could rightly have had no other name than Dante.

This special glory of Italy was born in our city in the year of the saving incarnation of the King of the universe 1265, when the Roman Empire was without a ruler, owing to the death of the aforesaid Frederick, and Pope Urban the Fourth was sitting in the chair of St. Peter. The family into which he was born was of a smiling fortune — smiling, I mean, if we consider the condition of the world that then obtained. I will omit all consideration of his infancy — whatever it may have been — wherein appeared many signs of the coming glory of his genius. But I will note that from his earliest boyhood, having already learned the rudiments of letters, he gave himself and all his time, not to youthful lust and indolence, after the fashion of the nobles of to-day, lolling at ease in the lap of his mother, but to continued study, in his native city, of the liberal arts, so that he became exceedingly expert therein. And as his mind and genius ripened with his years, he devoted himself, not to lucrative pursuits, whereto every one in general now hastens, but, with a laudable desire for perpetual fame, scorning transitory riches, he freely dedicated himself to the acquisition of a complete knowledge of poetic creations and of their exposition by rules of art. In this exercise he became closely intimate with Virgil, Horace, Ovid, Statius, and with every other famous poet. And not only did he delight to know them, but he strove to imitate them in lofty song, even as his works demonstrate, whereof we shall speak at the proper time.

He perceived that poetical creations are not vain and simple fables or marvels, as many blockheads suppose, but that beneath them are hid the sweetest fruits of historical and philosophical truth, so that the conceptions of the poets cannot be fully understood without history and moral and natural philosophy. Proportionately distributing his time, he therefore strove to master history by himself, and philosophy under divers teachers, though not without long study and toil. And, possessed by the sweetness of knowing the truth of the things shut up by Heaven, and finding naught else in life more dear than this, he utterly abandoned all other temporal cares, and devoted himself wholly to this alone. And to the end that no region of philosophy should remain unvisited by him, he penetrated with acute genius into the profoundest depths of theology. Nor was the result far distant from the aim. Unmindful of heat and cold, vigils and fasts, and every other physical hardship, by assiduous study he grew to such knowledge of the Divine Essence and of the other Separate Intelligences as can be compassed here by the human intellect. And as by application various sciences were learned by him at various periods, so he mastered them in various studies under various teachers.

The first rudiments of knowledge, as stated above, he received in his native city. Thence he went to Bologna, as to a place richer in such food. And, when verging on old age, he went to Paris, where in many disputations he displayed the loftiness of his genius with so great glory to himself that his auditors still marvel when they speak thereof. For studies so many and so excellent he deservedly won the highest titles, and while he lived some ever called him poet, others philosopher, and many theologian. But since the victory is more glorious to the victor, the greater the might of the vanquished, I deem it fitting to make known from how surging and tempestuous a sea, buffeted now this way, now that, triumphant alike over waves and opposing winds, he won the blessed haven of the glorious titles aforenamed.

§ 3. DANTE'S LOVE FOR BEATRICE, AND HIS MARRIAGE.

Studies in general, and speculative studies in particular — to which, as has been shown, our Dante wholly applied himself — usually demand solitude, remoteness from care, and tranquillity of mind. Instead of this retirement and quiet, Dante had, almost from the beginning of his life down to the day of his death, a violent and insufferable passion of love, a wife, domestic and public cares, exile, and poverty, not to mention those more particular cares which these necessarily involve. The former I deem it fitting to explain in detail, in order that their burden may appear the greater.

In that season wherein the sweetness of heaven reclothes the earth with all its adornments, and makes her all smiling with varied flowers scattered among green leaves, the custom obtained in our city that men and women should keep festival in different gatherings, each person in his neighborhood. And so it chanced that among others Folco Portinari, a man held in great esteem among his fellow-citizens, on the first day of May gathered his neighbors in his house for a feast. Now among these came the aforementioned Alighieri, followed by Dante, who was still in his ninth year; for little children are wont to follow their fathers, especially to places of festival. And mingling here in the house of the feast-giver with others of his own age, of whom there were many, both boys and girls, when the first tables had been served he boyishly entered with the others into the games, so far as his tender age permitted.

Now amid the throng of children was a little daughter of the aforesaid Folco, whose name was Bice, though he always called her by her full name, Beatrice. She was, it may be, eight years old, very graceful for her age, full gentle and pleasing in her actions, and much more serious and modest in her words and ways than her few years required. Her features were most delicate and perfectly proportioned, and, in addition to their beauty, full of such pure loveliness that many thought her almost a little angel. She, then, such as I picture her, or it may be far more beautiful, appeared at this feast to the eyes of our Dante; not, I suppose, for the first time, but for the first time with power to inspire him with love. And he, though still a child, received the lovely image of her into his heart with so great affection that it never left him from that day forward so long as he lived.

Now just what this affection was no one knows, but certainly it is true that Dante at an early age became a most ardent servitor of love. It may have been a harmony of temperaments or of characters, or a special influence of heaven that worked thereto, or that which we know is experienced at festivals, where because of the sweetness of the music, the general happiness, and the delicacy of the dishes and wines, the minds, not only of youths but even of mature men, expand and are prone to be caught readily by whatever pleases them. But passing over the accidents of youth, I say that the flames of love multiplied with years in such measure that naught else gave him gladness, or comfort, or peace, save the sight of Beatrice. Forsaking, therefore, all other matters, with the utmost solicitude he went wherever he thought he might see her, as if he were to attain from her face and her eyes all his happiness and complete consolation.

O insensate judgment of lovers! who but they would think to check the flames by adding to the fuel? Dante himself in his Vita Nuova in part makes known how many and of what nature were the thoughts, the sighs, the tears, and the other grievous passions that he later suffered by reason of this love, wherefore I do not care to rehearse them more in detail. This much alone I do not wish to pass over without mention, namely, that according as he himself writes, and as others to whom his passion was known bear witness, this love was most virtuous, nor did there ever appear by look or word or sign any sensual appetite either in the lover or in the thing beloved; no little marvel to the present world, from which all innocent pleasure has so fled, and which is so accustomed to have the thing that pleases it conform to its lust before it has concluded to love it, that he who loves otherwise has become a miracle, even as a thing most rare.

If such love for so long season could interrupt his eating, his sleep, and every quietness, how great an enemy must we think it to have been to his sacred studies and to his genius? Certainly no mean one, although many maintain that it urged his genius on, and argue for proof from his graceful rimed compositions in the Florentine idiom, written in praise of his beloved and for the expression of his ardors and amorous conceits. But truly I should not agree with this, unless I first admitted that ornate writing is the most essential part of every science — which is not true.

As every one may plainly perceive, there is nothing stable in this world, and, if anything is subject to change, it is our life. A trifle too much cold or heat within us, not to mention countless other accidents and possibilities, easily leads us from existence to non-existence. Nor is gentle birth privileged against this, nor riches, nor youth, nor any other worldly dignity. Dante must needs experience the force of this general law by another's death before he did by his own. The most beautiful Beatrice was near the end of her twenty-fourth year when, as it pleased Him who governs all things, she left the sufferings of this world, and passed to the glory that her virtues had prepared for her. By her departure Dante was thrown into such sorrow, such grief and tears, that many of those nearest him, both relatives and friends, believed that death alone would end them. They expected that this would shortly come to pass, seeing that he gave no ear to the comfort and consolation offered him. The days were like the nights, and the nights like the days. Not an hour of them passed without groans, and sighs, and an abundant quantity of tears. His eyes seemed two copious springs of welling water, so that most men wondered whence he received moisture enough for his weeping.

But even as we see that sufferings through long experience become easy to bear, and that similarly all things in time diminish and cease, so it came to pass that in the course of several months Dante seemed to remember without weeping that Beatrice was dead. And with truer judgment, as grief somewhat gave place to reason, he came to recognize that neither weeping, nor sighs, nor aught else could restore his lost lady to him, wherefore he prepared to sustain the loss of her presence with greater patience. Nor was it long, now that the tears had ceased, before the sighs, which were already near their end, began in great measure to depart without returning.

Through weeping and the pain that his heart felt within, and through lack of any care of himself, he had become outwardly almost a savage thing to look upon — lean, unshaven, and almost utterly transformed from that which he was wont to be formerly; so that his aspect moved to pity not only his acquaintances but all others who saw him, although he let himself be seen but little by any one save his friends while this so tearful state endured. Their compassion and fear of worse to come made his relatives attentive to his comfort. And when they saw that his tears had somewhat ceased, and knew that the burning sighs gave a little respite to his troubled bosom, they began again to solicit the broken-hearted one with consolations that had long been unheeded. And though up to that hour he had obstinately closed his ears to every one, he now began not only to open them somewhat, but willingly to listen to that which was said for his comfort.

When his relatives perceived this, to the end that they might not only completely draw him from his sorrow but might also restore him to happiness, they took counsel together to give him a wife. They thought that as the lost lady had been the cause of sadness, so the newly acquired one might be the occasion of joy. And having found a young girl who was suited to his condition, they unfolded their purpose to Dante, employing those arguments that seemed to them most convincing. Not to touch particularly on each point, after a long and continued struggle, the natural result followed their reasoning with him, and he was married.

O blind intellects! O darkened understandings! O vain reasoning of mortal men! how frequently are results contrary to your opinions, and for the most part not without cause! What man under pretense of the excessive heat would lead one from the soft air of Italy to the burning sands of Libya in order that he might cool himself, or from the island of Cyprus to the eternal shades of the Rhodopean Mountains in order that he might be warmed? What physician would strive to expel an acute fever by means of fire, or a chill from the marrow of the bones with ice or snow? Surely none save he who thinks to assuage the sorrows of love by means of a new bride. They who hope to do this do not know the nature of love, nor how it adds every other passion to its own. In vain is aid or counsel brought against its power, if once it has taken firm root in the heart of him who has long loved. Even as in the first stages every little resistance avails, so in its later growth the greater checks are frequently wont to work harm. But we must return to our subject, and concede for the moment that there may be things that in themselves can make one forget the troubles of love.

What, in truth, will he have done who, in order to free me from one trying thought, plunges me into a thousand more grievous still? Truly naught else, save that by adding to my ill he will make me wish to return to that from which he drew me. We see this happen to most of those who, in order to escape from or be relieved of troubles, blindly marry, or are married by others. They do not perceive that, though clear of one perplexity, they have entered into a thousand, until experience proves it to them when they are no longer able, though repentant, to turn back. His relatives and friends gave Dante a wife, that his tears for Beatrice might cease. I do not know that, as a result of this — although his tears passed away, or rather, perhaps, had already departed — the flame of love also passed away, and indeed I do not believe that such was the case. But, granting that it was extinguished, many fresh and more grievous trials might befall.

Accustomed to pursue his sacred studies far into the night, as often as was his pleasure he discoursed with kings, emperors, and other most exalted princes, disputed with philosophers, and delighted in the most agreeable of poets; and, through listening to the sufferings of others, he allayed his own. But now he is bound to withdraw from this illustrious company whenever his new lady wishes him to listen to the talk of such women as she chooses, with whom he must not only agree against his pleasure, but whom he must praise, if he would not add to his troubles. It had been his custom, whenever the vulgar crowd wearied him, to retire to some solitary spot, and there in speculation to discover what spirit moves the heavens, whence comes life to animals, what are the causes of things; to forecast strange inventions or compose something that should make him live after death among future generations. But now not only is he drawn from these sweet contemplations as often as it pleases his new lady, but he must consort with company ill fitted for such things. He who was free to laugh or weep, to sigh or sing, as sweet or bitter passions moved him, now does not dare, for he must needs give account to his lady, not only of greater things, but even of every little sigh, explaining what produced it, whence it came, and whither it went. For she takes his light-heartedness as evidence of love for another, and his sadness, of hatred for herself.

O the incalculable weariness of having to live and converse, and finally to grow old and die, with so suspicious a creature! I prefer to pass over the new and heavy cares which the unwonted must bear, especially in our city; namely, the provision of clothes, ornaments, and roomfuls of needless trifles, which women make themselves believe are necessary to proper living; the provision of men-servants, maid-servants, nurses, and chambermaids; the furnishing of banquets, gifts, and presents, which must be made to the bride's relatives, since husbands wish that their wives should think they love these persons. Moreover, there are many other things that free men never knew before. And I now come to things that cannot be evaded.

Who doubts that the judgment of the people concerns itself with one's wife, as to whether she be fair or no? And if she be reputed beautiful, who doubts that she straightway will have many admirers, who will importunately besiege her fickle mind, one with his good looks, another with his noble birth, this one with marvelous flattery, that one with presents, and still another with his pleasing ways? What is desired by many is hardly defended from every one, and the purity of women need be overthrown but once to make themselves infamous and their husbands forever miserable. And if, through the ill-luck of him who leads her home, she be not fair, inasmuch as we frequently see the most beautiful women soon become tiresome, what may we think with regard to these plain women, save that not only they themselves, but every place where they may be found, will be held in hatred by those who must always have them for their own? Hence arises their wrath. Nor is any brute more cruel than an angry woman, nay, nor so cruel. No man can feel safe who commits himself to one who thinks she has reason to be wroth. And they all think that.

What shall I say of their ways? If I were to show how and to how great an extent wives run counter to the peace and repose of men, I should stretch my discourse too far. It therefore suffices to speak of one thing alone, common to nearly all women. They reflect that good conduct on the part of the meanest servant retains him in the household, and that bad conduct leads to his dismissal. So they think that if they themselves do well, their fate is only that of a servant, and they feel that they are ladies only so long as, while doing ill, they yet escape the end which menials reach. But why should I describe in detail what most of us know? I deem it better to keep silent than to offend the lovely women by speaking. Who does not know that a purchaser, before he buys, makes trial of everything save of a wife, and that this exception occurs through fear that she may displease him before he leads her home? Whoso takes a wife must needs have her not such as he would choose, but such as fortune grants him.

And if these things are true, as he knows who has proved them, we may imagine how much unhappiness is hidden in rooms that are reputed places of delight by those whose eyes cannot pierce the walls. Assuredly I do not affirm that these things fell to the lot of Dante; for I do not know that they did. But, whether things like these or others were the cause, true it is that when once he had parted from his wife, who had been given him as a consolation in his troubles, he never would go to her, nor let her come to him, albeit he was the father of several children by her. Let no one suppose that I would conclude from what has been said above that men should not marry. On the contrary, I decidedly commend it, but not for every one. Philosophers should leave it to wealthy fools, to noblemen, and to peasants, while they themselves find delight in philosophy, a far better bride than any other.

§ 4. FAMILY CARES, HONORS, AND EXILE OF DANTE.

It is the general nature of things temporal that one thing entails another. Domestic cares drew Dante to public ones, where the vain honors that are attached to state positions so bewildered him that, without noting whence he had come and whither he was bound, with free rein he almost completely surrendered himself to the management of these matters. And therein fortune was so favorable to him that no legation was heard or answered, no law established or repealed, no peace made nor public war undertaken, nor, in short, was any deliberation of weight entered upon, until Dante had first given his opinion relative thereto. On him all public faith, all hope, and, in a word, all things human and divine seemed to rest. But although Fortune, the subverter of our counsels and the foe of all human stability, kept him at the summit of her wheel for several years of glorious rule, she brought him to an end far different from his beginning, since he trusted her immoderately.

In Dante's time the citizens of Florence were perversely divided into two factions, and by the operations of astute and prudent leaders each party was very powerful, so that sometimes one ruled and sometimes the other, to the displeasure of its defeated rival. In his wish to unite the divided body of his republic, Dante brought all genius, all art, all study to bear, showing the wiser citizens how great things soon perish through discord, and how little things through harmony have infinite growth. Finding, however, that his auditors' minds were unyielding and that his labor was in vain, and believing it the judgment of God, he at first purposed to drop entirely all public affairs and live a private life. But afterwards he was drawn on by the sweetness of glory, by the empty favor of the populace, and by the persuasions of the chief citizens, coupled with his own belief that, should the occasion offer, he could accomplish much more good for his city if he were great in public affairs than he could in his private capacity completely removed therefrom.

O fond desire of human splendors, how much stronger is thy power than he who has not known thee can believe! This man, mature as he was, bred, nurtured, and trained in the sacred bosom of philosophy, before whose eyes was the downfall of kings ancient and modern, the desolation of kingdoms, provinces, and cities, and the furious onslaughts of fortune, though he sought naught else than the highest, lacked either the knowledge or the power to defend himself from thy charms.

Dante decided, then, to pursue the fleeting honor and false glory of public office. Perceiving that he could not support by himself a third party, which, in itself just, should overthrow the injustice of the two others and reduce them to unity, he allied himself with that faction which seemed to him to possess most of justice and reason — working always for that which he recognized as salutary to his country and her citizens. But human counsels are commonly defeated by the powers of heaven. Hatred and enmities arose, though without just cause, and waxed greater day by day; so that many times the citizens rushed to arms, to their utmost confusion. They purposed to end the struggle by fire and sword, and were so blinded by wrath that they did not see that they themselves would perish miserably thereby.

After each of the factions had given many proofs of their strength to their mutual loss, the time came when the secret counsels of threatening Fortune were to be disclosed. Rumor, who reports both the true and the false, announced that the foes of Dante's faction were strengthened by wise and wonderful designs and by an immense multitude of armed men, and by this means so terrified the leaders of his party that she banished from their minds all consideration, all forethought, all reason, save how to flee in safety. Together with them Dante, instantly precipitated from the chief rule of his city, beheld himself not only brought low to the earth, but banished from his country. Not many days after this expulsion, when the populace had already rushed to the houses of the exiles, and had furiously pillaged and gutted them, the victors reorganized the city after their pleasure, condemning all the leaders of their adversaries to perpetual exile as capital enemies of the republic, and with them Dante, not as one of the lesser leaders, but as it were the chief one. Their real property was meanwhile confiscated or alienated to the victors.

§ 5. DANTE'S FLIGHT FROM FLORENCE AND HIS WANDERINGS.

In such wise, then, Dante left that city whereof not only he was a citizen, but of which his ancestors had been the rebuilders. He left his wife there, together with his children, whose youthful age ill adapted them for flight. At ease concerning his wife, for he knew that she was related to one of the leaders of the opposing faction, but uncertain of his own course, he wandered now here, now there, throughout Tuscany.

Under the title of her dowry, his wife with difficulty defended a small portion of his possessions from the fury of the citizens, and from the fruits thereof obtained a meagre support for herself and her little children. Therefore Dante in poverty was forced to get his living by a kind of industry to which he was a stranger.

O what righteous indignation must he repress, more bitter than death for him to bear, while hope promised him that his exile would be short — and then the return! But, after leaving Verona, whither he had first fled and where he had been graciously received by Messer Alberto della Scala, he tarried year after year, contrary to his expectation, first with the Count Salvatico in the Casentino, then with the Marquis Moruello Malaspina in Lunigiana, and finally with the della Faggiuola in the mountains near Urbino, most suitably honored in each case according to the times and the means of his host. Thence he later departed to Bologna, and from there, after a short stay, he went on to Padua, and then back again to Verona. But perceiving that the way of return was closed on every side, and that his hope was more vain from day to day, he abandoned not only Tuscany but all Italy, and, crossing the mountains that divide it from the province of Gaul, he made his way as best he could to Paris. There he gave his whole time to the study of philosophy and theology, though likewise regathering to himself such parts of the other sciences as had gone from him by reason of his adversities.

While he was thus spending his time in study, it came to pass, beyond his expectation, that Henry, Count of Luxemburg, at the desire and command of

Clement V., who was pope at this time, was elected King of the Romans, and was afterwards crowned Emperor. When Dante heard that he had left Germany in order to subjugate Italy, which in parts was rebellious to his Majesty, and that he was already besieging Brescia with a powerful force, believing, for many reasons, that the Emperor would be victor, he conceived the hope of returning to Florence by means of Henry's power and justice, although he knew that Florence was opposed to him. Wherefore, recrossing the Alps, he joined the many enemies of the Florentine party, and by embassies and letters strove to draw the Emperor from the siege of Brescia, in order that he might turn against Florence, who was the principal member of his enemies. He showed him that if she were overcome, he would have little or no trouble in securing free and unimpeded possession and dominion of all Italy.

But although Dante and others of the same purpose succeeded in drawing Henry thither, his coming did not have the expected result, for the resistance was far stronger than they had anticipated. And so, without having accomplished anything worthy of mention, the Emperor left, almost in despair, and directed his way toward Rome. And though in one part and another he achieved much, righted many things, and planned to do more, his too early death ruined the whole. As a consequence of his death every one who had looked to him lost courage, and especially Dante. Without making further effort toward his return, he crossed the Apennines and entered Romagna, where his last day, which was to end all his troubles, awaited him.

At that time the Lord of Ravenna, that famous and ancient city of Romagna, was a noble knight by the name of Guido Novello da Polenta. Trained in liberal studies, he greatly honored men of worth, and especially those who excelled in knowledge. When it came to his ears that Dante was then unexpectedly in Romagna and stood in great despair, he resolved to receive and honor him, for of his worth he had known by reputation long before. Nor did the lord wait for this to be asked of him, but reflecting what shame good men must feel in asking favors, he generously came to Dante with proffers, asking as a special favor that which he knew Dante in time must ask of him, namely, that Dante should find it his pleasure to reside with him.

Since, then, the two desires, that of the invited one and that of the host, concurred in the same end, and since the liberality of the noble knight was especially pleasing to Dante, and, on the other hand, since need pressed him, without waiting for further invitation he went to Ravenna. Here he was honorably received by the lord of the city, who revived his fallen hope by kindly encouragement, gave him an abundance of suitable things, and kept the poet with him for several years, even to the end of Dante's life.

Neither amorous desires, nor tears of grief, nor household cares, nor the tempting glory of public office, nor miserable exile, nor insufferable poverty, could ever by their power divert Dante from his main intent, that of sacred studies. For, as will be seen later when separate mention is made of his works, in the midst of whatever was most cruel of the aforementioned troubles, he will be found to have employed himself in composition. And if in spite of the many and great obstacles recounted above, by force of genius and perseverance he became so illustrious as we see him to be, what may we think he would have become with as many allies as others have, or at least with no enemies or very few? Certainly I do not know, but, were it permitted, I should say he would have become a god on earth.

§ 6. HIS DEATH AND FUNERAL HONORS.

Since all hope, though not the desire, of ever returning to Florence was gone, Dante continued in Ravenna several years, under the protection of its gracious lord. And here he taught and trained many scholars in poetry, and especially in the vernacular, which he first, in my opinion, exalted and made esteemed among us Italians, even as Homer did his tongue among the Greeks, and Virgil his among the Latins. Although the vulgar tongue is supposed to have originated some time before him, none thought or dared to make the language an instrument of any artistic matter, save in the numbering of syllables, and in the consonance of its endings. They employed it, rather, in the light things of love. Dante showed in effect that every lofty subject could be treated of in this medium, and made our vulgar tongue above all others glorious.

But even as the appointed hour comes for every man, so Dante also, at or near the middle of his fifty-sixth year, fell ill. And having humbly and devoutly received the sacraments of the Church according to the Christian religion, and having reconciled himself to God in contrition for all that he, as a mortal, had committed against His pleasure, in the month of September in the year of Christ 1321, on the day whereon the Exaltation of the Holy Cross is celebrated by the Church, not without great sorrow on the part of the aforesaid Guido and in general of all the other citizens of Ravenna, he rendered to his Creator his weary spirit, the which, I doubt not, was received in the arms of his most noble Beatrice, with whom, in the sight of Him who is the highest Good, having left behind him the miseries of the present life, he now lives most blissfully in that life to whose felicity we believe there is no end.

The noble-minded knight had the body of Dante placed upon a bier and adorned with a poet's ornaments, and this he had borne on the shoulders of the most eminent citizens of Ravenna to the convent of the Minor Friars in that city, with the honor he thought due to such a person. And thereupon he caused the body, followed thus far by the lamentings of nearly the whole city, to be placed in a stone sarcophagus, in which it lies to this day. Returning to the house where Dante had resided, he made, according to the custom of Ravenna, a long and elaborate discourse, both as a tribute to the virtue and high learning of the deceased, and by way of consolation to the friends whom he left behind in bitter grief. Guido purposed, if his life and fortune should continue, to honor him with so magnificent a sepulchre that if no merit of his own should render himself memorable to posterity, this of itself would do so.

This praiseworthy proposal soon became known to certain most excellent poets of Romagna who were living at that time. Thereupon, both to publish their own ability and to show their good will toward the dead poet, as well as to win the love and favor of the lord who was known to desire it, each one wrote verses which, placed for an epitaph upon the proposed tomb, by their fitting praises should testify to posterity who it was that lay therein. They sent these verses to the noble lord, but he, not long after, lost his station through great misfortune, and died at Bologna; and the erection of the tomb and the inscription of the proffered verses thereon were for this reason left undone.

These verses were shown to me some time afterwards, and finding that they had not been used, owing to the event already mentioned, and reflecting that this present composition, though not a tomb for Dante's body, is, nevertheless, as that would have been, a perpetual preserver of his memory, I have deemed it appropriate to insert the verses at this place. But inasmuch as only one of the many poems composed would have been engraven on the marble, I think it is necessary to subjoin but one here. Wherefore, having examined them all, I consider the most worthy in form and thought to be the fourteen lines written by Master Giovanni del Virgilio, at that time a great and famous poet of Bologna, and an intimate friend of Dante. These are the verses: —

Theologus Dantes, nullius dogmatis expers,
  Quod foveat claro philosophia sinu:
Gloria musarum, vulgo gratissimus auctor,
  Hic jacet, et fama pulsat utrumque polum:
Qui loca defunctis gladiis regnumque gemellis
  Distribuit, laicis rhetoricisque modis.
Pascua Pieriis demum resonabat avenis;
  Atropos heu letum[1] livida rupit opus.
Huic ingrata tulit tristem Florentia fructum,
  Exilium, vati patria cruda suo.

[1] For *laetum.*

Quem pia Guidonis gremio Ravenna Novelli
  Gaudet honorati continuisse ducis,
Mille trecentenis ter septem Numinis annis,
  Ad sua septembris idibus astra redit.

§ 8.[1] APPEARANCE, HABITS, AND CHARACTERISTICS OF DANTE.

Such as described above was the end of Dante's life, worn out by his various studies. And since I think I have adequately shown, according to my promise, his amorous flames, his domestic and public cares, his miserable exile, and his death, I deem it proper to proceed to speak of his bodily stature, of his external appearance, and in general of the most conspicuous customs observed by him in his life. I shall then immediately pass to his notable works, composed in a time rent by the fierce whirlwind which has been briefly described above.

Our poet was of moderate height, and, after reaching maturity, was accustomed to walk somewhat bowed, with a slow and gentle pace, clad always in such sober dress as befitted his ripe years. His face was long, his nose aquiline, and his eyes rather large than small. His jaws were large, and the lower lip protruded beyond the upper. His complexion was dark, his hair and beard thick, black, and curled, and his expression ever melancholy and thoughtful. And thus it chanced one day in Verona, when the fame of his works had spread everywhere, particularly that part of his Commedia entitled the Inferno, and when he was known by sight to many, both men and women, that, as he was passing before a doorway where sat a group of women, one of them softly said to the others, — but not

[1] § 7 is a digression to rebuke the Florentines.

so softly but that she was distinctly heard by Dante and such as accompanied him, — "Do you see the man who goes down into hell and returns when he pleases, and brings back tidings of them that are below?" To which one of the others naïvely answered, "You must indeed say true. Do you not see how his beard is crisped, and his color darkened, by the heat and smoke down there?" Hearing these words spoken behind him, and knowing that they came from the innocent belief of the women, he was pleased, and, smiling a little as if content that they should hold such an opinion, he passed on.

In both his domestic and his public demeanor he was admirably composed and orderly, and in all things courteous and civil beyond any other. In food and drink he was most temperate, both in partaking of them at the appointed hours and in not passing the limits of necessity. Nor did he show more epicurism in respect of one thing than another. He praised delicate viands, but ate chiefly of plain dishes, and censured beyond measure those who bestow a great part of their attention upon possessing choice things, and upon the extremely careful preparation of the same, affirming that such persons do not eat to live, but rather live to eat.

None was more vigilant than he in study and in whatever else he undertook, insomuch that his wife and family were annoyed thereby, until they grew accustomed to his ways, and after that they paid no heed thereto. He rarely spoke unless questioned, and then thoughtfully, and in a voice suited to the matter whereof he treated. When, however, there was cause, he was eloquent and fluent in speech, and possessed of an excellent and ready delivery. In his youth he took the greatest delight in music and song, and enjoyed the friendship and intimacy of all the best singers and musicians of his time. Led on by this delight he composed many poems, which he made them clothe in pleasing and masterly melody.

How devoted a vassal to love Dante was, has already been shown. It is the firm belief of all that this love inspired his genius to compose poetry in the vulgar tongue, first through imitation, afterwards through a desire for glory and for a more perfect manifestation of his feelings. By a careful training of himself in the vernacular, he not only surpassed all his contemporaries, but so elucidated and beautified the language that he made then, and has made since, and will make in the future, many persons eager to be expert therein. He delighted also in being alone and removed from people, to the end that his meditation might not be disturbed. If, moreover, any particularly pleasing contemplation came upon him when he was in company, it mattered not what it was that was asked of him, he would never answer the question until he had ended or abandoned his train of thought. This peculiarity often showed itself when he was at table, or in travel with companions, and elsewhere.

In his studies he was most assiduous, insomuch that while he was occupied therewith no news that he heard could divert him from them. Some trustworthy persons relate, anent this complete devotion of his to the thing that pleased him, that once, when he chanced to be at an apothecary's shop in Siena, there was brought him a little book, very famous among men of understanding, but which he had not yet seen, although it had been promised him. He did not have, as it happened, room to place it elsewhere, so, lying breast downwards upon a bench in front of the apothecary's, he laid the book before him and began to read with great eagerness. Now a little later in this same neighborhood, by reason of some general festival of the Sienese, there took place a grand tournament of young noblemen which created among the bystanders a great uproar, — such noise as many instruments and applauding voices are wont to produce. And though many other things were done to attract attention, such as dancing by fair ladies and numerous games of youths, none saw Dante move from his position, or once lift his eyes from his book. Indeed, although he had taken his station there about the hour of three, it was after six before, having examined and summarized all the points of the book, he rose from his position. Yet he afterwards declared to some who asked him how he could keep from watching so fine a festival as had taken place before him, that he had heard nothing. Whereupon to the first wonder of the questioners was not unduly added a second.

Moreover this poet possessed marvelous capacity, a most retentive memory, and a keen intellect. Indeed, when he was at Paris, in a disputation *de quolibet* held there in the schools of theology, wherein fourteen different theses were being maintained by various able men on divers subjects, Dante without a break gathered all the theses together in their sequence, with the arguments *pro* and *con* that were advanced by his opponents, and then, following the same order, recited them, subtly solved them, and refuted the counter arguments, — a feat that was reputed all but a miracle by them that stood by. He was possessed also of exalted genius and subtle invention, as his works, to those that understand them, reveal far more clearly than could any words of mine.

He had a consuming love for honor and fame, perchance a greater love than befitted his noble nature. But indeed what life is so humble as not to be touched by the sweetness of glory? It was due to this desire, I suppose, that he loved poetry beyond any other study. For he saw that, while philosophy surpasses all other studies in nobility, yet its excellence can be communicated to but few, and besides there are already many famous philosophers throughout the world; whereas poetry is more obvious and more delightful to every one, and poets are exceeding rare. So he hoped through poetry to obtain the unusual and splendid honor of coronation with the laurel, and therefore dedicated himself to its study and composition.

And surely his desire had been fulfilled, if fortune had been so gracious as to permit him ever to return to Florence, where alone, at the font of San Giovanni, he was minded to be crowned, in order that there, where in baptism he had received his first name, now by coronation he might receive his second. But things so turned out that, albeit his gifts would have enabled him to receive the honor of the laurel wherever he pleased (the which rite does not increase knowledge, but is its ornament and true witness of its acquisition), yet since he ever waited for that return which never was to be, he was unwilling to receive the much-coveted honor anywhere else, and so at length died without achieving it.

But inasmuch as frequent question is made among readers as to what poetry is and what poets are, whence the word is derived and why poets are crowned with the laurel, and since few seem to have explained these matters, it pleases me to make a digression here, in which I may throw some light on the subject, returning as soon as I am able to my theme.

§ 12.[1] QUALITIES AND DEFECTS OF DANTE.

Our poet, in addition to what has been said above, was of a lofty and disdainful spirit. On one occasion a friend, moved by entreaties, labored that Dante might return to Florence — which thing the poet desired above all else — but he found no way thereto with those who then held the government in their hands save that Dante should remain in prison for a certain time, and after that be presented as a subject for mercy at some public solemnity in our principal church, whereby he should be free and exempt from all sentences previously passed upon him. But this seemed to Dante a fitting procedure for abject, if not infamous, men and for no others. Therefore, notwithstanding his great desire, he chose to remain in exile rather than return home by such a road. O laudable and magnanimous scorn, how manfully hast thou acted in repressing the ardent desire to return, when it was only possible by a way unworthy of a man nourished in the bosom of philosophy!

Dante in many similar ways set great store by himself, and, as his contemporaries report, did not deem himself worth less than in truth he was. This trait, among other times, appeared once notably, when he was with his party at the head of the government of the

[1] § 9. A Digression Concerning Poetry. § 10. On the Difference between Poetry and Theology. § 11. On the Laurel bestowed on Poets.

republic. The faction that was out of power had, through Pope Boniface VIII., summoned a brother or relative of Philip, King of France, whose name was Charles, to direct the affairs of the city. All the chiefs of the party to which Dante held were assembled in council to look to this matter, and there among other things they provided that an embassy should be sent to the pope, who was then at Rome, in order to persuade him to oppose the coming of the said Charles, or to make him come with the consent of the ruling party. When they came to consider who should be the head of this embassy, all agreed on Dante. To their request he replied, after quietly meditating on it for a while, "If I go, who stays? And if I stay, who goes?" as if he alone was of worth among them all, and as if the others were nothing worth except through him. These words were understood and remembered, but that which followed from them is not pertinent to the present subject, wherefore I leave it and pass on.

Furthermore, this excellent man was most undaunted in all his adversities. In one thing alone he was, I do not know whether I should say passionate, or merely impatient: to wit, that after he went into exile he devoted himself much more to party affairs than befitted his quality, and more than he was willing to have others believe. To the end that it may be clear for what party he was so vehement and determined, it seems to me that I ought to write something further.

I believe it was the just anger of God which permitted, a long time ago, that nearly all Tuscany and Lombardy should be divided into two parties. Whence they received these names I do not know, but one was called, and is still called, the Guelf party, and the other the Ghibelline. Of such power and reverence were these two names in the foolish minds of many, that, in order to defend his party against the other, it was not hard for a man to lose all his possessions, nay, and finally his life too, if there were need. Under these titles the Italian cities sustained most grievous oppression and vicissitudes, and among them our city, which was as it were the head, now of one party, and now of the other, according as the citizens changed. Dante's ancestors, for example, were twice, as Guelfs, exiled by the Ghibellines, and it was under the title of Guelf that he held the reins of the republic in Florence. It was not, however, by the Ghibellines, but by the Guelfs, that he was banished. And when he found that he could not return, his sympathies changed, so that none was a fiercer Ghibelline and more violent adversary of the Guelfs than he.

Now that for which I am most ashamed in the service of his memory is that, according to the common report in Romagna, any feeble woman or child, in speaking of parties and condemning the Ghibellines, could move him to such rage that he would have been led to throw stones if the speaker had not become silent. This bitterness continued even to his death. I am ashamed to sully the reputation of so great a man by the mention of any fault in him, but my purpose to some extent requires it, for if I am silent about the things less worthy of praise, I shall destroy much faith in the laudable qualities already mentioned. I ask, therefore, the pardon of Dante, who perchance, while I am writing this, looks down at me with scornful eye from some high region of heaven.

Amid so great virtue, amid so much learning, as

we have seen was the portion of this wondrous poet, licentiousness found a large place; and this not only in his youth, but also in his maturity. Although this vice is natural, common, and in a certain sense necessary, it not only cannot be commended, but cannot even be decently excused. But what mortal shall be the just judge to condemn it? Not I. O little strength! O bestial appetite of men! What influence cannot women have over us if they will, since without caring they have so much? They possess charm, beauty, natural desire, and many other qualities that continually work in their behalf in the hearts of men.

To show that this is true, let us pass over what Jupiter did for the sake of Europa, Hercules for Iole, and Paris for Helen, since these are matters of poetry, and many of little judgment would call them fables. But let the matter be illustrated by instances fitting for none to deny. Was there yet more than one woman in the world when our first father, breaking the commandment given him by the very mouth of God, yielded to her persuasions? In truth there was but one. And David, notwithstanding the fact that he had many wives, no sooner caught sight of Bathsheba than for her sake he forgot God, his own kingdom, himself, and his honor, becoming first an adulterer and then a homicide. What may we think he would have done, had she laid any commands upon him? And did not Solomon, to whose wisdom none ever attained save the Son of God, forsake Him who had made him wise, and kneel to adore Balaam in order to please a woman? What did Herod? What did many others, led by naught else save their pleasure? Among so many and so great ones, then, our poet may pass on, not excused, but accused with a brow much less drawn than if he were alone. Let this recital of his more notable customs suffice for the present.

§ 14.[1] ON CERTAIN INCIDENTS RELATING TO THE DIVINA COMMEDIA.

The first part of the poem, a wonderful invention, Dante entitled the Inferno. He wrote it not in the manner of a pagan, but as a most Christian poet; a thing which had never before been done under this title. And now when he was most intent on his glorious work and had completed the first seven cantos, occurred the grievous misfortune of his banishment, or flight, as it is proper to call it. As a result, he abandoned this work of his and all else, and wandered uncertain of himself for many years among divers friends and lords.

But even as we certainly must believe that Fortune can work nothing contrary to what God ordains, whereby she can divert the force of its destined end, though she can perhaps delay it, so it happened that some one found the seven cantos that Dante had composed. He made the discovery while searching for some needed document among the chests of Dante's things, which had been hastily removed into sacred places at the time when the ungrateful and lawless multitude, more eager for booty than for just revenge, tumultuously rushed to his house.

This person read the cantos with admiration, though he did not know what they were; and, impelled by his exceeding delight in them, he carefully withdrew

[1] § 13. On the Different Works written by Dante.

them from the place where they lay, and brought them to one of our citizens, by name Dino di Messer Lambertuccio, a famous poet of that time, and a man of high intelligence. Upon reading them, Dino marveled no less than he who had brought them, both because of their beautiful, polished, and ornate style, and because of the depth of meaning that he seemed to discover hidden under the beautiful covering of words.

By reason of these qualities, and of the place where the cantos were found, Dino and the other deemed them to be the work of Dante, as in truth they were. Troubled because the work was unfinished, and unable of themselves to imagine its issue, they determined to find out where Dante was and to send him what they had found, in order that he might, if possible, give the contemplated end to so fine a beginning.

They found, after some investigation, that he was with the Marquis Moruello. Accordingly they wrote of their desire, not to Dante, but to the Marquis, and forwarded the seven cantos. When the latter, who was a man of great understanding, read them, he greatly praised them to himself, and, showing them to Dante, asked him if he knew whose work they were. Dante, recognizing them at once, replied that they were his own. Whereupon the Marquis begged of him that it might be his pleasure not to leave so lofty a beginning without its fitting end. "I naturally supposed," said Dante, "that, in the general ruin of my things, these and many other books of mine were lost. Both from this belief and from the multitude of other troubles that came upon me by reason of my exile, I had utterly abandoned the high design laid hold of for this work. But since fortune unexpectedly has restored the work to me, and since it is agreeable to you, I will try to recall the original idea, and proceed according as grace shall be given me." And so after a time and not without toil he resumed the interrupted subject, and wrote: —

Io dico, seguitando, che assai prima, etc.,

where the coupling of the parts of the work may be clearly recognized upon close examination.

When Dante had thus recommenced the great work, he did not finish it, as many might think, without frequent interruptions. Indeed many times, according as the seriousness of supervening events demanded, he put it aside, sometimes for months, again for years, unable to accomplish anything on it. Nor could he make such haste that death did not overtake him before he was able to publish all of it.

It was his custom, when he had finished six or eight cantos, more or less, to send them, from wherever he might be, before any other person saw them, to Messer Cane della Scala, whom he held in reverence beyond all other men. After he had seen them, Dante would make a copy of the cantos for whoever wished them. In such wise he had sent Messer Cane all save the last thirteen cantos — and these he had written — when he died without making any provision therefor. And although his children and disciples made frequent search for many months among his papers, to see if he had put an end to his work, in no way could they find the remaining cantos. All his friends were therefore distressed that God had not lent him to the world at least long enough for him to complete the little of his work that remained. And since they could not find the cantos, they abandoned further search in despair.

Dante's two sons, Jacopo and Piero, both of whom were poets, being persuaded thereto by their friends, resolved to complete their father's work, so far as in them lay, that it might not remain unfinished. But just at this time Jacopo, who was much more fervent in this matter than his brother, saw a remarkable vision, that not only put an end to his foolish presumption, but revealed to him where the thirteen cantos were that were missing.

An excellent man of Ravenna by the name of Piero Giardino, long time a disciple of Dante, related that eight months after the death of his master the aforesaid Jacopo came to him one night near the hour of dawn, and told him that in his sleep a little while before on this same night he had seen Dante, his father, draw near to him. He was clad in the whitest raiment, and his face shone with unwonted light. The son in his dream asked him if he were living, and heard him reply, "Yes, not in our life, but in the true." Again he seemed to question him, asking if he had finished his poem before passing to that true life, and, if he had completed it, where was the missing part which they had never been able to find. And again he seemed to hear in answer, "Yes, I finished it." And then it seemed to him that his father took him by the hand and led him to the room where he was wont to sleep when alive, and touching a spot there, said, "Here is that for which thou hast so long sought." And with these words his sleep and his father left him.

Jacopo said that he could not postpone coming to Messer Piero to tell him what he had seen, in order that together they might go and search the place — which he kept exactly in his memory — and learn whether it was a true spirit or a false delusion that had revealed this to him. While there still remained a good part of the night they set out together, and, coming to the designated spot, they found a matting fastened to the wall. Gently lifting this, they discovered a little opening which neither of them had ever seen or known of before. Therein they found some writings, all mildewed by the dampness of the wall, and on the point of rotting had they remained there a little longer. Carefully cleaning them of the mould, they read them, and found that they were the long-sought thirteen cantos. With great joy, therefore, they copied them, and sent them first, according to the custom of the author, to Messer Cane, and then attached them, as was fitting, to the incomplete work. In such wise the poem that had been many years in composition was finished.

§ 16.[1] OF THE BOOK DE MONARCHIA AND OTHER WORKS.

At the coming of the Emperor Henry VII., this illustrious author wrote another book, in Latin prose, called the De Monarchia. This he divided into three books, in accordance with three questions which he settled therein. In the first book he proves by argument of logic that the Empire is necessary for the well-being of the world. This is his first point. In the second book, proceeding by arguments drawn from history, he shows that Rome rightly holds the title of

[1] § 15. Why the Commedia was written in the Vulgar Tongue.
§ 17. Explanation of the Dream of Dante's Mother.

the Empire. This is his second point. In the third book by theological arguments he proves that the authority of the Empire proceeds directly from God, and not through the mediation of any vicar, as the clergy appear to maintain. This is his third point.

This book, several years after the death of its author, was condemned by Cardinal Beltrando of Poggetto, papal legate in the parts of Lombardy, during the pontificate of John XXII. The reason of the condemnation was this. Louis, Duke of Bavaria, had been chosen King of the Romans by the electors of Germany, and came to Rome for his coronation, against the pleasure of the aforenamed Pope John. And while there, against ecclesiastical ordinances he created pope a minor friar called Brother Piero della Corvara, besides many cardinals and bishops; and had himself crowned there by this new pontiff.

Now inasmuch as his authority was questioned in many cases, he and his followers, having found this book by Dante, began to make use of its arguments to defend themselves and their authority; whereby the book, which was scarcely known up to this time, became very famous. Afterwards, however, when Louis had returned to Germany, and his followers, especially the clergy, began to decline and disperse, the aforesaid Cardinal, since there was none to oppose him therein, seized the book and condemned it in public to the flames, charging that it contained heretical matters.

In like manner he attempted to burn the bones of the author, and would have done so, to the eternal infamy and confusion of his own memory, had he not been opposed by a good and noble Florentine knight, by name Pino della Tosa. This man and Messer Ostagio da Polenta were great in the sight of the Cardinal, and happened to be in Bologna where this matter was being mooted.

Besides the foregoing, Dante composed two very beautiful eclogues, which he dedicated and sent, in reply to certain verses, to Master Giovanni del Virgilio, of whom mention has already been made. He composed also a comment in prose in the Florentine vulgar tongue on three of his elaborated canzoni. Although he seems to have had the intention, when he began, of commenting on them all, nevertheless, owing either to change of plan or to lack of time, we find no more than these three treated of by him. This comment he entitled the Convivio, a very beautiful and admirable little work.

Later, when already near his death, he wrote a little book in Latin prose which he entitled De Vulgari Eloquentia, wherein he purposed to give instruction in the writing of rime to whoever wished to undertake it. Though he seems to have had in mind to compose four parts to this little work, either he was overtaken by death before he finished it, or the other parts have been lost, since only two remain. This excellent poet also wrote many letters in Latin prose, whereof several are still extant. Moreover he composed many elaborated canzoni, sonnets, and *ballate*, both on love and on morals, in addition to those that appear in the Vita Nuova, but of these I do not care at present to make especial mention.

In such matters, then, as are told of above, this illustrious man cousumed what time he could steal from amorous sighs, piteous tears, private and public cares, and from the various fluctuations of hostile fortune, — works much more acceptable to God and man than the deceits, frauds, falsehoods, robberies, and treacheries which the majority of men practice to-day, seeking as they do by different ways one and the same goal, namely, to become rich, as if on that rested all good, all honor, all felicity.

III

FILIPPO VILLANI'S DE VITA ET MORIBUS DANTIS INSIGNIS COMICI

"THE life and character of Dante the distinguished comedian!" is the curious title of the next document we have of the poet's deeds. Filippo Villani, the author, was a nephew of the great chronicler, a lawyer of renown, who lectured on the Divina Commedia in Florence, and who also wrote a work entitled, Liber de Civitatis Florentinae Famosis Civibus. The Lives are between thirty and forty in number, and are written in Latin. That of Dante is the longest, though occupying but a few pages. He draws chiefly from Boccaccio, but contradicts his statement that *lussuria* had a large place in Dante, saying that the poet was *vitae continentissimae, cibi potusque parcissimus.* He also informs us that Dante studied theology in Paris. The most important and original contribution Villani has given us is an account of Dante's last illness. "He was sent by his patron Guido Novello da Polenta on an embassy to Venice, but the Venetians, dreading (says Villani) the power of his eloquence, repeatedly refused to grant him an audience. At the last, being sick with fever, he begged them to convey him back to Ravenna by sea; but they, increasing in their fury against him, utterly refused this, so that he had to undertake the fatiguing and unhealthy journey by land. This so aggravated the fever from which he was suffering that he died in a few days after his arrival at Ravenna. We have some details about his burial, especially that *apud vestibulum Fratrum Minorum eminenti conditus est sepulcro.*"[1]

Villani gives us very little, excepting the Venetian Embassy, that is not more fully stated in the Life by Boccaccio.

[1] *Dante and His Early Biographers*, p. 61.

IV

THE LIFE OF DANTE BY LIONARDO BRUNI ARETINO

"A MUCH more original character[1] and critical value belong to the next of the Early Biographies which we have to consider, that of Lionardo Bruni, commonly known from the name of his birthplace as Lionardo Aretino. Born in 1369 and dying in 1444, he was thus a little more than a century later than Dante, and about half a century later than Boccaccio. He was well acquainted with both Latin and Greek literature, and translated several Greek works, parts of Aristotle, Plato, Demosthenes, etc., and was able to address a Greek oration to the Greek Emperor and Patriarch at the Council of Constance. He filled important political posts at Rome and at Florence, and, regarding him as a biographer of Dante, it is interesting to note that he was at the Council of Constance in attendance on Pope John XXIII., at which Council there was also present John of Serravalle, who, at the instance of the two English bishops, Hallam and Bubwith (also present at the Council), wrote a commentary on the Commedia, which including a brief biography of its author, the chief interest of which is the novel and unsupported assertion of Dante's visit to England, and to London and Oxford in particular. Lionardo, who, as we shall presently see, is entirely ignorant of any such journey, and by implication excludes the possibility of it, must doubtless have met Serravalle and his patrons at the Council. It is curious to speculate whether they compared notes or otherwise discoursed together about the sub-

[1] *Dante and His Early Biographers*, Dr. Edward Moore, pp. 64–66.

ject of their common literary labors. Lionardo was a somewhat voluminous writer on a variety of subjects, some of his works being in Latin and some in Italian.

"His chief work is a Historia Florentina from the earliest times to 1404.

"In the particular work with which we are concerned he begins by taking his readers into his confidence in a very pleasant and lively manner. 'I had just completed,' he says, 'a few days ago a somewhat laborious work, and I felt the need of some literary recreation, for variation in the subjects of study is quite as necessary as variety in one's diet. Just as I was thinking about this, I chanced to take up again the Life of Dante by Boccaccio, a book which I had indeed formerly read with much care. It struck me that Boccaccio, excellent man and charming writer though he is, had written the life of the sublime poet as though he had been undertaking another Filocolo, Filostrato, or Fiammetta' (referring to well-known light works of Boccaccio). Indeed he seems to write with the idea that a man is born into the world for nothing else than to qualify himself for a place in the Decameron. Consequently, Boccaccio has recorded numerous trivialities about the life of Dante, but has neglected the weightier and more serious parts of his life. 'I propose, therefore,' says Lionardo, 'to write for my diversion a new life of Dante, paying greater attention to the significant events. I do this not in disparagement of Boccaccio, but that I may compose a supplement to his work.'"

Dante's ancestors[1] belonged to one of the oldest Florentine families. Indeed the poet in certain passages seems to imply that they were among those Romans who founded Florence. But this is most doubtful, — mere supposition, as it seems to me. His

[1] *The Earliest Lives of Dante*, trans. by James Robinson Smith. Yale Studies in English, A. S. Cook, editor: Henry Holt & Co. Used by permission.

great-great-grandfather, as I am informed, was Messer Cacciaguida, a Florentine knight who served under the Emperor Conrad. This Messer Cacciaguida had two brothers, Moronto and Eliseo. We do not read of any succession from Moronto, but from Eliseo sprang the family of the Elisei, who, however, possibly bore this name previously. From Messer Cacciaguida came the Aldighieri, so called from one of his sons, who received the name from the family of his mother.

Messer Cacciaguida, his brothers, and their ancestors lived almost at the corner of the Porta San Piero, where it is first entered from the Mercato Vecchio, in houses still called of the Elisei, since their ancient title has remained to them. The Aldighieri, who were descended from Messer Cacciaguida, dwelt in the piazza at the rear of San Martino del Vescovo, opposite the street that leads to the houses of the Sacchetti. On the other side their dwellings extend toward those of the Donati and of the Giuochi.

Dante was born in the year of our Lord 1265, shortly after the return to Florence of the Guelfs, who had been in exile because of the defeat at Monteaperti. In his boyhood he received a liberal education under teachers of letters, and at once gave evidence of a great natural capacity equal to excellent things. At this time he lost his father, but, encouraged by his relatives and by Brunetto Latini, a most worthy man for those times, he devoted himself not only to literature but to other liberal studies, omitting nothing that pertains to the making of an excellent man.

He did not, however, renounce the world and shut himself up to ease, but associated and conversed with youths of his own age. Courteous, spirited, and full of courage, he took part in every youthful exercise; and in the great and memorable battle of Campaldino, Dante, young but well esteemed, fought vigorously, mounted and in the front rank. Here he incurred the utmost peril, for the first engagement was between the cavalry, in which the horse of the Aretines defeated and overthrew with such violence the horse of the Florentines that the latter, repulsed and routed, were obliged to fall back upon their infantry.

This rout, however, lost the battle for the Aretines. For their victorious horsemen, pursuing those who fled, left their infantry far behind, so that thenceforth they nowhere fought in unison, but the cavalry fought alone without the infantry, and the infantry alone without the cavalry. But on the Florentine side the contrary took place, for, since their cavalry had retreated to their infantry, they were able to advance in a body, and easily overthrew first the horse and then the foot-soldiers of the enemy.

Dante gives a description of the battle in one of his letters. He states that he was in the fight, and draws a plan of the field. And for our better information we must understand that the Uberti, Lamberti, Abati, and all the other Florentine exiles sided with the Aretines in this battle, and that all the exiles of Arezzo, nobles and commoners of the Guelfs, all of whom were in banishment at this time, fought with the Florentines. For this reason the words in the Palace read: "The Ghibellines defeated at Certomondo," and not, "The Aretines defeated;" to the end that those Aretines who shared the victory with the Commune might have no reason to complain.

Returning then to our subject, I repeat that Dante

fought valiantly for his country on this occasion. And I could wish that our Boccaccio had made mention of this virtue rather than of love at nine, and the like trivialities which he tells of this great man. But what use is there in speaking? "The tongue points where the tooth pains," and "Whose taste runs to drinking, his talk runs to wines."

When Dante returned home from this battle, he devoted himself more fervently than ever to his studies, yet omitted naught of polite and social intercourse. It was remarkable that, although he studied incessantly, none would have supposed from his happy manner and youthful way of speaking that he studied at all. In view of this, I wish to denounce the false opinion of many ignorant persons who think that no one is a student save he who buries himself in solitude and ease. I have never seen one of these muffled recluses who knew three letters. The great and lofty genius has no need of such tortures. Indeed, it is a most true and absolute conclusion that they who do not learn quickly, never learn. Therefore to estrange and absent one's self from society is peculiar to those whose poor minds unfit them for knowledge of any kind.

It was not only in social intercourse with men that Dante moved, since in his youth he took to himself a wife. She was a lady of the Donati family, called Madonna Gemma. By her he had several children, as we shall see in another part of this work. At this point Boccaccio loses all patience, and says that wives are hindrances to study, forgetting that Socrates, the noblest philosopher that ever lived, had a wife and children, and held public offices in his city. And

Aristotle, beyond whose wisdom and learning it is impossible to go, was twice married, and had children and great riches. Moreover, Cicero, Varro, and Seneca, all consummate Latin philosophers, had wives, and held offices of government in the republic. So Boccaccio may pardon me, for his judgments on this matter are both false and feeble. Man, according to all the philosophers, is a social animal. The first union, by the multiplication whereof the city arises, is that of husband and wife. Nothing can be perfect where this does not obtain, for only this kind of love is natural, lawful, and allowable.

Dante, then, took a wife, and living the honest, studious life of a citizen, was considerably employed in the republic, and at length, when he had attained to the required age, was made one of the Priors, not chosen by lot as at present, but elected by vote, as was then the rule. With him in this office were Messer Palmieri degli Altoviti, Neri di Messer Jacopo degli Alberti, and others.

This priorate, of the year 1300, was the cause of Dante's banishment and of all the misfortunes of his life, as he himself states in one of his letters in the following words: "All my troubles and hardships had their cause and rise in the disastrous meetings held during my priorate. Albeit in wisdom I was not worthy of that office, nevertheless I was not unworthy of it in fidelity and in age, since ten years had elapsed since the battle of Campaldino, wherein the Ghibelline party was almost utterly defeated and effaced, and on that occasion I was present, no child at arms, and felt at first great fear, but in the end the greatest joy by reason of the various fortunes of that battle." These are Dante's own words. I wish now to give in detail the cause of his banishment, since it is a matter worthy our attention, and Boccaccio passes over it so briefly that perchance it was not so well known to him as it is to me by reason of the history I have written.

The city of Florence, which formerly had been divided by the many dissensions of Guelfs and Ghibellines, finally passed into the hands of the Guelfs, and remained for a long period in that condition. But now among the Guelfs themselves, who ruled the republic, another curse of parties arose, namely, the factions of the Bianchi and Neri. This infection first appeared among the Pistojans, particularly in the family of the Cancellieri. And when all Pistoja was divided, the Florentines, by way of remedy, ordered the leaders of these factions to come to Florence, in order that they might not cause further disturbance at home.

This remedy worked less good to the Pistojans by the removal of their chiefs than harm to the Florentines, who contracted this pestilence. For, since the leaders had many relatives and friends in Florence, from whom they received divers favors, they at once kindled a greater fire of discord than they had left behind them in Pistoja. And inasmuch as the affair was treated of *publice et privatim*, the evil seed spread to a marvelous degree, so that the whole city took sides. There was scarcely a house, noble or plebeian, that was not divided against itself, nor was there a man of any prominence or family that did not subscribe to one of these two parties. The division extended even to brothers of the same blood, one holding to this side, the other to that.

The troubles, which already had lasted several

months, were multiplied not only by words, but by mean and spiteful deeds. These were begun by the youths, but were taken up by men of maturity, until the whole city was in confusion and suspense. At this point, while Dante was still of the Priors, the Neri faction held a meeting in the Church of Santa Trinità. The proceedings were profoundly secret, but the main plan was to treat with Boniface VIII., who was pope at that time, to the end that he should send Charles of Valois, of the royal house of France, to pacify and reform the city.

When the other faction, the Bianchi, heard about the conference, they immediately conceived the greatest distrust thereof. They took up arms, gathered together their allies, and, marching to the Priors, complained of the conference in that it had deliberated in private on public affairs. This was done, they declared, in order to banish them, the Bianchi, from Florence, and they therefore demanded that the Priors should punish this presumptuous outrage.

They who had held the meeting, fearing, in turn, the Bianchi, took up arms, complained to the Priors that their adversaries had armed and fortified themselves without the public consent, and affirmed that the Bianchi under various pretexts wished to banish them. They asked the Priors to punish them, therefore, as disturbers of the public peace.

Both parties were provided with armed men and with their allies. Suspicion and terror were at their height, and the actual peril was very great. The city being in arms and in a turmoil, the Priors, at Dante's suggestion, took the precaution of fortifying themselves behind the multitude of the people. And when they were thus secured, they confined within bounds the leaders of the two factions. Of the Neri faction, Messer Corso Donati, Messer Geri Spini, Messer Giacchinotto de' Pazzi, Messer Rosso della Tosa, and others were sent to the Castello della Pieve in the province of Perugia. Of the Bianchi faction were Messer Gentile and Messer Torrigiano de' Cerchi, Guido Cavalcanti, Baschiera della Tosa, Baldinaccio Adimari, Naldo di Messer Lottino Gherardini, and others. These men were confined within bounds at Serezzana.

This action caused much trouble to Dante. Although he defended himself as a man without a party, yet it was thought that he inclined to the Bianchi, and that he disapproved of the scheme proposed in Santa Trinità of calling Charles of Valois to Florence, believing that it was likely to bring discord and calamity on the city. To add to this ill-feeling, those citizens who were confined at Serezzana suddenly returned to Florence, while those who had been sent to the Castello della Pieve remained outside. With regard to this matter Dante explained that he was not a Prior at the time when the men of Serezzana were recalled, and that therefore he was not to be held accountable. He declared, furthermore, that their return was due to the sickness and death of Guido Cavalcanti, who had fallen ill at Serezzana owing to the bad climate, and died shortly afterward.

This unequal state of things led the Pope to send Charles to Florence. Being honorably received into the city out of respect to the papacy and the house of France, he straightway recalled those citizens who were still confined within bounds, and later banished all the Bianchi faction. The reason of this was a plot that was disclosed by his baron, Messer Piero Ferranti. This man said that three gentlemen of the Bianchi party, namely, Naldo di Messer Lottino Gherardini, Baschiera della Tosa, and Baldinaccio Adimari, had requested him to try and prevail upon Charles of Valois to keep their party at the head of the state, and that they promised to make him governor of Prato in return. The baron produced the written petition and promise with their seals affixed. This original document I have seen, since it lies to-day in the Palace with other public writings, but in my opinion it is not above suspicion, and indeed I feel quite certain that it was forged. Be that as it may, the banishment of all the Bianchi party followed, Charles professing great indignation at their request and promise.

Dante was not in Florence at this time, but at Rome, whither he had been sent shortly before as ambassador to the Pope, to offer him the peace and concord of the citizens. Nevertheless, through the anger of those Neri who had been banished during his priorate, his house was attacked, everything was pillaged, and his estate was laid waste. Banishment was decreed for him and for Messer Palmieri Altoviti, not by reason of any wrong committed, but for contumacy in failing to appear.

The manner of decreeing the banishment was this. They enacted a perverse and iniquitous law with retrospective action, which declared it the power and duty of the Podestà of Florence to recognize past offenses committed by a Prior when in office, although acquittal had followed at the time. Under this law Messer Cante de' Gabbrielli, Podestà of Florence, summoned Dante to trial. And since he was absent from the city, and did not appear, he was condemned and banished, and his goods were confiscated, although they already had been plundered and laid waste.

We have given the cause and the circumstances of Dante's banishment; we shall now speak of his life in exile. When Dante heard of his ruin, he at once left Rome, where he was ambassador, and, journeying with all haste, he came to Siena. Here he learned more definitely of his misfortune, and seeing no recourse, he decided to throw in his lot with the other exiles. He first joined them in a meeting held at Gorgonza, where among the many things discussed they fixed on Arezzo as their headquarters. There they made a large camp, and created the Count Alessandro da Romena their captain, together with twelve councilors, among whom was Dante. They remained here from hope to hope till the year 1304, and then, making a great gathering of all their allies, they planned to reënter Florence with an exceeding great multitude, assembled not only from Arezzo, but from Bologna and Pistoja. Arriving unexpectedly, they immediately captured one of the gates and occupied part of the city. But in the end they were forced to retire with no advantage.

Since this great hope had failed, Dante, deeming it wrong to waste more time, left Arezzo for Verona. Here he was most courteously received by the Lords della Scala, and tarried with them for some time. And now in all humility he endeavored by good deeds and upright conduct to obtain the favor of returning to Florence through the voluntary action of the government. Devoting himself resolutely to this end, he wrote frequently to individual citizens in power and also to the people, among others one long letter which began, "Populе mee, quid feci tibi?"

But while he was still hoping to return by the way of pardon, the election of Henry of Luxemburg as Emperor occurred. This election, and the coming of Henry, filled all Italy with the hope of a great change, and Dante himself could no longer keep to his plan of waiting for pardon. With his pride of spirit aroused, he began to speak evil of the rulers of the state, calling them caitiffs and criminals, and threatening them at the hands of the Emperor with deserved punishment. From this, he said, there was clearly no possible escape for them.

Yet so great was the reverence he felt for his country, that when the Emperor had marched against Florence and was encamped near the gate, Dante would not be present, as he writes, although he had urged the Emperor's coming. And when Henry died the following summer at Buonconvento, Dante lost all hope, for he himself had destroyed all chance of pardon by speaking and writing against the citizens in power, and no force remained whereon he could place further assurance. Void of hope, therefore, and in great poverty, he passed the remainder of his life tarrying in divers parts of Lombardy, Tuscany, and Romagna, under the protection of various lords, until finally he settled down at Ravenna, where he died.

Since we have told of his public troubles, and under this head have shown the course of his life, we will now speak of his domestic affairs, and of his habits and studies. Previous to his banishment from Florence, although he was not a man of great wealth, yet he was not poor, for he possessed a moderate patrimony, large enough to admit of comfortable living. He had one brother, Francisco Alighieri, a wife, as already mentioned, and several children, whose descendants remain to this day, as we shall show later. He owned good houses in Florence, adjoining those of Gieri di Messer Bello, his kinsman; possessions also in Camerata, in the Piacentina, and in the plain of Ripoli; and, as he writes, many pieces of valuable furniture.

He was a man of great refinement; of medium height, and a pleasant but deeply serious face. He spoke only seldom, and then slowly, but was very subtle in his replies. His portrait may be seen in Santa Croce, near the centre of the church, on the left hand as you approach the high altar, a most faithful painting by an excellent artist of that time. He delighted in music and singing, and drew exceedingly well. He wrote a finished hand, making thin, long, and perfectly formed letters, as I have seen in some of his correspondence. In his youth he associated with young lovers, and he, too, was filled with a like passion, not through evil desire, but out of the gentleness of his heart. And in his tender years he began to write love verses, as may be seen in his short work in the vernacular called the Vita Nuova.

His chief study was poetry: not dry, poor, or fantastic poetry, but such as is impregnated, enriched, and confirmed by true knowledge and many disciplines. . . .

Dante writes that riming began about one hundred and fifty years before his time. The first in Italy to practice it were Guido Guinizzelli of Bologna, the "Joyous Knight" Guitone d'Arrezzo, Bonagiunta da Lucca, and Guido da Messina [Guido delle Colonne]. Dante so far excelled all of these in knowledge, delicacy, and graceful elegance that good judges believe that in the use of rime he will never be surpassed. And truly wonderful is the sweetness and sublimity of his wise, pithy, and serious verse, with its variety and affluence, its knowledge of philosophy, its references to ancient history, and such familiarity with modern history that he seems to have been present at every event. These excellent qualities, unfolded with the gentleness of rime, take captive the mind of every reader, and especially of such as have the greatest understanding.

His invention, which was marvelous, was laid hold of with great genius, comprehending, as it does, description of the world, the heavens, and the planets, of men, the rewards and punishments of human life, happiness and misery, and the middle way that lies between these two extremes. I believe that there never was any one who took a larger or more fertile subject by which to deliver the mind of all its conceptions through the different spirits who discourse on diverse causes of things, on different countries, and on various chances of fortune.

Dante began this, his chief work, before his expulsion, and completed it afterwards in exile, as the work itself clearly reveals. He also wrote moral canzoni and sonnets. His canzoni are perfect, polished, graceful, and full of high sentiment. All of them begin in noble fashion, like the one that commences —

> O Love that drawest from the Heaven thy power
> Even as the sun his splendor,

wherein there is a subtle philosophical comparison between the effects of the sun and the effects of love. Another begins —

> Three Ladies round about my heart have come.

Still another begins —

Ye Ladies that have cognizance of Love.

And in many other canzoni he is equally subtle, scholarly, and polished. In his sonnets he does not show the same power.

So much for his works in the vernacular; but he also wrote in Latin prose and verse: in prose, a book entitled the De Monarchia, written in unadorned fashion, with no beauty of style; also a book entitled De Vulgari Eloquentia, and many letters. In Latin verse he wrote several eclogues, and the beginning of the Commedia in hexameters, but, as he did not succeed with the style, he pursued it no further.

Dante died at Ravenna in the year 1321. He left, among others, one son by name Piero, who studied law and showed himself a man of ability. Thanks to his own powers and to the remembrance in which his father was held, he attained to great distinction and wealth, and maintained his position at Verona with considerable state. This Messer Piero had a son named Dante, who in turn had a son Lionardo, who is still living and has several children. A short time ago Lionardo came to Florence with other young men of Verona, well and honorably appointed, and visited me as a friend to the memory of his great-grandfather, Dante. I showed him the houses of the poet and of his ancestors, and called his attention to many things that were new to him because he and his family had been estranged from their fatherland. And thus Fortune turns this world, and shifts its inhabitants with the revolutions of her wheel.

Of the value of this life by Lionardo Bruni, Dr. Moore says: "We feel that we have here the work of a serious and intelligent historian, who avoids repeating gossip, and for the most part also mere current tradition, — possibly some might say that he does this too rigidly, alarmed by the warning example of Boccaccio; one too who knows how to make use of letters, archives, and other documents in order to verify or test his statements; one, finally, who can secure both these merits without becoming dull, since his work is often enlivened by gleams of humor and touches of sympathy."[1]

There are two other Lives of Dante which Dr. Moore mentions: one by Giannozzo Manetti, who lived from 1396 to 1459, and whose work is thus summarized: "This prolix and rather pretentious work has added little either to our knowledge or to our pleasure. Its only feature of originality is displayed in the inventive enterprise of the author, while the rest is a mere *réchauffé* of Boccaccio and Lionardo, with occasional scraps from Villani." The Life by Filelfo (1426–1480) depends for its authority on the author's own "lively imagination, unembarrassed by any reference to documents, except when he is servilely copying the very language of Lionardo, Boccaccio, or others of his predecessors."

[1] *Dante and His Early Biographers*, p. 81.

V

WHAT IS DEFINITELY KNOWN

HAVING given a comprehensive survey of the earliest sources of our knowledge of Dante, we subjoin the most succinct and authoritative statement we have been able to find of what the sifting processes of five hundred years have found to be true of the external events of his life.

PROFESSOR NORTON'S NARRATIVE OF DANTE'S LIFE.[1]

Dante was born in Florence, in May or June, 1265. Of his family little is positively known.[2] It was not among the nobles of the city, but it had place among the well-to-do citizens who formed the body of the state and the main support of the Guelf party. Of Dante's early years, and the course of his education, nothing is known save what he himself tells us in his various writings, or what may be inferred from them. Lionardo Bruni, eminent as an historian and as a public man, who wrote a Life of Dante about a hundred years after his death, cites a letter of which we have no other knowledge, in which, if the letter be

[1] *Library of the World's Best Literature*, article on Dante. (By permission.)

[2] In the *Paradiso* (canto xv.) he introduces his great-great-grandfather Cacciaguida, who tells of himself that he followed the Emperor Conrad to fight against the Mohammedans, was made a knight by him, and was slain in the war.

genuine, the poet says that he took part in the battle of Campaldino, fought in June, 1289. The words are: "At the battle of Campaldino, in which the Ghibelline party was almost all slain and undone, I found myself not a child in arms, and I experienced great fear, and finally the greatest joy, because of the shifting fortunes of the fight."[1] It seems likely that Dante was present, probably under arms, in the latter part of the same summer, at the surrender to the Florentines of the Pisan stronghold of Caprona, where, he says (Inferno, xxi. 94–96), "I saw the foot soldiers afraid, who came out under compact from Caprona, seeing themselves among so many enemies."

Years passed before any other event in Dante's life is noted with a certain date. An imperfect record preserved in the Florentine archives mentions his taking part in a discussion in the so-called Council of a Hundred Men, on the 5th of June, 1296. This is of importance as indicating that he had before this time become a member of one of the twelve Arts, — enrollment in one of which was required for the acquisition of the right to exercise political functions in the state, — and also as indicating that he had a place in the chief of those councils by which public measures were discussed and decided. The Art of which he was a member was that of the physicians and druggists (*medici e speziali*), an Art whose dealings included commerce in many of the products of the East.

Not far from this time, but whether before or after 1296 is uncertain, he married. His wife was Gemma dei Donati. The Donati were a powerful family among

[1] *Vide* p. 119.

the *grandi* of the city, and played a leading part in the stormy life of Florence. Of Gemma nothing is known but her marriage.

Between 1297 and 1299, Dante, together with his brother Francesco, as appears from existing documentary evidence, were borrowers of considerable sums of money; and the largest of the debts thus incurred seem not to have been discharged till 1332, eleven years after his death, when they were paid by his sons Jacopo and Pietro.

In May, 1299, he was sent as envoy from Florence to the little, not very distant, city of San Gemignano, to urge its community to take part in a general council of the Guelf communes of Tuscany.

In the next year, 1300, he was elected one of the six Priors of Florence, to hold office from the 15th of June to the 15th of August. The Priors, together with the "gonfalonier of justice" (who had command of the body of one thousand men who stood at their service), formed the chief magistracy of the city. Florence had such jealousy of its rulers that the Priors held office but two months, so that in the course of each year thirty-six of the citizens were elected to this magistracy. The outgoing Priors, associated with twelve of the leading citizens, — two from each of the *sestieri*, or wards, of the city, — chose their successors. Neither continuity nor steady vigor of policy was possible with an administration so shifting and of such varied composition, which by its very constitution was exposed at all times to intrigue and to attack. It was no wonder that Florence lay open to the reproach that her counsels were such that what she spun in October did not reach to mid-November (Purgatory, vi. 142–144).

His election to the priorate was the most important event in Dante's public life. "All my ills and all my troubles," he declared, "had occasion and beginning from my misfortunate election to the priorate, of which, though I was not worthy in respect of wisdom, yet I was not unworthy in fidelity and in age." [1]

The year 1300 was disastrous not only for Dante, but for Florence. She was, at the end of the thirteenth century, by far the most flourishing and powerful city of Tuscany, full of vitality and energy, and beautiful as she was strong. She was not free from civil discord, but the predominance of the Guelf party was so complete within her walls that she suffered little from the strife between Guelf and Ghibelline, which for almost a century had divided Italy into two hostile camps. In the main the Guelf party was that of the common people and the industrious classes, and in general it afforded support to the Papacy as against the Empire, while it received, in return, support from the popes. The Ghibellines, on the other hand, were mainly of the noble class, and maintainers of the Empire. The growth of the industry and commerce of Florence in the last half of the century had resulted in the establishment of the popular power, and in the suppression of the Ghibelline interest. But a bitter quarrel broke out in one of the great families in the neighboring Guelf city of Pistoia, a quarrel which raged so furiously that Florence feared that it would result in the gain of power by the Ghibellines, and she adopted the fatal policy of compelling the heads of the contending factions to take up their residence within her walls.

[1] From the letter already referred to, cited by Lionardo Bruni, p. 119.

The result was that she herself became the seat of discord. Each of the two factions found ardent adherents, and, adopting the names by which they had been distinguished in Pistoia, Florence was almost instantly ablaze with the passionate quarrel between the Whites and the Blacks (Bianchi and Neri). The flames burned so high that the Pope, Boniface VIII., intervened to quench them. His intervention was vain.

It was just at this time that Dante became Prior. The need of action to restore peace to the city was imperative, and the Priors took the step of banishing the leaders of both divisions. Among those of the Bianchi was Dante's own nearest friend, Guido Cavalcante. The measure was insufficient to secure tranquillity and order. The city was in constant tumult; its conditions went from bad to worse. But in spite of civil broils, common affairs must still be attended to, and from a document preserved in the Archives at Florence we learn that on the 28th April, 1301, Dante was appointed superintendent, without salary, of works undertaken for the widening, straightening, and paving of the street of San Procolo, and making it safe for travel. On the 13th of the same month he took part in a discussion, in the Council of the Heads of the twelve greater Arts, as to the mode of procedure in the election of future Priors. On the 18th of June, in the Council of the Hundred Men, he advised against providing the Pope with a force of one hundred men which had been asked for; and again in September of the same year there is record, for the last time, of his taking part in the Council, in a discussion in regard "to the conservation of the Ordinances of Justice and the Statutes of the People."

These notices of the part taken by Dante in public affairs seem at first sight comparatively slight and unimportant; but were one constructing an ideal biography of him, it would be hard to devise records more appropriate to the character and principles of the man as they appear from his writings. The sense of the duty of the individual to the community of which he forms a part was one of his strongest convictions; and his being put in charge of the opening of the street of San Procolo, and making it safe for travel, "eo quod popularis comitatus absque strepitu et briga magnatum et potentum possunt secure venire ad dominos priores et vexilliferum justitiae cum expedit" (so that the common people may, without uproar and harassing of magnates and mighty men, have access whenever it be desirable to the Lord Priors and the Standard-Bearer of Justice), affords a comment on his own criticism of his fellow-citizens, whose disposition to shirk the burden of public duty is more than once the subject of his satire. "Many refuse the common burden, but thy people, my Florence, eagerly replies without being called on, and cries, 'I load myself'" (Purgatory, vi. 133–135). His counsel against providing the Pope with troops was in conformity with his fixed political conviction that the function of the papacy was to be confined to the spiritual government of mankind; and nothing could be more striking, as a chance incident, than that the last occasion on which he, whose heart was set on justice, took part in the counsels of his city, should have been for the discussion of the means for "the conservation of the ordinances of justice and the statutes of the people."

In the course of events in 1300 and 1301 the Bianchi proved the stronger of the two factions by which the city was divided, they resisted with success the efforts of the Pope in support of their rivals, and they were charged by their enemies with intent to restore the rule of the city to the Ghibellines. While affairs were in this state, Charles of Valois, brother to the king of France, Philip the Fair, was passing through Italy with a troop of horsemen to join Charles II. of Naples,[1] in the attempt to regain Sicily from the hands of Frederic of Aragon. The Pope favored the expedition, and held out flattering promises to Charles. The latter reached Anagni, where Boniface was residing, in September, 1301. Here it was arranged that before proceeding to Sicily, Charles should undertake to reduce to obedience the refractory opponents of the Pope in Tuscany. The title of the Pacifier of Tuscany was bestowed on him, and he moved toward Florence with his own troop and a considerable additional force of men-at-arms. He was met on his way by deputies from Florence, to whom he made fair promises; and trusting to his good faith, the Florentines opened their gates to him and he entered the city on All Saints' Day (November 1st), 1301.

Charles had hardly established himself in his quarters before he cast his pledges to the wind. The exiled Neri, with his connivance, broke into the city, and for six days worked their will upon their enemies, slaying many of them, pillaging and burning their houses, while Charles looked on with apparent unconcern at the widespread ruin and devastation. New

[1] Charles II. of Naples was the cousin of Philip III., the Bold, of France, the father of Charles of Valois; and in 1290 Charles of Valois had married his daughter.

Priors, all of them from the party of the Neri, entered upon office in mid-November, and a new Podestà, Cante dei Gabrielli of Agobbio, was charged with the administration of justice. The persecution of the Bianchi was carried on with consistent thoroughness: many were imprisoned, many fined, Charles sharing in the sums exacted from them. On the 27th of January, 1302, a decree was issued by the Podestà condemning five persons, one of whom was Dante, to fine and banishment on account of crimes alleged to have been committed by them while holding office as Priors. "According to public report," said the decree, "they committed barratry, sought illicit gains, and practiced unjust extortions of money or goods." These general charges are set forth with elaborate legal phraseology, and with much repetition of phrase, but without statement of specific instances. The most important of them are that the accused had spent money of the commune in opposing the Pope, in resistance to the coming of Charles of Valois, and against the peace of the city and the Guelf party; that they had promoted discord in the city of Pistoia, and had caused the expulsion from that city of the Neri, the faithful adherents of the Holy Roman Church; and that they had caused Pistoia to break its union with Florence, and to refuse subjection to the Church and to Charles the Pacificator of Tuscany. These being the charges, the decree proceeded to declare that the accused, having been summoned to appear within a fixed time before the Podestà and his court to make their defense, under penalty for non-appearance of five thousand florins each, and having failed to do so, were now condemned to pay this sum and to restore their illicit gains; and if this were not done within three days from the publication of this sentence against them, all their possessions (*bona*) should be seized and destroyed; and should they make the required payment, they were nevertheless to stand banished from Tuscany for two years; and for perpetual memory of their misdeeds their names were to be inscribed in the Statutes of the People, and as swindlers and barrators they were never to hold office or benefice within the city or district of Florence.

Six weeks later, on the 10th of March, another decree of the Podestà was published, declaring the five citizens named in the preceding decree, together with ten others, to have practically confessed their guilt by their contumacy in non-appearance when summoned, and condemning them, if at any time any one of them should come into the power of Florence, to be burned to death ("Talis perveniens igne comburatur sic quod moriatur").[1]

From this time forth till his death Dante was an exile. The character of the decrees is such that the charges brought against him have no force, and leave no suspicion resting upon his actions as an officer of the State. They are the outcome and expression of the bitterness of party rage, and they testify clearly only to his having been one of the leaders of the party opposed to the pretensions of the Pope, and desirous to maintain the freedom of Florence from foreign intervention.

In April Charles left Florence, "having finished," says Villani, the eye-witness of these events, "that for

[1] These decrees and the other public documents relating to Dante are to be found in various publications. They have all been collected and edited by Professor George R. Carpenter, in the tenth and eleventh Annual Reports of the Dante Society, Cambridge, Massachusetts, 1891, 1892.

which he had come, namely, under pretext of peace, having driven the White party from Florence; but from this proceeded many calamities and dangers to our city."

The course of Dante's external life in exile is hardly less obscure than that of his early days. Much concerning it may be inferred with some degree of probability from passages in his own writings, or from what is reported by others; but of actual certain facts there are few. For a time he seems to have remained with his companions in exile, of whom there were hundreds, but he soon separated himself from them in grave dissatisfaction, making a party by himself (Paradiso, xvii. 69), and found shelter at the court of the Scaligeri at Verona. In August, 1306, he was among the witnesses to a contract at Padua. In October of the same year he was with Franceschino, Marchese Malespina, in the district called the Lunigiana, and empowered by him as his special procurator and envoy to establish the terms of peace for him and his brothers with the Bishop of Luni. His gratitude to the Malespini for their hospitality and good-will toward him is proved by one of the most splendid compliments ever paid in verse or prose, the magnificent eulogium of this great and powerful house with which the eighth canto of the Purgatory closes. How long Dante remained with the Malespini, and whither he went after leaving them, is unknown. At some period of his exile he was at Lucca (Purgatorio, xxiv. 45); Villani states that he was at Bologna, and afterwards at Paris, and in many parts of the world. He wandered far and wide in Italy, and it may well be that in the course of his years of exile he went to Paris, drawn thither by the opportunities of learning which the University afforded, but nothing is known definitely of his going.

In 1311 the mists which obscure the greater part of Dante's life in exile are dispelled for a moment by three letters of unquestioned authenticity, and we gain a clear view of the poet. In 1310 Henry of Luxemburg, a man who touched the imagination of his contemporaries by his striking presence and chivalric accomplishments as well as by his high character and generous aims, "a man just, religious, and strenuous in arms," having been elected Emperor, as Henry VII., prepared to enter Italy, with intent to confirm the imperial rights and to restore order to the distracted land. The Pope, Clement V., favored his coming, and the prospect opened by it was hailed not only by the Ghibellines with joy, but by a large part of the Guelfs as well; with the hope that the long discord and confusion, from which all had suffered, might be brought to end, and give place to tranquillity and justice. Dante exulted in this new hope; and on the coming of the Emperor, late in 1310, he addressed an animated appeal to the rulers and people of Italy exhorting them in impassioned words to rise up and do reverence to him whom the Lord of heaven and earth had ordained for their king. "Behold, now is the accepted time; rejoice, O Italy, dry thy tears; efface, O most beautiful, the traces of mourning; for he is at hand who shall deliver thee."

The first welcome of Henry was ardent, and with fair auspices he assumed at Milan, in January, 1311, the Iron Crown, the crown of the king of Italy. Here at Milan Dante presented himself, and here with full heart he did homage upon his knees to the Emperor.

But the popular welcome proved hollow; the illusions of hope speedily began to vanish; revolt broke out in many cities of Lombardy; Florence remained obdurate, and with great preparations for resistance put herself at the head of the enemies of the Emperor. Dante, disappointed and indignant, could not keep silence. He wrote a letter headed "Dante Alaghieri, a Florentine and undeservedly in exile, to the most wicked Florentines within the city." It begins with calm and eloquent words in regard to the divine foundation of the imperial power, and to the sufferings of Italy due to her having been left without its control to her own undivided will. Then it breaks forth in passionate denunciation of Florence for her impious arrogance in venturing to rise up in mad rebellion against the minister of God; and, warning her of the calamities which her blind obstinacy is preparing for her, it closes with threats of her impending ruin and desolation. This letter is dated from the springs of the Arno, on the 31st of March.

The growing force of the opposition which he encountered delayed the progress of Henry. Dante, impatient of delay, eager to see the accomplishment of his hope, on the 16th of April addressed Henry himself in a letter of exalted prophetic exhortation, full of biblical language, and of illustrations drawn from sacred and profane story, urging him not to tarry, but trusting in God, to go out to meet and to slay the Goliath that stood against him. "Then the Philistines will flee, and Israel will be delivered, and we, exiles in Babylon, who groan as we remember the holy Jerusalem, shall then, as citizens breathing in peace, recall in joy the miseries of confusion." But all was in vain.

The drama which had opened with such brilliant expectations was advancing to a tragic close. Italy became more confused and distracted than ever. One sad event followed after another. In May the brother of the Emperor fell at the siege of Brescia; in September his dearly loved wife Margarita, "a holy and good woman," died at Genoa. The forces hostile to him grew more and more formidable. He succeeded, however, in entering Rome in May, 1312, but his enemies held half of the city, and the streets became the scene of bloody battles; St. Peter's was closed to him, and Henry, worn and disheartened and in peril, was compelled to submit to be ingloriously crowned at St. John Lateran. With diminished strength and with loss of influence he withdrew to Tuscany, and laid ineffectual siege to Florence. Month after month dragged along with miserable continuance of futile war. In the summer of 1313, collecting all his forces, Henry prepared to move southward against the King of Naples. But he was seized with illness, and on the 24th of August he died at Buonconvento, not far from Siena. With his death died the hope of union and of peace for Italy. His work, undertaken with high purpose and courage, had wholly failed. He had come to set Italy straight before she was ready (Paradiso, xxxi. 137). The clouds darkened over her. For Dante the cup of bitterness overflowed.

How Dante was busied, where he was abiding, during the last two years of Henry's stay in Italy, we have no knowledge. One striking fact relating to him is all that is recorded. In the summer of 1311 the Guelfs in Florence, in order to strengthen themselves against the Emperor, determined to relieve from ban and to recall from exile many of their banished fellow-citizens, confident that on returning home they would strengthen the city in its resistance against the Emperor. But to the general amnesty which was issued on the 2d of September there were large exceptions; and impressive evidence of the multitude of the exiles is afforded by the fact that more than a thousand were expressly excluded from the benefit of pardon, and were to remain banished and condemned as before. In the list of those thus still regarded as enemies of Florence stands the name of Dante.

The death of the Emperor was followed eight months later by that of the Pope, Clement V., under whom the papal throne had been removed from Rome to Avignon. There seemed a chance, if but feeble, that a new pope might restore the Church to the city which was its proper home, and thus at least one of the wounds of Italy be healed. The Conclave was bitterly divided; month after month went by without a choice, the fate of the Church and of Italy hanging uncertain in the balance. Dante, in whom religion and patriotism combined as a single passion, saw with grief that the return of the Church to Italy was likely to be lost through the selfishness, the jealousies, and the avarice of her chief prelates; and under the impulse of the deepest feeling he addressed a letter of remonstrance, reproach, and exhortation to the Italian cardinals, who formed but a small minority in the Conclave, but who might by union and persistence still secure the election of a pope favorable to the return. This letter is full of a noble but too vehement zeal. "It is for you, being one at heart, to fight manfully for the Bride of Christ; for the seat of the Bride, which is Rome; for our Italy, and in a word, for the whole commonwealth of pilgrims upon earth." But words were in vain; and after a struggle kept up for two years and three months, a pope was at last elected who was to fix the seat of the papacy only the more firmly at Avignon. Once more Dante had to bear the pain of disappointment of hopes in which selfishness had no part.

And now for years he disappears from sight. What his life was he tells in a most touching passage near the beginning of his Convito: "From the time when it pleased the citizens of Florence, the fairest and most famous daughter of Rome, to cast me out from her sweetest bosom (in which I had been born and nourished even to the summit of my life, and in which, at good peace with them, I desire with all my heart to repose my weary soul, and to end the time which is allotted to me), through almost all the regions to which our tongue extends I have gone a pilgrim, almost a beggar, displaying against my will the wound of fortune, which is wont often to be imputed unjustly to [the discredit of] him who is wounded. Truly I have been a bark without sail and without rudder, borne to divers ports and bays and shores by that dry wind which grievous poverty breathes forth, and I have appeared mean in the eyes of many who perchance, through some report, had imagined me in other form; and not only has my person been lowered in their sight, but every work of mine, whether done or to be done, has been held in less esteem."

Once more, and for the last time, during these wanderings he heard the voice of Florence addressed to him, and still in anger. A decree was issued [1] on the

[1] This decree was pronounced in a General Council of the Commune

6th of November, 1315, renewing the condemnation and banishment of numerous citizens, denounced as Ghibellines and rebels, including among them Dante Aldighieri and his sons. The persons named in this decree are charged with contumacy, and with the commission of ill deeds against the good state of the Commune of Florence and the Guelf party; and it is ordered that "if any of them shall fall into the power of the Commune he shall be taken to the place of Justice and there be beheaded." The motive is unknown which led to the inclusion in this decree of the sons of Dante, of whom there were two, now youths respectively a little more or a little less than twenty years old.[1]

It is probable that the last years of Dante's life were passed in Ravenna, under the protection of Guido da Polenta, lord of the city. It was here that he died, on September 14th, 1321. His two sons were with him, and probably also his daughter Beatrice. He was in his fifty-seventh year when he went from suffering and from exile to peace (Paradiso, x. 128).

Such are the few absolute facts known concerning the external events of Dante's life. A multitude of

by the vicar of King Robert of Naples, into whose hands the Florentines had given themselves in 1313 for a term of five years, — extended afterwards to eight, — with the hope that by his authority order might be preserved within the city.

[1] Among the letters ascribed to Dante is one, much noted, in reply to a letter from a friend in Florence, in regard to terms of absolution on which he might secure his readmission to Florence. It is of very doubtful authenticity. It has no external evidence to support it, and the internal evidence of its rhetorical form and sentimental tone is all against it. It belongs in the same class with the famous letter of Fra Ilario, and like that, seems not unlikely to have been an invention of Boccaccio's.

statements, often with much circumstantial detail, concerning other incidents, have been made by his biographers; a few rest upon a foundation of probability, but the mass are guesswork. There is no need to report them; for small as the sum of our actual knowledge is, it is enough for defining the field within which his spiritual life was enacted, and for showing the conditions under which his work was done, and by which its character was largely determined.

CHAPTER III

DANTE'S PERSONAL APPEARANCE

PORTRAITS AND MASK [1]

In his Life of Dante, Boccaccio, the earliest of the biographers of the poet, describes him in these words: "Our poet was of middle height, and after reaching mature years he went somewhat stooping; his gait was grave and sedate; always clothed in most becoming garments, his dress was suited to the ripeness of his years; his face was long, his nose aquiline, his eyes rather large than small, his jaw heavy, and his under lip prominent; his complexion was dark, and his hair and beard thick, black, and crisp, and his countenance was always sad and thoughtful. . . . His manners, whether in public or at home, were wonderfully composed and restrained, and in all his ways he was more courteous and civil than any one else." [2]

Such was Dante as he appeared in his later years to those from whose recollections of him Boccaccio drew this description.

But Boccaccio, had he chosen so to do, might have drawn another portrait of Dante, not the author of the Divine Comedy, but the author of the New Life. The likeness of the youthful Dante was familiar to those Florentines who had never looked on the living presence of their greatest citizen.

On the altar wall of the chapel of the Palace of the Podestà (now the Bargello) Giotto had painted a grand religious composition, in which, after the fashion of the

[1] Professor Charles Eliot Norton, *On the Original Portraits of Dante.* (By permission.)

[2] *Vide* p. 95.

times, he exalted the glory of Florence by the introduction of some of her most famous citizens into the assembly of the blessed in Paradise. "The head of Christ, full of dignity, appears above, and lower down, the escutcheon of Florence, supported by angels, with two rows of saints, male and female, attendant to the right and left, in front of whom stand a company of the *magnates* of the city, headed by two crowned personages, close to one of whom, to the right, stands Dante, a pomegranate in his hand, and wearing the graceful falling cap of the day."[1] The date when this picture was painted is uncertain, but Giotto represented his friend in it as a youth, such as he may have been in the first flush of early fame, at the season of the beginning of their memorable friendship.

Of all the portraits of the revival of art, there is none comparable in interest to this likeness of the supreme poet by the supreme artist of mediæval Europe. It was due to no accident of fortune that these men were contemporaries, and of the same country; but it was a fortunate and delightful incident that they were so brought together by sympathy of genius and by favoring circumstance as to become friends, to love and honor each other in life, and to celebrate each other through all time in their respective works. The story of their friendship is known only in its outline, but that it began when they were young is certain, and that it lasted till death divided them is a tradition which finds ready acceptance.

It was probably between 1290 and 1300, when Giotto was just rising to unrivaled fame, that this painting was executed. There is no contemporary record

[1] Lord Lindsay's *History of Christian Art*, vol. ii. p. 174.

of it, the earliest known reference to it being that by Filippo Villani, who died about 1404. Gianozzo Manetti, who died in 1459, also mentions it, and Vasari, in his Life of Giotto, published in 1550, says, that Giotto "became so good an imitator of nature, that he altogether discarded the stiff Greek manner, and revived the modern and good art of painting, introducing exact drawing from nature of living persons, which for more than two hundred years had not been practiced, or if indeed any one had tried it, he had not succeeded very happily, nor anything like so well as Giotto. And he portrayed among other persons, as may even now be seen, in the chapel of the Palace of the Podestà in Florence, Dante Alighieri, his contemporary and greatest friend, who was not less famous a poet than Giotto was painter in those days. . . . In the same chapel is the portrait by the same hand of Ser Brunetto Latini, the master of Dante, and of Messer Corso Donati, a great citizen of those times."[1]

One might have supposed that such a picture as this would have been among the most carefully protected and jealously prized treasures of Florence. But such was not the case. The shameful neglect of many of the best and most interesting works of the earlier period of art, which accompanied and was one of the symptoms of the moral and political decline of Italy during the sixteenth and seventeenth centuries, ex-

[1] Since this essay was written, careful investigations made by eminent Florentine authorities have shown that Vasari was probably mistaken in ascribing the portrait of Dante to Giotto. It is now commonly assigned to his pupil Taddeo Gaddi, who is supposed to have painted it in 1337, the year after Giotto's death. It does not seem improbable that he had a drawing by his master of Dante in early life from which to work.

tended to this as to other of the noblest paintings of Giotto. Florence, in losing consciousness of present worth, lost care for the memorials of her past honor, dignity, and distinction. The Palace of the Podestà, no longer needed for the dwelling of the chief magistrate of a free city, was turned into a jail for common criminals, and what had once been its beautiful and sacred chapel was occupied as a larder or storeroom. The walls, adorned with paintings more precious than gold, were covered with whitewash, and the fresco of Giotto was swept over by the brush of the plasterer. It was not only thus hidden from the sight of those unworthy indeed to behold it, but it almost disappeared from memory also; and from the time of Vasari down to that of Moreni, a Florentine antiquary, in the early part of the present century, hardly a mention of it occurs. In a note found among his papers, Moreni laments that he had spent two years of his life in unavailing efforts to recover the portrait of Dante, and the other portions of the fresco of Giotto in the Bargello, mentioned by Vasari; that others before him had made a like effort, and had failed in like manner; and that he hoped that better times would come, in which this painting, of such historic and artistic interest, would again be sought for, and at length recovered. Stimulated by these words, three gentlemen, one an American, Mr. Richard Henry Wilde, one an Englishman, Mr. Seymour Kirkup, and one an Italian, Signor G. Aubrey Bezzi, all scholars devoted to the study of Dante, undertook new researches, in 1840, and, after many hindrances on the part of the government, which were at length successfully overcome, the work of removing the crust of plaster from the walls of the ancient chapel was entrusted to the Florentine painter, Marini. This new and well-directed search did not fail. After some months' labor the fresco was found,[1] almost uninjured, under the whitewash that had protected while concealing it, and at length the likeness of Dante was uncovered.

"But," says Mr. Kirkup, in a letter published in the Spectator (London), May 11, 1850, "the eye of the beautiful profile was wanting. There was a hole an inch deep, or an inch and a half. Marini said it was a nail. It did seem precisely the damage of a nail drawn out. Afterwards Marini filled the hole and made a new eye, too little and ill designed, and then he retouched the whole face and clothes, to the great damage of the expression and character. The likeness of the face, and the three colors in which Dante was dressed, the same with those of Beatrice, those of young Italy, white, green, and red, stand no more; the green is turned to chocolate color; moreover, the form of the cap is lost and confounded.

"I desired to make a drawing. It was denied me. But I obtained the means to be shut up in the prison for a morning; and not only did I make a drawing, but a tracing also, and with the two I then made a facsimile sufficiently careful. Luckily it was before the *rifacimento*."

This fac-simile afterwards passed into the hands of Lord Vernon, well known for his interest in all Dantesque studies, and by his permission it has been admirably reproduced in chromo-lithography under the auspices of the Arundel Society. The reproduction is entirely satisfactory as a presentation of the

[1] July 21, 1840.

authentic portrait of the youthful Dante, in the state in which it was when Mr. Kirkup was so fortunate as to gain admission to it.

This portrait by Giotto is the only likeness of Dante known to have been made of the poet during his life, and is of inestimable value on this account. But there exists also a mask, concerning which there is a tradition that it was taken from the face of the dead poet, and which, if its genuineness could be established, would not be of inferior interest to the early portrait. But there is no trustworthy historic testimony concerning it, and its authority as a likeness depends upon the evidence of truth which its own character affords. On the very threshold of the inquiry concerning it, we are met with the doubt whether the art of taking casts was practiced at the time of Dante's death. In his Life of Andrea del Verrocchio, Vasari says that this art began to come into use in his time, that is, about the middle of the fifteenth century; and Bottari refers to the likeness of Brunelleschi, who died in 1446, which was taken in this manner, and was preserved in the office of the Works of the Cathedral at Florence. It is not impossible that so simple an art may have been sometimes practiced at an earlier period;[1] and if so, there is no inherent improbability in the supposition that Guido Novello, the friend and protector of Dante at Ravenna, may, at the time of the poet's death, have had a mask taken to serve as a model for the head of a statue intended to form part of the monument which he proposed to erect in honor of Dante. And it may further be supposed, that, this design failing, owing to the fall of Guido

[1] Pliny refers to the taking of casts of the face of the dead.

from power before its accomplishment, the mask may have been preserved at Ravenna, till we first catch a trace of it nearly three centuries later.

There is in the Magliabecchiana Library at Florence an autograph manuscript by Giovanni Cinelli, a Florentine antiquary who died in 1706, entitled La Toscana letterata, ovvero Istoria degli Scrittori Fiorentini, which contains a life of Dante. In the course of the biography Cinelli states that the Archbishop of Ravenna caused the head of the poet which had adorned his sepulchre to be taken therefrom, and that it came into the possession of the famous sculptor, Gian Bologna, who left it at his death, in 1606, to his pupil, Pietro Tacca. "One day Tacca showed it, with other curiosities, to the Duchess Sforza, who, having wrapped it in a scarf of green cloth, carried it away, and God knows into whose hands the precious object has fallen, or where it is to be found. . . . On account of its singular beauty, it had often been drawn by the scholars of Tacca." It has been supposed that this head was the original mask from which the casts now existing are derived. Mr. Seymour Kirkup, in a note on this passage from Cinelli, says that "there are three masks of Dante at Florence, all of which have been judged by the first Roman and Florentine sculptors to have been taken from life [that is, from the face after death], — the slight differences noticeable between them being such as might occur in casts made from the original mask." One of these casts was given to Mr. Kirkup by the sculptor Bartolini, another belonged to the late sculptor Professor Ricci,[1] and the

[1] "The mask possessed by Ricci, who made use of it for the purposes of his statue of Dante in Santa Croce in Florence, eventually also passed into the hands of Kirkup." (Toynbee.)

third is in the possession of the Marchese Torrigani.[1]

In the absence of historical evidence in regard to this mask, some support is given to the belief in its genuineness by the fact that it appears to be the type of the greater number of the portraits of Dante executed from the fourteenth to the sixteenth century, and was adopted by Raffaelle as the original from which he drew the likeness which has done most to make the features of the poet familiar to the world.

The character of the mask itself affords, however, the only really satisfactory ground for confidence in the truth of the tradition concerning it. It was plainly taken as a cast from a face after death. It has none of the characteristics which a fictitious and imaginative representation of the sort would be likely to present. It bears no trace of being a work of skillful and deceptive art. The difference in the fall of the two half-closed eyelids, the difference between the sides of the face, the slight deflection in the line of the nose, the droop of the corners of the mouth, and other delicate, but none the less convincing, indications combine to show that it was in all probability taken directly from nature. The countenance, moreover, and expression are worthy of Dante; no ideal forms could so answer to the face of him who had led a life apart from the world in which he dwelt, and had been conducted by love and faith along hard, painful, and solitary ways, to behold —

L' alto trionfo del regno verace.

The mask conforms entirely to the description by Boccaccio of the poet's countenance, save that it is

[1] Now in the Uffizi Gallery.

THE DEATH MASK

beardless, and this difference is to be accounted for by the fact that to obtain the cast the beard must have been removed.[1]

The face is one of the most pathetic upon which human eyes ever looked, for it exhibits in its expression the conflict between the strong nature of the man and the hard dealings of fortune, — between the idea of his life and its practical experience. Strength is the most striking attribute of the countenance, displayed alike in the broad forehead, the masculine nose, the firm lips, the heavy jaw and wide chin; and this strength, resulting from the main forms of the features, is enforced by the strength of the lines of expression. The look is grave and stern almost to grimness; there is a scornful lift to the eyebrow, and a contraction of the forehead as from painful thought; but obscured under this look, yet not lost, are the marks of tenderness, refinement, and self-mastery, which, in combination with more obvious characteristics, give to the countenance of the dead poet an ineffable dignity and melancholy. There is neither weakness nor failure here. It is the image of the strong fortress of a strong soul "buttressed on conscience and impregnable will," battered by the blows of enemies without and within, bearing upon its walls the dints of many a siege, but standing firm and unshaken against all attacks until the warfare was at an end.

The intrinsic evidence for the truth of this likeness, from its correspondence, not only with the description of the poet, but with the imagination that we form of him from his life and works, is strongly confirmed by

[1] *Purg.* xxxi. 68; also page 96 of this book.

a comparison of the mask with the portrait by Giotto. So far as I am aware, this comparison has not hitherto been made in a manner to exhibit effectively the resemblance between the two. A direct comparison between the painting and the mask, owing to the difficulty of reducing the forms of the latter to a plain surface of light and shade, is unsatisfactory. But by taking a photograph from the mask, in the same position as that in which the face is painted by Giotto, and placing it alongside of the fac-simile from the painting, a very remarkable similarity becomes at once apparent. In the two accompanying photographs the striking resemblance between them is not to be mistaken. The differences are only such as must exist between the portrait of a man in the freshness of a happy youth and the portrait of him in his age, after much experience and many trials. Dante was fifty-six years old at the time of his death, when the mask was taken; the portrait by Giotto represents him as not much past twenty. There is an interval of at least thirty years between the two. And what years they had been for him!

The interest of this comparison lies not only in the mutual support which the portraits afford each other, in the assurance each gives that the other is genuine, but also in their joint illustration of the life and character of Dante. As Giotto painted him, he is the lover of Beatrice, the gay companion of princes, the friend of poets, and himself already the most famous writer of love verses in Italy. There is an almost feminine softness in the lines of the face, with a sweet and serious tenderness well befitting the lover, and the author of the sonnets and canzoni which were in a

THE BARGELLO PORTRAIT

Drawn by Mr. Seymour Kirkup before it was retouched by Marini.

THE DEATH MASK

few years to be gathered into the incomparable record of his New Life. It is the face of Dante in the May-time of youthful hope, in that serene season of promise and of joy, which was so soon to reach its fore-ordained close in the death of her who had made life new and beautiful for him, and to the love and honor of whom he dedicated his soul and gave all his future years. It is the same face with that of the mask; but the one is the face of a youth, "with all triumphant splendor on his brow," the other of a man, burdened with "the dust and injury of age." The forms and features are alike, but as to the later face, —

> That time of year thou mayst in it behold
> When yellow leaves, or none, or few, do hang
> Upon those boughs which shake against the cold,
> Bare ruined choirs, where late the sweet birds sang.

The face of the youth is grave, as with the shadow of distant sorrow; the face of the man is solemn, as of one who had gone —

> Per tutti i cerchi del dolente regno.

The one is the young poet of Florence, the other the supreme poet of the world,[1] —

> Che al divino dall' umano,
> All' eterno dal tempo era venuto.

[1] "In 1864, in view of the approaching celebration in Florence of the sixth centenary of Dante's birth, the Minister of Public Instruction commissioned Gaetano Milanesi and Luigi Passerini to report upon the most authentic portrait of the poet, as it was proposed to have a medallion executed in commemoration of the centenary. Milanesi and Passerini communicated the results of their investigations to the Minister in a letter which was published in the *Giornale del Centenario* for 20th July, 1864. After stating their doubts with regard to the Bargello portrait, and disposing of the claims of two other portraits contained in MSS. preserved in Florence, they go on to say: 'Very precious on the other hand is the portrait prefixed to Codex 1040 in the Riccardi Library, which contains the minor poems of Dante,

together with those of Messer Bindi Bonichi, and which appears from the arms and initials to have belonged to Paolo di Jacopo Giannotti, who was born in 1430. This portrait, which is about half the size of life, is in water-color, and represents the poet with his characteristic features at the age of rather more than forty. It is free from the exaggeration of later artists, who, by giving undue prominence to the nose and under lip and chin, make Dante's profile resemble that of a hideous old woman. In our opinion this portrait is to be preferred to any other, especially for the purposes of a medallion.'[1]

"Cavalcaselle, among other authorities, declined to accept these conclusions. Checcacci, on the contrary, who carefully compared the Riccardi portrait with a very exact copy of that in the Bargello, asserted that if the difference of age be taken into consideration, the two resemble each other 'like two drops of water': 'The Bargello portrait lacks the wrinkles of the other, while the coloring is more fresh, and the prominence of the lower lip is less marked, but the nose, which does not change with advancing years, is identical, as are the shape and color of the eyes, and the shape of the skull, which may be distinguished in both portraits.' He added further that the sculptor Dupré was greatly struck with the Riccardi portrait, which he considered might be the work of Giotto himself, and that he availed himself of it for the medallion which he was commissioned to execute in commemoration of the centenary." (Toynbee.)

The portrait in the Santa Maria Novella which Prof. Chiappelli has recently asserted to be of Dante, while interesting, throws no new light on the appearance of the poet, as it was painted after 1350, much later than the so-called Giotto portrait. (D)

[1] This portrait is reproduced as the frontispiece of this book.

Sixth Centenary Medallion

CHAPTER IV

THE VITA NUOVA

I

LYRICAL POETRY BEFORE DANTE [1]

It was in southern France that the intellectual life of Europe first awoke. In that land of fertile soil and fair skies a new sense of the joy of living began to stir in men's hearts after the cheerless night of the Dark Ages. They saw that the world was good to dwell in and that existence had its zest. Especially did they become aware of the shapeliness of the human form, and discarding the loose sacks which monkish prejudice had designed to conceal it, they modeled their apparel to reveal its grace. With the throwing off of the ascetic ideals, woman was elevated from the degrading position she had held, and by a natural reaction became the object of chivalrous devotion. The awakening of nobler love, and the growing pleasure in life and its beauty, produced inevitably a fresh outburst of song. The ballad singers gave place to the troubadours. Many of these were men of talent, culture, and high birth, who easily compelled their flexible and rhythmic language to express in melodious strains their knightly passions. Their songs may seem to us vapid after the chill of so many centuries, and they are undoubtedly lacking in that vividness that so often reveals genius in the ruder ages.

[1] For much of the material used in this short account I am indebted to Gaspary's *Italian Literature to the Death of Dante*, trans. by H. Oelsner, a book of great valne. (D.)

Their forms of expression, moreover, are unnatural and cumbrously artificial, but the power of their exaggerated sentiments, wedded to the harmony of their musical verse, gave them great influence among a people not trained to refined criticism. Yet their intrinsic merit is not great, and they owe their interest to the contrast with the sterility that preceded them, and to the deep impression they made on the singers who came after them.

In Italy the period of literary activity was much later in its coming than in France. This seems strange when we consider the intense activity of her political life, the strife of her factions, the hot debates of her ambitious republics with the emperors. One would naturally think that such seething, tumultuous life would find appropriate literary expression. The chief reason seems to lie in the slow development of the Italian tongue. Italy was the home of the Latin race, and here longer than elsewhere the stately language of the Roman refused to be moulded into a vernacular. There cannot be a living literature without a living language. Not after Charlemagne was a grammatical Latin spoken in Italy, and not until the beginning of the thirteenth century do we find any Italian literary production. During the four intervening centuries the sweet Italian tongue was forming. A document of the year 960 contains a sentence in the vulgar speech. We have also a Sardinian document, and a formula of confession from central Italy, which are almost entirely in the speech of the common people. These, with some Italian inscriptions and other Sardinian documents belonging to the twelfth century, are all we have to mark the transition period.

Northern Italy, being contiguous to southern France, soon felt the thrill of the latter's poetic impulse. But the poets of Lombardy, not being original enough to sing in their native tongue, although that speech was capable of expressing musically any thought of theirs, servilely imitated the troubadours of Provence, both in subject-matter, form, and language.

To the Sicilian school of poets is usually given the honor of first using the vernacular in song. But why ignore St. Francis' Hymn to the Sun, — a lyrical outburst of a soul of the finest fibre and noblest compass? It possessed that to which the poets in the brilliant circle surrounding Frederick II. were strangers, — genuine spontaneity. Even after the lapse of seven centuries we can still feel the swing of its cadences and catch the glow of its spiritual fervor. Yet this canticle of St. Francis, which his followers sang as God's minstrels from village to village, while it undoubtedly exerted wide influence, is not in the line of the historical development of Italian lyrical poetry. This passes through Sicily rather than through Umbria. In the hands of the troubadours of the court of Frederick the national language became pliant and flexible, fitted for the hand of the master when he comes. But while entrusting their lyrics to the national tongue, and rendering valuable service by giving to lyrical poetry a basis of metrical form, the Sicilians still worked to the models coming from Provence. As the chivalrous ideals of southern France were hardly at home in a court where the emperor kept a harem, guarded by eunuchs, the verse growing out of such conditions was conventional and artificial, lacking all vital inspiration.

It was in Tuscany that Italian song found its most congenial field. The free cities, with their fermenting life, their vigorous aspirations, their joy in an awakening sense of power, must needs usher in a new era of song. The first important figure we meet is Guittone of Arezzo, whose best poem was written in 1260, five years before Dante's birth, in celebration of the battle of Monteaperti. Dante twice speaks of him in the Purgatorio (xxiv. 56, xxvi. 124), each time slightingly, as one who wrote not close to the emotion of his heart. Guittone brought the Provençal-Sicilian ideals into Tuscany, and in modeling his poems after conceptions alien to the soil of his native province, brought forth a highly artificial product, which Dante with his passionate love of reality could not but condemn. Yet in his time he was held in great esteem, and his influence upon literature was not insignificant. He died in 1294, when Dante was in his thirtieth year, and when most of the verse of the Vita Nuova had been written.

The transition from the old school to the new, from the artificial to the natural, comes with Guido Guinicelli, the greatest poet of his generation, whom Dante willingly acknowledged to be "the father of me and of others my betters, who ever used sweet and graceful rhymes of love."[1] Of the life of this justly famous man we know but little. His home was in Bologna, and we find him mentioned in documents from 1266. In 1274 he went into exile for adhering to the Ghibelline cause, and died two years later. His early literary compositions show the distinct influence of Guittone, and his ideals were fashioned after

[1] *Purg.* xxvi. 97.

the manner of the Sicilian school; consequently his poems are stiff and conventional. But a new spirit was working in Italy. Under the authority of Frederick II. a new translation of Aristotle was made, and thus a knowledge of his teachings was widely spread. Thomas Aquinas, the Dumb Ox, was fulfilling the prophecy that his lowings would be heard over Europe. While Guinicelli was still in Bologna this Doctor Angelicus came to the University to lecture. The eager mind of the young poet quickly absorbed these enriching influences, and a deep new note is heard in his verse.

The school of poetry which he inaugurated had two distinguishing characteristics. Its ideals were spiritual, and were described with an intensity of passion which gave to the style a naturalness and beauty which was impossible to the poets of the old school. The troubadours had sung of love, but it was an earthly passion between man and woman, couched in complimentary phrases, and stiff with meretricious flattery. It was a love distinctively sensuous and human, a devotion of a knight to his lady, of a youth to a maiden.

In the new movement the lady loved is but a symbol of truth and beauty; through her the lover beholds the loftiest good and his affection leads him to the heights of blessedness. Love is purged of all that is of the earth, earthy, and becomes pure and spiritual. The lady is to the ecstatic poet the image of God's eternal love, the embodiment of divine beauty, the inspirer of the soul to seek the paths of noblest life. Poetry is thus the utterance of the soul's loftiest yearnings, rather than the vehicle through which a love-sick heart pours its plaint. Poetry becomes spiritual allegory; its images are freighted with deep philosophical meanings; its words are rich with mystic significance. This is chivalrous love of woman carried to its highest point; it is philosophy wrought into forms of beauty; it is religion clothing itself in sweet and graceful imagery.

The ardor of spiritual love could not fail to break up the hard forms of the earlier school and bring in a "sweet new style." The change to greater naturalness Dante himself expresses in his own inimitable way. On the ledge of the gluttons, meeting Bonagiunta, who inquires if it is the author of the new rhymes beginning "Ladies that have intelligence of Love" who has come, Dante replies: "I am one who, when love inspires me, take note, and go setting it forth after the fashion which he dictates within me." "O brother," said he, "now I see the knot which kept back the Notary, and Guittone, and me, short of the sweet new style that I hear. Truly I see how your pens go close following the dictator, which surely befell not with ours." [1]

Writing only when love dictated and following close to the genuine feeling, gave to the new school of which Dante became the most distinguished representative its "sweet new style." Guido Guinicelli's canzone "Of the Gentle Heart" marks the turning from the conventional school to the natural, from the poetry of chivalrous love to the poetry of spiritual passion. Its doctrine of true nobleness is adopted by Dante in the Convito. Several times it is quoted in De Vulgari Eloquentia as a perfect type of the highest poetry. Its mystical conception of love Dante made his own

[1] *Purg.* xxiv. 52–60.

and developed it in the verse of the Vita Nuova. As it occupies such a prominent place in the history of Italian lyrical poetry, and so profoundly influenced Dante, we quote it in full.

OF THE GENTLE HEART.[1]

Within the gentle heart Love shelters him,
As birds within the green shade of the grove.
Before the gentle heart, in nature's scheme,
Love was not, nor the gentle heart ere Love.
For with the sun, at once,
So sprang the light immediately; nor was
Its birth before the sun's.
And Love hath his effect in gentleness
Of very self; even as
Within the middle fire the heat's excess.

The fire of Love comes to the gentle heart
Like as its virtue to a precious stone;
To which no star its influence can impart
Till it is made a pure thing by the sun:
For when the sun hath smit
From out its essence that which there was vile,
The star endoweth it.
And so the heart created by God's breath
Pure, true, and clean from guile,
A woman, like a Star, enamoreth.

In gentle heart Love for like reason is
For which the lamp's high flame is fanned and bow'd:
Clear, piercing bright, it shines for its own bliss;
Nor would it burn there else, it is so proud.
For evil natures meet
With Love as it were water met with fire,
As cold abhorring heat.
Through gentle heart Love doth a track divine, —
Like knowing like; the same
As diamond through iron in the mine.

The sun strikes full upon the mud all day:
It remains vile, nor the sun's worth is less.

[1] *Dante and his Circle*, D. G. Rossetti, p. 187. Little, Brown, and Company. (By permission.)

"By race I am gentle," the proud man doth say:
He is the mud, the sun is gentleness.
Let no man predicate
That aught the name of gentleness should have,
Even in a king's estate,
Except the heart there be a gentle man's.
The star-beam lights the wave,—
Heaven holds the star and the star's radiance.

God, in the understanding of high Heaven,
Burns more than in our sight the living sun:
There to behold His Face unveiled is given;
And Heaven, whose will is homage paid to One,
Fulfils the things which live
In God from the beginning excellent.
So should my lady give
That truth which in her eyes is glorified,
On which her heart is bent,
To me whose service waiteth at her side.

My lady, God shall ask, "What daredst thou?"
(When my soul stands with all her acts review'd)
"Thou passedst Heaven, into My sight, as now,
To make Me of vain love similitude.
To Me doth praise belong,
And to the Queen of all the realm of grace
Who slayeth fraud and wrong."
Then may I plead: "As though from Thee he came,
Love wore an angel's face:
Lord, if I love her, count it not my shame."

The Provençal solution of the origin, nature, and influence of Love was that it springs from seeing and pleasing. "The image of beauty," says Gaspary,[1] "penetrates through the eyes into the soul, takes root in the heart and occupies the thoughts, which is nothing but a superficial statement, describing the subject without fathoming it. In Guido's canzone, an entirely new conception takes the place of this well-worn succession

[1] *Italian Literature to the Death of Dante*, trans. by H. Oelsner, p. 101.

of phrases. Love seeks its place in the noble heart, as the bird in the foliage; nobility of heart and love are one and inseparable as the sun and its splendor; as the star imparts its magic power to the jewel when the sun has purified it from all gross matter, in the same way the image of the beloved lady inflames the heart, which nature has created noble and pure; and, as fire by water, so, too, every impure feeling is extinguished by the contact of love; the sentiment inspired by the loved lady shall fill him who is her devoted slave, even as the power of the Deity is transmitted into the heavenly intelligences. — To such a degree has the conception of love changed; the earthly passion has become transfigured, and has been brought into contact with the sublimest ideas known to man; it is a philosophical conception of love, and the similes that serve to illustrate and to explain it in so elaborate and diversified a manner, show no traces of the old repertory." The poetry of Platonic love which Guinicelli introduced and which was further elaborated by Guido Cavalcanti and Cino of Pistoia, finds its highest and finest expression in Dante's Vita Nuova, in which a simple Florentine maiden stands transfigured in the light of his intense spiritual passion. Of the lofty, mystical love, based on such a slight foundation of fact, no one has written more illuminatingly than Gaspary.

II

THE MEANING AND CHARACTER OF THE VITA NUOVA[1]

THE great event of Dante's youth is his love, and the figure that dominates everything and fills his entire life is Beatrice. He saw her for the first time when they both were children, he nine and she eight years of age. She appeared to him "clothed in a most noble color, a humble and subdued red, girded and adorned as became her very youthful age." And his life-spirit began to tremble violently; for he has found one who will dominate him. From that time he feels himself urged on to seek the place where he may see this "youthful angel." One day, after the lapse of another space of nine years from the day of the first meeting, she appears to him again, robed in the purest white, between two other ladies, and "passing along the way, she turned her eyes . . . and by her ineffable courtesy . . . she saluted him in such virtuous wise, that he appeared to behold the highest degree of bliss." It was the first time that her voice reached his ear, and it fills him with such joy, that he is as it were intoxicated, and takes refuge from the intercourse of man in the solitude of his chamber. He falls asleep and has a dream. On waking he puts it down in verse, and this was the origin of Dante's first sonnet: —

[1] Gaspary's *History of Early Italian Literature to the Death of Dante*, trans. by H. Oelsner, pp. 221–232. Bell & Sons. (By permission.)

A ciascun' alma presa e gentil core,
  Nel cui cospetto viene il dir presente,
  A ciò che mi riscrivan suo parvente,
  Salute in lor signor, cioè Amore.
Già eran quasi ch' atterzate l' ore
  Del tempo che ogni stella è più lucente,
  Quando m' apparve Amor subitamente,
  Cui essenza membrar mi dà orrore.
Allegro mi sembrava Amor, tenendo
  Mio cor in mano, e nelle braccia avea
  Madonna involta in un drappo, dormendo.
Poi la svegliava, e d' esto core ardendo
  Lei paventosa umilmente pascea;
  Appresso gir ne lo vedea piangendo.[1]

The poem is addressed to the lovers, that is, to the poets, and demands an explanation of the dream. In these verses, written by Dante at the age of eighteen, we have an allegory in the form of a vision, a psychological process symbolically represented, — Amore giving the loved one to eat of the poet's heart; images these, which appear to us grotesque, but which are full of significance and rich in ideas. Here we have again the poetic manner of the new Florentine school, and so we can understand how Dante da Majano, the representative of the old Provençal manner, received the sonnet in a hostile spirit and answered it in an indecent and scoffing manner, while Guido Cavalcanti congratulated the new poet from his heart, and from that time remained the dearest of his friends.

[1] To every captive soul and noble heart, that comes to see the present song, so that they may write me back their opinion, greeting in the name of Love, their lord. Already had a third almost of the time passed, in which each star shines brightest, when suddenly Amore appeared to me, to recall whose being fills me with horror. Joyous seemed Amore to me, holding my heart in his hand, and in his arms he held Madonna sleeping, wound in a cloth. Then he woke her, and of this glowing heart he gently gave her to eat, she showing signs of fear. Then I saw him go his way weeping.

Of his love Dante has told us himself in a little book called La Vita Nuova (The New Life), a prose narrative interspersed with the poems that owe their origin to the feelings which are treated in them, and which are interpreted in the prose sections. The "new life" is that life which began for the poet with the first ray of love. This love of Dante is ethereal and pure, and is elevated high above sensuality. The loved one is the ideal that has come to life, something divine, descended from heaven, in order to impart to the world a ray of the splendor of Paradise. She appears to him robed in the "noblest color," she appears to him robed in "the whitest color" — it is truly an apparition, something from above that has come down to him. Quite at the beginning she is "that very youthful angel," and then always "that most noble one." He scarcely ventures from time to time to call her by her own name of Beatrice, though this name, too, has its lofty meaning: she is one who spreads around her bliss (*beatitudine*).

The story of Dante's love is a very simple one. The events are all so insignificant. She passes him in the street and greets him; he sees her with other ladies at a wedding banquet, and she scoffs at him; he learns from the ladies how she laments over her father's death. Such are the events narrated: but they all become significant in the heart of the worshiper. It is an inner history of emotions, touching in its tenderness and sincere religious feeling. A breath of this pure worship communicates itself to us, so that it does not appear to us exaggerated.

This love in its extreme chastity is timid; it conceals itself from the eyes of others and remains for a long time a secret. So great, indeed, is Dante's fear lest his sacred feelings be exposed to profane looks, that, when he cannot hide the passions that burn within him, he makes people believe that another woman is the cause of them. Twice he finds a beautiful woman, who thus serves him as it were as a screen. On her he turns his eyes when he meets her, to her apparently his verses are addressed. The splendor of the divinity herself does not permit to look at her; her presence dazzles and confounds him — almost robs him of his senses. However, on the second occasion he carries this dissimulation so far that it is taken for truth by the people, and also by Beatrice, who for a time withholds her greeting from him.

The tone of the whole narrative is solemn, almost religious. The poet is fond of applying biblical words to his case. Thus he begins one sonnet with the lines: "O voi che per la via d' amor passate, Attendete e guardate, S' egli è dolore alcun quanto il mio grave;" and these are the words of Jeremiah: "O vos omnes qui transitis per viam, attendite et videte, si est dolor sicut dolor meus." — "Quomodo sedet sola civitas," he exclaims in the words of the same prophet, after Beatrice's death, and this event is, in the prophetic vision (cap. 23), accompanied by terrible natural disturbances, like the death of Christ. Take, for example, the beginning of the narrative: "Nine times already since my birth had the heaven of light (*i. e.* of the sun) returned to almost the same point, in respect to its own revolution, when before my eyes appeared for the first time the glorious mistress of my mind, who was called by many Beatrice, without their knowing what they called thus" (meaning, without their knowing that she actually was Beatrice, the dispenser of bliss). Or again, in cap. 5: "One day it happened that this most noble lady sat in a place where one heard words of the Queen of glory (Mary), and I was in a spot from which I saw my happiness." He avoids the mere name of the thing, and employs instead some circumlocution, because the other appeared to him too vulgar. The city of Florence is never named; it is called "the city in which my mistress was set by the Highest Lord" (cap. 6), or "the city in which was born, lived and died the most noble lady" (cap. 41). Beatrice's brother is not designated by this term, but as follows: "And this one was so closely connected with this glorious one by blood relationship, that no one was nearer to her." Such a method of exposition cannot condescend to a description of the objects: these are touched only in the most general way. Beatrice is always being celebrated: her eyes, her smile, and her mouth are extolled; but it is their influence and power that are insisted on, not their external appearance. Of the surroundings of the loved one, of the localities and people, we are given only a few cursory hints. We have here an existence that lies entirely apart from actual events; these are shown now and again from a distance, but only iu order to give an impulse to the rich inner life. Events are here assigned a different standard for their relative importance from that prevailing in ordinary life.

Beatrice is the ideal of Platonic love; the passion for her is the way leading to virtue and to God. "When she appeared anywhere," Dante says (cap. 11), "there remained to me no enemy in the world, through hoping for her wondrous greeting; rather was

I imbued with the flame of charity, that made me forgive all who had offended me, and if any one had then asked me for anything, my reply would have been only 'Love,' with a countenance clothed with humility." She spreads about her as it were an atmosphere of purity. Wherever she appears, all eyes are turned on her, and when she greets any one, his heart trembles, he lowers his countenance and sighs over his faults. Hate and anger flee from before her, nothing ignoble persists in her presence, and the ladies that accompany her appear more amiable and more virtuous when they are illumined by her radiance. Beatrice's nature is more that of an angel than of a woman. In her there is nothing earthly, and she takes no part in earthly things; as on angels' wings she is lightly wafted through this life, till she flies back to that other life whence she came. A presentiment of her death pervades the entire narrative from the beginning, from the very first sonnet. The angels demand her, and it is only God's mercy that can refuse her for a time, to console the world and the lover.

What is the goal of the lover's desire? Not possession; for how can a man wish to possess that which he does not consider earthly? Those who can ask why Dante did not marry Beatrice have not rightly understood the nature of this passion. Her look, her greeting, these are all that he ardently longs for, and in these he sees the fulfillment of his wishes. And when she denies him her greeting, he is happy in considering and extolling her perfection. "With what object dost thou love thy mistress, seeing that thou canst not endure her presence?" the ladies ask him (cap. 18), and he replies: "The aim of this my love was formerly the greeting of this lady . . . and in it dwelt the happiness and the end of all my desires. But since it pleased her to withhold it from me, my lord Amore has, in his mercy, set all my happiness in that which cannot be taken from me." And being asked what that might be, he says: "In those words that extol my lady." There is nothing said as to whether she returned his love; and we are scarcely told whether she knew anything about it. The divinity feels no passion; enough if he can worship it. It is true that his imagination once carries him away, and he dreams of a fabulous happiness, — of being together with the loved one, in a boat, on the solitary sea, without being disturbed by the cold world, and accompanied only by his dearest friends. This mood gave rise to the sonnet, "Guido, vorrei che tu e Lapo ed io;" but this beautiful poem, in which the mystic veil is for once rent asunder, was excluded from the collection of the Vita Nuova, — it would not have harmonized with the general note of that book.

Beatrice represents in its highest perfection that ideal of spiritual love, which had been celebrated previously in the verses of Guido Guinicelli and of Guido Cavalcanti. With his first sonnet, Dante had joined the new Florentine school of poetry, that of the *dolce stil nuovo;* with his first poem of greater importance, the sonnet "Donne che avete intelletto d' amore," he took the place in it that was due to him. This shows no great innovation as yet, and Dante can scarcely have intended to claim such for himself, when he makes Buonagiunta Urbiciani say in the Purgatorio (xxiv. 49): —

But say if him I here behold, who forth
Evoked the new-invented rhymes, beginning:
Ladies, that have intelligence of love.

The conventionalism of the school reappears with Dante. Here we have again Amore, the ruler of the soul, and the soul itself in abstractions and personifications, while grief and death are personified too. The psychological processes are depicted in the traditional manner, that is to say, not as such, not as inner occurrences, but in a materialized and symbolical form. The spirits of life and love and the thoughts come, go, fly, speak, and struggle with each other in an entirely substantial manner. The soul speaks with death, and complains of it as of a person, that is accordingly endowed with all personal attributes. The parting soul embraces the spirits, who weep because they lose its company (in the canzone, "E' m' incresce di me sì duramente"). If we desire to obtain a clear idea of the relation between Dante's lyrical poetry and that hailing from Bologna, we have only to read the sonnet concerning the origin of love (Vita Nuova, cap. 20). Dante, too, was asked by a friend to solve the famous problem, and he replied as follows: —

Amore e 'l cor gentil sono una cosa,
  Sì come 'l Saggio in suo dittato pone;
  E così esser l' un sanza l' altro osa,
  Com' alma razional sanza ragione.
Fagli Natura, quando è amorosa,
  Amor per sire e 'l cor per sua magione,
  Dentro allo qual dormendo si riposa
  Tal volta brieve e tal lunga stagione.
Beltate appare in saggia donna pui,
  Che piace agli occhi sì che dentro al core
  Nasce un disio della cosa piacente.

E tanto dura talora in costui,
Che fa svegliar lo spirito d' amore,
E simil face in donna uomo valente.[1]

We may note here the grace of the expression, and a certain vivacity in the image that reveals the poet and, as it were, transforms the abstract theme into a little drama. But the idea is in harmony with the spirit of the school; the sage introduced in the sonnet is no other than Guido Guinicelli, and his poem, the canzone concerning Amore and the *cor gentile*. From this piece Dante borrowed the idea that a noble heart could not exist without love, nor love without a noble heart; the rest is nothing but the old theory of seeing and pleasing, so that Dante did not even display more genius in treating the question than so many others.

Dante shared with his predecessors their mode of thought, their theoretical convictions as to the essence and character of poetry, their conception of love, and their entire poetical apparatus. What distinguished him from and raised him above them was his superior poetic gift. He did not create the language, but he had mastered it more thoroughly than all the others. He treats the same themes in the same manner; but they are consecrated afresh and endowed with originality by reason of the depth of his feeling. He employs the traditional forms, but the subjects treated

[1] Amore and the noble heart are one, as the sage says in his poem; and one can be without the other as little as a rational soul without reason. Nature makes them when she is full of love, Amore as lord, and the heart as his dwelling, in which sleeping he rests, now for a short and now for a long while. Beauty appears thereupon in a virtuous lady, who pleases the eyes, so that within the heart is born a desire for the pleasing object. And at times this lasts so long in him, that it awakes the spirit of love; and the same is caused in a woman by a virtuous man.

have been experienced by himself: they come from the heart and are often expressed with delightful tenderness and sincerity. Immediate inspiration by the feelings he himself designated, in the verses of the Purgatorio mentioned above, is the distinctive mark of his poetry.

Filled with this deep sincerity and warmed by true feeling, in spite of all its idealism, is the tender, ethereal image of the loved one as it appears to us in the ballad, "Io mi son pargoletta bella e nuova," a poem that does not belong to the collection of the Vita Nuova, but which undoubtedly refers to Beatrice. This image of the loved one is pure and sacred as that of a Madonna, and yet graceful, almost child-like, in its ingenuousness. She is an angel come from heaven, and wishes soon to return thither; but first she desires to show us a ray of her light, a ray of the heavenly place whence she came. Her eyes are bright with all the virtues of the stars, and no charms were denied her by the Creator, when he set her in the world. And she rejoices in her beauty and purity, and communicates some of it to the others. She smiles, and her smile tells of her home, of Paradise. The qualities attributed by the poet to his beloved in extolling her are the same as were regularly celebrated ever since Guinicelli wrote. However, we have no mere repetition of commonplaces, but a deeply felt enthusiasm pervades this glorification and gave birth to some of the most fragrant blossoms of Italian lyrical poetry, such as the sonnets "Negli occhi porta la mia donna amore," "Vede perfettamente ogni salute," and especially the following one: —

Tanto gentile e tanto onesta pare
  La donna mia, quand' ella altrui saluta,
  Ch' ogni lingua divien tremando muta,
  E gli occhi non l' ardiscon di guardare.
Ella sen va sentendosi laudare,
  Benignamente d' umiltà vestuta,
  E par che sia una cosa venuta
  Di cielo in terra a miracol mostrare.
Mostrasi sì piacente a chi la mira,
  Che dà per gli occhi una dolcezza al core,
  Che 'ntender non la può chi non la prova.
E par che della sua labbia si muova
  Un spirito soave pien d' amore,
  Che va dicendo all' anima: sospira.[1]

In this sigh of the soul spiritualized passion has found its true expression. The beloved is transfigured, but she has not become an abstraction: the ideal does not tear itself away from the concrete image of the beauty in which it is incorporated. We see the lady, full of grace and virtue, go her way adorned with all her charms.

The first poem of Dante was a vision; so, too, was his last, his great work. And in the Vita Nuova, in general, visions play no small part. The dream was regarded by the age as significant and prophetic; it is the form corresponding to a feeling of presentiment that passes over into the other world. A vision

[1] So noble and so honorable appears my lady, when she greets any one, that every tongue trembling becomes dumb, and the eyes do not dare to look at her. She goes her way when she hears herself praised, gently clothed with humility, and she appears as a being come from heaven to earth in order to show us a miracle. So pleasing she shows herself to him who beholds her, that through the eyes she sends a joy into the heart, that only he can understand who experiences it himself. And from her lip appears to move a gentle spirit full of love, that says to the soul: "Sigh." — There may be a connection between this sonnet and Guido Cavalcanti's "Chi è quella che vien."

is depicted in the canzone that is rightly considered to be the most perfect poem of this first period of Dante's lyrical work. It begins with the words, "Donna pietosa e di novella etade." Here it is pain that unfetters the poetry and frees it from all conventional elements. Once, while the poet himself is ill, the thought comes to him that Beatrice, too, will die, and that he will lose her. Thereupon he falls asleep and dreams that she is really dead. And he sees women going about weeping and with unbound tresses. He sees the sun darkened and the moon appear, and the birds falling from the air and the earth trembling, and one of his friends appears to him with discolored face and cries to him: "What art thou doing? Dost thou not know the tidings? Dead is thy mistress that was so beautiful."

Che fai? non sai novella?
Morta è la donna tua, ch' era sì bella.

And he raises his eyes streaming with blood, and sees the angels returning to heaven "even as a rain of manna," and before themselves they have a little cloud, and all sing "Hosanna": —

E vedea (che parean poggia di manna)
Gli angeli che tornavan suso in cielo,
Ed una nuvoletta avean davanti,
Dopo la qual cantavan tutti Osanna.

And thereupon he goes to behold the mortal remains of his beloved, and sees women covering her with a veil, and over her was spread such true gentleness, that she seemed to say, "I am in peace." When he has seen that, he, too, begins to call on Death, to beseech and extol him; for henceforth he must be full of charm, and must show compassion, not wrath, since he has been in that most beautiful lady:—

> Morte, assai dolce ti tegno;
> Tu dei omai esser cosa gentile,
> Poichè tu se' nella mia donna stata,
> E dei aver pietate e non disdegno.

The poem is moving in its simplicity. A whole world of feeling, of painful recollections, is compressed in those few words, "Morta è la donna tua, ch' era sì bella," and we can already recognize the poet of the Commedia and his capacity to bring before our soul, in a few traits, a complete image, instinct with feeling:—

> Ed avea seco umiltà sì verace
> Che parla che dicesse: io son in pace.

The figure of the departed one lies at rest, in such calm repose that we long for her peace. It was thus that painters depicted the death of the saints.

It is curious, considering this piece, that Beatrice's death itself should not have inspired any poem of distinction. The canzone, "Gli occhi dolenti per pietà del core," which refers to it, contains, perhaps, only two of these expressive and touching verses:—

> Chiamo Beatrice, e dico: Or se' tu morta!
> E mentre ch' io la chiamo, mi conforta.

Beatrice died on June 9th, 1290, in her twenty-fourth or twenty-fifth year. The Vita Nuova, that is to say, the collection of the poems and the addition of the prose text, was not begun till after her death. It is everywhere plain that the commentary is much later than the poems, as, for instance, in the case of the very first sonnet. The true meaning of the dream, says Dante, with reference to the presentiment of his beloved's death contained in the last verse, was not seen by any one at the time; but now it is plain to the dullest, that is to say, the prophecy is now fulfilled and Beatrice is no more. The close of the narrative goes more than a year beyond Beatrice's death. That brings us to the year 1292 as the date of the composition of the book, and this agrees with what Dante says in the Convivio (i. 1) that it was written at the beginning of his youth, that is to say, after the twenty-fifth year, and almost exactly with the words of Boccaccio in his Vita di Dante, to the effect that the author wrote it when he was "about twenty-six years old" — more correct would have been, "at the age of twenty-six." Another opinion, according to which the Vita Nuova belongs to the year 1300, I regard as refuted, after Fornaciari's examination of the facts.

Love in so transfigured and exalted a form as it is represented in the Vita Nuova, that intimate fusion of a symbol and a concrete being, became difficult to understand in later ages. Many doubted whether this love had ever been actually felt, while others could not conceive that the object of it was a mortal person, and consequently endeavored to regard Dante's Beatrice as a mere symbol and allegory, as the personification of the poet's own thoughts, not having any basis on an actual personality. Boccaccio relates in his Vita di Dante, that the lady celebrated by the poet was the daughter of Folco Portinari, and this statement is repeated in his Dante commentary (lez. viii. p. 224), with the addition, that the authority for it rests with a trustworthy person, who had known Beatrice, and been connected with her in very close blood relationship. Of this Bice Portinari we know from the will of her father, that on January 15th, 1288, the date at which the document was drawn up, she was the wife of Messer Simone de' Bardi. That Dante should have loved and celebrated a married woman can cause but little surprise, in view of the manners of the age; the troubadours always extolled married women, and the Italian poets probably did likewise, though in their case we have no positive testimony. It was just from these relations that chivalrous love took its origin, as Gaston Paris has demonstrated in such a brilliant manner, and the mystical and spiritual love had nothing to alter in this respect. Dante's passion was for the angel, not for the earthly woman; her marriage belonged to her earthly existence, with which the poet was not concerned. We must beware of confounding our age with that of Dante. What a terrible event for the poets of our day is the marriage of the loved one to another! What tempests in the heart, what complaints, what despair! Dante does not allude to the event by a single word. But it would be wrong to deduce from this fact that it never took place; it was merely something of which that poetry took no heed, and which could find no place in it. Accordingly we have no valid reasons for doubting Boccaccio's statement. The houses of the Portinari were close to those of the Alaghieri, and Folco Portinari died on December 31st, 1289, which date tallies very well with the passage in the Vita Nuova which treats of the death of Beatrice's father. It is true that Boccaccio was the first to identify Beatrice with the one of the Portinari family, but there is nothing strange in that. Love affairs are not set out in official documents, and the report may well have been handed down by tradition till some one wrote the biography of the poet.

III

ON THE STRUCTURE OF THE VITA NUOVA [1]

It is to be observed upon close examination, that the poems of the Vita Nuova are arranged in such order as to suggest an intention on the part of Dante to give his work a symmetrical structure. If the arrangement be accidental, or governed simply by the relation of the poems to the sequence of the events described in the narrative which connects them, it is certainly curious that they happened to fall into such order as to give to the little book a surprising regularity of construction.

The succession of the thirty-one poems of the New Life is as follows: —

5 sonnets,	3 sonnets,
1 ballad,	1 imperfect canzone,
4 sonnets,	1 canzone,
1 canzone,	1 sonnet,
4 sonnets,	1 imperfect canzone,
1 canzone,	8 sonnets.

At first sight no regularity appears in their order, but a little analysis reveals it. The most important poems, not only from their form and length, but also from their substance, are the three canzoni. Now it will be observed that the first canzone is preceded by ten and followed by four minor poems. The second

[1] Charles Eliot Norton, Essay III. in translation of *The New Life.* Houghton, Mifflin & Co. (By permission.)

canzone, which is by far the most elaborate poem of the whole, stands alone, holding the central place in the volume. The third canzone is preceded by four and followed by ten minor poems, like the first in inverse order. Thus this arrangement appears as follows: —

10 minor poems,	4 minor poems,
1 canzone,	1 canzone,
4 minor poems,	10 minor poems.
1 canzone,	

Here, leaving the central canzone to stand by itself, we have three series of ten poems each. It will be observed further, that the first and the third canzone stand at the same distance from the central poem, and that ten minor poems separate the one from the beginning, the other from the end of the book, and in each instance nine of these poems are sonnets. It is worth remark, that while the first canzone is followed by four sonnets, and the third is preceded by three sonnets and an imperfect canzone, this imperfect canzone is a single stanza, which has the same number of lines, and the same arrangement of its lines in respect to rhyme, as a sonnet, differing in this respect from the other canzoni. It may be fairly classed as a sonnet, its only difference from one being in the name that Dante has given to it.

The symmetrical construction now appears still more clearly: —

10 minor poems, all but one of them sonnets,	4 sonnets,
1 canzone,	1 canzone,
4 sonnets,	10 minor poems, all but one of them sonnets.
1 canzone,	

It may be taken as evidence that this regularity of arrangement was intentional, that a comparison of the first with the third canzone shows them to be mutually related, one being the balance of the other. The first begins: —

> Donne ch' avete intelletto d' amore
> Io vo' con voi della mia donna dire;

and the last line of its first stanza is —

> Chè non è cosa da parlarne altrui.

In the first stanza of the third there is a distinct reference to these words: —

> E perchè mi ricorda ch' io parlai
> Della mia donna, mentre che vivia,
> Donne gentili, volentier con vui,
> Non vo' parlarne altrui
> Se non a cor gentil che 'n donna sia.

The second stanza of the first canzone relates to the desire which is felt in Heaven for Beatrice. The corresponding stanza of the third declares that it was this desire for her which led to her being taken from the world. The third stanza of the one relates to the operation of her virtues and beauties upon earth; of the other, to the remembrance of them. There is a similarity of expression to be traced throughout.

In the last stanza, technically called the *commiato*, or dismissal, in which the poem is personified and sent on its way, in the first canzone it is called *figliuola d' amor;* in the third, *figliuola di tristizia.* One was the daughter of love, the other of sorrow; one was the poem recording Beatrice's life, the other her death. It is thus that one is made to serve as the complement and balance of the other in the structure of the New Life.

It may be possible to trace a similar relation between some of the minor poems of the beginning and the end of the volume; but I have not observed it, if it exists.

The second canzone is, as I have said, the most important poem in the volume, from the force of imagination displayed in it, as well as from its serving to connect the life of Beatrice with her death; and thus it holds, as of right, its central position in relation to the poems which precede and follow it.

But another, not less numerically symmetrical, division of these poems, no longer according to their form but according to their subject, may be observed by the careful reader. The first ten of them relate to the beginning of Dante's love, and to his own early experiences as a lover. At their close he says that it seemed to him he had said enough of his own state, and that it behoved him to take up *a new theme*, and that he thereupon resolved thenceforth to make the praise of his lady his sole theme (cc. xvii., xviii.). This theme is the ruling motive of the next ten poems. The last of them is interrupted by the death of Beatrice, and thereafter he takes up, as he again says, *a new theme*, and the next ten poems are devoted to his affliction, to the episode of the gentle lady, and to his return to his faithful love of Beatrice. One poem, the last, remains. It differs from all the rest; he calls it *a new thing*. It is the consummation of his experience of love in the vision of his lady in glory.

It is to be noted as a peculiarity of this final poem, and an indication of its composition at a later period than those which precede it, that whereas the visions which they report have reference, without exception, to things which the poet had experienced, or seen, or fancied, when awake, thus appearing to be dependent on previous waking excitements, the vision related in this sonnet seems, on the contrary, to have had its origin in no external circumstance, but to be the result of a purely internal condition of feeling. It was a *new* Intelligence that led his sigh upwards,— a new Intelligence which prepared him for his vision at Easter in 1300.

If a reason be inquired for that might lead Dante thus symmetrically to arrange the poems of this little book in a triple series of ten around a central unit, or in a triple series of ten followed by a single poem in which he is guided to Heaven by a new Intelligence, it may perhaps be found in the value which he set upon ten as the perfect number; while in the three times repeated series, culminating in a single central or final poem, he may have pleased himself with some fanciful analogy to that three and one on which he dwells in the passage in which he treats of the friendliness of the number nine to Beatrice. At any rate, as he there says, "This is the reason which I see for it, and which best pleases me; though perchance a more subtile reason might be seen therein by a more subtile person." [1]

[1] For an inquiry into the statements of a symmetrical arrangement of the lyrics by Gabriel Rossetti, Araux, and Federzoni, and for a defense and further elaboration of Professor Norton's theory, vide *The Symmetrical Structure of Dante's Vita Nuova*, by Kenneth McKenzie, in Publications of the Modern Language Association of America, vol. xviii. No. 2 (1903). (D.)

CHAPTER V

DANTE'S MINOR WORKS

DANTE'S MINOR WORKS

I. IL CONVITO [1]

AFTER the death of Beatrice, Dante, seeking comfort from his grief, turned for solace to the Consolations of Philosophy by Boethius, and to Cicero's treatise On Friendship. Becoming absorbed in his reading and studies, he rapidly acquires knowledge, and for love of it all other things are forgotten. By means of his great natural talents he masters the science and philosophy of his time. The enlarged vision which these give him, together with the new temper of mind which they induce, profoundly modify his lyrical compositions. The Middle Ages had a strong tendency towards symbolism. This is forcibly exemplified in the worship of the Roman church, where every garment worn by the priest, the candles, the ceremonials, had a religious significance, and were intended to teach some truth. Upon symbolism far more than on preaching the church relied to convey spiritual instruction to the common people. This same tendency finds expression in the literature of the period. Spiritual abstractions and philosophic ideas are presented in allegorical form that they may appeal to the imagination, for in the untrained the imagination affords a broader avenue to the will than does the reason. Moreover allegory is delightful in itself. Its hidden and problematical meanings afford genuine pleasure to minds enamored of mystery and subtlety. From Dante's lyrical genius, now steeped in

[1] For an interesting discussion of the phase in Dante's experience represented by the *Convito*, *vide* Wicksteed's translation of Witte's *Dantes Trilogie*, in *Essays on Dante* (Houghton, Mifflin & Co.), especially the Appendix, pp. 423–432.

scholastic lore, a new type of poetry, more didactic and richer in hidden meanings than the sonnets and canzoni of the Vita Nuova, is inevitable, and as a result we have Il Convito, or Il Convivio (The Banquet).

Dante's[1] object in the book was twofold. His opening words are a translation of what Matthew Arnold calls "that buoyant and immortal sentence with which Aristotle begins his Metaphysics:" "All mankind naturally desire knowledge." But few can attain to what is desired by all, and innumerable are they who live always famished for want of this food. "Oh, blessed are the few who sit at that table where the bread of the angels is eaten, and wretched they who have food in common with the herds." "I, therefore, who do not sit at the blessed table, but having fled from the pasture of the crowd, gather up at the feet of those who sit at it what falls from them, and through the sweetness I taste in that which little by little I pick up, know the wretched life of those whom I have left behind me, and moved with pity for them, not forgetting myself, have reserved something for these wretched ones." These crumbs were the substance of the banquet which he proposed to spread for them. It was to have fourteen courses, and each of these courses was to have for its principal viand a canzone of which the subject should be Love and Virtue, and the bread served with each course was to be the exposition of these poems,— poems which for want of this exposition lay under the shadow of obscurity, so that by many their beauty was more esteemed than their goodness. They were in appearance mere poems of

[1] Charles Eliot Norton, *Library of the World's Best Literature*, essay on Dante. (By permission.)

love, but under this aspect they concealed their true meaning, for the lady of his love was none other than Philosophy herself, and not sensual passion but virtue was their moving cause. The fear of reproach to which this misinterpretation might give occasion, and the desire to impart teaching which others could not give, were the two motives of his work.

There is much in the method and style of the Convito which in its cumbrous artificiality exhibits an early stage in the exposition of thought in literary form, but Dante's earnestness of purpose is apparent in many passages of manly simplicity, and inspires life into the dry bones of his formal scholasticism. The book is a mingling of biographical narrative, shaped largely by the ideals of the imagination, with expositions of philosophical doctrine, disquisitions on matters of science, and discussion of moral truths. But one controlling purpose runs through all, to help men to attain that knowledge which shall lead them into the paths of righteousness.

For his theory of knowledge is, that it is the natural and innate desire of the soul, as essential to its own perfection in its ultimate union with God. The use of the reason, through which he partakes of the Divine nature, is the true life of man. Its right use in the pursuit of knowledge leads to philosophy, which is, as its name signifies, the love of wisdom, and its end is the attainment of virtue. It is because of imperfect knowledge that the love of man is turned to fallacious objects of desire, and his reason is perverted. Knowledge, then, is the prime source of good; ignorance, of evil. Through knowledge to wisdom is the true path of the soul in this life on her return to her Maker, to know whom is her native desire and her perfect beatitude.

In the exposition of these truths in their various relations a multitude of topics of interest are touched upon, and a multitude of opinions expressed which exhibit the character of Dante's mind and the vast extent of the acquisitions by which his studies had enriched it. The intensity of his moral convictions and the firmness of his moral principles are no less striking in the discourse than the nobility of his genius and the breadth of his intellectual view. Limited and erroneous as are many of his scientific conceptions, there is little trace of superstition or bigotry in his opinions; and though his speculations rest on a false conception of the universe, the revolting dogmas of the common mediæval theology in respect to the human and the Divine nature find no place in them. The mingling of fancy with fact, the unsoundness of the premises from which conclusions are drawn, the errors in belief and in argument, do not affect the main object of his writing, and the Convito may still be read with sympathy and with profit, as a treatise of moral doctrine by a man the loftiness of whose intelligence rose superior to the hampering limitations of his age.

In its general character and in its biographical revelations the Banquet[1] forms a connecting link between the New Life and the Divine Comedy. It is not possible to frame a complete reconciliation between all the statements of the Banquet in respect to Dante's

[1] Although two of the Canzoni were well known before 1300, the prose comments did not assume their present form until after Dante left his fellow exiles and before the invasion of Italy by Henry VII. Toynbee assigns the date between April, 1307, and May, 1309; Scartazzini between 1308 and 1310. (D.)

experience after the death of Beatrice, and the narrative of them in the New Life; nor is it necessary, if we allow due place to the poetic and allegoric interpretation of events natural to Dante's genius. In the last part of the New Life he tells of his infidelity to Beatrice, in yielding himself to the attraction of a compassionate lady, in whose sight he found consolation. But the infidelity was of short duration, and, repenting it, he returned with renewed devotion to his only love. In the Convito he tells us that the compassionate lady was no living person, but was the image of Philosophy, in whose teaching he had found comfort; and the poems which he then wrote and which had the form, and were in the terms of, poems of Love, were properly to be understood as addressed — not to any earthly lady, but — to the lady of the understanding, the most noble and beautiful Philosophy, the daughter of God. And as this image of Philosophy, as the fairest of women, whose eyes and whose smile reveal the joys of Paradise, gradually took clear form, it coalesced with the image of Beatrice herself, she who on earth had been the type to her lover of the beauty of eternal things, and who had revealed to him the Creator in his creature. But now having become one of the blessed in heaven, with a spiritual beauty transcending all earthly charm, she was no longer merely a type of heavenly things, but herself the guide to the knowledge of them, and the divinely commissioned revealer of the wisdom of God. She, looking on the face of God, reflected its light upon him who loved her. She was one with Divine Philosophy, and as such she appears, in living form, in the Divine Comedy, and discloses to her lover the truth which is the native desire of the soul, and in the attainment of which is beatitude.

It is this conception which forms the bond of union between the New Life, the Banquet, and the Divine Comedy, and not merely as literary compositions but as autobiographical records. Dante's life and his work are not to be regarded apart; they form a single whole, and they possess a dramatic development of unparalleled consistency and unity. The course of the events of his life shaped itself in accordance with an ideal of the imagination, and to this ideal his works correspond. His first writing, in his poems of love and in the story of the New Life, forms as it were the first act of a drama which proceeds from act to act in its presentation of his life, with just proportion and due sequence, to its climax and final scene in the last words of the Divine Comedy. It is as if Fate had foreordained the dramatic unity of his life and work, and impressing her decree upon his imagination, had made him her more or less conscious instrument in its fulfillment.

Had Dante written only his prose treatises and his minor poems, he would still have come down to us as the most commanding literary figure of the Middle Ages, the first modern with a true literary sense, the writer of love verses whose imagination was at once more delicate and more profound than that of any among the long train of his successors, save Shakespeare alone, and more free from sensual stain than that of Shakespeare; the poet of sweetest strain and fullest control of the resources of his art, the scholar of largest acquisition and of completest mastery over his acquisitions, and the moralist with higher ideals of conduct and more enlightened conceptions of duty than any other of the period to which he belonged. All this he would have been, and this would have secured for him a place among the immortals. But all this has but a comparatively small part in raising him to the station which he actually occupies, and in giving to him the influence which he still exerts. It was in the Divine Comedy that his genius found its full expression, and it is to this supreme poem that all his other work serves as substructure.

II. DE MONARCHIA

To assign a date to the De Monarchia is difficult. Some place it before the year 1300, because, like the Vita Nuova, it contains no mention of Dante's exile; others think it written on the occasion of the entrance of Henry VII. into Italy; while others place it near the close of Dante's life. As the book contains few personal references, and no intimations of the conditions under which it was written, it is as unimportant as it is difficult to fix the time of its composition. Its great worth arises from its exposition of Dante's lofty political ideals, and its statement of the principles upon which his ideals rested. The book has the defects of the time in its unsound arguments, its strained analogies, its fanciful propositions; but it is the noblest statement of the most exalted political dreams of the Middle Ages, and as such occupies an important place in the history of governmental speculation. James Bryce, in his history of the Holy Roman Empire,[1] has given what is, perhaps, the best statement of its contents and significance.[2]

[1] *The Holy Roman Empire*, James Bryce, pp. 219–224. The notes are Mr. Bryce's. (By permission.)

[2] See Boccaccio's account of how the book fared after Dante's death, pp. 108, 109.

The career of Henry the Seventh in Italy [A. D. 1308–1313] is the most remarkable illustration of the Emperor's position; and imperialist doctrines are set forth most strikingly in the treatise which the greatest spirit of the age wrote to herald or commemorate the advent of that hero, the De Monarchia of Dante. Rudolf, Adolf of Nassau, Albert of Hapsburg, none of them crossed the Alps or attempted to aid the Italian Ghibellines who battled away in the name of their throne. Concerned only to restore order and aggrandize his house, and thinking apparently that nothing more was to be made of the imperial crown, Rudolf was content never to receive it, and purchased the Pope's good-will by surrendering his jurisdiction in the capital and his claims over the bequest of the Countess Matilda. Henry the Luxemburger ventured on a bolder course, — urged perhaps only by his lofty and chivalrous spirit, perhaps in despair at effecting anything with his slender resources against the princes of Germany. Crossing from his Burgundian dominions with a scanty following of knights, and descending from the Cenis upon Turin, he found his prerogative higher in men's belief after sixty years of neglect than it had stood under the last Hohenstaufen. The cities of Lombardy opened their gates; Milan decreed a vast subsidy; Guelf and Ghibelline exiles alike were restored, and imperial vicars appointed everywhere. Supported by the Avignonese pontiff, who dreaded the restless ambition of his French neighbor, King Philip IV., Henry had the interdict of the Church as well as the ban of the Empire at his command. But the illusion of success vanished as soon as men, recovering from their first impression, began to be again governed by their ordinary passions and interests, and not by an imaginative reverence for the glories of the past. Tumults and revolts broke out in Lombardy; at Rome the King of Naples held St. Peter's, and the coronation must take place in St. John Lateran, on the southern bank of the Tiber. The hostility of the Guelfic league, headed by the Florentines, Guelfs even against the Pope, obliged Henry to depart from his impartial and republican policy, and to purchase the aid of the Ghibelline chiefs by granting them the government of cities. With few troops, and encompassed by enemies, the heroic Emperor sustained an unequal struggle for a year longer, till, in A. D. 1313, he sank beneath the fevers of the deadly Tuscan summer. His German followers believed, nor has history wholly rejected the tale, that poison was given him by a Dominican monk in sacramental wine.

Others after him descended from the Alps, but they came, like Lewis the Fourth, Rupert, Sigismund, at the behest of a faction, which found them useful tools for a time, then flung them away in scorn; or like Charles the Fourth and Frederick the Third, as the humble minions of a French or Italian priest. With Henry the Seventh ends the history of the Empire in Italy, and Dante's book is an epitaph instead of a prophecy. A sketch of its argument will convey a notion of the feelings with which the noblest Ghibellines fought, as well as of the spirit in which the Middle Age was accustomed to handle such subjects.

Weary of the endless strife of princes and cities; of the factions within every city against each other;

seeing municipal freedom, the only mitigation of turbulence, vanish with the rise of domestic tyrants, Dante raises a passionate cry for some power to still the tempest, not to quench liberty or supersede local self-government, but to correct and moderate them, to restore unity and peace to hapless Italy. His reasoning is throughout closely syllogistic; he is alternately the jurist, the theologian, the scholastic metaphysician. The poet of the Divina Commedia is betrayed only by the compressed energy of diction, by his clear vision of the unseen, rarely by a glowing metaphor.

Monarchy is first proved to be the true and rightful form of government.[1] Men's objects are best attained during universal peace. This is possible only under a monarch. And as he is the image of the Divine unity, so man is through him made one, and brought most near to God. There must, in every system of forces, be a *primum mobile;* to be perfect, every organization must have a centre, into which all is gathered, by which all is controlled.[2] Justice is best secured by a supreme arbiter of disputes, himself unsolicited by ambition, since his dominion is already bounded only by ocean. Man is best and happiest when he is most free; to be free is to exist for one's own sake. To this grandest end does the monarch and he alone guide us; other forms of government are perverted,[3] and exist

[1] More than half a century earlier the envoys of the Norwegian king, in urging the chiefs of the republic of Iceland assembled at their Althing to accept Hakon as their suzerain, had argued that monarchy was the only rightful form of government, and had appealed to the fact that in all continental Europe there was no such thing as an absolutely independent republic.

[2] Suggesting the celestial hierarchies of Dionysius the Areopagite.

[3] Quoting Aristotle's *Politics*.

for the benefit of some class; he seeks the good of all alike, being to that very end appointed.[1]

Abstract arguments are then confirmed from history. Since the world began there has been but one period of perfect peace, and but one of perfect monarchy, that, namely, which existed at our Lord's birth, under the sceptre of Augustus; since then the heathen have raged, and the kings of the earth have stood up; they have set themselves against their Lord, and his anointed the Roman prince.[2] The universal dominion, the need for which has been thus established, is then proved to belong to the Romans. Justice is the will of God, a will to exalt Rome shown through her whole history.[3] Her virtues deserved honor. Virgil is quoted to prove those of Æneas, who by descent and marriage was the heir of three continents: of Asia, through Assaracus and Creusa; of Africa, by Electra (mother of Dardanus and daughter of Atlas) and Dido; of Europe, by Dardanus and Lavinia. God's favor was approved in the fall of the shields to Numa, in the miraculous deliverance of the capital from the Gauls, in the hailstorm after Cannæ. Justice is also the advantage of the state, — that advantage was the constant object of the virtuous Cincinnatus and the other heroes of the republic. They conquered the world for its own good, and therefore justly, as Cicero attests;[4] so that their sway was not so much *imperium* as

[1] "Non enim cives propter consules nec gens propter regem, sed e converso consules propter cives, rex propter gentem."

[2] "Reges et principes in hoc unico concordantes, ut adversentur Domino suo et uncto suo Romano Principi," having quoted "Quare fremuerunt gentes."

[3] Especially in the opportune death of Alexander the Great.

[4] Cic. *De Off.*, ii. "Ita ut illud patrocinium orbis terrarum potius quam imperium poterat nominari."

patrocinium orbis terrarum. Nature herself, the fountain of all right, had, by their geographical position and by the gift of a genius so vigorous, marked them out for universal dominion: —

Excudent alii spirantia mollius aera,
Credo equidem: vivos ducent de marmore vultus;
Orabunt causas melius, coelique meatus
Describent radio, et surgentia sidera dicent:
Tu regere imperio populos, Romane, memento;
Hae tibi erunt artes; pacisque imponere morem,
Parcere subiectis, et debellare superbos.

Finally, the right of war asserted, Christ's birth, and death under Pilate, ratified their government. For Christian doctrine requires that the procurator should have been a lawful judge,[1] which he was not unless Tiberius was a lawful Emperor.

The relations of the imperial and papal power are then examined, and the passages of Scripture (tradition being rejected), to which the advocates of the papacy appeal, are elaborately explained away. The argument from the sun and moon [2] does not hold, since both lights existed before man's creation, and at a time when, as still sinless, he needed no controlling powers. Else *accidentia* would have preceded *propria*

[1] "Si Pilati imperium non de iure fuit, peccatum in Christo non fuit adeo punitum."

[2] There is a curious seal of the Emperor Otto IV. (figured in J. M. Heineccius, *De veteribus Germanorum atque aliarum nationum sigillis*), on which the sun and moon are represented over the head of the Emperor. Heineccius says he cannot explain it, but there seems to be no reason why we should not take the device as typifying the accord of the spiritual and temporal powers which was brought about at the accession of Otto, the Guelfic leader, and the favored candidate of Pope Innocent III.

The analogy between the lights of heaven and the potentates of earth is one which mediæval writers are very fond of. It seems to have originated with Gregory VII.

in creation. The moon, too, does not receive her being nor all her light from the sun, but so much only as makes her more effective. So there is no reason why the temporal should not be aided in a corresponding measure by the spiritual authority. This difficult text disposed of, others fall more easily: Levi and Judah, Samuel and Saul, the incense and gold offered by the Magi,[1] the two swords, the power of binding and loosing given to Peter. Constantine's donation was illegal. No single Emperor nor Pope can disturb the everlasting foundations of their respective thrones. The one had no right to bestow, nor the other to receive, such a gift. Leo the Third gave the Empire to Charles wrongfully: "Usurpatio iuris non facit ius." It is alleged that all things of one kind are reducible to one individual, and so all men to the Pope. But Emperor and Pope differ in kind, and so far as they are men, are reducible only to God, on whom the Empire immediately depends; for it existed before Peter's see, and was recognized by Paul when he appealed to Cæsar. The temporal power of the papacy can have been given neither by natural law, nor divine ordinance, nor universal consent: nay, it is against its own form and essence, — the life of Christ, who said, "My kingdom is not of this world."

Man's nature is twofold: corruptible and incorruptible. He has therefore two ends, active virtue on earth, and the enjoyment of the sight of God hereafter; the one to be attained by practice conformed to the precepts of philosophy, the other by the theo-

[1] Typifying the spiritual and temporal powers. Dante meets this by distinguishing the homage paid to Christ from that which his vicar can rightfully demand.

logical virtues. Hence two guides are needed, the Pontiff and the Emperor, the latter of whom, in order that he may direct mankind in accordance with the teachings of philosophy to temporal blessedness, must preserve universal peace in the world. Thus are the two powers equally ordained of God, and the Emperor, though supreme in all that pertains to the secular world, is in some things dependent on the Pontiff, since earthly happiness is subordinate to eternal. "Let Cæsar, therefore, show toward Peter the reverence wherewith a firstborn son honors his father, that, being illumined by the light of his paternal favor, he may the more excellently shine forth upon the whole world, to the rule of which he has been appointed by Him alone who is of all things, both spiritual and temporal, the King and Governor." So ends the treatise.

Dante's arguments are not stranger than his omissions. No suspicion is breathed against Constantine's donation; no proof is adduced, for no doubt is felt, that the Empire of Henry the Seventh is the legitimate continuation of that which had been swayed by Augustus and Justinian. Yet Henry was a German, sprung from Rome's barbarian foes, the elected of those who had neither part nor share in Italy and her capital.

III. DE VULGARI ELOQUENTIA.

Concerning the significance of this book, George Saintsbury, the distinguished critic, says:[1] "It is in

[1] *History of Criticism*, vol. i. bk. iii. c. ii.

two different ways a document of the very highest value, even before its intrinsic worth is considered at all. In the first place, there is the importance of date, which gives us in it the first critical treatise on the literary use of the vernacular, at exactly the point when the various vernaculars of Europe had finished, more or less, their first stage. Secondly, there is the importance of authorship, in that we have, as is hardly anywhere else the case, the greatest creative writer, not merely of one literature but of a whole period of the European world, betaking himself to criticism. If Shakespeare had written the Discoveries instead of Ben Jonson, the only possible analogue would have been supplied. Even Homer could not have given us a third, for he could hardly have had the literature to work upon. — I am prepared to claim for it, not merely the position of the most important critical document between Longinus and the seventeenth century at least, but one of intrinsic importance on a line with that of the very greatest critical documents of all history. — That the book has remained so long unknown, and that even after its belated publication it attracted little attention, and has for the most part been misunderstood, or not understood at all, is no doubt in part connected with the fact of its extraordinary precocity. On the very threshold of modern literature, Dante anticipates and follows out methods which have not been reached by all, or by many, who have had the advantage of access to the mighty chambers whereof the house has since been built and is still a-building."

Its Nature.[1]

What Dante did in order to acquire for the Italian tongue a position superior to the Latin, with which it was struggling for literary priority, is one of his finest and most brilliant achievements. How true his instinct was in this may be seen from the example of Petrarca, who, coming later, gave the preference again to the Latin, and of whom nothing has survived save what was written in Italian. For the matter of that, Dante himself only gradually shook off the prejudice of his age in favor of Latin, nor did he ever free himself from it entirely. The Vita Nuova was apparently, according to the statement in cap. 31, written in Italian at the instigation of Guido Cavalcanti, to whom the book is dedicated; but in cap. 25 we still find the opinion expressed that only love matters should be treated in the *volgare*, that being done solely in order that women might understand them. In the Convivio more nobility is granted to the Latin, because it is "permanent and incorruptible" (while the *volgare* is "not stable and corruptible"), because it is more beautiful, because it follows art (and the *volgare* only custom), and because it is always able to express things for which the *volgare* does not suffice. One of the reasons given for the employment of allegory in the first canzone is that no poem in the *volgare* appeared worthy to extol philosophy, unless some veil were used. Nevertheless, Dante already at that time composed his canzoni on virtue in Italian; he writes on the highest questions of philosophy in the *volgare*,

[1] Gaspary's *History of Early Italian Literature*, trans. by H. Oelsner, pp. 253–259. (By permission.)

which he defends and extols in words that come from the heart. The development of his ideas was therefore notable. The little book De Eloquentia Vulgari adopts practically the same standpoint; in addition to love, arms and virtue are designated as proper subjects for treatment in the Italian language. The *volgare* is here called more noble even than Latin, in direct contradiction to the Convivio. At the same time, as D'Ovidio rightly remarked, so vague an expression as *nobile* must not be interpreted in too pedantic a spirit: according to the author's particular object or point of view, his opinion might lean one way or the other. The Latin poets, called *magni et regulares*, are, in this treatise, still invariably distinguished from those that write in the *volgare*, because the former proceed according to art, the latter according to chance. That Dante composed this very book on the Italian language in Latin may be due to the fact that in it he addressed those that despised the *volgare*, who only read Latin works, and to whom he had, therefore, to speak in this language, so as to be able to refute their opinions. This book, too, belongs to the period of exile, to which it contains an allusion (i. 6). The Convivio mentions it only as a projected work (i. 5): "This will be treated more fully in another place, in a book which, with God's help, I mean to write concerning the vulgar speech." The treatise, however, contains an historical allusion (i. 12) which assigns it a date prior to the year 1305, namely, the mention of John of Montferrat (who died in January, 1305) as a living man. And so the words in the Convivio probably mean that the book, as such, did not exist, that is to say, it was not yet completed and published, which does not exclude the possibility of its having been partially finished. That is the explanation of D'Ovidio and Fraticelli.

But this work of Dante's also remained unfinished, the reason being unknown. It was intended to comprise at least four books, as the fourth is several times referred to in advance (ii. 4, 8), but it breaks off in the middle of the fourteenth chapter of the second book. The original title is De Eloquentia Vulgari, this being Dante's own designation in the text of the treatise itself (at the beginning and end of i. 1) and in the Convivio. Later it was called De Vulgari Eloquio, by Giovanni Villani, for example. But this did not show any misunderstanding of the author's plan; for Dante really intended to treat of the vulgar tongue, and not merely of the poetic style, as has often been assumed. Only the fact of the non-completion of the work might produce the impression that it was meant to be nothing more than a *Poetica;* but the author says expressly at the beginning that the *eloquentia vulgaris* was necessary for all, and that not only men, but women and children also strove to attain it, and at the end of the first book he says that he proposes treating the other *vulgaria* after the *vulgare illustre*, descending down to the speech that is proper to one family only. Accordingly, the precepts concerning poetic style and form constituted only a subdivision of the entire work, and Dante's *eloquentia* stands for language, or at the outside for eloquence in general.[1]

[1] In the same way Pietro Allighieri, in the *Commentarium*, edited by Nannucci, p. 84, employs *eloquentia* in the sense of "speech": "Rhadamanthus vero iudicat de *eloquentia*, utrum sit vera, ficta vel otiosa; unde 'Rhadamanthus,' id est 'iudicans verba.'"

Following the custom of his time, Dante begins with the origin of language itself, and answers the questions why it was given to man and to man alone, and not to the angels and animals; he also discusses which was the language of Adam, and decides in favor of Hebrew. Then he comes to speak of the confusion of Babel and of the origin of the various languages and families of languages, of which he distinguishes three in Europe. One of them is that of the Romance idioms, the common basis and original unity of which he therefore recognizes, though he does not explain correctly. According to Dante there are three Romance languages, too, which he distinguishes in the manner that has become so usual, according to their affirmative particle, into the languages of *oc*, *oïl*, and *sì*. Are we to assume that Spanish and Portuguese were really unknown to him, or was it again his predilection for the symbolical number three asserting itself? He puts the *Hispani* down as representatives of the *lingua d'oc*, whereas, of course, only their two northeastern provinces belong to this domain. The separate languages are again subdivided; people speak differently in the various districts, in the various towns, at times even in the various quarters of the same town. The cause of this is, as Dante thought, the change to which all human things are subjected, and which is, in the case of language, effected variously in the various localities. And so men no longer understand one another, and no longer understand what their ancestors spoke, and the need arises for a universal language, uninfluenced by remoteness of time or place. As such a language the *Grammatica*, that is, Latin, was invented, which is unchangeable because it "was regulated by the agreement of many nations" (i. 9). And so, according to Dante's opinion, the Romance languages do not derive from the Latin; on the contrary, the Latin is a later invention, an artificial product, as opposed to those products of nature. The vulgar tongue is very old; it is the natural speech of man, which he learns without rules from those around him, when he first begins to form words; grammar, the Latin language, is acquired by dint of study, and only by a few.

Further on, Dante asks himself which of the three Romance languages should be awarded the precedence. He does not come to a decision, as each of them can boast of its special literary productions; two points, however, appear to decide him in favor of the Italian, namely, its closer resemblance to the language of grammar (Latin) commou to them all, and its employment as the organ of the most perfect lyrical poetry, that of the *dolce stil nuovo*. But Italy possesses several different *vulgaria*, many dialects, of which the author distinguishes fourteen principal ones, divided into two great classes, east and west of the chain of the Apennines. Now, which of these is the noble Italian *vulgare*, which he compared with the other Romance languages, to which he even awarded a certain precedence? Dante goes through the dialects one by one, quotes from each some words by way of specimen, and comparing them with the literary type that he has in mind, he rejects them all, with his impatient and passionate temperament, and inveighs against nearly all of them with bitter words, even against the Tuscan; the Tuscans, indeed, come in for special abuse, since they maintain that they possess the noble language, whereas they write and speak more faultily than the rest. But, nevertheless, in the course of his researches, he found traces of that higher *vulgare* in the most various districts, in Sicily, Apulia, Tuscany, Bologna, in isolated instances also in Romagna, Lombardy, and Venetia, namely, in the court poets who rejected the particular idiom of their province, and everywhere employed the same expressions. This is Dante's famous doctrine of a national language, that was to be common to every district of the country, not identical with any one of the dialects, and superior to them all. Nowadays we also say that no dialects correspond exactly to the literary language; but, at the same time, we recognize that the relation in which the latter stands to the single dialects is very various, that this literary language is based on one of these dialects, from which it arose by merely eliminating certain elements, whereas it is distinguished from the others by its phonetics and forms. As D'Ovidio noted, Dante was not yet able to draw this distinction, the distinction between language and style; he denominated both of them as *lingua*, and did not recognize that the literary language he employed was derived from the Tuscan, in spite of the divergencies detected by him. Nor could he realize this fact, seeing that, according to his convictions, the literary language, as the higher and the more excellent, must also be the earliest in point of time, and the dialects a corruption of this pure type, whose existence he demonstrates *a priori* by means of a scholastic deduction. In all classes of things, he says, there is a simple fundamental standard by which they are measured, — as, for numbers, one; for colors, white; for human actions, virtue, and so on. In the same way, the fundamental standard for the *vulgaria* is this language common to all of them. Just as there is a *vulgare* of Cremona, so there is one of the whole of Lombardy, further, one of the entire left portion of Italy, and, finally, one of the whole of Italy; and, just as the first is the Cremonese, the second the Lombard, and the third a *Semilatium* (l. *Semilatinum?*), so we call the fourth the *Latinum vulgare*, the Italian. For us this universal fundamental type is merely an abstraction, which has no existence save in the particular case. But for Dante the universals possess reality, and accordingly there is no need for him to ask how this type is obtained, and whence the universal language derives, in which the best poets of every province wrote.

After obtaining his universal language in this manner, Dante extols it with enthusiastic epithets. It is the *vulgare illustre*, *cardinale*, *aulicum*, *curiale*, that is to say, the noble and perfect language of poetry, the source of fame and honor, and the court language, that of cultured society. It is true that there is no court in Italy at which it is employed, but there are the members of an ideal court, that is to say, the most distinguished men of the nation, and especially the leading poets, who thus feel themselves united by the bond of an intellectual companionship in the same way as elsewhere courts are bound together through the efforts of the prince. But this *vulgare illustre* must not be employed indiscriminately for every kind of literary production. Dante distinguishes three species of style, — the tragic, comic, and elegiac, — which terms must be taken not in the classical, but in the widely different mediæval sense, as a distinction based on the greater or lesser degree of sublimity and solemnity contained in the poem. The *vulgare illustre* is adapted only to tragic subjects and to the highest styles, to which belongs the canzone, that loftiest and most solemn form of poetry, while the ballad and sonnet stand lower and adopt the *vulgare mediocre.* And so Dante's *vulgare illustre*, from a literary point of view, consists of nothing but the canzone, and we can understand how it is that, in certain sonnets of the correspondence type, and especially in the Commedia, he could be more free in the use of idiomatic forms, nay, even employ words which he had specially blamed in the treatise, but only with reference to the noblest type of the *vulgare illustre.*

In the remaining chapters of the second book (ii. 5 *sqq.*), the author deals with the stylistic and metrical peculiarities of the canzone. The severe and in reality somewhat exclusive nature of his selection, in the matter of word construction, reveals to us the inflexible taste of an aristocratic form of art. But the instructions are here inadequate, and those who had not mastered the subject before, could have learnt but little from them. More interesting, and very important for our knowledge of the old metrical laws, are the data concerning the structure of the poem, the verse, the stanza and its divisions, and the terminology of the time. The unwritten portion of the book was to treat the sonnet and the ballad.

Dante's work contains a number of errors. Although his fundamental idea rises above the general prejudice, yet he cannot free himself from it in all its details, and although he sets himself the solution of an important problem, yet he does not really succeed in solving it; for his method could not fail to be shackled by the errors that belonged to the teaching of his time. But it is just this fundamental idea that reveals to us the boldness of his mind. He was the first among his countrymen to put a conscious theory in the place of the irregular use of the *volgare;* his little book contains the first scientific treatment of the Italian language, and it is at the same time the first example of a regular *Ars poëtica* for any vulgar tongue, after the manner of those that had previously been compiled for Latin only. And thus, owing to Dante's original intellect, Italian poetry, that began latest among the Romance languages, first and almost at its commencement came to be combined with reflection and with the theory of art.

IV. THE QUAESTIO DE AQUA ET TERRA.[1]

On one occasion, when Dante was in Mantua, there arose a certain question regarding the place and figure of the two elements, water and earth. The point of this question was, whether the water, in its sphere, or in its natural circumference, was in any part higher than the earth emerging from the waters and usually denominated the "habitable quadrant." Some argued in the affirmative, adducing many grounds in support of their opinion. Whence Dante, "having from his childhood been continually nurtured in the love of truth, could not bear to leave said question undiscussed." And so, both from love of the truth, and still more from hatred of falsehood, he "resolved to demonstrate the truth regarding that question, and to answer the arguments

[1] *Dante Handbook*, Scartazzini and Davidson, p. 255. (Ginn & Co.) (By permission.)

raised on the other side." Having, therefore, repaired to Verona, he there discussed this question, "in the chapel of St. Helena, in the presence of all the clergy of Verona," and further, "he resolved to leave written with his own fingers, what had been settled by him, and to put down in black and white the form of the whole dispute."

The order of inquiry is as follows: In the first place, it is shown to be impossible that the water in any part of its circumference should be higher than this land which emerges and is uncovered. In the second place, it is proved that this emerging land is everywhere higher than the total surface of the sea. In the third place, an objection is stated to the things demonstrated, and this objection is met and answered. In the fourth place, the final and efficient cause of this elevation or emergence of the land is shown; and, finally, the contrary arguments are answered.

This work of Dante's has been undeservedly neglected, although it is a most important document for the history of the sciences, and a monument of the vastness of Dante's genius and knowledge.[1]

V. THE ECLOGUES

While Dante[2] was at Ravenna, Giovanni del Virgilio, a celebrated professor of Latin literature at

[1] Dr. Edward Moore in the second series of his *Studies in Dante* has gone exhaustively into the question of the authenticity of this book, and considers it from the hand of Dante, though possibly corrupted in some of its details. In the Twenty-first Annual Report of the Dante Society (Cambridge, Mass.), there is an excellent translation and discussion of this work by Alain C. White. (D.)

[2] *Dante Handbook*, Scartazzini and Davidson, p. 259. *Dante and Giovanni del Virgilio*, Wicksteed and Gardner (Constable) contains corrected text, translation, and valuable discussion of the Eclogues. (D.)

Bologna, invited him, in a Latin ode, to come to Bologna, praising him for his Comedy, but, at the same time, blaming him for having written it in the vulgar tongue. He then exhorted him to win the laurel by writing Latin poems. Dante replied in a Latin eclogue, without entering into any literary discussion, courteously praised him for his poetical studies, adding that he disdained to accept the poetic crown at Bologna, because that city was opposed to the empire, and that his sole desire was to bind his head with his country's laurel, when he should have published, in its completeness, The Comedy,[1] of which he promised to send him soon ten cantos.

Giovanni replied in another eclogue, urging Dante to set his mind at rest and to cherish the hope of returning to his country, and inviting him to come to Bologna, where the scholars were eagerly waiting for him, and where he would meet, among other persons, the poet Albertino Mussato. Dante replied in a second eclogue, saying that he disdained to go to Bologna, all the more that he feared Robert, King of Naples.

These two eclogues are of great value both because they show us the genial side of Dante's nature and because they help us fix the dates of the completion of the Inferno and Purgatorio. In the first eclogue (lines 48–51) Dante promises that "when the bodies that flow round the world, and

[1] We have a charming description of Dante's love for the *Paradiso* and of the fitfulness of his inspiration in this first Eclogue (lines 57–64, Wicksteed and Gardner's translation). "I have," said I, "one sheep, thou knowest, most loved; so full of milk she scarce can bear her udders; even now under a mighty rock she chews the late-cropped grass: associate with no flock, familiar with no pen; of her own will she ever comes, ne'er must be driven to the milking pail. Her do I think to milk with ready hands; from her ten measures will I fill and send to Mopsur." (D.)

they that dwell among the stars, shall be shown forth in my song, even as the lower realms, then shall I joy to bind my brow with ivy and with laurel." This indicates that in 1318 or 1319 the Inferno and Purgatorio were written and the Paradiso was in preparation.

VI. THE LETTERS

The question of the genuineness of the letters attributed to Dante has not yet been settled. There are eleven which are entitled to careful investigation. Of these the letter to Henry VII. is the only one that may pass unchallenged. In the Vita Nuova (xxxi) Dante refers to a letter which he wrote to the chief persons of the land on the occasion of the death of Beatrice. If this is a statement of fact, the letter is lost, as is also the one mentioned by Bruni (p. 117), describing the battle of Campaldino. Giovanni Villani (p. 62) speaks of three noble epistles: one to the Florentine government, another to the Emperor Henry, the third to the Italian Cardinals. Boccaccio also refers to three in the Laurentian MS.

The epistle to Niccolò da Prato has nothing to show that it is connected with Dante. The one to the Counts of Romena is either a forgery, or wrongly ascribed to him. The letter to Marquis Moroello Malaspina is of questionable authenticity. The alleged epistle to Cino da Pistoia, in which neither the name Cino nor Dante occurs, is also much debated. The one to the Princes and People of Italy is generally considered authentic. There are strong reasons for the belief that the letter to the Florentines, mentioned by Bruni (p. 124), is genuine. The epistle to Henry VII. is of undoubted authenticity. Probably the one to Guido da Polenta is spurious. The letter to the Italian Cardinals, noted by Villani, is probably genuine. The epistle to a Florentine friend is justly under suspicion. The letter to Can Grande is the longest and most interesting of all Dante's letters, and while it is subject to vigorous onslaught its genuineness seems highly probable. How thoroughly this letter, which is printed in full, pp. 262–286, is impregnated with Dante's thought and shaped by his manner of expression is brought out by Mr. Latham's notes.

CHAPTER VI

THE DIVINA COMMEDIA

I

THE DIVINA COMMEDIA[1]

Oft have I seen at some cathedral door
 A laborer, pausing in the dust and heat,
 Lay down his burden, and with reverent feet
 Enter, and cross himself, and on the floor
Kneel to repeat his paternoster o'er;
 Far off the noises of the world retreat;
 The loud vociferations of the street
 Become an undistinguishable roar.
So, as I enter here from day to day,
 And leave my burden at this minster gate,
 Kneeling in prayer, and not ashamed to pray,
The tumult of the time disconsolate
 To inarticulate murmurs dies away,
 While the eternal ages watch and wait.

How strange the sculptures that adorn these towers!
 This crowd of statues, in whose folded sleeves
 Birds build their nests; while canopied with leaves
 Parvis and portal bloom like trellised bowers,
And the vast minster seems a cross of flowers!
 But fiends and dragons on the gargoyled eaves
 Watch the dead Christ between the living thieves,
 And, underneath, the traitor Judas lowers!
Ah! from what agonies of heart and brain,
 What exultations trampling on despair,
 What tenderness, what tears, what hate of wrong,
What passionate outcry of a soul in pain,
 Uprose this poem of the earth and air,
 This mediæval miracle of song!

[1] Henry W. Longfellow. Taken from Longfellow's translation of *The Divine Comedy*, Houghton, Mifflin & Co.

I enter, and I see thee in the gloom
Of the long aisles, O poet saturnine!
And strive to make my steps keep pace with thine.
The air is filled with some unknown perfume;
The congregation of the dead make room
For thee to pass; the votive tapers shine;
Like rooks that haunt Ravenna's groves of pine,
The hovering echoes fly from tomb to tomb.
From the confessionals I hear arise
Rehearsals of forgotten tragedies,
And lamentations from the crypts below;
And then a voice celestial that begins
With the pathetic words, "Although your sins
As scarlet be," and ends with "as the snow."

With snow-white veil, and garments as of flame,
She stands before thee, who so long ago
Filled thy young heart with passion and the woe
From which thy song in all its splendors came;
And while with stern rebuke she speaks thy name,
The ice about thy heart melts as the snow
On mountain heights, and in swift overflow
Comes gushing from thy lips in sobs of shame.
Thou makest full confession; and a gleam
As of the dawn on some dark forest cast,
Seems on thy lifted forehead to increase;
Lethe and Eunoë — the remembered dream
And the forgotten sorrow — bring at last
That perfect pardon which is perfect peace.

I lift mine eyes, and all the windows blaze
With forms of saints and holy men who died,
Here martyred and hereafter glorified;
And the great Rose upon its leaves displays
Christ's Triumph, and the angelic roundelays,
With splendor upon splendor multiplied;
And Beatrice again at Dante's side
No more rebukes, but smiles her words of praise.

And then the organ sounds, and unseen choirs
    Sing the old Latin hymns of peace and love
    And benedictions of the Holy Ghost;
And the melodious bells among the spires
    O'er all the house-tops and through heaven above
    Proclaim the elevation of the Host!

O star of morning and of liberty!
    O bringer of the light, whose splendor shines
    Above the darkness of the Apennines,
    Forerunner of the day that is to be!
The voices of the city and the sea,
    The voices of the mountains and the pines,
    Repeat thy song, till the familiar lines
    Are footpaths for the thought of Italy!
Thy fame is blown abroad from all the heights,
    Through all the nations; and a sound is heard,
    As of a mighty wind, and men devout,
Strangers of Rome, and the new proselytes,
    In their own language hear thy wondrous word,
    And many are amazed and many doubt.

II

THE DIVINA COMMEDIA[1]

I. DATE OF COMPOSITION.

THE dates when the different books were written cannot be definitely fixed. Boccaccio's account of the finding of the first seven cantos of the Inferno may indicate that previous to his exile Dante had made notes and sketches which were afterwards worked into the Commedia. It is quite certain that the poem took shape between the death of Clement V. and the end of Dante's life. "From internal allusions (such as Clement's death, April 20th, 1314, in Inf. xix. 79; the failure of Henry VII., in Purg. vii. 96; the pontificate of John XXII., in Par. xxvii. 58), together with the evidence furnished by Dante's first eclogue to Giovanni del Virgilio,[2] in which it appears that both the Inferno and the Purgatorio were completed in 1318 or 1319, and Boccaccio's story of the finding of the last thirteen cantos, it would seem that the Inferno and the Purgatorio were finished between 1314 and 1318 or 1319, the Paradiso between 1316 and Sept. 14th, 1321."[3]

[1] We do not know what name Dante intended to give the work. In the letter to Can Grande he calls it a "Comedy." Some editions style it "Le terza rime di Dante;" others the "Vision of Dante Alighieri." The title *Divina Commedia* appears in some of the earliest manuscripts.

[2] Pp. 220, 221.

[3] *Dante*, E. G. Gardner, in Temple Primers.

The date of the action of the poem is in the jubilee year 1300, when Dante was in his thirty-fifth year. His journey began on Good Friday and continued for a week, ending Thursday evening.

II. ITS STRUCTURE.[1]

There exists no poetical work elaborated with such consummate art as this. The smallest detail is worked out; it resembles a technical work, every iron joint, every nail of which has been considered before. Even the number of the words seems to have been counted. The mystical properties of numbers, on which such stress is laid in the Vita Nuova, where the number Nine, that of the miraculous, recurs ever and again, and Beatrice herself is called a Nine, that is, a wonder whose root is in the Trinity — these properties are worked out to the utmost in the structure of the Divine Comedy. The numbers Three, that of the threefold Deity, Nine, that of wonder and second birth, and Ten, the number of the Perfect, are the basis of its construction. Three are the rhymes, three verses form a stanza, three animals rise to terrify Dante, three holy women intervene for him, three guides lead him. Three in number are the realms, and correspondingly the whole poem is divided into three parts; the book opens with an introductory canto, then follow ninety-nine cantos, thirty-three for each of the three realms, corresponding to the years of Christ's life on earth, so that the whole number of the cantos is an hundred, the number of the Whole. Each of the three realms is divided into ten regions: Hell into Limbo and the nine circles; Purgatory into

[1] *Dante and his Time*, p. 270. Karl Federn. McClure, Phillips & Co.

three preparatory divisions and the seven circles of the capital sins; in Paradise there are nine heavens and as the tenth region the Heaven of perfect light, the Empyrean. Even verses and words seem to have been counted, for the number of the words is 99,542; and of verses Hell contains 4720, Purgatory 35 more, and Paradise again 3 more. And each of the three parts ends with the word "stars."

III. THE TERZA RIMA.[1]

Each canto is composed of from thirty-eight to fifty-three terzine or terzette, continuous measures of three normally hendecasyllabic lines, woven together by the rhymes of the middle lines, with an extra line or *tornello* rhyming with the second line of the last terzina to close the canto: —

ABA, BCB, CDC, DED — XYX, YZYZ.

This *terza rima* seems to be derived from one of the rather numerous forms of the Italian *serventese*, or *sermontese*, a species of poem introduced from Provence in the latter half of the thirteenth century. The Provençal *sirventes* was a serviceable composition employed mainly for satirical, political, and ethical purposes, in contrast with the stately and "tragical" canzone of Love. Although the Italians extended its range of subject and developed its metres, no one before Dante had used it for a great poem or had transfigured it into this superb new measure, at once lyrical and epical. In his hand, indeed, the "thing became a trumpet," sounding from earth to heaven, to call the dead to judgment.

[1] *Dante*, E. G. Gardner, Temple Primers, p. 86.

III

DANTE'S COSMOGRAPHY[1]

THE sacred documents of our religion are clear enough in expressing the dependent relation of the whole firmament to the earth. When the story of creation makes the Almighty say, "Let there be lights in the firmament of heaven, to divide the day from the night, and let them be for signs, and for seasons, and for days, and for years, and let them be for lights in the firmament of the heaven, to give light upon the earth," or when Joshua commands, "Sun, stand thou still in Gibeon, and thou, moon, in the valley of Ajalon," we may talk, if we choose, of an "accommodation" to the human conceptions of those ancient days.

Not so, however, when we find the relation of all created things to the Creator determined by events which have taken place upon our earth, by the fall, the redemption, and the second coming of the Christ. The Saviour himself declares, "Heaven and earth shall pass away, but my words shall not pass away." The Apostle Peter says yet more distinctly that "the heavens that now are, and the earth . . . have been stored up for fire, being reserved against the day of

[1] *Essays on Dante*, by Dr. Karl Witte, trans. by C. Mabel Lawrence, and edited by Philip A. Wicksteed. Houghton, Mifflin & Co. The essay is found in Witte's *Dante-Forschungen*, vol. ii. pp. 161–182 (1878). The notes are Mr. Wicksteed's. (By permission.)

judgment and destruction of ungodly men;" and further on he adds, "The heavens shall pass away with a great noise, and the elements shall be dissolved with fervent heat, and the earth and the works that are therein shall be burned up." "But," he continues, "according to His promise, we look for new heavens and a new earth, wherein dwelleth righteousness."

In the Middle Ages all this was united with the special conceptions of ancient astronomy, which had taken its rise amongst the great Greek astronomers of the third century before Christ, and was systematized mainly by the Alexandrian Ptolemy in the second century of the Christian era, further details being added by Arabian scholars, especially under the Sassanid dynasty in Spain. The doubts which the Samian Aristarchus had already thrown on the central position of the earth were passed over by antiquity, just as they were by the Middle Ages when propounded by the celebrated Ibn Roschd, or Averroës as we are accustomed to call him, and a little later on by Alphonso the Wise, king of Castile.

Right down into the sixteenth century the conviction remained unshaken that the earth was fixed at the middle point of the universe. All the heavenly spheres circled round it as their centre. It was the lowest point of the universe, towards which all bodies possessing material weight were drawn. The two heavy elements formed the body of the earth and the two light ones encompassed it; for beyond the sphere of air lay that of fire, the true home of that element towards which all upleaping flames aspire, only being kept back by the matter on which they feed. From that high region of fire the thunderstorms tore off fragments of the element, and hurled them to earth as lightning.

Far beyond the sphere of fire came the seven planets, each of which had a heaven to itself, the moon counting as the undermost of the planets. The sun was in the middle, between the three inner and the three outer planets, and although only reckoned as one of the planets, he was the source of light to the whole universe, for not only our earth, and the planets (as we also believe), but the fixed stars too received their light from him. Hence the poet calls him[1] "the greatest of all ministers of nature, who stamps the world with the virtue of the heaven, and gives the measure of time unto us."

Beyond Saturn (the most distant planet known till the year 1781) lay the heaven of the fixed stars. Attempts had been made to number them in early times. Eratosthenes counted 675, and for more than a thousand years science rested in Ptolemy's 1022 — only about a fifth of the number now given as visible to the naked eye, and less than a hundredth of the number marked on our modern astronomical maps. According to Aristotle there was nothing beyond this eighth heaven. Each heaven had a "proper" or special motion of its own, from west to east; and as the distance from the earth, the centre of the universe, increased, this movement became slower and slower, till the heaven of the fixed stars only revolved once in 36,000 years.

But the path of the planets as actually observed was not adequately expressed by their supposed revolution in company with the heavens called after their

[1] *Par.* x. 28.

names. The astronomers were driven to assume for each planet a second revolution whereby it revolved round a fixed invisible point in its own (already revolving) heaven, somewhat as, according to modern astronomy, the moon, besides accompanying the earth in her course round the sun, herself revolves round the earth. This second movement of the planets was called the epicyclic revolution. This theory, however fanciful and involved it may sound to us, corresponds so closely with the actual phenomena presented by the heavenly bodies, that it enabled the observer to predict every eclipse or conjunction of planets to the minute. Such accuracy was reached that in 1560, long before the new doctrine of Copernicus had gained acceptance, the punctual occurrence of an eclipse of the sun at the moment predicted moved Tycho Brahe, then fourteen years old, with such reverence for astronomy that he resolved from that hour to dedicate all the powers of his mind to her alone.

But the motions of these eight heavens, with their epicycles, leave unexplained just the one phenomenon which the least observant must perforce notice, — the daily rising and setting of the sun, moon, and stars. Ptolemy explained this[1] by the theory of a ninth heaven, embracing all the others, sweeping them all round (though without interfering with their own

[1] Not, of course, that it had not been observed or accounted for before. But till his time it had been identified with the movement of the fixed stars. Ptolemy observed that it did not quite coincide therewith, and so separated out the "proper" motion of the starry sphere (see above, p. 233, end of second paragraph) which corresponds to what is now known as the "precession of the equinoxes." Then he took away from the eighth sphere the function of originating the daily motion common to all, and gave it to a now first recognized ninth heaven.

special motions) in its inconceivably swift revolution completed every twenty-four hours. It is both the source and the limit of all motion and of all change. Beyond it lies the eternal, unchanging peace of God, to which the Christian astronomers assigned a tenth heaven, the Empyrean, "the heaven that is pure light; light intellectual full of love, love of the good full of joy, joy that transcends all sweetness," as the poet describes it.[1] The ninth heaven, which the eye cannot perceive, and which is therefore called the crystalline or transparent heaven, the poet names[2] "the royal mantle of all the swathings of the universe, which most burns and quickens in the breath and ways of God."

Every one knows that this assumption of a number of heavens is not without support in Holy Scripture. In the Old Testament (as in the original Greek of the Lord's Prayer) the "heavens" are often spoken of in the plural, and the Apostle Paul not only says that he was caught up to the *third* heaven, but evidently places the Paradise to which he was further transported, in order to hear unutterable words, beyond it.

And now that we have taken a general survey of the cosmography of the Middle Ages, let us return again to earth, and examine its place in the universe, by preference under Dante's guidance. We are told in the Apocalyptic vision of St. John that after the war which Michael and his angels waged against the Dragon, the "Old Serpent, called the Devil and Satan, which deceiveth the whole world, he was cast out into the earth, and his angels were cast

[1] *Par.* xxx. 39. [2] *Par.* xxiii. 112.

out with him" (Rev. xii. 7–10). This passage was regarded not as prophecy, but as a record of what had already taken place. Under Satan's leadership certain of the angels fell. They uplifted themselves, almost as soon as they were made, against their Creator, and being overcome in the strife were thereupon hurled down to the newly formed earth. At that time there were great continents rising above the sea in the opposite hemisphere to ours; but as Virgil tells Dante when they have arrived at the other side (the south side) of the centre of the earth,[1] "From *this direction* he fell down from heaven; and the land which erst spread itself out on this side the world, in terror of him, now made a veil of the ocean, and came up in our hemisphere; and (to flee him, I take it) the land which appears on this side [*i. e.* the Mount of Purgatory] left the space empty here and rushed up backwards."

Ever since then, earth's surface, stretching from the Pillars of Hercules round to the East Indies, has been a waste of waters as yet unsailed by any who has returned to tell the tale.

One mountain alone rises out of this sea, the highest of all on earth, so lofty indeed that it towers above all changes of our atmosphere, so that there is neither rain nor snow, storm nor lightning, on its summit; and since the first pair left it it has ne'er been trodden by the foot of man. One man, indeed, set out to explore the unknown world which lay beyond the Straits of Gibraltar. It was Ulysses, who had returned from his long wanderings, but could not be at peace in his tiny fatherland. Further and further West he sailed with his companions.[2]

[1] *Inf.* xxxiv. 121. [2] *Inf.* xxvi. 130.

"Five times was rekindled, and as often quenched the light that comes down from the moon, since we had entered on the high emprise, when there appeared to us a mountain, brown by distance, and methought it loftier than I had e'er seen one before. We were rejoiced, but soon it turned to wailing; for from that new land arose a squall and smote the foremost quarter of our vessel. Three times it made her swirl with all the waters; then at the fourth it lifted up her poop; down plunged her prow, as was the will of One, until the sea again closed over us."

On the summit of this mountain, which is heaped like a funeral barrow above Satan, lies the *Garden of Eden*, planted by God. It is watched by the angel with the fiery sword, and is guarded from men by the wide stretch of the ocean and the precipitous sides of the mountain. Here Adam was placed and Eve was shaped by God; and from hence, within a few hours of their creation, tempted to disobedience by that same serpent, they exiled themselves.

At the exact antipodes of the Garden of Eden, and in the centre, as the Middle Ages supposed, of the inhabited world, lies Jerusalem, and the hill on which the Christ bruised the head of the Old Serpent, and by his sacrificial death lifted off the curse which had spread over that hemisphere also at the fall of man.

Jerusalem lies in the middle of the *inhabited earth*, but at the Eastern limit of *Christendom*. The quadrant from Jerusalem to the Ganges is in the hands of the Heathen and Moslem. Only the Western quadrant is Christian, extending to the shores of the Atlantic, where the Apostle James, like another Hercules, erected as it were a pillar in Compostella that marks the confines alike of the Church and of the inhabited world. In the middle, again, of these Christian lands lies Rome, the burial-place of the two chief Apostles, destined from the beginning of time to be the seat of St. Peter's successors and the centre of the Church of Christ.

Jerusalem, with the crust of earth, miles in thickness, on which its walls are reared, covers and seals up a huge cavity which stretches down below it, in darkness and horror, right to the centre of the earth. Satan was hurled not merely down to the earth but deep into its bowels, even to the dead centre, the pivot of the universe, the deepest point of all, and the furthest removed from the presence and light of God. Sin and weight answer to one another. As flame, which is not subject to the law of gravitation, tends upward to its home in the heaven of fire, so the soul, when freed from sin, rises to God, its source. But as a stone is drawn downwards by its weight, so sin drags the soul weighted by it down to the Father of sin in his dark kingdom of torment and estrangement from God. This huge cavity between the crust of the earth and its centre, where Satan abides in gruesome majesty, is Hell. It is divided into numerous circles, corresponding with the sins which meet with their reward in it; but the deeper we go the deeper is the negation of light and warmth, until finally the souls of traitors, nearest of all to Satan, are frozen, with wailing and gnashing of teeth, into the ice whereto the waters of Hell are congealed. And these waters themselves are a product of sin. The tears extorted from the sinners, the blood shed by tyrants and murderers, all the filth of the sinful world, flow down below by secret conduits and are then transformed into instruments of torment.

This nether world of unrepentant sinners is closed upon them forever. Since Christ descended into Hell to preach to the spirits in prison (1 Pet. iii. 19) and to release the patriarchs, the number of spirits in Hell has indeed increased, from day to day, but not one has ever been able to free himself again from its fetters.

On the other hand, the ban which closed the gate of Eden is done away by the death of Christ; not indeed for the living, who may be pious but are not sinless, but for the Christian souls that have expired in faith and penitence. The Roman Catholic doctrine teaches, it is true, that even these still bear the stain of earthly sin; but they are permitted to wash it away by prayer and penance till at last they become worthy, like the first pair before the fall, of the Earthly Paradise. So this mount of purification, Purgatory, forms the counterpart to the funnel of Hell. The circles of Hell begin with mere defect of the true faith, and descend through the lighter sins which are still worthy of pity, to heavier and still heavier ones, ending in rebellious hatred of God. In Purgatory we pass from repentance, as yet inadequate, first through the heavier sins and then through the errors which mislead the nobler instincts, from which indeed they rise.

In the Southern hemisphere a beautiful constellation, invisible in ours, lights the souls who come thither for purification. The poet, on his arrival there, says:[1] —

"I turned me to the right hand, and heedfully I gazed upon the other pole, and saw four stars ne'er looked upon save by the primal folk. The heaven seemed to gladden in their flames. O widowed region

[1] *Purg.* i. 22.

of the North, since thou art shorn of looking upon them!"

At the beginning of the sixteenth century Amerigo Vespucci, and subsequently Andrea Corsali, enjoyed the magnificent spectacle of the Southern Cross, and ever since it has been frequently assumed (as it was by Vespucci himself) that the four stars of the Divine Comedy signify this jewel of the Southern skies. Some have imagined that Dante anticipated the knowledge of them by the spirit of prophecy, and others have supposed that Pisan or other navigators brought home from their wanderings the report of this constellation. In recent times Alexander von Humboldt, and subsequently Oscar Peschel, have thought the question worthy of special discussion. As a matter of fact there was no need to assume that Dante heard the report from otherwise unknown voyagers who had been driven as far as Cape Verde or beyond; for soon after 1290 Marco Polo had visited Java and Sumatra, whence such an observant student of the heavens could not fail to note the imposing spectacle of the Southern Cross. Now when Dante wrote the second part of his poem, Polo, who was never weary of recounting his adventures, had been back in Venice, his native city, for twenty years. It is therefore highly probable, at any rate, that in describing the four stars the poet had in mind the wonderful constellation of which he had heard. It remains unquestionable, however, that here as elsewhere he has given an allegorical meaning to actual phenomena, and in this case the symbolic meaning is the most prominent.

For the four stars are taken by him to mean what we call the four moral or cardinal virtues, — Wisdom,

Justice, Temperance, and Fortitude. In the progress of the ascent these four morning stars find their counterpart in three evening stars, which represent the three Christian or theological virtues, Faith, Hope, and Charity.[1]

The spirits on the Mount of Purgatory likewise suffer torment; but it is now penance, not punishment. And the higher we ascend the more endurable the sufferings grow. The very climbing itself, which at first is toilsome and breathless, becomes painless, nay, pleasant, as when a ship is carried down stream by a favorable breeze. The guilt washed away by penance drips down from this mountain and gnaws its way into the bowels of the earth, there to swell the volume of the waters of Hell.

At the summit of the mountain we find the Garden of Eden, depicted in glowing colors, after the scriptural account, with all manner of trees beautiful to look on, and good for food, with the breath of morning whispering among their branches and birds plying their art in varying melody. But it is not rain nor dew that fosters the growth of the trees and flowers of this garden. The moist exhalations of earth and the dews which they deposit, the fury of storm and thunder, all these bear the character of change, for which there is no room in Paradise. Streams of living water springing up in Eden irrigate the garden. And as the breeze, following the motion of heaven, passes from east to west through the tree-tops and strikes the shrubs and grasses, it bears away their seeds, and strews them here and there over the face of the earth.[2]

[1] *Purg.* viii. 89.

[2] *Purg.* xxviii. 109.

The smitten plant hath power to impregnate the breeze with its virtue, and the breeze as it circles scatters it around. And the rest of the earth, according as itself and its heaven make it worthy, conceives and bears diverse growths of diverse virtues. Henceforth it should not seem a wonder, this being heard, should any plant take root there without visible seed."

My respected hearers will perceive how the poet seems in these lines to have a premonition of the microscopic fungus spore, pollen, and infusorial germs, which play so prominent a part in the natural science of our day.

Where then in this garden, with its beautiful trees full of pleasant fruits, is man, for whom God planted it all? We have seen how Christ has reopened it to the spirits of the redeemed purified by penance; but their dwelling-place is no longer on earth, — no, not even in the Earthly Paradise. They have lost their sins, and with them their material weight; and were they now to cling to earth, it would be as strange as if a living flame, instead of rising upwards, were to creep along the ground.[1] The sinless souls are not retained even by the joys of the Earthly Paradise, but rise upwards to Heaven.

But Heaven, too, is an organized whole, with degrees and distinctions, according to the particular qualities for which each spirit was conspicuous. The seven grades of the punishment of Hell,[2] and the seven terraces of the Mount of Purgatory, find their counterpart here in the spheres of the seven planets. A

[1] *Par.* i. 139.

[2] Not reckoning the Virtuous Heathen and the Heretics, who stand in a sense outside the sevenfold ethical division of Hell and raise the total number of circles to nine.

separate company of the blessed is assigned to each; those who vowed themselves to God are in the chaste moon; in Mercury are those who strove after intellectual perfection; in Venus, those who were inflamed with heavenly love; in the sun, the source of all light, the theologians who sank deep into the light of God; in Mars, those who fought for Christ; in Jupiter, the source of all justice according to the Ancients, the righteous rulers; and finally, the holy hermits in Saturn, who pursues his slow course far removed from the other planets.

The Greek astronomers had handed down the belief that since the sun was far larger than the earth, the shadow cast in space by the latter would taper to a point, and they calculated that it would just reach to the sphere of Venus. Beyond Venus there is nothing but the pure light of heaven, but the memories and lighter blemishes of earth extend up to her orb. We spoke just now of errors, which, sinful though they are, yet bear witness to nobility of soul. In the same way virtues, even while pleasing to God, may have some earthly alloy. The moon is the symbol of chastity, but she is not spotless, and her inconstancy reveals itself in ceaseless change. So, too, the bride of Christ, instead of staking all on the preservation of her vow, may yield to external pressure. Yet if her will has but remained faithful, her weakness will not be imputed to her, and she will yet attain to bliss. The scholars, orators, and poets to whom Mercury is assigned are not free from the thirst for personal renown; and, again, spiritual love may be twin sister to her earthly counterpart. Thus these three planets represent lower degrees of blessedness, but all Heaven is

Paradise, and the spirits in these spheres do not feel themselves less blessed because of their lower place. One of them answers the poet's question on this very point:[1]—

"Brother, the virtue of love quiets our will, for it makes us wish only for that we have, and feel no other thirst. Did we desire to be more aloft, our longings were at discord with His will who decrees we should be here. . . . So that the way we rank from threshold to threshold through the realm, pleases all the realm even as its king, who draws our wills in his. And his will is our peace; it is that sea to which all moves that it creates or that nature makes."

The harmonies which strike the poet's ear as soon as he has passed the sphere of fire do not arise, then, as Cicero once made his Scipio dream, from the rush of the planets through the ringing ether, but from the songs of praise raised by the blessed spirits, differing in the different heavens according to their gifts.

But while the planets are peopled now with blessed spirits, this could not have been so, according to the Church, either in heathen times or under the Old Covenant. Were they then nothing before the redemption but soulless balls of fire? For the Christian poet could not offer his tribute of praise to the silent majesty with which Helios guided his golden chariot; and neither have I, let me confess it, ever been able to feel the lofty poetry which our own Schiller finds in the thought of a driver following the same road day in, day out, for one millennium after another, even though he had a golden chariot!

In the conception of the Middle Ages, however, the

[1] *Par.* iii. 70.

stars were anything but soulless balls of fire. Aristotle himself had said that where motion was there must life be also, for only death is motionless. The most perfect form of movement, in that it is capable of endless continuance, is the circular motion exemplified in the movement of the heavens. Now the starry or highest heaven, by whose movement that of all the others is conditioned, is moved by a supernal Being proceeding from God, an Intelligence. Elsewhere Aristotle adopts the popular idea which named the planets after the gods and assumed other beings, besides this supreme Intelligence, who ruled the special motions of the planets. The Neoplatonists, followed by the Arabians, expanded these suggestions, until finally the Schoolmen of the thirteenth century worked them up into such a form as fitted them to become an organic part of the Christian conception of Heaven.

The "Intelligences" became "Angels," whose various hierarchies ruled the nine revolving heavens. The motions of these heavens are, as already indicated, manifold, but each movement is guided by one or more angels. The presiding spirits of the planets, however, perform their functions in a fashion widely differing from that attributed in heathen times to the deities from whom the planets took their names. Helios, in his golden chariot, turned his gaze earthwards, now on Clymene, on Daphne, or some other nymph, now on the wide-browed cattle of his friend Admetus. The moon-goddess Diana let her eye rest on the fair sleeper Endymion, while the warm-blooded Venus now looked in the Firmament on Mars or Mercury, and now smiled on Adonis, or descended to the groves of Ida, where the longing Anchises awaited her.

But in the system of the mediæval Church the eyes of those who rule the stars are ever directed upwards. The whole being of the legions of angels consists in losing themselves in God. The task of each one is to apprehend God's essence in his own special way, under the special aspect and in the special direction indicated individually to him. It is because of this apprehension that they bear the name of *Intelligences.* Here, as usual, the Schoolmen overrefine, and are overconfident in exhaustively apportioning the different aspects under which God is contemplated by the hierarchies and choirs of angels, as elaborated by the inventive faculty of the ancient Church from the faint suggestions of Scripture.

Next to the Empyrean, which embraces the whole of creation and is itself the very fullness of God, comes, as we saw above, the transparent crystalline heaven invisible to the eye. It is the heaven of the Seraphim, who see deepest of all the angels into the secrets of the Creator. And each of the constituent parts of this heaven, each indwelling seraph, has such yearning toward each point of the Empyrean, in other words, such longing to comprehend the whole being of God, that this heaven revolves ceaselessly under the canopy of the highest with a speed unapproached by any other, completing its revolution in four-and-twenty hours, and sweeping all the lower heavens with it. And it is this same thirst to apprehend which causes the motion of all the spheres. Wherefore it is said in the schools: "By *apprehending* the Intelligences move the Heavens and the Planets."

But while the eyes of the guiding spirits of the Heavens are directed upward, the power of their knowledge radiates all around them, and into the lower spheres. Hence the often-recurring image by which they are spoken of as Mirrors of God. The poet says in one place:[1]—

"He whose wisdom transcendeth all, made the heavens, and so gave them guides that every part glows upon every part with even distribution of its light."

And elsewhere:[2]—

"The primal light which over-rays it all (*i. e.* the angelic nature) is received thereby in as many ways as are in number the splendors to which it is revealed. Wherefore, since affection conforms to the act of apprehension, the sweetness of love boils or is tepid in them diversely. Behold now the height and breadth of the Eternal Worth, since it hath made itself so many mirrors wherein it breaks itself, remaining in itself one as before."

This conception of the heavenly bodies, each receiving from above and radiating and attracting below, is no other than a spiritual version of Newton's law of gravitation, on which the equilibrium and movement of the heavenly bodies depend.[3] "These orders all gaze upwards, and so work victoriously downwards that all are drawn and all do draw towards God."

But this conception and reflection of theirs is not confined to spiritually apprehending and illuminating. Inseparably united with it, and with the revolution of the heavens which it causes, is the radiation of divine powers and influences even down to our earth. Birth, growth, and decay follow one another on earth in accordance with eternal laws. The elements combine into

[1] *Inf.* vii. 73. [2] *Par.* xxix. 136. [3] *Par.* xxviii. 127.

all the manifold forms of the three realms of Nature. But the degree of perfection with which each individual creature comes into existence and develops itself depends upon the heavenly influences. While even the most favorable constellations are powerless to give a higher form to bad material and unfit seed, yet even noble seed comes to naught under adverse stars. The manifold combinations brought about by the endless motions of the heavenly spheres and the bodies they support are the essential condition of an organized and organic life; for uniformity in the individuals would preclude it. Like these changing influences of the stars, which defy all human interference, are the workings of Fortune, whose wheel may be likened to the circles in which the planets roll.[1]

"In like manner hath he ordained to earthly splendors a general administrix and guide, in due time to interchange fallacious blessings from folk to folk, from one class to another, beyond resistance of the wit of man. Wherefore one folk hath sway, another languisheth, after her judgment who doth lie concealed like to a serpent in the grass. . . . This is she who is so crucified just by the ones who ought to give her praise, but give her wrongfully their blame and ill report. But she is blessed and heareth not this, exultant with the other primal creatures doth she roll her sphere, and, blessed, doth rejoice."

Now all these combinations of the elements under the influences of the stars, these "contingencies," as the Schoolmen called them, were intended and *foreseen* by God; but it is only indirectly that they *proceed* from him. The only thing that, in the progress of creation,

[1] *Inf.* vii. 77.

daily and hourly proceeds immediately from God, is the Soul which he breathes into every single child before its birth. This is why all "contingencies" are destined to be resolved and to fall to pieces. They are given over to change, decay, and destruction. But the human soul, which emanates from God himself, is immortal and eternal. On the journey through the planets the poet's guide says to him:[1] —

"The Good which moves and satisfies all the realm thou art climbing, frames its providence into a virtuous power in these great bodies; and not only are created things provided for in the mind that in itself is perfect, but they together with their means of safety. Wherefore whatsoe'er this bow doth shoot, lights as disposed to a provided end, even as a thing directed to its mark. Were this not so, the heaven thou art traversing would produce such effects as make not works of art but ruins. . . . The circling nature which is seal to the mortal wax, plies its art well, but maketh no distinction betwixt one abode and other. Wherefore it comes that Esau parts from Jacob in the seed; and from so base a father is Quirinus born he is assigned to Mars. The begotten nature would ever make its path like to its generators, did not divine provision overrule."

And in like manner he says elsewhere:[2] —

"Seldom does human goodness mount up through the branches; and this He wills who gives it, that from Him it may be asked for."

Are we then to believe in astrological fatalism? Are the nature, the virtues, and the vices of each in-

[1] *Par.* viii. 97–108, and 127–135.
[2] *Purg.* vii. 121.

dividual and his lot in life unconditionally fixed by the stars under whose influence he came into the world? Do the consequences of our decisions and our actions depend on the positions of the planets?

This belief was widely held during the Middle Ages, and my hearers will remember how long it maintained itself, — so long, indeed, that it has many echoes even in our modern forms of speech. Dante most emphatically contradicts it:[1] —

"Ye mortals refer all causes to the Heaven, as though it swept all with it of necessity. If it were so, free choice in you would not exist, and there would be no justice in your reaping joy for good and misery for evil. The Heaven does give rise to impulses within you, — I say not all of them, but if I did say all, yet light is given you for goodness and for wickedness, and free will, which, if it endure the toil in its first conflicts with the Heaven, then if it be well nurtured conquers all. To Greater Power and to Better Nature ye lie in free subjection, and that it is which doth create in you the mind o'er which the Heaven hath not charge. Wherefore if the present world goes off the track, in you lieth the cause; in you it must be sought."

We have seen the Intelligences moving the nine heavens and thereby bringing their influence to bear on the destinies of earth. Are they then confined each to his special heaven as an actual dwelling-place? — We must answer this question in the negative. Each angel enjoys, in the Empyrean, the immediate presence and sight of God, and it is only the forces radiating from him and from his apprehension of God

[1] *Purg.* xvi. 67.

which are reflected in the stars. Nor is it otherwise with the souls of the blessed. The Heaven of highest light is the true home of all; all are permitted to gaze on the face of God, only the measure of sight is determined by their capacity and deserts, and the Heaven to which they are, so to speak, outwardly assigned,[1] is a symbol of this measure.

And thus, spiritually and ultimately, the whole of this cosmography comes to be, as it were, reversed. We have been depicting the whole God-filled heaven, wherein is his city and his lofty throne, as the outermost, embracing all the others. But again, God is the sole kernel of the universe, round which the whole creation must revolve in a widening series of circles. God, says one of the Schoolmen, is indeed a circle; but a circle whose centre is everywhere and its bounding circumference nowhere. Thus, if we picture the heaven of God as stretching beyond all conceivable extension, yet may God equally be conceived as the absolutely indivisible unit, the mathematical point which occupies no space at all. The poet depicts this inverted conception, if we may so call it, thus:[2]—

"A point I saw that rayed out light so keen that the sight on which it blazed must needs close itself against its piercing power. And whichever star seems smallest seen from here, had seemed a moon compared with it, as star compares with star. Perchance so close as Halo seems to gird the light that paints her when the sustaining moisture is most dense, e'en at such distance round the point a fire-circle whirled so rapidly it

[1] And apparently assigned only on the special occasion when they come to meet Dante and his guide, *Par.* iv. 28 *seq.*

[2] *Par.* xxviii. 16.

had surpassed that motion which most swiftest girds the universe; and this was by another girt around, that by a third, the third too by a fourth, by a fifth the fourth, then by a sixth the fifth. Above followed the seventh, already spread so wide that Juno's messenger, complete, had been too strait to hold it. And so the eighth and ninth; and each one moved more slow according as in number 't was more distant from the unit: and that one had its flame most clear from which the pure spark was least distant; I believe because it plunged the deepest in the truth thereof."

Thus we have followed the poet in his ascent, and have, I hope, returned unharmed to the point whence we started, I mean to your own well-grounded conception of the construction of the universe. For our last vision has been not alien from the teaching of Copernicus — a vision, not indeed of the planets themselves, but of the Spirits that move them, circling around the sun, only in the place of the physical Sun the poet has placed "the Sun of the angels," God.

IV

THE CHRONOLOGY OF THE DIVINA COMMEDIA

I. THE INFERNO.[1]

THE chronology of the Divine Comedy has been discussed still more elaborately than the topography and the division of sins; and all that this note attempts is to set forth in plain terms the view which approves itself to the writer. References are given to the passages which support the statements made; but there is no attempt to defend the interpretation adopted against other views.

The year of the Vision is 1300, Inf. i. 1; xxi. 112–114; Purg. ii. 98, 99; Parad. ix. 40. The sun is exactly in the equinoctial point at spring, the change of his position during the action of the poem being ignored, Inf. i. 38–40; Parad. x. 7–33; and less precisely Parad. i. 37–44. The night on which Dante loses himself in the forest is the night preceding the anniversary of the death of Christ, Inf. xxi. 112–114. At some period during that night the moon is at the full, Inf. xx. 127; and (as will presently appear) a comparison of Inf. xx. 124–126 with xxi. 112–114, together with a reference to Purg. ix. 1–9, indicates that

[1] *The Inferno*, Temple Classics, J. M. Dent & Co. Written by P. H. Wicksteed. (By permission.) For full discussion *vide* Dr. Edward Moore's *Time References in the Divina Commedia*.

the precise moment of full moou coincided with the sunrise at the end of the night in question. We have then the following data: the sun is in the equinox, the moon is at the full; and it is the night preceding the anniversary of the crucifixion.

There is no day in the year 1300 which meets all these conditions. We are therefore in the presence of an ideal date, combiniug all the phenomena which we are accustomed to associate with Easter, but not corresponding to any actual day in the calendar. All discussions as to whether we are to call the day that Dante spent in the attempt to climb the mountain the 25th March or the 8th April (both of which, in the year 1300, were Fridays) are therefore otiose.

The sun is rising, on Friday morning, when Dante begins his attempt to scale the mountain, Inf. i. 37–40; it is Friday evening when he starts with Virgil on his journey, ii. 1–3; all the stars which were mounting as the poets entered the gate of Hell are descending as they pass from the 4th to the 5th circle, vii. 98, 99; that is to say, it is midnight between Friday and Saturday. As they descend from the 6th to the 7th circle the constellation of Pisces (which at the spring equinox immediately precedes the sun) is on the horizon, xi. 113; that is to say, it is somewhere between 4 and 6 A. M. on the Saturday morning. They are on the centre of the bridge over the 4th bolgia of the 8th circle as the moon sets (Jerusalem time), xx. 124–126. Now according to the rule given by Brunetto Latini, we are to allow fifty-two minutes' retardation for the moon in every twenty-four hours; that is to say, if the moon sets at sunrise one day, she will set fifty-two minutes after sunrise the

PIANTA DELL' INFERNO

E ITINERARIO DI DANTE

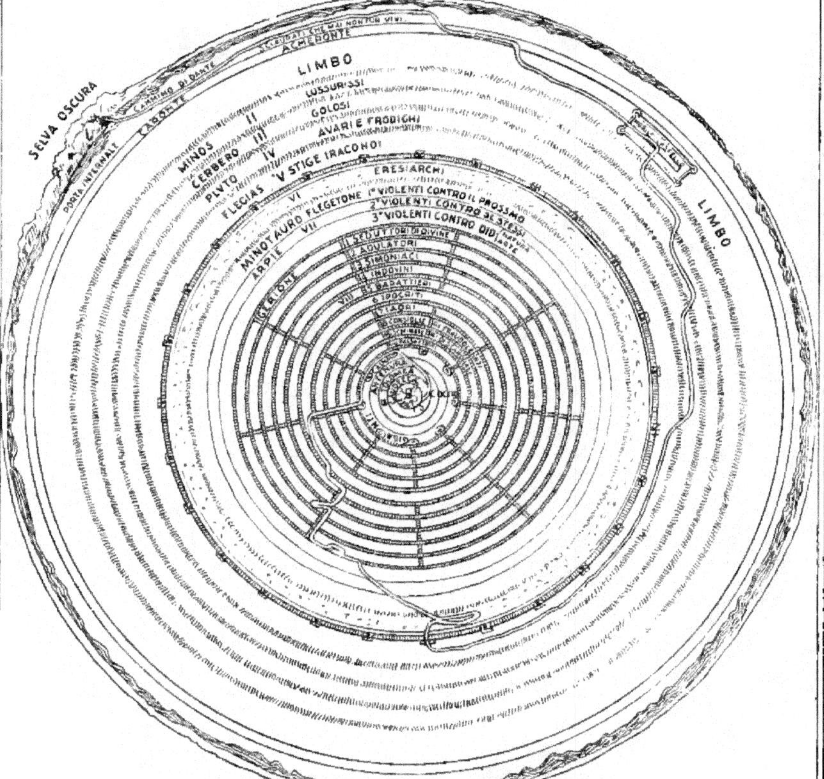

From "La materia della Divina Commedia di Dante Alighieri dichiarata in vi tavole. Dal Duca Michelangelo Caetani di Sermoneta."

next. If then (see above) we suppose the moon to have been full at the moment of sunrise on Friday morning, we shall have six o'clock on Friday morning and 6.52 on Saturday morning for moonset. This will give us eight minutes to seven as the moment at which the two poets stood on the middle of the bridge over the 4th bolgia. The next eight minutes are crowded; so crowded, indeed, as to constitute a serious difficulty in the system of interpretation here adopted, for the poets are already in conference with the demons on the inner side of bolgia 5 by seven o'clock, xxi. 112–114 (compared with Conv. iv. 23, 103–107). In mitigation of the difficulty, however, it may be noted that the 5th bolgia, like some at least of the others, appears to be very narrow, xxii. 145–150. The moon is under their feet as they stand over the middle of the 9th bolgia, xxix. 10, which, allowing for the further retardation of the moon, will give the time as a little past one o'clock on Saturday afternoon. They have come close to Satan at nightfall, six o'clock on Saturday evening, xxxiv. 68, 69; and they spend an hour and a half first in clambering down Satan's sides, to the dead centre of the universe, then turning round and clambering up again toward the antipodes of Jerusalem.

It is therefore 7.30 in the morning in the hemisphere under which they now are (7.30 in the evening in the hemisphere which they have left), when they begin their ascent of the tunnel that leads from the central regions to the foot of Mount Purgatory, xxxiv. 96. This ascent occupies them till nearly dawn of the next day. The period of this ascent therefore corresponds to the greater part of the night between

Saturday and Sunday and of the day of Easter Sunday by Jerusalem time. By Purgatory time it is day and night, not night and day. It is simplest to regard the period as Easter Sunday and Sunday night;

TABLE I.

Reproduced by kind permission from The Time References in the Divina Commedia, by Rev. Edward Moore, D. D.

		SELVA OSCURA.	Th.	All night.	i. 21.
		TRE FIERE, &c.	Fr.	All day.	i. 37, &c.
CIRCLE	I.		"	Nightfall.	ii. 1.
"	II.				
"	III.				
"	IV.		"	Midnight.	vii. 98.
"	V.				
"	VI.		Sat.	4 A. M.	xi. 113.
"	VII.	1 GIRONE.			
		2 "			
		3 "			
"	VIII.	1 BOLGIA.			
		2 "			
		3 "			
		4 "	"	6 A. M.	xx. 125.
		5 "	"	7 A. M.	xxi. 112.
		6 "			
		7 "			
		8 "			
		9 "	"	1 P. M.	xxix. 10.
		10 "			
"	IX.	CAINA.			
		ANTENORA.			
		TOLOMEA.			
		GIUDECCA.	"	7.30 P. M.	xxxiv. 96.

but some prefer to regard it as Saturday (over again) and Saturday night.[1] It depends on whether we regard the Sunday, or other day, as beginning with sunrise at Purgatory and going all round the world with the sun till he rises in Purgatory again; or as run-

[1] This is the reckoning reproduced in Table II., p. 258.

ning in like manner from sunrise to sunrise at Jerusalem, rather than Purgatory. In the former case it will be found that after spending three days and three nights on the Mount of Purgatory and six hours in the Earthly Paradise, Dante rises to Heaven at midday on Thursday, and goes round the world with Thursday till he is about over Italy as the sun sets in Jerusalem, Parad. xxvii. 79–87, on Thursday evening. If the other view be taken we shall say that it is noonday on Wednesday (not Thursday) when Dante rises to Heaven, and that he goes round with Wednesday till he is over the meridian of Jerusalem, when the day changes to Thursday.

In any case the action of the Divine Comedy lasts just a week, and ends on the Thursday evening.

II. THE PURGATORIO.[1]

It is near sunrise when the poets issue at the eastern base of the Mount of Purgatory (i. 19–21), and close upon sunrise, 6 A. M., as they leave Cato (i. 107–117). The stars in mid heaven have disappeared when the souls are discharged from the angel's boat (ii. 55–57), though shadows are not yet distinctly visible, since the souls recognize Dante as a living man only by his breathing (ii. 67, 68). The sun is up and the hour of vespers, 3 P. M., has already arrived in Italy, as the poets turn westward again toward the mountain (iii. 16–26). The conversation with Manfred is over about 9.20 A. M. (iv. 15). It is noonday when Dante has finished his conversation with Belacqua (iv. 137–139); that is to say, the sun

[1] *The Purgatorio*, Temple Classics, J. M. Dent & Co. Written by P. H. Wicksteed. (By permission.)

is in the north; and since the poets are almost on the due east portion of the mountain, it is not long ere the sun disappears behind the hill (vi. 51). So Dante

Table II.

From Dr. Moore's Time References in the Divina Commedia. (By permission.)

EASTER-DAY, APRIL 10.	ANTE-PURGATORY.	1. 19-21	c. 4 A. M.
		107-115	c. 5 A. M.
		2. 1	c. 5.15 A. M., sunrise.
		55-7	6 A. M.
		3. 16, 25	6 to 6.30 A. M.
		4. 15	c. 9 A. M.
		138	Noon.
		7. 43	Day declining.
		85	"Poco sole."
		8. 1	Just after sunset.
		49	c. 7.30 P. M.
		9. 1-9	c. 8.45 P. M.
MONDAY, 11.	PURGATORY.	13, 52	Before dawn.
		44	c. 7.30 A. M.
	CORNICE I.	10. 14	c. 8.30 A. M.
		12. 81	c. Noon.
	" II.	15. 1	3 P. M.
	" III.	141	c. 6 P. M.
		17. 9-12	c. 6.30 P. M.
	" IV.	62, 72	Twilight.
		18. 76	Towards midnight.
TUESDAY, 12.	" V.	19. 1-6	c. 4.30 A. M.
		37	Full daylight.
	" VI.	22. 118	11 A. M.
		25. 1-3	c. 2 P. M.
	" VII.	26. 4-6	c. 4 or 5 P. M.
		27. 1-5	c. 6 P. M.
		61	Sunset.
		70	Twilight.
		89	Starlight.
WEDNESDAY, 13.	EARTHLY PARADISE.	94	Before dawn.
		109, &c.	Sunrise.
		133	Sun fully up.
		33. 103	Noon.

casts no shadow, and is not recognized as a living man by Sordello, with whom Virgil converses till day is declining (vii. 43). At sunset the souls in the valley of the kings sing their evening hymn (viii. 1–18); very soon after which the poets descend (descent being possible after sunset, though they could not have ascended, cf. vii. 58, 59) into the valley, as twilight deepens (viii. 43–51). Taking the moment of full moon to have been at sunrise on the Friday morning, it is now 3x24 hours since full moon, and the retardation of the moon is therefore 3x52 minutes = 2 hours 36 minutes; and the moon, therefore, has passed through the Scales and is 36 minutes deep in Scorpion. The first stars of Scorpion, then, and the glow of the lunar aurora are on the horizon, and it is just over 8.30 P. M. on what (with the reservations indicated in the chronological note on the Inferno) we may call Monday evening,[1] when Dante falls asleep (ix. 1–12). Before dawn on the next morning Dante has a vision of the eagle, and is in point of fact carried up by Lucia near to the gate of Purgatory (ix. 13–63), where he awakes at about 8 A. M. (ix. 44). The retardation of the moon is now three hours and two minutes, and when they issue upon the first terrace she has already set (x. 13–16). It is therefore about 9 A. M. About 12 o'clock noon they reach the stair to the second circle (xii. 80, 81). When the poets pass from the second to the third terrace they are walking westward and have therefore reached the northern quarter of the mount, and it is 3 o'clock in the afternoon (xv. 1–9); and their direction has not sensibly changed when they meet the wrathful (xv. 139). The sun has already set at the base of the mountain (xvii. 12) when the final visions of the circle of the wrathful come upon Dante, and he sets to the poets, high up on the mountain, just as they have completed the ascent of the stair to the fourth circle

[1] Sunday according to Table II.

(xvii. 70–75). By comparing these data, it will be seen that the poets traverse portions of the first three circles, constituting all together a quadrant or a little more, during the day. They start on the eastern side of the mountain, and end at the north, or a little west of it, and have spent about three hours in each circle. About three hours more are occupied by Virgil's discourse, which ends towards midnight, when the moon, which rose at 9.28, a good way south of east, now first appears due east, or a trifle north of due east, from behind the mountain (xviii. 76–81). Before dawn (xix. 1–6) on what we may call Wednesday,[1] Dante has his vision of the Siren, and it is full daylight when he wakes. They still travel due, or nearly due, west, with the newly risen sun at their backs (xix. 37–39). They swiftly pass the fourth circle and reach the fifth, in which they stay so long that it is after ten when they reach the sixth circle (xxii. 115–120). Though they are now well to the west of the mountain, the sun has traveled with them, so that Dante casts a shadow (xxiii. 114). Indeed it is after 2 o'clock when they reach the stair which leads to the seventh circle (xxv. 1–3), so that by this time shadows are visible on the mountain from near the northeast to near the southwest of its surface. As Dante converses with the shades on the seventh terrace the sun is almost due west; the poet is walking nearly due south, the sun on the right and the flame glowing redder under his shadow at the left (xxvi. 1–9). And the position is not perceptibly changed when the angel of the circle appears to them as the sun sets at the base of the mountain (xxvii.

[1] Tuesday in Table II.

1–6); nor have they mounted many stairs after passing through the flame, before the sun, exactly behind them, sets on the higher regions of the mount where they now are (xxvii. 61–69). Before sunrise (xxvii. 94–96) on the day we may call Thursday,[1] Dante sees Leah in his vision, and wakes at dawn of day (xxvii. 109–114). The sun shines full upon their faces as they enter the Earthly Paradise from the western point, facing east (xxvii. 133); and it is noonday (xxxiii. 103–105) as they reach the source of Lethe and Eunoë.

In the Paradiso we have passed from time to eternity, yet Dante intends us to understand from one or two hints which he gives (Par. xxii. 124–154, xxvii. 82–87) that time is still passing on earth, and that when he returned to it, he found it to be the evening of Thursday, April 14th.

[1] Wednesday.

V

DANTE'S STATEMENT OF THE MEANING OF THE POEM

Letter to Can Grande.[1]

To the magnificent and victorious lord, the Lord Can Grande della Scala, Vicar General of the Most Holy Roman Empire in the city of Verona and the town of Vicenza, his most devoted Dante Alighieri, a Florentine by birth, but not by character, desires a life happy throughout the duration of many years, and a perpetual augmentation of his glorious name.

1. The glorious renown of your magnificence, which Fame proclaimeth abroad on never resting wing,[2] leadeth different men to such opposite conclusions, that it emboldeneth some to hope for good fortune and driveth others to fear for their very existence.[3] Indeed, I once thought such a renown, too lofty for modern deeds, somewhat beyond the truth and

[1] *Dante's Eleven Letters*, translated by Chas. S. Latham. Houghton, Mifflin & Co. The notes also are Mr. Latham's. The authenticity of this letter is disputed by some, bnt is generally accepted. (Used by permission.)

[2] Interea pavidam volitans pennata per urbem
Nuncia Fama ruit.
(*Æneid*, ix. 473, 4.)

[3] On him rely, and on his benefits;
By him shall many people be transformed,
Changing condition rich and mendicant.
(*Paradiso*, xvii. 88–90.)

excessive. But that a long uncertainty might not keep me in too great suspense, as the Queen of the East sought Jerusalem,[1] as Pallas sought Helicon, so sought I Verona to examine with faithful eyes the things that I had heard. And there I beheld your splendor; and likewise I beheld and enjoyed your bounty. And even as at first I had suspected an excess in the reports, so afterward I recognized that the excess was in the deeds themselves. And thus it came to pass, that as before from hearsay alone I had been, with a certain subjugation of spirit, your well-wisher, so on first seeing you I became both your most devoted servant and your friend.

2. Nor do I think I shall incur the imputation of presumption in assuming the name of friend, as some perchance might object, since those of unequal rank are united by the sacred bond of friendship no less than equals. For if one chooseth to glance at pleasant and profitable friendships, very frequently it will be evident to him that persons of preëminence have been united with their inferiors; and if his glance is turned to true friendship — friendship for its own sake — will it not be acknowledged that many a time men obscure in fortune but distinguished in virtue have been the friends of illustrious and most great princes? And why not? Since even the friendship of God and man is in no way hindered by disparity? But if this assertion should seem unbecoming to any one, let him hearken to the Holy Ghost, who doth avow that certain men have been made participators in his friendship; for in the Book of Wisdom in regard to wisdom it is written: "For she is a treasure unto men

[1] 1 Kings x.; 2 Chron. ix.

that never faileth; which they that use become partakers of the friendship of God."[1] But the ignorance of the herd formeth judgments without discretion;[2] and even as it thinketh the sun is a foot in magnitude, so in regard to the one thing and the other it is deceived by its credulity.[3] But to those to whom it is given to know the best that is in us, it is not befitting to follow in the steps of the vulgar: nay, rather, they are bound to oppose their errors; for as they are vigorous in reason and intellect and endowed with a certain divine freedom, they are held in check by no custom. Nor is this to be marveled at, since they are not guided by the laws, but the laws by them. It is clear therefore that what I said above — that I am your most devoted servant and friend — is in no wise presumptuous.

3. Accordingly, preferring your friendship to all things, I wish to guard it like a most precious treasure with earnest forethought and studied care. And thus, since it is taught in the dogmas of moral philosophy[4]

[1] Wisdom, vii. 14.

[2] Cf. *Convito*, i. 11; iv. 8: "The most beautiful branch that springs from the root of reason is discernment."

[3] Cf. *Convito*, iv. 8: "For we know that to most people the sun appears to be a foot in diameter."

[4] Aristotle, *Ethics*, ix. 1, *in init.* See also *Convito*, iii. 1: "As there can be no friendship between those who are dissimilar, where we see friendship there must be likeness. . . . Whence we must know that (as the Philosopher says in the Ninth of the *Ethics*), in the friendship of persons of unequal station, some mutual relation is necessary for its preservation which should reduce that dissimilarity as much as possible, as in the case of master and servant. For although the servant cannot render to his master such benefits as he receives from him, he ought, nevertheless, to return the best he can by such solicitude and promptness, that that which is unlike in itself becomes like by the demonstrations of good-will, which show friendship, and confirm and preserve it."

that friendship becometh equal and is preserved by some proportion, it is my sacred duty to preserve the proportion in return for the benefits conferred upon me. And on this account time and time again I have carefully looked over the little things that I could give you, and separated and examined them each by each, seeking the most worthy and pleasing for you. Nor did I find anything more suitable even for your preëminence than the sublime Canticle of the Comedy which is graced with the title of "Paradise;" and that with the present letter, as dedicated with a proper inscription, I inscribe, offer, and, in fine, commend to you.

4. In like manner my ardent affection will not permit me to pass over simply in silence, that in this gift more honor and fame may seem to be conferred upon my Lord than upon the gift;[1] of a truth even in its title I have seemed, to those who have given the matter sufficient attention, to express a presage of the increasing glory of your name; and this is of design. But new to your favor, for which I thirst, and considering my life of small account, I will press forward to my proposed goal. Therefore, since I have completed the epistolary formula, I will attempt briefly, after the manner of a commentator,[2] to say something as an introduction to the work offered.

5. In the Second of the Metaphysics[3] the Philosopher spoke thus: "A thing hath a relation to truth according to the relation it hath to existence,"

[1] *Convito*, i. 8: "Therefore, for a change in things to be praiseworthy, it must always be for the better, because it ought to be superlatively praiseworthy; and this the gift cannot be, unless it becomes more precious by its transfer; and it cannot become more precious unless it be more useful to the receiver than to the giver."

[2] [See Giuliani, *Le opere latine di Dante Alighieri*, ii. 184.]

[3] A careful reading of the Second of the *Metaphysics* does not reveal this passage.

the meaning of which is this: that the truth of a thing, which subsisteth in truth as in its subject, is the perfect likeness of the thing as it is. Indeed, of those things that exist certain are of such a kind that they have their being absolute in themselves; certain others are so made that they have their being dependent on something else in a certain relation, as existing at the same time and being connected with something else; just as father and son, master and servant, double and half, whole and part, and things of a like sort, inasmuch as they are such, are related. And inasmuch as their existence is dependent on something else, it doth follow as a consequence that their truth will be dependent on something else; for if the half is unknown, the double is never known; and thus in regard to the others.

6. To those, then, who wish to give any introduction to a part of any work whatsoever, it is necessary to give some conception of the whole of which it is a part. Therefore, I also, wishing to write something in the manner of an introduction of the part of the comedy above named, thought something ought to be said first in regard to the whole work, in order that there might be an easier and more perfect entrance to the part. Six, therefore, are the things that are to be sought at the beginning of every doctrinal work; that is to say, *the subject*, *the agent*, *the form*, *the aim*, *the title of the book*, *and the kind of philosophy*. Of these there are three in which the part, which I have purposed to dedicate to you, differs from the whole: namely, *the subject*, *the form*, *and the title;* but in the others there is no diversity, as will be evident to whosoever examineth them. Therefore, for a consid-

eration of the whole, these three things must be examined separately; and when this hath been done, enough will be shown for an introduction to the part. Then we will examine the other three, not only in respect to the whole, but also in respect to that part which I offer you.

7. For the clearness, therefore, of what I shall say, it must be understood that the meaning of this work is not simple, but rather can be said to be of many significations, that is, of several meanings; for there is one meaning that is derived from the letter, and another that is derived from the things indicated by the letter. The first is called *literal*, but the second *allegorical* or *mystical*. That this method of expounding may be more clearly set forth, we can consider it in these lines: "When Israel went out of Egypt, the house of Jacob from a people of strange language; Judah was his sanctuary and Israel his dominion." For if we consider the *letter* alone, the departure of the children of Israel from Egypt in the time of Moses is signified; if the *allegory*, our redemption accomplished in Christ is signified; if the *moral meaning*, the conversion of the soul from the sorrow and misery of sin to a state of grace is signified; if the *anagogical*, the departure of the sanctified soul from the slavery of this corruption to the liberty of everlasting glory is signified. And although these mystical meanings are called by various names, they can in general all be said to be allegorical, since they differ from the literal or historic; for the word *Allegoria* is derived from the Greek ἀλλοῖος, which in Latin is *alienum* or *diversum*.[1]

[1] Cf. *Convito*, ii. 1: "I say that, as has been stated in the first

8. Now that these things have been explained, it is evident that the subject around which the alternate meanings revolve must be double.[1] And therefore the subject of this work must be understood as taken ac-

chapter, this explanation should be both literal and allegorical. And to understand this, we should know that books can be understood, and ought to be explained, in four principal senses. One is called *literal*, and this it is which goes no further than the letter, such as the simple narration of the thing of which you treat. . . .

"The second is called *allegorical*, and this is the meaning hidden under the cloak of fables, and is a truth concealed beneath a fair fiction; as when Ovid says that Orpheus with his lute tamed wild beasts, and moved trees and rocks; which means that the wise man, with the instrument of his voice, softens and humbles cruel hearts, and moves at his will those who live neither for science nor for art, and those who, having no rational life whatever, are almost like stones. . . . The theologians, however, take this meaning differently from the poets; but because I intend to follow here the method of the poets, I shall take the allegorical meaning according to their usage.

"The third sense is called *moral;* and this readers should carefully gather from all writings, for the benefit of themselves and their descendants; it is such as we may gather from the Gospel, when Christ went up into the mountain to be transfigured, and of the twelve apostles took with Him but three; which in the moral sense may be understood thus, that in most secret things we should have few companions.

"The fourth sense is called *anagogical* [or mystical], that is, beyond sense; and this is when a book is spiritually expounded, which, although [a narration] in its literal sense, by the things signified refers to the supernal things of the eternal glory; as we may see in that psalm of the Prophet, where he says that when Israel went out of Egypt Judæa became holy and free. Which, although manifestly true according to the letter, is nevertheless true also in its spiritual meaning, — that the soul, in forsaking its sins, becomes holy and free in its powers."

Compare also the *Summa Theologica* of St. Thomas Aquinas, Ques. i. art. x.

[1] Cf. *Convito*, ii. 1: "In everything, natural or artificial, it is impossible to have *form* without a previous preparation of the subject which should take that form; as it is impossible to have the form *gold*, unless the matter, that is, the subject, be not first prepared and made ready."

cording to the letter, and then as interpreted according to the allegorical meaning. The subject, then, of the whole work, taken according to the letter alone, is simply a consideration of the state of souls after death; for from and around this the action of the whole work turneth. But if the work is considered according to its allegorical meaning, the subject is man, liable to the reward or punishment of Justice, according as through the freedom of the will he is deserving or undeserving.

9. The *form* then is double: the form of the treatise, and the form of treating it. The form of the treatise is triple, according to its threefold division. The first division is where the whole work is divided into three canticles; the second is where each canticle is divided into cantos; the third is where each canto is divided into rhythms. The form or method of treating is *poetic*, *figurative*, *descriptive*, *digressive*, *transumptive*, and, in addition, *explanatory*, *divisible*, *probative*, *condemnatory*, and *explicit in examples*.

10. The title of the book is: "Here beginneth the Comedy of Dante Alighieri, a Florentine by birth, but not by character." And for the comprehension of this it must be understood that the word "comedy" is derived from κώμη, *village*, and ᾠδή, which meaneth *song;* hence comedy is, as it were, a *village song*. Comedy is in truth a certain kind of poetical narrative that differeth from all others. It differeth from Tragedy in its subject-matter, — in this way, that Tragedy in its beginning is admirable and quiet, in its ending or catastrophe foul and horrible; and because of this the word "tragedy" is derived from τράγος, which meaneth *goat*, and ᾠδή. Tragedy is, then, as it were, a *goatish*

song; that is, foul like a goat, as doth appear in the tragedies of Seneca. Comedy, indeed, beginneth with some adverse circumstances, but its theme hath a happy termination, as doth appear in the comedies of Terence. And hence certain writers were accustomed to say in their salutations in place of a greeting, "A tragic beginning and a comic ending." Likewise they differ in their style of language, for Tragedy is lofty and sublime, Comedy, mild and humble, — as Horace says in his Poetica,[1] where he concedeth that sometimes comedians speak like tragedians and conversely:

> Interdum tamen et vocem comoedia tollit,
> Iratusque Chremes tumido delitigat ore;
> Et tragicus plerumque dolet sermone pedestri.

From this it is evident why the present work is called a comedy. For if we consider the theme, in its beginning it is horrible and foul, because it is Hell; in its ending, fortunate, desirable, and joyful, because it is Paradise; and if we consider the style of language, the style is careless and humble, because it is the vulgar tongue, in which even housewives hold converse.[2] There are also other kinds of poetic narration: namely, the bucolic song, the elegy, the satire, and the votive hymn, as likewise can be seen in the Poetica of Horace; but of these at present nothing need be said.

[1] Verses 93–95: —

> Yet comedy sometimes will raise her note.
> See Chremes, how he swells his angry throat!
> And when a tragic hero tells his woes,
> The terms he chooses are akin to prose.
>
> (Conington.)

[2] Cf. *Convito*, i. 5; also *De Eloquentia Vulgari*, i. 1: "We call that the vulgar tongue, which, without any rules whatever, we learn as children from our nurses."

11. Now it must be evident in what manner the part offered you is to be assigned. For if the subject of the whole work, taken according to the letter, is the state of souls after death considered not in a special but in a general sense, it is manifest that in this part the subject is the same state treated in a special sense, namely: the state of the souls of the blessed after death. And if the subject of the whole work, allegorically considered, is man, liable to the reward or punishment of Justice, according as through the freedom of the will he is deserving or undeserving, it is manifest that the subject in this part is restricted, and is man, liable to the reward of Justice, according as he is deserving.

12. And thus the form of the part is evident in that assigned to the whole, for if the form of the whole treatise is triple, in this part it is only double, namely: the division of the canticle and the canto. The first division cannot apply to this, since this is a part of the first division.

13. The *title of the book* is also evident. For if the title of the whole book is: Here beginneth the Comedy, etc., as above, the title of this part will be: Here beginneth the Third Canticle of the Comedy of Dante, which is called Paradise.

14. Now that these three things in which the part differeth from the whole have been inquired into, the other three in which there is no variation from the whole must be considered. The *agent*, then, of the whole and of the part is he who hath been named and who throughout appears as the agent.[1]

[1] That Dante considered himself a prophet, an agent through whom valuable and eternal truths were to be stated, is evident in many

15. The *aim* of the whole and of the part may be manifold; that is to say, near and remote. But omitting all subtle investigation, it can be briefly stated that the aim of the whole and of the part is to remove those living in this life from a state of misery and to guide them to a state of happiness.

16. Now the *kind of philosophy* under which we proceed in the whole and in the part is moral philosophy or ethics; because the whole was undertaken not for speculation but for practice. For although in some place or passage it may be handled in the manner of speculative philosophy, this is not for the sake of speculative philosophy, but for the sake of practical needs; since, as the Philosopher saith in the Second of the Metaphysics, "practical men speculate somewhat now and then."

17. These things premised, we must enter upon the interpretation of the letter, after something of a preamble; but first we must announce that the interpretation of the letter is no more than revealing the form of the work. This part, therefore, or the third Canticle, which is called Paradise, is divided principally into two parts: namely, into a *prologue* and a *principal part.* The second part beginneth here: —

To mortal men by passages diverse.

18. In regard to the first part it is to be understood that although it may be called an *exordium* in ordinary discourse, speaking properly it ought to be

places. Cf. *Convito*, i. 2: "First, any speaking of one's self seems unlawful. . . . The rhetoricians will not allow any one to speak of himself unnecessarily." See also *Purg.* xxx. 62: —

When at the sound I turned of my own name,
Which of necessity is here recorded.

called nothing but a *prologue ;* and the Philosopher[1] seemeth to allude to this in the Third of the Rhetoric, where he saith that "the proem is the beginning in a rhetorical oration, as the prologue is in poetry, and the prelude in fluting."[2] It is also to be first noted that this preamble, which may ordinarily be called an exordium, is composed in one manner by the poets, in another by the rhetoricians. For the rhetoricians were accustomed to forecast what was to be said in order to prepare the mind of the listener; but the poets not only do this, but after it they also pronounce something of an invocation. And this is befitting in them, since they have need of a great invocation, inasmuch as something above the ordinary powers of men is to be sought from the supernal essences: a certain gift almost divine. Therefore the present prologue is divided into two parts; in the first is forecast what is to be said; in the second Apollo is invoked. The second part beginneth here: —

O good Apollo, for this last emprise.

19. In regard to the first part it is to be noted that three things are required for a good beginning, as Tullius says in the New Rhetoric,[3] namely: that the auditor should be rendered well-disposed, attentive, and docile; and this is especially needed in a subject of the marvelous kind, as Tullius himself says. Since, therefore, the theme around which the present treatise turneth is marvelous, on that account these three things in the beginning of the exordium or prologue aim to recall one to the marvelous. For he

[1] Dante always refers to Aristotle as "the Philosopher," "the master of those who know." See *Inf.* iv. 131.

[2] *Rhet.* iii. 14, *in init.*

[3] Cicero, *De Inventione*, i. 15.

saith that he will speak of those things that he saw in the first heaven of which he had power to retain the remembrance. And in these words all those three things are comprehended; for by the utility of the things to be said benevolence is excited;[1] by their marvelous character, attention; by their possibility, docility.[2] He alludeth to their utility when he saith that he is about to tell those things that are especially alluring to human desires, namely: the joys of Paradise; he toucheth on their marvelous character when he doth promise to say things so arduous and sublime, namely: the nature of the Kingdom of Heaven; he showeth their possibility when he saith that he shall speak of those things of which he had the power to retain the remembrance, for if he, others also would have the power. All these things are touched upon in those words where he saith that he had been in the first heaven and that he doth wish to relate of the Kingdom of Heaven whatever he had the power to retain, like a treasure, in his mind. Having then observed the excellence and perfection of the first part of the Prologue, let us enter on the interpretation of the letter.

20. He saith, then, that *The glory of Him who moveth everything*, which is God, *doth shine in every corner of the Universe*, but *in one part more and in*

[1] *Convito*, iv. 2: "If the hearer be not well disposed, even good words will be badly received."

[2] Cf. *Convito*, ii. 1: "But because in every kind of discourse the speaker ought to think of persuading, that is, of *charming*, his audience, and that which is the first of all persuasions, as the rhetoricians assert, is the most potent of any to render the listener attentive, the promising to relate new and great things, therefore I follow up my prayer for an audience with this persuasion, announcing to them my intention to relate *new* things."

another less.[1] That he shineth everywhere, reason and authority likewise clearly show. Reason thus: Everything that doth exist either receiveth its being from itself or from something else. But it is evident that to receive its being from itself is not allowable save to One: namely, to the First, or Beginning, which is God. And since the act of being does not denote an existence of necessity *per se*, and since an existence of necessity *per se* appertaineth to One alone, namely, to the First or Beginning, which is the Cause of all things; therefore all things that exist, with the exception of that One, receive their being from something else. If therefore the most remote, or any entity whatsoever in the universe be taken, it is evident that it doth receive its being from something else; and that this, from which it doth receive it, oweth its existence to itself or to something else. If to itself, then it is first; if to something else, that in like manner doth receive its existence from itself or from something else. And thus it might be continued indefinitely among active causes, as proved in the Second of the Metaphysics;[2] but since this is impossible,

[1] Cf. *Convito*, iii. 7: "And here we must know that the Divine goodness descends upon all things, otherwise they could not exist; but although this goodness springs from that Principle which is most simple, it is received in divers ways, and in greater or less degree according to the virtue of the recipients. Whence it is written in the book of *Causes*, 'The Primal Goodness sendeth His bounties unto all things in an affluence.' None the less does each thing receive of this affluence according to the manner of its power and its being."

[2] Aristotle, *Metaphysics*, ii. (that is, Book i. the Less): "But, truly, that there is, at least, some first principle, and that the causes of entities are not infinite, either in a progress in straightforward direction, or according to form, is evident. For neither, as of matter, is it possible that this particular entity proceed from this to infinity; for instance, flesh, indeed, from earth, and earth from air, and air from

recourse must be had to the First, which is God. And thus everything that doth exist receiveth its being mediately or immediately from Him; inasmuch as the second cause, proceeding from the first, hath influence upon the object caused in the manner of a looking-glass that receiveth and reflecteth the ray; since the first is the greater cause. And this is written in the book De Causis:[1] "that every primary cause hath greater influence upon the object caused by it than a universal second cause." But this hath relation to being.

21. Now in what relateth to the essence I demonstrate thus: Every essence except the First hath been caused; otherwise there would be many things which would exist of necessity *per se*, which is impossible. Whatever is, hath been caused either by nature or

fire, and this without ever coming to a standstill. Nor can there an infinite progression take place with the origin of the principle of motion; as, for instance, that man should have been moved by the air, and this by the sun, and the sun by discord; and of this that there should be no end. Nor, in like manner, can this infinite progression take place with the final cause, — that walking, for instance, should be gone through for the sake of health, and this for the sake of enjoyment, and this enjoyment for the sake of something else; and similarly, that one thing invariably should subsist on account of another. And, in like manner, is it the case with the formal cause. For of media, to which externally there is something last and first, it is necessary that what is first should be a cause of those things which are subsequent to it."

[1] *Beati Alberti Magni Opera*, Lugduni, 1651, vol. 5, p. 567, *Liber de Causis et Processu Universitatis*, bk. ii. (*De terminatione causarum*), Tr. i. cap. 5, *in init.:* "Ex omnibus his facile probatur quod causa primaria universalis plus influit super causatum suum quam causa secondaria."

Cf. also *Convito*, iii. 2: "Every substantial form proceeds from its First Cause, which is God, as is written in the book of *Causes*, and it is not differentiated by this [First Cause], which is most simple, but by secondary causes, and by the matter into which it descends."

mind; and what hath been caused by nature, as a consequence hath been caused by mind, since nature is a work of mind. Therefore everything that hath been caused, hath been caused by some mind, mediate or immediate. Since therefore the virtue is inherent in the essence whose virtue it is, it doth proceed wholly from the essence that causeth, if this is intelligent. And thus, in the same manner as before it was necessary to go to the First Cause of being itself, so now recourse must be had to the First Cause of the essence and virtue. Wherefore it is evident that every essence and virtue proceeds from the First, and that the lower intelligences receive the light as from a sun and reflect the rays of what is higher than they to what is lower, after the manner of looking-glasses;[1] which Dionysius seemeth to touch upon clearly enough when he speaketh of the celestial hierarchy.[2] And therefore it is written in the book De Causis[3] that "every intelligence is full of forms." It is evident, then, in what manner reason doth manifest that the divine

[1] Cf. *Convito*, iii. 14: "Here we must observe that the first Agent, that is, God, gives to all things of His power, either by direct rays or by reflected splendor. Wherefore the Divine Light shines directly upon the Intelligences, and upon others is reflected from these first illuminated Intelligences."

[2] Dionysius, the Areopagite. Modern criticism now believes, however, that he did not write this work. See D' Ancona, *I precursori di Dante*, p. 23, note. "Ed. Ant. 1643, i. pag. 142, 143. Versio Corderii: 'Conclusum igitur a nobis, quomodo illa quidem antiquissima, quae Deo praesto, est intelligentiarum distributio, ab ipsamet primitus initiante illuminatione consecrata, immediate illi intendendo, secretiori simul et manifestiori divini Principatus, illustratione purgetur et illuminetur atque perficiatur.' Cf. Albertum Magnum, I. 1, ii. 2, cap. 17, pag. 599." (Witte.)

[3] *Beati Alberti Magni opera*, Tr. ii. cap. 21, *in init.*: "From what is said before it is easily seen that every intelligence which is in itself and in its substance intelligence, is active and full of forms."

light — that is, the divine goodness, wisdom, and virtue — shineth everywhere.

22. Even as knowledge, so likewise authority proveth. For the Holy Ghost saith through Jeremiah:[1] "Do not I fill heaven and earth?" and in the Psalms:[2] "Whither shall I go from thy spirit? or whither shall I flee from thy presence? If I ascend up into heaven thou art there; if I make my bed in hell, behold, thou art there. If I take the wings," etc. And the Book of Wisdom[3] saith that "the spirit of the Lord filleth the universe;" and the forty-second of Ecclesiasticus:[4] "And the work thereof is full of the glory of the Lord." And this is also confirmed in the writings of the pagans, for Lucan in his ninth book saith:[5] "Jove is whatever thou seest and wherever thou turnest."

23. Therefore it is well said, when the author saith that the divine ray, or the divine glory, *doth penetrate the universe and shine*. It *doth penetrate*, as touching the essence; it *shineth*, as touching the existence. Likewise what he doth append in regard to *more* and *less* is manifestly true, since we see one thing that existeth in a more exalted station and another in a more lowly; as is evident in regard to the heavens and the elements, the one of which is in truth incorruptible, but the others corruptible.

24. And after he hath premised this truth, he proceedeth to speak of Paradise, by circumlocution, and saith that *he was within that heaven which receiveth*

[1] Jer. xxiii. 24.
[2] Psalm cxxxix. 7–9.
[3] Wisdom i. 7.
[4] Eccles. xlii. 16.
[5] "Jupiter est quodcumque vides quocumque moveris." (*Pharsalia*, ix. 580.)

most of the glory of God, or *of his light*. And from this it is to be understood that that is the highest heaven, containing all bodies and contained by none, within which all bodies move, whilst it remaineth in sempiternal quiet and receiveth its virtue from no corporeal substance. And it is called the Empyrean, which is the same as a heaven glowing with fire or heat; not because there is in it a material fire or heat, but a spiritual, which is holy love or charity.

25. Likewise that it doth receive *more* of the divine light can be proved by two arguments. First, because it containeth all things and is contained by none; second, by its sempiternal quiet or peace. In respect to the first it is proved thus: as containing, it doth hold a natural relation toward what is contained, like that of the mould to the plastic substance, as is held in the Fourth of the Physics.[1] But in the natural relation of the whole universe, the first heaven containeth all things; therefore it doth hold to all things the relationship of mould to the plastic substance, which is to say, that it holdeth the relation of a cause. And since all power of causing is a certain ray that streameth from the First Cause, which is God, it is manifest that that heaven which hath more the nature of a cause receiveth more of the divine light.

26. In respect to the second the proof is as follows. Everything that moveth doth move on account of some-

[1] "Dante seems to have referred to chapter 4, Tr. 35, where, according to Argyropulus, we read: 'Propterea quod continet (locus) videtur forma esse: in eodem enim sunt extrema continentis et contenti. Sunt igitur utraque termini, sed non ejusdem; sed forma quidem rei, locus autem continentis corporis.' See also *De Coelo*, iv. cap. 4, Tr. 35: 'Dicimus autem id quidem, quod continet, formae esse; quod autem continetur materiae.'" (Witte.)

thing which it hath not and which is the goal of its motion. Even as the heaven of the moon is moved on account of some part of it which hath not that whereto it is moved, and because any part of it whatsoever, when its place hath not been gained (which is impossible), is moved to another, hence it is that this heaven doth always move and is never at rest, as it desires to be.[1] And what I say of the heaven of the moon is to be understood of all heavens, save the first. Everything, therefore, that moveth hath some defect, and hath not its whole being complete in itself. Therefore that heaven, which is moved by none, hath in itself, and in every part whatsoever of it, whatever it can have in a perfect measure, to such a degree that it requireth not motion for its perfection. And since all perfection is a ray of the First, which existeth in the highest degree of perfection, it is manifest that the First Heaven receiveth more of the First Light, which is God. Nevertheless this reasoning seemeth to argue to the confutation of the antecedent, inasmuch as it doth not prove simply and according to the *form* of arguing; but if we consider its *material*, it proveth well, because a sempiternal heaven is treated of in which a defect would be eternized. Therefore if God did not give it motion, it is evident that He did not give it material defective in anything.[2] And according to this suppo-

[1] Cf. *Convito*, iii. 15: "And the reason is this — that as everything by nature desires its own perfection, without this it cannot be content, that is, blest; for man, whatever other things he may possess, without this would he filled with a desire which cannot coexist with blessedness, because blessedness is a perfect thing and desire an imperfect, seeing that no one desires that which he has, but that which he has not, and here is a manifest defect."

[2] See *Convito*, iii. 6: "Where we must understand that everything

sition the argument doth hold by reason of its material; and a like manner of arguing is as if I should say, "If he is a man he can laugh;" for in all convertible propositions a like reasoning doth hold on account of the material. Thus therefore it is evident that when he saith, *Within that heaven which most His light receives*, he purposeth to speak of Paradise or the Empyrean Heaven.[1]

27. Likewise, in agreement with the foregoing reason the Philosopher in the First of the De Coelo[2] saith that heaven "hath a material so much the more exalted than its inferiors as it is the more removed from the things that are here." In addition to this can be adduced also what the Apostle saith to the Ephesians[3] of Christ: "That ascended up far above all heavens, that he might fill all things." This is the heaven of the delights of the Lord of which it is

desires above all its own perfection; and in this finds every desire satisfied, and for this [end] all things are desired."

[1] See *Convito*, ii. 4: "However, beyond all these, the Catholics place the Empyrean Heaven, which is as much as to say the Heaven of *Flame*, or *Luminous* Heaven; and they hold it to be immovable, because it has within itself, in every part, that which its matter demands. And this is the reason that the *Primum Mobile* moves with immense velocity; because the fervent longing of all its parts to be united to those of this [tenth and] most divine and quiet heaven, makes it revolve with so much desire that its velocity is almost incomprehensible. And this quiet and peaceful heaven, is the abode of that Supreme Deity who alone doth perfectly behold Himself. This is the abode of the beatified spirits, according to the holy Church, who cannot lie. . . . This is the supreme edifice of the universe, in which all the world is included, and beyond which is nothing; and it is not in space, but was formed solely in the Primal Mind, which the Greeks called *Protonoe*. This is that magnificence of which the Psalmist spake, when he says to God, 'Thy magnificence is exalted above the heavens.'" See also *Convito*, ii. 15.

[2] Aristotle, *De Coelo*, i. 2.

[3] Eph. iv. 10.

said against Lucifer by Ezekiel,[1] "Thou sealest up the sum, full of wisdom, and perfect in beauty: thou hast been among the delights of the paradise of God."

28. And after he hath said that he was in that part of Paradise, he continueth with his paraphrases, and saith that he —

> things beheld which to repeat
> Nor knows, nor can, who from above descends.

And he giveth the cause when he saith that "our intellect ingulphs itself so far" in its desire, which is God, —

> That after it the memory cannot go.

For the comprehension of these things it must be understood, that when the human intellect is exalted in this life, on account of the natural relation and affinity that it hath to the separate intellectual substance, it is exalted to such a degree that after return the memory waxeth feeble, because it hath transcended human bounds. And this is suggested to us by the Apostle, where in speaking to the Corinthians[2] he saith: "And I know such a man (whether in the body, or out of the body, I cannot tell: God knoweth), how that he was caught up into Paradise, and heard unspeakable words, which it is not lawful for a man to utter." Lo then! when the intellect had transcended human bounds in its exaltation, it did not remember what had passed exterior to it. This is again suggested to us in Matthew,[3] where the three disciples fell on their faces, and afterwards told none of it, as though they had forgotten. And in Ezekiel[4] it is written: "And when I saw it, I fell

[1] Ezek. xxviii. 12.
[2] 2 Cor. xii. 3, 4.
[3] Matt. xvii. 6, 7.
[4] Ezek. i. 28.

upon my face." And wherein these examples do not suffice for the invidious,[1] let them read Richard of Saint Victor, in the book De Contemplatione;[2] let them read Bernard, in the book De Consideratione;[3] let them read Augustine, in the book De Quantitate Animae;[4] and they will be disdainful no longer. But if they should rail at the ordering of so great an exaltation through the fault of the speaker, let them read Daniel,[5] wherein they will find that even

[1] *Convito*, i. 4: "Equality, with the wicked, causes envy; and envy causes perverted judgment, because it will not permit reason to argue in favor of the thing envied, and the judicatory power then becomes like a judge who hears but one side. Therefore, when such people see a famous person, they immediately become envious, because they see themselves with equal members and equal powers, and fear that the excellency of the other person will cause them to be less esteemed, and thus they not only misjudge, being swayed by passion, but by their calumnies cause others to misjudge." Cf. also *Convito*, i. 11: "The envious man then argues, not by blaming him who speaks for not knowing how to speak, but by blaming the material in which he works, in order (by disparaging the work from that side) to take away the honor and fame of the speaker; as he who should blame the blade of a sword, not for the sake of condemning the blade, but all the work of the master."

[2] "*De arca mystica, in quo de contemplatione*, etc., lib. iv. cap. 12 (ed. Ven. 1506, 8): 'Quaedam namque ejusmodi sunt, quae humanam intelligentiam excedunt, et humana ratione investigari non possunt, et inde, uti superius jam dictum est, praeter rationem non sunt, etc.'" (Witte.)

[3] "*De consideratione ad Eugenium*, lib. v. (ed. Spirens, 1501, 4): 'Ad omnium maximus (viator), qui spreto ipso usu rerum et sensuum, quantum quidem humanae fragilitati fas est, non ascensoriis gradibus, sed inopinatis excessibus avolare interdum contemplando ad illa sublimia consuevit. Ad hoc ultimum genus illos pertinere reor excessus Pauli, etc.'" (Witte.)

[4] "Cap. 76 (*Opp. Paris*, 1689, f. T. i. pag. 436): 'Jam vero in ipsa visione veritatis, quae septimus atque ultimus animae gradus est, neque jam gradus, sed quaedam mansio, quo illis gradibus pervenitur, quae sint gaudia, quae perfruitio summi et veri boni, cujus serenitatis atque aeternitatis afflatus, quid ego dicam?'" (Witte.)

[5] Dan. ii. 3.

Nebuchadnezzar by divine inspiration saw something terrible to sinners, and then forgot it. For He "who maketh his sun to rise on the evil and on the good, and sendeth rain on the just and on the unjust,"[1] — sometimes compassionately, for their conversion, sometimes severely, for their punishment, — more or less, according as it pleaseth Him, doth manifest His glory even to those who live evilly.

29. He beheld therefore, as he saith, some things which to repeat nor knows, nor can, who from above descends. In truth, it must be carefully noted that he saith, *nor knows*, and *nor can.* He *knoweth not*, because he hath forgotten ; he *cannot*, because even if he doth remember and retaineth the idea, words are nevertheless lacking. For we behold many things with the intellect for which the vocal symbols are wanting ;[2] and Plato suggesteth this sufficiently in his books by the use of metaphors ; for he beheld many things by the light of the intellect which he was unable to express in fitting words.

30. After this he saith that he will tell *whatever of the holy realm he had the power to treasure in his mind*, and this he saith is *the subject of his song ;* and of what sort and how many these matters are will appear in the principal part.

[1] Matt. v. 45.

[2] See Canzone ii. in the *Convito :* —

> Wherefore if my rhymes are defective
> . . . .
> For that is guilty my weak understanding
> And our own tongue, which has not strength
> To encompass all. . . .

That is, as Dante explains further on, iii. 3, the reason is that language cannot completely render account of that which the understanding sees.

31. Then when he saith, "O good Apollo," etc., he doth make his invocation. And this part is divided into two parts: in the first, in making his invocation he doth make a petition; in the second, he doth persuade Apollo of what he hath asked, first promising a certain reward. The second part beginneth here: "O power divine." The first part is divided into two parts: in the first he seeketh the divine aid; in the second he toucheth on the necessity of his position, which is its justification; and it beginneth here: "One summit of Parnassus hitherto," etc.

32. This is the signification of the second part of the prologue in general. In particular I will not expound it at present; for poverty presseth so hard upon me that I must needs abandon these and other matters useful for the public good. But I hope of your magnificence that other means may be given me of continuing with a useful exposition.

33. Of the principal part, which was divided even as the whole prologue, nothing will be said at present, either in respect to its division or its signification, save this: that it will proceed ascending from heaven to heaven, and will tell of the souls of the blessed found in each sphere, and that true blessedness consisteth in knowing the source of truth; as doth appear in St. John [1] where he saith: "This is true blessedness, that they might know thee, the true God," etc.; and in Boethius,[2] in the Third of De Consolatione, where he saith: "To see Thee is our end." Hence it is that many things that have a great utility and delight will be asked from these souls, as from those beholding all truth, in order to reveal the glory of their blessed-

[1] John xvii. 3. [2] *De Consolatione*, iii. 9 (ed. Peiper).

ness. And because when the Source or First, which is God, hath been found, there is nothing to be sought beyond (since He is the Alpha and Omega, which is the Beginning and the End, as the vision of Saint John doth demonstrate,[1]) the treatise draweth to a close in God, who is blessed throughout all the ages.

[1] Rev. i. 8; xxi. 6; xxii. 13.

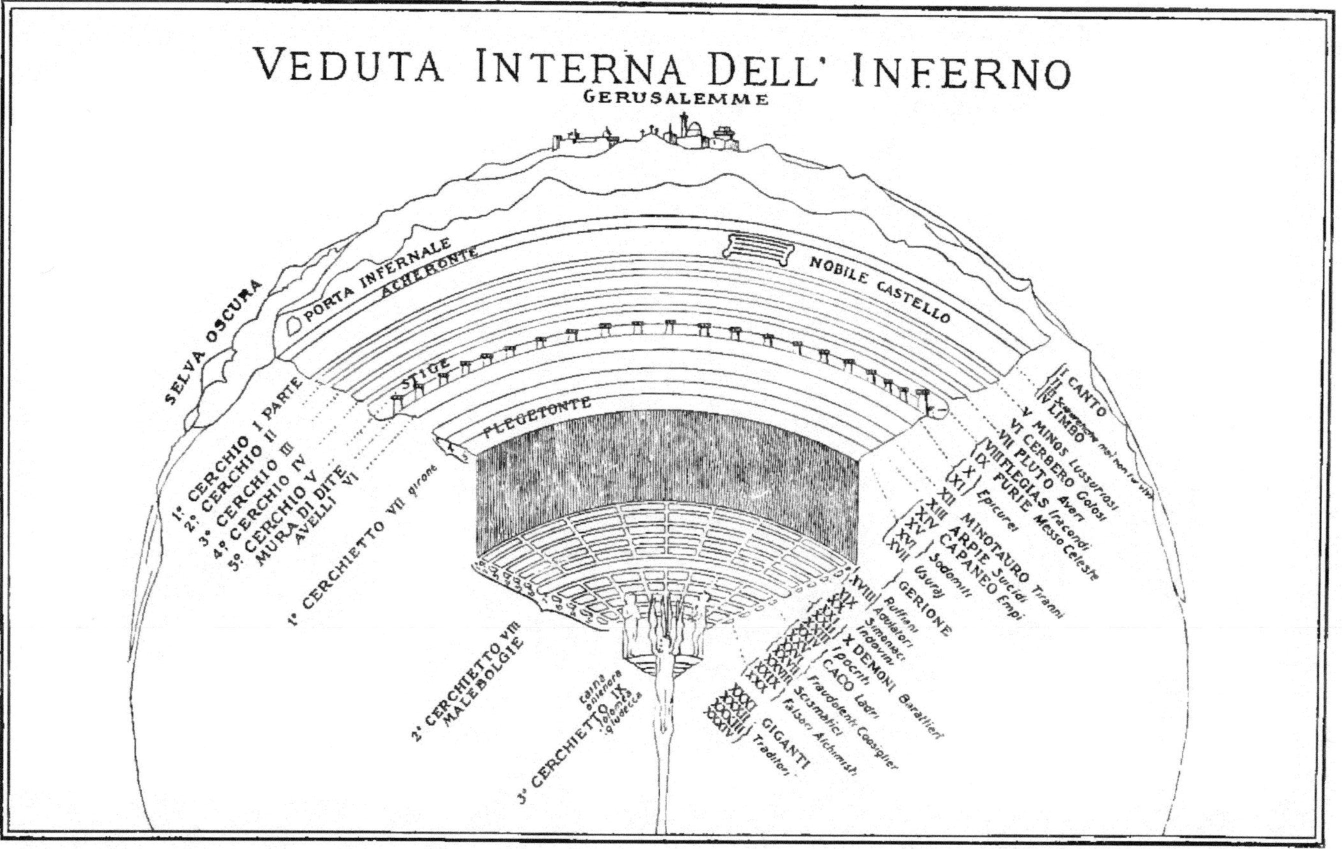

From "La materia della Divina Commedia di Dante Alighieri dichiarata in vi tavole. Dal Duca Michelangelo Caetani di Sermoneta."

VI

THE MORAL TOPOGRAPHY OF THE INFERNO[1]

HELL is a vast pit or funnel piercing down to the centre of the earth, formed when Lucifer and his angels were hurled down from Heaven. It lies beneath the inhabited world, whose centre is Jerusalem and Mount Calvary; its base toward the earth, and its apex at the centre. It is divided into nine concentric circles, the lower of which are separated by immense precipices — circles that grow more narrow in circumference, more intense and horrible in suffering, until the last is reached where Lucifer is fixed in the ice at the earth's centre, at the farthest point from God, gazing upward in defiance towards Jerusalem, where his power was overthrown at the cross (cf. Inf. xxxiv. 106–126).

"There are two elements in sin," writes St. Thomas Aquinas: "the conversion to a perishable good, which is the material element in sin; and the aversion from the imperishable good, which is the formal and completing element in sin." In Dante's Purgatory the material element is purged away. In his Hell sin is considered mainly on the side of this formal element, its aversion from the Supreme Good; and its enormity is revealed in the hideousness of its effects. The

[1] E. G. Gardner, *Dante*, Temple Classics, p. 92. *Vide* Dante's Cosmography, p. 236.

Table III.

Classification of Sins in the Inferno. (D.)

Division	Class	Circle	Subdivision	Deadly sin
	Neutrals	0		
	Limbo: unbaptized	1		
I. Incontinence	Carnal sinners	2		i. Luxury.
	Gluttonous	3		ii. Gluttony.
	Avaricious and prodigal	4		iii. Avarice.
	Wrathful and sullen or slothful	5		iv. Sloth (?), v. Anger.
	Heretics	6		vi. Envy (?).
II. Violence or Bestiality		7	i. Violent against others	
			ii. " " themselves and goods	
			iii. " " God and nature	
III. Fraud or Malice	Simple Fraud	8	i. Pandars and seducers	
			ii. Flatterers	
			iii. Simonists	
			iv. Diviners	
			v. Barrators	
			vi. Hypocrites	
			vii. Thieves	
			viii. Evil counselors	
			ix. Sowers of discord and schism	
			x. Forgers	
	Treachery	9	i. Caina. Treacherous to kindred	vii. Pride (?).
			ii. Antenora. " " country	
			iii. Tolomea. " " hospitality	
			iv. Giudecca. " " lords and benefactors	

ethic. system of the Inferno, as set forth in Canto xi., corresponds to Aristotle's threefold division of things to be morally avoided: Incontinence, Bestiality, Malice. Dante equates Bestiality and Malice with the Ciceronian Violence and Fraud, by which injurv is done. Thus there is the upper Hell of sins proceeding from the irrational part of the soul, divided into five circles. The lower Hell of Bestiality and Malice is the terrible city of Dis, the true kingdom of Lucile in which, after the intermediate sixth circle, co nesohree great circles, each divided into a number of sub divisions, and each separated by a chasm from the one above; the seventh circle of Violence and Bestiality; followed by two circles of Malice — the eight of simple fraud, and the ninth of treachery. There is such dispute as to how far Dante further equates this division with the seven capital sins recognized by the Church. Although actual deeds are considered in her, rather than the sinful propensities that lead to there it seems plausible to recognize in Incontinence the five lesser capital sins: Luxury, Gluttony, Avarice, Sloth (though the treatment of this sin in the Inferno is questionable), and Anger; and to regard the whole of the three circles of the city of Dis as proceeding from and being the visible effects of envy and pride, the sins proper to devils according to St. Thomas, — seen in their supreme degree in him whose pride made him rebel against his Maker, and whose envy brought death into the world.

VII

THE NATURE OF THE VERGIL OF THE DIVINA COMMEDIA

THE reasons which led Dante to choose Vergil for his guide were numerous. In the first place Vergil was Dante's favorite author and the greatest poet with whom he was acquainted. Being a great poet himself, Dante appreciated the art of Vergil in a way which no other man of the Middle Ages had ever been able to do, and looked on him as his master in style. He admired him further as the singer of the glories of Italy and as a poet of Italian feeling. It was through Vergil again that Dante had brought to maturity his lofty ideal of the Empire and all the elevated poetry which that implied, and in the formation of this ideal Vergil had served him not merely as theorist, but also as actual historical witness both by the subject of his poem and by the period to which it belonged. Then, by following the system of allegorical interpretation which was in vogue in the Middle Ages, Dante found in the Æneid just that account of the soul's progress toward perfection which was the subject of his own poem. Once more, in his conception of the relation between reason and faith and the power of the intellect, unenlightened by revelation, to

[1] *Vergil in the Middle Ages.* Domenico Comparetti, trans. by E. F. M. Benecke. The selections are taken from chapter xv. (By permission.)

attain great truths, Vergil stood out preëminently among the great names of antiquity as the one who, according to mediæval ideas, appeared the purest and the nearest the Christ, of whom he had been, however unconsciously, a prophet. And finally, in the construction of his great poem, Dante derived the main idea and many of the details from Vergil, and made more use of him than of any other writer in the course of his work.

All this will, I trust, make it clear that the office of guide assigned by Dante to Vergil is a thoroughly genuine one, and that the choice of Vergil for this purpose is not, as is generally considered, a mere freak of the imagination determined by external causes, but has just as true a psychological reason as the choice of his other guide, Beatrice. And it is further necessary to bear in mind the essential fact that Dante's is a creative genius, not in the field of science, but in that of poetry, and that therefore, while admiring intellectual greatness in every form, if called upon to choose as his associate between a philosopher and a poet, he could not fail to choose the latter. Hence those with whom in his poem he spends much time are always artists and poets, such as Vergil, Statius, Sordello, Arnaldo, and Casella, while the five men *di cotanto senno*, whom he meets in Limbo, are all poets. It is as poet that he regards himself in the moments of his strongest emotions; this is his supreme merit, by which he hopes to obtain that return from exile *al bell' ovile ov' io dormii agnello;* and it is a poet's crown which he aspires to take in his *bel San Giovanni*, where first he was admitted into the Christian communion: —

Con altra voce omai, con altro vello
Ritornerò poeta, ed in sul fonte
Di mio battesmo prenderò il cappello.

His nature and his predilections as poet, qualities in which his guide shared, are all brought out in that passage where both of them suddenly discover, to their great confusion, that they have been forgetting the serious object of their journey in listening to a fascinating song.

Those scholars who have discussed the subject of the Dantesque Vergil have generally found it quite natural that, in searching for some character of antiquity who might be the symbol of human reason as independent of revelation, Dante should have lighted upon Vergil, owing to that general reputation for omniscience and semi-Christianity which the latter enjoyed in the Middle Ages. No one has stopped to inquire why Dante, as a schoolman, should not rather have chosen Aristotle. In Dante's time, as he himself expressly states, the *maestro di color che sanno* was Aristotle, not Vergil, and omniscience was quite as generally attributed to him as to the latter; Dante, like the rest, would regard Aristotle as the supreme authority on philosophy and as the prince of human reason, and, as every one knows, in the region proper to scholasticism his fame far surpassed that of Vergil. Legends as to his wisdom were not wanting; he, too, was believed to have come as near being a Christian as was possible before the coming of Christ, and his prospects of salvation were seriously discussed; Dante, moreover, in the theoretical part of his scheme of the empire, had not failed to make use of the authority of Aristotle. But Aristotle was a Greek and no Roman, and entirely alien to Dante as poet, who never therefore felt that familiarity with him that he felt with Vergil, and consequently could not, on such an occasion as this, have chosen him for his guide.

The purely popular reputation of a literary man could not be of any account to one who held art so high as Dante did, and had so lofty a conception of the ancient poets. In matters of art and intellect Dante is an intense aristocrat. But even in the literary tradition there were things connected with Vergil which were not in accord with the lofty conception which Dante had formed of him, or the symbolical manner in which he wished to employ his name; and hence he has purified him from more than one stain which made him obnoxious to Christian eyes. Vergil is certainly not an obscene poet — indeed he is distinguished among the rest for his refinement and reserve, but yet the loves of which he sings in the Bucolics and even in the Æneid had troubled the conscience of more than one mediæval ascetic, who hence condemned his poetry as something sensual and lascivious; there were besides certain statements in his Biography, supported by various passages of the Bucolics, according to which Vergil should have been placed in the circle of those who sin contrary to nature, among whom Dante had not hesitated to place both Priscian and his own master Brunetto. And again, when it came to be a question of the purity of Vergil's doctrine, though it was the general mediæval view that the great Latin poet had come very near adopting the principles of Christianity, yet it was felt that, as a pagan, he had fallen into certain unavoidable errors, chiefly Epicurean. This had been animadverted upon already, by Fulgentius, and agrees too with Vergil's biography, which describes him as the pupil of an Epicurean, and also with the fact that certain Epicurean principles do actually occur in his works, as was indeed only natural in a poet living at a period when these principles were in such favor among the Romans. All these matters Dante has entirely ignored, either because he considered them as unimportant blemishes on so great a reputation, or else because his system of allegorical interpretation permitted him to be blind to faults that others saw. In the circle of those who sin against nature Vergil does not utter a word, and the affection with which Dante there addresses his master Brunetto shows that in such cases great merit could induce him to overlook certain faults. Of the Epicurean philosophy, Dante has no direct or adequate knowledge. He knows from Cicero's De Finibus that Epicurus regarded pleasure as the highest good; but he only knows this vaguely. The principal fault for which he condemns the Epicureans is that they *L' anima col corpo morta fanno*, but of this he could not accuse Vergil, who had himself described the kingdom of the dead, and who speaks to him in this canto of the Epicureans without any suggestion of sharing their errors. Such a method of idealization is characteristic of Dante, and is not confined to his treatment of Vergil; for, regarding as he does everything on its abstract side, he considers in each case merely what is truly typical and essential, and is thus enabled to ignore those imperfections or deviations which would have troubled a smaller mind. Thus the suicide Cato does not appear in the circle of those who have sinned against themselves, but occupies that lofty and exalted position which every one knows. And thus too in the idea of Rome and the empire, which Dante follows so assiduously throughout his poem, there appear the great ideal types of Æneas, Cæsar, Augustus, Trajan, and Justinian; but those brutal types of ancient Emperors, such as Nero, whom historical tradition and mediæval legend alike would not have suffered to be placed anywhere but among the damned, are not so much as mentioned.

Vergil appears in the Divina Commedia as far more definitely Christian than he does in the mediæval tradition; but there is always a clear line drawn between what he was while alive, and what he has become after death. Vergil speaks always as the soul of one dead, who has spent many centuries in the place which his deeds have deserved; at his death the veil fell from his eyes, and the life beyond the grave revealed to him those truths which he had not known before and made him understand his error, which, though involuntary, was fatal, and the just consequences which it entailed. This is no special privilege of Vergil's; it is a knowledge which he shares with all the dead, not excluding the damned. This is the Christian view, not peculiar to Dante, and in that respect the Vergil of Dante agrees with the Vergil of Fulgentius. In Fulgentius, too, Vergil speaks as a shade brought up from the dead; as he has another object in coming, he does not describe what is his condition there, but it is clear that he has learned to know certain truths and to recognize certain errors, and that the subject is to him a painful and humiliating one, on which he does not care to dwell. But the

Vergil of Dante, being different alike in character and intention, enlarges far more on what death has taught him; he knows that the gods whom he worshiped in his time are *falsi e bugiardi;* he knows what is the nature of the Christian God of whom he was formerly ignorant, and when Dante adjures him —

> Per quel Dio che tu non conoscesti,

he knows that this God is *una sustanzia in tre persone*, and knows the benefits of the "partorir Maria." These and similar things Vergil knows for the same reason that makes him acquainted with many facts subsequent to his life upon earth, even in matters relating to Dante's contemporaries, or that renders him familiar with various earlier facts with which he could not have been familiar in his lifetime, as when he speaks of Nimrod, or quotes Genesis in the same breath as Aristotle. All that he has learned makes him reflect sadly on his own condition and on that of Aristotle, Plato, and so many other great men among the ancients, who have lost eternal bliss because they did not know that which without revelation it was impossible to know. But if the Christian truths which Vergil mentions or explains have been revealed to him by death, this does not imply that his knowledge of them is like that of any dead man; when Dante gave a symbolical value to the name of a real personage of well-known characteristics, he could not represent the ultramundane wisdom of this personage as entirely independent of or diverse from his wisdom during his life upon earth. Hence between the two lives of Vergil there is continuity, and never opposition. What Vergil has learned after death does not induce him to disclaim anything that his reason had taught him during his lifetime; a good instance of this is when Dante raises a doubt, and Vergil explains that his line, —

Desine fata deum flecti sperare precando,

if properly understood, in no way contradicts the Christian doctrine of the efficacy of prayer for the souls in Purgatory. This harmony is always preserved as far as possible in that ideal region to which the symbolical Vergil belongs, while certain inevitable deviations from it are deliberately passed over in silence. Thus, while Dante has taken from Vergil the main idea of his journey among the dead, he has notably altered it in matter of detail to suit his own views and the exigencies of Christian tradition; but no emphasis is ever laid on these differences in any part of the poem. Dante distinguishes clearly in the work of the ancient poets between the idea expressed, whether literally or figuratively, and the poetical expression in which it is clothed; and thus he too makes use of mythological names and images, not only as symbols, but also as purely poetical elements. Of the journey of Æneas to the shades he has adopted what he considers the fundamental idea, while of the merely formal and fanciful parts he has taken some and omitted or altered others, without however this method of treatment becoming in any way a subject of discussion between him and Vergil in the course of their entirely ideal association.

The conception of a purification of the spirit and an intuition of great truths, arrived at by sole force of character without external aid, would necessarily, when applied to a man who already had a literary and learned reputation, of itself lead to a further conception of exceptional wisdom and vast and encyclopædic learning. And hence the Vergil of Dante is as learned as the Vergil of Macrobius, Fulgentius, or any other mediæval writer. Dante's Vergil has only occasion to display certain sides of his universal knowledge, but it is none the less clear that this knowledge is virtually universal and only limited in the direction where that of Beatrice begins; moreover, what he knows as a shade harmonizes with his previous knowledge as a man, for Vergil, it must not be forgotten, however much he may appear as ideal or symbol, yet always retains his historical reality as man and as poet. Hence that omniscience which we find attributed throughout the Middle Ages to Vergil appears also in Dante, to whom this idea presented itself not merely in connection with his poem, but also independently of it, as an evident and perfectly reasonable fact; for in reality the nature and the proportions of mediæval knowledge were such that it was possible, and even necessary, to conceive of the perfect scholar as a man of encyclopædic learning, and the tendency, moreover, of the scholars of the time, and of Dante among them, was entirely towards polymathy. It was the habit of the Middle Ages to look upon the ancient poets as scholars and philosophers; Dante too regards them as such, but he differs from his contemporaries in never forgetting that they are also, and principally, poets. It is just the depth of thought in their poetry which attracts him as a poet to the ancients, at the head of whom is Vergil. Vergil therefore, as the greatest ancient poet, is the most learned, and the mediæval idea comes out strongly in such expressions as "virtù somma," "quel savio gentil che tutto seppe," "tu che onori ogni scienza ed arte," "mar di tutto senno," and the like. This reputation for learning belongs to Vergil principally among the poets; in the other classes of the great men of ancient times appear others who are no less learned than he; for, as we have already noticed, Dante is enthusiastic for every illustrious name of antiquity, and shows great joy at finding himself in Limbo with these "spiriti magni," of whom he says, "Che del vederli in me stesso m' esalto." Dante was able to draw a distinction where the mediæval monks could not, and with him Vergil, though not yet returned entirely to his true position, is yet well on the way to return. If therefore the choice of Vergil as representative of human reason corresponds to the position which he occupies in the mediæval tradition, yet the more elevated conception of antiquity peculiar to Dante shows that the true explanation of that choice lies in those personal and subjective reasons of which we have already spoken. . . .

When we consider the various requirements of the poem, which necessitated Vergil's appearing as at once an inhabitant of Limbo, a servant of Beatrice, and a symbol, we may well feel surprise, not merely at the harmony brought about among these varied and apparently incongruous characteristics, but still more at the fact that after all the Vergil of Dante is far nearer the historical truth than any previous mediæval conception of him had ever been. In fact, the Vergil of Dante is not merely the Vergil of the biography, but also the Vergil apparent to the reader of his poetry. . . .

The delicacy of the touch with which Dante has delineated his figure of Vergil is brought out by certain light shadows which, without depriving Vergil of any characteristic essential to his purity, yet serve to show that he is farther from perfection than various others among the great men of antiquity. Not only does Dante admit that there were men before the coming of Christ more perfect than Vergil, but he even derives from the lines of the Æneid itself the idea of contrasting its author with Cato and with that Ripheus, to whom, because he is described as —

> "iustissimus unus,
> Qui fuit in Teucris et servantissimus aequi,"

he assigns a place in Paradise. The type of Cato, delineated in a masterly manner and idealized after the traditional manner, holy, majestic, and venerable, but severe and stoical, an *atrox animus*, deprived of every human feeling, is higher in a noteworthy degree than that of Vergil, alike in its nature and its rewards. To such a height as this Vergil could not attain, and Dante therefore, with a skill all his own, not merely shows him as being on more equal terms with himself before his purification than Cato is, but also, without introducing any historical or realistic element from the biography, by merely developing his character, shows him to be susceptible to certain slight errors of judgment of which neither Cato nor still less Beatrice would have been capable. An instance of this is the passage in which Vergil suffers himself to be beguiled by the song of Casella; but a more characteristic example of the contrast between the two types is where Vergil, in speaking to Cato, thinks to move him by an appeal to his Marcia, an appeal which Cato quietly and severely puts aside, showing by the sole regard which he has for the "Heavenly Lady who moves and rules" Vergil's movements how great is the difference in the degrees of purification to which their two souls have attained.

These various gradations in purification and perfection form the first principle which determines the behavior of those who guide or encounter Dante on his journey. Thus Vergil, who is without the Christian faith, leads him readily through the Inferno, but in Purgatory, where the more exclusively Christian element of grace comes into play, he feels uncertain and in many cases ignorant, and has to ask the way of others. This is that part of the road toward perfection which he could never traverse in its entirety or with security, lacking the escort of the *tre sante virtu*. At a certain point therefore they are joined by Statius, who is represented as a sort of emanation of Vergil, seeing that he had become through the latter's agency not merely a poet but also a Christian, as Vergil himself would have been had he been born after Christ. And here there is introduced with great ingenuity for the first time the mediæval idea of the prophecy of Christ contained in the Fourth Eclogue. Vergil, who was a prophet of Christ without knowing it, and does not so much as speak of Christ throughout the poem, finds as it were a supplement for this defect in Statius, who, having been born after Christ, was able to understand the meaning of the prophecy and to become by its means converted to Christianity.

Such then is the principal idea which regulates the nature and the limits of the Vergil of the Divina Commedia. Dante has his one well-known idea for the better ordering of mankind; he aspires not merely to perfect himself, he aspires also to realize that ideal of human society which he considers to be most in harmony with the laws of justice, morality, and religion, and hence most adapted for the development of the individual. The distinction between spiritual and temporal, between Pope and Emperor, forms the basis of this idea, which in its turn forms the basis of the Divina Commedia. Æneas and Paul have been Dante's two predecessors on his journey, and at the bottom of the universe he finds associated, as the worst sinners of whom it is possible to conceive, the betrayers of Christ and of Cæsar. This order of things is represented, not as a project of Dante's own, but as a fact determined by the will of God, made evident in great part by reason and by history, and confirmed by faith; it appears therefore as the ideal which Dante finds present to the minds of all the honest dead, and especially of his guides. It is evident that all that part of this ideal which referred to the Empire and the Temporal Power would be included in the knowledge of Vergil, and would appear in his works literally as well as allegorically. Vergil, historically, was a contemporary of the good Augustus and of the peaceful beginnings of the Empire, and withal near in time to that great event, whereby Providence was preparing Rome to become

> lo loco santo
> U 'siede il successor del maggior Piero;

he was, besides, the singer of universal empire. But in addition to this, he had also written allegorically of the contemplative life, and had in this respect too understood the most perfect order of human society.

It would be as unjust, therefore, to say that Vergil represents in Dante only the imperial idea, as it would be to maintain that the Divina Commedia contains nothing but Dante's political views. The historical character of Vergil could not fail to bring him into close connection with the idea of the Empire, but this idea, which was in Dante's case the outcome of profound speculation, was necessarily also contained in the symbol of Vergil, because, according to Dante, human reason was necessarily bound to acknowledge the legitimacy of the Roman empire and the perfection of his great ideal for the regeneration of society.

An examination of mediæval tradition, with the view of discovering to what extent it had preceded Dante in associating Vergil with the imperial idea, will show that here too the great poet found nothing but the bare elements upon which to work. The idea of the empire was, as we have seen, common in the Middle Ages, and had been the aim of many princes, but none of them had, like Dante, developed this idea into a political theory having its basis in a vast system of speculation which included the whole history of mankind. It would be vain to search in the Middle Ages for any other writer in whom Vergil and the imperial idea are historically and philosophically so closely combined as is the case in Dante.

VIII

STRUCTURE AND MORAL SIGNIFICANCE OF PURGATORY[1]

PURGATORY is a steep mountain of surpassing height, on the only land rising out of the sea in the southern hemisphere. Like Hell, it was formed when Lucifer and his followers were cast out of Heaven. To escape him the earth rushed up to form this mountain, and left void the cavern through which Dante ascended (Inf. xxxiv. 125). It is the exact antipodes of Jerusalem and Mount Calvary, rises beyond atmospheric changes, and is crowned by the Earthly Paradise, scene of man's fall and symbol of blessedness of this life.[2]

In the literal sense the Purgatorio is the essential Purgatory of separated spirits, expiating and exorcising, paying the debt of temporal punishment that remains after the guilt has been forgiven, purging away the material element after the formal element has been remitted.[3] In the allegorical sense it represents the moral purgatory of repentant sinners in this world; and has for subject man, by penance and good works, becoming free from the tyranny of vice, attaining to intellectual and moral freedom. . . . Dante spends part of four days, with three nights, in this portion of his pilgrimage; for Purgatory is the symbol of the

[1] E. G. Gardner, *Dante*, Temple Primers, pp. 101 ff.
[2] *Vide* pp. 239–242. [3] *Vide* p. 287.

From "La materia della Divina Commedia di Dante Alighieri dichiarata in vi tavole. Dal Duca Michelangelo Caetani di Sermoneta."

life of man, and the life of man has four periods.[1] At the end of each day Dante rests and sleeps; before dawn on each day except the first, a vision prepares him for the work of the day — the work which cannot commence or proceed save in the light of the sun, for man can advance no step in this spiritual expiation without the light of God's grace. But the fourth day does not close, like the other three, in night; for it corresponds to that fourth and last stage of man's life, in which the soul "returns to God, as to that port whence she set out, when she came to enter upon the sea of this life" (Conv. iv. 28). There are three main divisions of the Mountain. From the shore to the gate of St. Peter is Ante-Purgatory, still subject to atmospheric changes. Within the gate is Purgatory proper, with its seven terraces bounded above by a ring of purifying flames. Thence the way leads up to the Earthly Paradise; for by these purgatorial pains the fall of Adam is repaired, and the soul of man regains the state of innocence.

In Ante-Purgatory Dante passes Easter Day and the following night. Here the souls of those who died in contumacy of the Church are detained at the foot of the mountain, and may not yet commence the ascent; and the negligent, who deferred their conversion, and who now have to defer their purification, are waiting humbly around the lower slopes. Here purgation has not yet commenced; this is the place where "time by time is restored" (Purg. xxiii. 84). . . .

Within the gate is Purgatory proper with its seven terraces, each devoted to the purgation of one of the seven capital sins, out of which other vices spring,

[1] *Convito*, iv. 23, 24.

especially by way of final causation (Aquinas). Whereas in the Inferno sin was considered in its manifold and multiform effects, in the Purgatorio it is regarded in its causes, and all referred to disordered love. The formal element, the aversion from the imperishable good, which is the essence of Hell, has been forgiven; the material element, the conversion to the good which perishes, the disordered love, is now to be purged from the soul. In the allegorical or moral sense, since every agent acts from some love, it is clear that a man's first business is to set love in order; and, indeed, the whole moral basis of Dante's Purgatory rests upon a line ascribed to St. Francis of Assisi: *Ordina quest' Amore, O tu che m' ami;* "set love in order, thou that lovest me." In the first three terraces, sins of the spirit are expiated; in the fourth terrace, sloth, which is both spiritual and carnal; in the fifth, sixth, seventh terraces, sins of the flesh. This purgation, which involves both pain of loss for a time and punishment of sense, is effected by turning with fervent love to God and detesting what hinders union with Him. Therefore, at the commencement of each terrace, examples are seen or heard of virtue contrary to the sin, in order to excite the suffering souls to extirpate its very roots; and at the end examples of its result or punishment (the "bit and bridle"). These examples are chosen with characteristic Dantesque impartiality alike from Scripture and legend or mythology; but in each case an example from the life of the Blessed Virgin is opposed to each deadly sin. At the end of each terrace stands an Angel — personification of one of the virtues opposed to the deadly sins. These seven Angels in their successive apparitions are among the divinest things of beauty in the Divine Comedy. It is only when the sin is completely purged away that man can contemplate the exceeding beauty, the "awful loveliness" of the contrary virtue.

The Earthly Paradise is the type of blessedness in this life (*De Mon.* iii. 16); it is the condition of innocence which man enjoyed before the fall, and, his will being free and right, he has no need of the directive authority of imperial and ecclesiastical powers, but is a crowned and mitred master of himself. Here Dante shows in apocalyptic imagery what God does for man's salvation by means of Church and Empire, and what man must do for himself, if he desires to attain spiritual freedom. The pageant is also prophetic of the degradation of the Church and State. The innocent soul is fitted to ascend to the stars by passing through the river Lethe, which washes away all memory of sin, and the river Eunoë, which restores the weakened energies and quickens the memory of all good done.

The probable symbolical meaning of the persons and objects introduced is as follows: Cato is the type of moral liberty; the "four holy lights aureoling his face" represent the four cardinal virtues, Prudence, Justice, Fortitude, Temperance; the three stars shining over the Valley of the Princes are the theological virtues, Faith, Hope, Charity; the Eagle is the type of the Spirit, and Lucia of Divine Grace; the three steps are the three parts of the sacrament of penance — confession, contrition, satisfaction; the Angel at the Gate of Justification is the Confessor, with the silver and gold keys of Judgment and Absolution; the seven P's signify Peccata, *i. e.* the seven mortal sins; Leah and Rachel are respectively the Active and the Contemplative life, both self-centred; Matilda is the Active Life made unselfish by Christian love; Vergil is human Reason enlightened by Divine Grace, and Beatrice is Divine Revelation; Lethe is the river of forgetfulness, and Eunoë the restorer of the good. (D.)

IX

THE MORAL TEACHING OF ST. THOMAS AQUINAS

ON HAPPINESS.[1]

Is happiness an activity of the speculative or of the practical understanding?

R. Happiness consists rather in the activity of the speculative understanding than of the practical, as is evident from three considerations. First from this, that if the happiness of man is an activity, it must be the best activity of man. Now the best activity of man is that of the best power working upon the best object; but the best power is the understanding, and the best object thereof is the Divine Good, which is not the object of the practical understanding, but of the speculative. Secondly, the same appears from this, that contemplation is especially sought after for its own sake. But the act of the practical understanding is not sought after for its own sake, but for the sake of the action, and the actions themselves are directed to some end. Hence it is manifest that the last end cannot consist in the active life that is proper to the practical understanding. Thirdly, the same appears from this, that in the contemplative life man is partaker with his betters, namely, with God and the

[1] *Aquinas Ethicus*, translated from the second part of the *Summa Theologica*, Jos. Rickaby, S. J., vol. i. p. 23. (By permission.)

angels, to whom he is assimilated by happiness; but in what concerns the active life other animals also after a fashion are partakers with men, albeit imperfectly. And therefore the last and perfect happiness which is expected in the world to come must consist mainly in contemplation. But imperfect happiness, such as can be had here, consists primarily and principally in contemplation, but secondarily in the activity of the practical understanding directing human actions and passions.

The practical understanding has a good which is outside of itself, but the speculative understanding has good within itself, to wit, the contemplation of truth; and if that good be perfect, the whole man is perfected thereby and becomes good. This good within itself the practical understanding has not, but directs a man towards it.

Does man's happiness consist in the vision of the Divine Essence? [1]

R. The last and the perfect happiness of man cannot be otherwise than in the vision of the Divine Essence. In evidence of this statement two points are to be considered: first, that man is not perfectly happy, so long as there remains anything for him to desire and seek; secondly, that the perfection of every power is determined by the nature of its object. Now the object of the intellect is the essence of a thing: hence the intellect attains to perfection so far as it knows the essence of what is before it. And therefore, when a man knows an effect, and knows that it has a cause, there is in him an outstanding natural

[1] Vol. i. p. 24.

desire of knowing the essence of the cause. If therefore a human intellect knows the essence of a created effect without knowing aught of God beyond the fact of His existence, the perfection of that intellect does not yet adequately reach the First Cause, but the intellect has an outstanding natural desire of searching into the said Cause: hence it is not yet perfectly happy. For perfect happiness, therefore, it is necessary that the intellect shall reach as far as the very essence of the First Cause.

Love [1] ranks above knowledge in moving, but knowledge goes before love in attaining; for nothing is loved but what is known, and therefore an end of understanding is first attained by the action of understanding, even as an end of sense is first attained by the action of sense.

Can man acquire happiness by the exercise of his own natural powers? [2]

R. Imperfect happiness, which can be had in this life, can be acquired by man through the exercise of his own natural powers. But the perfect happiness of man consists in the Vision of the Divine Essence. Now to see God by essence is above the nature, not only of man but of every creature. For the natural knowledge of every creature whatever is according to the mode of its substance. But every knowledge that is according to the mode of a created substance falls short of the vision of the Divine Essence, which infinitely exceeds every created substance. Hence neither man nor any creature can gain final happiness by the exercise of his own natural powers.

[1] Vol. i. p. 22.

[2] Vol. i. p. 36.

THE CARDINAL VIRTUES.

The formal principle of virtue is rational good; and that may be considered in two ways — in one way as consisting in the mere consideration of reason; and in that way there will be one principal virtue, which is called *prudence:* in another way according as a rational order is established in some matter, and that, either in the matter of actions, and so there is *justice;* or in the matter of passions, and so there must be two virtues. For rational order must be established in the matter of the passions with regard to their repugnance to reason. Now this repugnance may be in two ways: in one way by passion impelling to something contrary to reason; and for that passion must be *temperate*, or repressed: hence *temperance* takes its name; in another way by passion holding back from that which reason dictates; and for that, man must put his foot down there where reason places him, not to budge from thence: and so *fortitude* gets its name. And in like manner according to subjects the same number is found. For we observe a fourfold subject of this virtue whereof we speak: to wit, the part *rational by essence*, which prudence perfects; and the part *rational by participation*, which is divided into three, namely, the *will*, the subject of justice; the *concupiscible* faculty, the subject of temperance; and the *irascible* faculty, the subject of fortitude.

THE THEOLOGICAL VIRTUES.[2]

By virtue man is perfected unto the acts whereby he is set in the way to happiness. Now there is a

[1] Vol. i. p. 179. [2] Vol. i. p. 182.

twofold happiness of man: one proportionate to human nature, whereunto man can arrive by the principles of his own nature. Another happiness there is exceeding the nature of man, whereunto man can arrive only by a divine virtue involving a certain participation in the Deity, according as it is said that by Christ we are made "partakers of the divine nature." And because this manner of happiness exceeds the capacities of human nature, the natural principles of human action, on which man proceeds to such well-doing as is in proportion with himself, suffice not to direct man unto the aforesaid happiness. Hence there must be superadded to man by the gift of God certain principles, whereby he may be put on the way to supernatural happiness, even as he is directed to his connatural end by natural principles, yet not without the divine aid. Such principles are called *theological virtues* both because they have God for their object, inasmuch as by them we are directed aright to God; as also because it is only by divine revelation in Holy Scriptures that such virtues are taught.

Are theological virtues distinct from virtues intellectual and moral?[1]

R. Habits are specifically distinct according to the formal difference of their objects. But the object of the theological virtues is God Himself, the last end of all things, as He transcends the knowledge of our reason: whereas the object of the intellectual and moral virtues is something that can be comprehended by human reason. Hence the theological virtues are specifically distinct from virtues moral and intellectual.

[1] Vol. i. p. 182.

The intellectual and moral virtues perfect the intellect and appetite of man according to the capacity of human nature, but the theological virtues supernaturally.

Are faith, hope, and charity fitly assigned as the theological virtues?[1]

R. The theological virtues set man in the way of supernatural happiness, as he is directed to his connatural end by a natural inclination. This latter direction is worked out in two ways: first, by way of the reason or intellect, as that power holds in its knowledge the general principles of rational procedure, theoretical and practical, known by the light of nature; secondly, by the rectitude of the will naturally tending to rational good. But both these agencies fall short of the order of supernatural good. Hence for both of them some supernatural addition was necessary to man, to direct him to a supernatural end. On the side of the intellect man receives the addition of certain supernatural principles, which are perceived by divine light; and these are the objects of divine belief, with which *faith* is conversant. Second, there is the will, which is directed to the supernatural end, both by way of an effective movement, directed thereto as to a point possible to gain, and this movement belongs to *hope;* and by way of a certain spiritual union, whereby the will is in a manner transformed into that end, which union and transformation are wrought by *charity.* For the appetite of every being has a natural motion and tendency toward an end connatural to itself; and that movement arises from some sort of conformity of the thing to its end.

[1] Vol. i. p. 182.

ON SIN.

Is that a proper division of sin, into sin against God, sin against self, and sin against one's neighbor?[1]

R. Sin is an inordinate act. Now there ought to be a threefold order in man: one in reference to the rule of reason, by which all our actions and passions should be regulated; another in reference to the rule of the divine law, by which man should be guided in all things. And if man were by nature a solitary animal, this twofold order would suffice. But because man is naturally a political and social animal, therefore there must be a third order to direct man in his dealings with other men in whose society he has to live. Of these orders the first contains the second, and goes beyond it. For whatever is contained under the order of reason is contained under the order of God; but there are things contained under the order of God that go beyond human reason, as the things of faith. Hence he who sins against such things is said to sin against God, as does the heretic, and the sacrilegious person, and the blasphemer. In like manner also the second order includes the third and goes beyond it; because in all things in which we have relations with our neighbor we must be guided by the rule of reason; but in some things we are guided by reason to our own concerns only, and not to those of our neighbor; and any sin committed in such matters is said to be committed by a man against self, as with the glutton, the debauchee, and the spendthrift. When, again, a man sins in matters in which

[1] Vol. i. p. 206.

he has relations with his neighbor, he is said to sin against his neighbor, as does the thief and the murderer.

This is a distinction according to objects which make different species of sin. The virtues also are thus distinguished in species. For it is obvious that by the theological virtues man is put in relation with God; by temperance and fortitude he deals with himself, and by justice with his neighbor.

To sin against God, in so far as the order of relation to God includes every human relation, is common to all sin; but in so far as the order of relation to God goes beyond the other two orders, in that way sin against God is a special kind of sin.

Does sin cause any stain on the soul?[1]

R. A stain properly so called is spoken of in material things, when some lustrous body loses its lustre by contact with another body, as in the case of clothes, gold and silver and the like. This is the image that must be kept to when we speak of a *stain* in spiritual things. Now the soul of man has a twofold lustre, one from the shining of the natural light of reason, whereby it is guided in its acts; the other from the shining of the divine light of wisdom and grace, whereby man is further perfected unto good and seemly action. Now there is a sort of contact of the soul, when it clings to any objects by love. But when it sins, it clings to objects in despite of the light of reason and of the divine law. It is just this loss of lustre, arising from such a contact, that is called metaphorically a *stain* on the soul.

[1] Vol. i. p. 251.

Does the stain remain on the soul after the act of sin?[1]

R. The stain of sin remains on the soul even when the act of sin passes. The reason is, because this stain signifies a certain lack of lustre, consequent upon a departure from reason or from the divine law. Wherefore, so long as the man remains out and away from this light, the stain of sin remains on him; but when he returns to the light of reason and the light divine, which return is the work of grace, then the stain ceases. But the mere cessation of the act of sin, whereby the man departed from the light of reason and the divine law, does not involve his immediate return to the state in which he had been, but some movement of the will contrary to the first movement is required; just as when one has moved away to a distance from another, he does not become near him again the instant the movement ceases, but has to come back by a contrary movement.

Does the liability to punishment remain after the sin?[2]

R. In sin there are two things to consider, the culpable act and the stain ensuing. It is plain that on the cessation of the act of sin liability to sin remains. For an act of sin makes a man liable as a transgressor of the order of divine justice, to which order he returns not otherwise than by a certain penal compensation, which brings him back to the equilibrium of justice; so that he who has indulged his own will beyond due bounds, acting against the commandment of God, suf-

[1] Vol. i. p. 251. [2] Vol. i. p. 256.

fers according to the order of divine justice, either spontaneously or reluctantly, something contrary to what he would wish. And the same is observed also in injuries done to men. Hence it is clear that when the act of sin or of injury done is at an end, the debt of punishment still remains. But if we speak of the taking away of sin as to the stain of it, evidently the stain of sin cannot be taken away from the soul except by the soul being united to God; as it was in separation from Him that the soul incurred that loss of its own lustre which is the meaning of a stain. Now the soul is united to God by the will. Hence the stain of sin cannot be taken out of man, unless the will of man accepts the order of divine justice, by either spontaneously taking upon itself punishment in compensation for the past fault, or patiently bearing the punishment inflicted by God; for in both ways punishment bears the character of satisfaction. Now the fact of being satisfactory takes off something of the nature of the punishment. For it is of the nature of punishment to be against the will. But satisfactory punishment, although absolutely considered it is against the will, yet is not actually against it as things actually stand; wherefore the punishment here is *absolutely* voluntary, but involuntary *in a restricted sense.* We must say then that after the removal of the stain of sin, there may remain a liability, not to punishment absolutely, but to punishment inasmuch as it is satisfactory.

Punishment absolutely, so called, is not due to the virtuous: still there may be due to them punishment in its satisfactory aspect; for this is also a point of virtue to make satisfaction for offenses to God or to man.

What is a mortal sin?[1]

R. That sin is called *mortal*, which takes away the spiritual life, which life is by charity, and by charity we have God dwelling in us. Hence that sin is mortal of its kind, which of its own nature is contrary to charity. . . . It is to be noticed, however, in all sins mortal of their kind, that they are not mortal except when they attain their full completeness. For the consummation of sin is in the consent of reason. We speak now of human sin, which cousists in a human act, the principle of which is reason. Hence if there be a beginning of sin in the sensitive appetite, and it reach not so far as the consent of reason, the sin is *venial* owing to the imperfection of the act; but if it reaches so far as the consent of reason, it is a mortal sin.

Is pride the most grievous of sins?[2]

R. There are two elements in sin: the turning to the good that perishes, which turning to is the material element in sin; and the turning away from the good that perishes not, which turning away is the formal and completely constituent element of sin. On the side of the turning to the perishable, pride has not the attribute of being the greatest of sins: because the height which the proud man inordinately affects has not of its own nature the greatest possible opposition to the good of virtue. But on the side of the turning from the imperishable, pride has the utmost grievousness: because in other sins man turns away from God either through ignorance, or through weak-

[1] Vol. i. p. 400. [2] Vol. ii. p. 366.

ness, or through desire of some other good; but pride involves a turning away from God merely because one will not be subject to God and to his rule. Hence Boethius says, that "while all vices fly from God; pride alone sets itself against God;" on which ground it is especially said that "God resisteth the proud." And therefore the turning away from God and from his commandments, which is a sort of appanage of other sins, belongs to pride as part and parcel of itself, since the act of pride is a contempt of God. And because what is part and parcel of a thing always takes precedence over what is a mere appanage of the same, it follows that pride is of its kind the most grievous of sins, because it exceeds them all in that turning away from God, which is the formal and crowning constituent of sin.

THE ACTIVE AND CONTEMPLATIVE LIFE.[1]

Is the active life better than the contemplative?

R. A thing may well be in itself more excellent, and in some respects be surpassed by another thing. We must say then the contemplative life, absolutely speaking, is better than the active. Which the Philosopher proves by eight reasons: of which the first is, because the contemplative life becomes a man in respect of the most excellent element in his nature, namely, his understanding. The second is, because the contemplative life can be more continuous, though not in its highest act. The third is, because the delight of the contemplative life is greater than that of the active. The fourth is, because in the contempla-

[1] Vol. ii. p. 386.

tive life man is more self-sufficient and needs fewer things. The fifth is, because the contemplative life is loved for its own sake, while the active life is directed to something ulterior to itself. The sixth is, because the contemplative life consists in a certain stillness and rest, according to the text: "Be still and see that I am God." The seventh is, because the contemplative life is formed upon divine things, but the active life upon human things. The eighth is, because the contemplative life is life according to that which is proper to man, namely, the intellect, whereas in the operations of the active life the lower powers concur, which are common to us with dumb animals. A ninth reason is added by our Lord, which is explained by Augustine: "From thee shall one day be taken away the burden of necessity, but the sweetness of truth is eternal." Relatively however, and in some particular case, the active life is rather to be chosen for the necessity of our present time, as also the Philosopher says: "Philosophy is better than riches, but riches are better to a man in need."

Is the active life of greater merit than the contemplative?

R. The root of merit is charity. Now since charity consists in the love of God and of our neighbor, and the love of God is in itself more meritorious than the love of our neighbor, it follows that what belongs more directly to the love of God is more meritorious of its kind than what directly belongs to the love of our neighbor for God. But the contemplative life directly and immediately appertains to the love of God, whereas the active life is more directly ordered to the love of our neighbor, being "busy about much serving." And therefore of its kind the contemplative life is of greater merit than the active. But it may happen that one individual merits more in the works of the active life than another in the works of the contemplative, if through an abounding love for God, to the end that His will may be fulfilled, and for His glory, this person endures to be separated from the sweetness of divine contemplation for a time; as did the Apostle, as Chrysostom expounds: "His whole heart was so flooded with the love of Christ, that even that which was otherwise his greatest desire, to be with Christ, he could bring himself to set aside for the good pleasure of Christ."

Outward labor works to the increase of our accidental reward; but the increase of merit, touching our essential reward, lies principally in charity, one sign of which is outward labor endured for Christ; but a much more express sign of it is the neglect of all that belongs to this life to devote one's self with delight to divine contemplation alone.

A sacrifice is spiritually offered to God when anything is rendered to Him. But of all the goods of man God most willingly accepts the good that consists of the soul of man, that is to be offered to Him in sacrifice. A man should offer himself to God, first his own soul, according to the text, "Have pity on thy own soul, pleasing God:" then the souls of others, according to the text, "He that heareth, let him say, Come." But the closer one unites his own or another's soul to God, the more acceptable is the sacrifice to God: hence it is more acceptable to God that one should apply his own and other souls to contemplation than to action.

Therefore Gregory's saying, "No sacrifice is more acceptable to God than zeal of souls," is not a preference of the merit of the active before that of the contemplative life, but a declaration that it is more meritorious to offer to God one's own and other souls than any exterior gifts whatever.

THE STATE OF PERFECTION.[1]

Is the perfection of Christian life to be looked for in charity especially?

R. Everything is said to be perfect inasmuch as it attains to its proper end, which is the ultimate perfection of the thing. But it is charity that unites us to God, the ultimate end of the human mind, because "he that abideth in charity abideth in God, and God in him." And therefore it is by charity especially that the perfection of Christian life is measured.

Can any one be perfect in this life?

R. The perfection of Christian life consists in charity. Now perfection implies what we may call a "universal thoroughness:" for that is perfect to which nothing is wanting. We may consider perfection therefore in three forms. One absolute, one total, as well on the part of the person loving as on the part of the object loved; so that God should be loved as much as He is lovable. Such perfection is not possible to any creature: God alone is capable of it, in whom good is found in its entirety and in its essence. There is another perfection where the totality is absolute on the part of the person loving, in that the whole power of

[1] Vol. ii. p. 395.

TABLE IV.

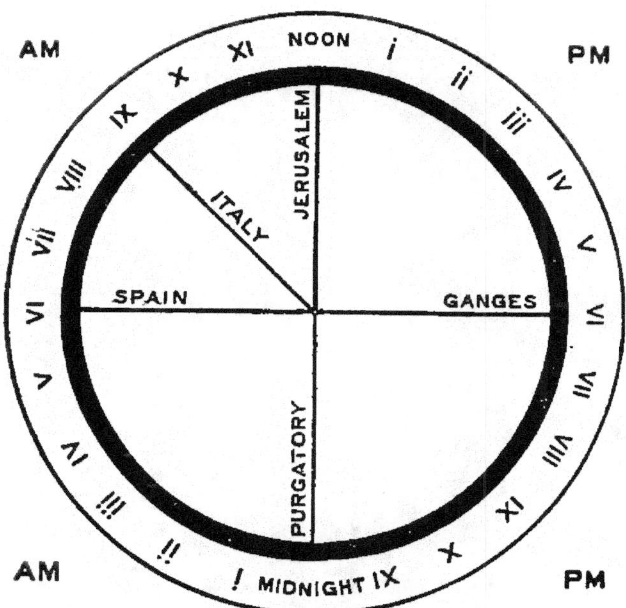

DIRECTIONS.—If the part of this diagram within the dark circle be cut out separately in cardboard, so that it can be made to revolve, it will be possible to see at a glance the simultaneous hours described in the Purgatorio, viz., ii. 1–9; iii. 25; iv. 138, 139; xv. 1–6; xxvii. 1–6.

his affection is ever absolutely fixed upon God; and such perfection is not possible on the way to heaven, but will be realized on our arrival in our heavenly home. There is a third perfection that is neither total as regards the object loved nor total on the part of the person loving. It does not involve a continual actual yearning after God, but only an exclusion of whatever is inconsistent with the motion of love toward God. So Augustine says: "The poison of charity is cupidity; and perfection is the absence of all cupidity." And such perfection can be had in this life, and that in two ways; in one way to the extent of excluding from the heart all that is contrary to charity, as is mortal sin; and without such perfection charity cannot be: consequently this perfection is of necessity to salvation. The other way goes to the extent of excluding from the heart, not only all that is contrary to charity, but also all that hinders the entire concentration of the heart upon God. Charity can exist without this perfection, as it exists in beginners and in proficients.

X

BEATRICE [1]

THAT Folco Portinari's daughter who married Simone dei Bardi was called Beatrice we are not prepared to deny; but the fact only concerns us in so far as it suggests an origin for the myth. Dante's love was certainly not called Beatrice. The poet no doubt called her so; but poets of all ages and of all countries have been in the habit of calling their ladies, not by their baptismal names, but by names of their own selection. Thus if Beatrice had been the real name of the love of Dante's youth, that he should call her by it would have been an exception to the rule. Indeed he indicates as much himself. No doubt there is still controversy as to the meaning of the words at the opening of the Vita Nuova, "La quale fu chiamata da molti Beatrice, i quali non sapeano che si chiamare;" but no controversy could have arisen but for the assumption that Beatrice was really her name. All artificialities set aside, the words mean, "Who was called Beatrice by many who did not know how to call her," that is, did not know her real name. But whatever be the meaning of the sentence, there can be no doubt of the poet's statement that many called her Beatrice. But if it was her real name, why not all? And if those

[1] *A Companion to Dante.* Scartazzini, translated by A. J. Butler. Macmillan & Co. (An argument to show that she was not Beatrice Portinari. Against the view here given, *vide* pp. 77 ff., 185 ff.)

who "non sapeano che si chiamare" called her Beatrice, what did they call her who "sapean che si chiamare"? Clearly the poet wants to make it plain at the outset that Beatrice was not his lady's baptismal name.

This is corroborated by another fact. The poet relates at length the trouble which he took to prevent the secret of his love from escaping. How then could he have brought himself both in the lifetime of his lady and immediately after her death to trumpet forth his secret? Only by admitting such irrational conduct can we escape from admitting that Beatrice was only a fictitious and assumed name, and that the name which she bore in real life may have been any but this.

Folco Portinari was a neighbor of Dante's parents; their houses were fifty paces apart. One would expect that the children, being of about the same age, would have seen each other frequently. Yet Dante says expressly that he never saw Beatrice until the end of his ninth year. Boccaccio feels this difficulty and gets out of it by remarking, "I do not think it can really have been the first time, but for the first time after she was capable of kindling the flame of love." Boccaccio may, of course, believe if he pleases that a child of eight years old is capable of kindling such a flame, but we prefer to take Dante's words in their literal sense, inferring from them that the girl whom Dante saw cannot have been his neighbor Beatrice Portinari.

With still greater preciseness he further assures us that he heard the voice of his Beatrice for the first time when as a maiden of about eighteen years she first saluted him. Therewith Boccaccio's whole idyl appears to collapse, unless we are to assume that Beatrice was dumb or Dante deaf until that date.

It must be admitted further that she was still unmarried when she refused her greeting to the poet, for it could not concern a married woman if he did pay his court to a maiden. One may further allow that neither in the Vita Nuova nor elsewhere in Dante's writings is any indication to be found that his Beatrice was married. No doubt some have wished to see a suggestion of this in Vita Nuova, § 14. But up to the present no proof has been produced that maidens were not allowed to join the wedding. On the other hand, we have in § 41 a very distinct intimation that Beatrice died unmarried. To every unprejudiced mind the sentence, "Where this most noble lady was born, lived, and died," implied that she had never left her parents' house. Folco Portinari's will, dated January 15, 1288, in which his daughter is described as wife of the Master Simone dei Bardi, would seem to show that she is older than the lady of Dante's love, for the latter would at that time have been only in the twenty-first year of her life. If, moreover, she had been a married woman, Dante's remark in § 29, that among other reasons for not speaking of the departure of his Beatrice he could not do it without praising himself, would seem out of place. The inspiration which he derived from her would in that case have been a ground for self-reproach rather than self-praise.

Folco Portinari died December 31, 1289, Dante's Beatrice some five or six months later. Her death is related in § 29, her father's in § 22; now if her father had been Folco, all that is recorded in the intervening sections must have taken place in the five months of mourning. We should be curious to know if any one is hardy enough to defend such a theory.

On the news of Beatrice's death Dante takes up his pen in order to write a letter of lamentation to the most eminent men of the city. The letter can scarcely have been finished, it is almost impossible that it can have been sent, but that the thought of it can have arisen in his soul is significant. Unless he were beside himself he can never have dreamt of writing a letter about the death of Simone dei Bardi's wife and publishing it throughout Florence, perhaps even beyond.

The nearest relation of the lady, her brother as has been universally assumed, entreats him to write a poem on her death. This would be conceivable if she died unmarried, always supposing that this nearest relation had been admitted to the secret of his love. But how the nearest relation of another man's deceased wife could have asked her adorer for a poem, conceive who may! The invitation would probably have taken another form.

Again, according to his own story, Dante mourned the death of his Beatrice for a long time, and that not in privacy but, as from his description it is impossible to doubt, in the full sight of man. Was he more likely to have done this for another man's wife or for one who would have been his if death had not torn her away. Further, the episode of the "noble lady" (Vita Nuova, §§ 36–40) remains, on the hypothesis that Dante's Beatrice was a married woman, an unsolved riddle. What would have been the meaning of all his self-accusations if all that he had to reproach himself with was disloyalty to another man's wife, and even the composition and publication of the Vita Nuova would be incomprehensible and in no way creditable to the poet's taste if we are really to assume that his Beatrice was a married woman. The rejoinder which has been made to objections based on the fact of the marriage of Beatrice Portinari by appeal to the manners of the time we may dismiss as trivial. We know all about the manners of the time and the poetry of the Troubadours. In the present case we have to do not only with love poems but also with a work which, though deeply imbued with mysticism, is written in prose. In the case of Dante we cannot recognize as possible the continued hymning of a married woman; but when it comes to collecting the hymns shortly after her death, furnishing them with a commentary which forms a love story in plain prose, and publishing the whole thing, it is more than any troubadour ever did. Even Boccaccio saw the improbability and tried to escape with a statement that in his riper years Dante was ashamed of his Vita Nuova. He might have had reason for being so if the object of his love, the heroine of his work, had been the wife of Bardi. But his own words (Conv. i. 1; Purg. xxx. 115) show pretty plainly that he felt no shame.

Among the grounds which induced him to compose the Convito, Dante mentions a care for his own good name. "I fear," he says, "the disgrace of having followed a passion such as he who reads the aforesaid odes can conceive to have had the lordship over me, which disgrace comes entirely to an end by what I am saying at the present about myself. For it shows that not passion but the love of virtue was the moving cause." The odes referred to are those which he addressed to the comforter who appeared to him after

Beatrice's death. Is it possible that Dante should have feared to come into disgrace if people had believed that after the death of a married woman he was in love with a maiden and yet feared no disgrace on the assumption that he had for years been enamored of another man's wife? If any one can reconcile himself to such an assumption it would be better to avoid all scientific inquiry and be content with tradition. But if we are to test the matter critically the fashion in which Dante expressed himself in the Convito in regard to his love affair should be decisive. To his love for his Beatrice he allows its full and complete value; it is only the second love that is not to be taken literally, but is rather a spiritual love for philosophy. Since, then, he is in no way anxious lest his first love should be made a reproach to him, it was clearly no illicit passion.

The magnificent vision at the end of the Purgatory points in the same direction. The reproofs which the poet puts into the mouth of Beatrice have no doubt a highly symbolical meaning, but so far as their form goes they are just such reproaches as a woman would address to a man whom she loves, and who has proved himself untrue to her. What right would Bardi's wife have to utter such? Surely no reader could ever have imagined that Beatrice was a married woman had it not been for tradition. In that case too we should have been spared the symbolical and idealistic systems.

But how did the tradition itself arise? It certainly goes back farther than Boccaccio; he found it already in existence. For the "credible person" to whom he appeals is assuredly no invention of his own. The testimony of this "credible person" is, however, rendered somewhat suspicious by the fact that he or she was one of Madonna Bardi's nearest relations. Forty or fifty years after the poet's death, when he had already attained a high fame, there must have been a strong temptation first to conjecture, then to say, and lastly to believe, that the Beatrice whom he had glorified and rendered immortal was no other than the narrator's mother, grandmother, sister, aunt, as the case might be. Yet we would not say either that Boccaccio's "credible person" was the first to set the tradition on foot. The person may have found it in existence, so that the question as to its origin is not yet solved.

The following solution has recently been suggested. On Dante's own showing he was talked about in connection with two ladies whom he pretended to love with a view of concealing his secret. One of these may well have been the Bardi-Portinari lady, and the gossip which he relates may afterwards have been made up into the tradition. The assumption involved in this acute and clever hypothesis is that in the first twenty years of the fourteenth century people in Florence should have troubled themselves to ascertain who was the fair lady who had aroused the enthusiasm of a fellow-citizen known to them as having been exiled and frequently condemned to death. Being unable to share this assumption, we must venture to attempt another solution. . . .

Even before the Vita Nuova was completed there may well have been some curiosity to know who was the object of the author's passion; there are indeed indications to this effect in the work itself. But he was quite able to guard his secret. Then he entered himself into family life, and took part in public affairs in the government of the state. During these years people would hardly have inquired any further with whom the statesman and father of a family had been in love in his young days. Then came his exile, and the question was even less likely to be asked. Thus the whole love story must have fallen into oblivion; even though in 1290 guesses might have been made at it. But now the poet published his Convito, and then the Commedia, which quickly sprang into renown. Then was kindled a lively interest in the question of the identity of the lady whom he so glorified. But if the secret had been so closely kept all these years, who would now be able to discover it? Conjecture was driven to fix itself on the name Beatrice. It was assumed that this was her real name; inquiries were made as to possible acquaintances or contemporaries so named, and who was found in his near neighborhood. "Beatrice Portinari, of course," said every one; "it would be no other." And perhaps after this fashion the tradition grew up.

Perhaps also in quite a different fashion. Who at the present day can ascertain the truth with any security? Just as the people of old could only conjecture as to the true Beatrice, so can we only conjecture with regard to the origin of the tradition regarding her.

XI

THE PARADISO: ITS ASTRONOMICAL AND RELIGIOUS CONCEPTIONS[1]

I. THE SUBLIME CANTICLE OF THE COMEDY.

THE Inferno is the most widely known portion of the Divine Comedy, and the Purgatorio the most human and natural because it best describes the present life in its weaknesses and its disciplines; yet Dante undoubtedly considered the Paradiso the supreme triumph of his prophetic and artistic genius, as well as the culmination of his thought. His theme here reaches the fullness of its grandeur, and to rise to the height of his great argument he realized that he taxed his powers to their utmost. In his dedication of it to Can Grande he called it "the sublime Canticle of the Comedy." He felt that he was constantly struggling with the ineffable, that the vision hopelessly transcended his speech. Into this consecrated poem he threw his whole soul. "It is no coasting voyage for a little barque, this which the intrepid prow goes cleaving, nor for a pilot who would spare himself,"[2] and he pleads that he may well be excused, if, under the ponderous burden, his mortal shoulder sometimes trembles. Greater task, indeed, never essayed poet or prophet. He sought to combine in a form of perfect

[1] *The Teachings of Dante*, Charles Allen Dinsmore, pp. 161 ff. Houghton, Mifflin & Co.

[2] *Par.* xxiii. 67–69.

beauty the Ptolemaic system of astronomy; the teachings of Dionysius the Areopagite regarding the celestial hierarchy; the current astrological dogma of stellar influences; the guesses of the crude science of the times; the cumbrous theology of Aquinas; the rapt vision of the mystics; his own personal experiences; his passionate love for Beatrice the Florentine maiden, and Beatrice the symbol of divine revelation; the whole process of the development of soul from the first look of faith to the final beatitude; and even to symbolize the Triune God Himself as He appears beyond all space and time. No wonder that as he embarks on the deeps of this untried sea he warns the thoughtless not to follow him.

O ye, who in some pretty little boat,
Eager to listen, have been following
Behind my ship, that singing sails along,
Turn back to look again upon your shores;
Do not put out to sea, lest peradventure,
In losing me, you might yourselves be lost.
The sea I sail has never yet been passed;
Minerva breathes, and pilots me Apollo,
And Muses nine point out to me the Bears.[1]

How well he succeeded in this most hazardous voyage is a matter of diverse opinion. Leigh Hunt, who was incapable of appreciating such a nature as Dante's and such a poem as the Divine Comedy, in his little book entitled Stories from the Italian Poets, says: "In Paradise we realize little but a fantastical assemblage of doctors and doubtful characters, far more angry and theological than celestial; giddy raptures of monks and inquisitors dancing in circles, and saints denouncing Popes and Florentines; in short, a heaven libeling itself with invectives against earth, and ter-

[1] *Par.* ii. 1-9.

minating in a great presumption." It must be confessed that there is much in this canticle that strikes one as ridiculous. When we behold the flaming spirit of the venerable Peter Damian, whirling like a millstone, making a centre of his middle, we are far more inclined to laugh at our own crude conception of the grotesque figure he makes, than to picture the beauty of the swiftly circling flame, and marvel at the vigorous spiritual life which his cyclonic gyrations were intended to suggest. Doubtless also the many quaint mediæval discussions regarding the spots on the moon, the influences of the planets on human destiny, the language Adam spoke, and the length of time he spent in Eden before he ate the fatal apple, have little interest to us, and are endured as one traverses the desert for the good that lies beyond. Yet we must remember that Dante distinctly states in his dedication of this portion of his work to Can Grande that when he deals in speculative philosophy, it is not for the sake of the philosophy, but for practical needs. Notwithstanding all that is scholastic and bizarre in the Paradiso its most careful students are generally agreed that it is the fitting crown of the great trilogy. "Every line of the Paradiso," says Ruskin, "is full of the most exquisite and spiritual expressions of Christian truths, and the poem is only less read than the Inferno because it requires far greater attention, and, perhaps for its full enjoyment, a holier heart."[1] In this wonderful book, which to Carlyle was full of "inarticulate music," poetry seems to reach quite its highest point. "It is a perpetual hymn of everlasting love," exclaims Shelley; "Dante's apotheosis of Bea-

[1] *Stones of Venice*, ii. 324.

trice and the gradations of his own love and her loveliness by which as by steps he feigns himself to have ascended to the throne of the Supreme Cause, is the most glorious imagination of modern poetry."[1] Not less pronounced is Hallam's judgment that it is the noblest expression of the poet's genius. Comparing Dante with Milton, he says: "The philosophical imagination of the forms in this third part of his poem, almost defecated from all sublunary things by long and solitary musing, spiritualizes all that it touches."[2]

II. THE THEME OF THE PARADISO.

In this canticle Dante seeks to describe the nature of the religious life, its dominant truths, its felicities, and its ultimate beatitude. He is not painting a rapturous picture of bliss to comfort and lure the soul of the believer, but is making a sober attempt to show the spiritual life in its meaning, development, and final glory. As he could not make known the true hideousness of sin without following it into the future where it made the full disclosure of itself; as the purgatorial process, although taking place in this world and in the next, has the scene laid after death that the completed work may be revealed; so the true life of man is delineated against the background of eternity. This affords a canvas large enough to portray the spiritual life when it has come to the fullness of its stature. It is not heaven he is describing, but the religious life. These temporal experiences he lifts into the eternal light and displays the fullness of their glory.

[1] *Defence of Poetry.*
[2] *Literature of Europe*, vol. iv. chap. v.

III. THE BEGINNINGS OF THE SPIRITUAL LIFE.

The first steps in the religious life find their descriptions in that wonderfully beautiful and significant scene in Purgatory where the poet meets Beatrice in the Terrestrial Paradise. When the soul comes face to face with the revealed truth of God, it sees its sin, repents of it, confesses it, and looks toward Christ for atoning mercy. Now it is ready to enter the way that leads toward the Highest. The penitent soul enters upon the spiritual life when it centres itself upon God. "Man," says Horace Bushnell, "finds his paradise when he is imparadised in God. It is not that he is squared to certain abstractions or perfected in his moral conformity to certain impersonal laws; but it is that he is filled with the sublime personality of God, and forever exalted by his inspiration, moving in the divine movement, rested on the divine centre, blessed in the divine beatitude."[1] Thus a New England preacher, though but vaguely familiar with Dante, describes exactly the experience the poet went through, when after squaring himself to the impersonal laws of Purgatory, he fixed his eyes upon the Sun — the symbol of God. With this steady gaze there came into his soul a new power, and day seemed to be added to day. Having centred his life on God, he now turns his gaze to Beatrice, the revealed truth. In this most impressive way does Dante give us his definition of faith. It is the look of the soul toward divine truth; it is that spiritual energy by which man commits himself to truth; it is a look that trustfully, without analysis, receives its object as a whole into the soul.

[1] *Sermons for the New Life*, pp. 41, 42.

IV. THE ASTRONOMICAL FRAMEWORK OF THE POEM.

The idea of describing the development of the Christian life an ascent from star to star was a sublime conception of artistic genius. According to the Ptolemaic system of astronomy the earth was the centre of the universe, being encompassed by a zone of air and that by a zone of fire. Beyond the sphere of fire were seven planets, each revolving within a heaven of its own. These seven encircling heavens were those of the Moon, Mercury, Venus, the Sun, Mars, Jupiter, and Saturn; above were the Fixed Stars; then came a crystalline heaven, originating all movement and called the Primum Mobile; and surrounding all was the Empyrean, — the place of eternal, unchanging peace.

As the Catholic Church taught that there were seven virtues, Dante employed the seven planets to represent them. The prevalent belief that the earth cast a shadow on the first three planets enabled him to mark the distinction between the three theological and the four cardinal virtues. It is only vaguely hinted that the first three stars typify faith, hope, and charity, since these virtues do not come to their full vigor except through moral discipline.[1] The last four clearly indicate the cardinal virtues, prudence, fortitude, justice, temperance. Dante believed that the penitent having begun to live the blessed life by faith, hope, and love, which are necessarily imperfect, is trained by the moral virtues into robust character. After the perfected character, and resulting from it,

[1] Many authorities question whether the first three planets have any reference to the theological virtues.

comes a completed faith, hope, and love. Having done the will he can know the teaching; therefore after ascending through these seven planets, in the eighth and ninth Dante learns the loftiest truths revealed to the faithful. In the eighth he is taught the important truths of redemption, and in the ninth the celestial mysteries. Being now faultless in character and creed, the tenth heaven receives him into the ultimate blessedness. Thus the astronomical order proved a most serviceable framework for the poet's symbolism.

V. TWO FUNDAMENTAL TRUTHS.

The prevailing system of astronomy also enabled one so adept in allegory to give singularly interesting expression to two most important truths. The three shadowed stars suggest that the shadow of earthly sins falls upon heaven, in accordance with the immemorial faith of Christian thinkers that men are rewarded in the hereafter according to their fidelity here. This shadow of time upon eternity has no other influence, however, than to affect the capacity for bliss, since all dwelling in the celestial sphere are perfectly happy. "Everywhere in heaven is paradise, although the grace of the Supreme Good rains not there in one measure."[1]

The four unshadowed planets he uses to teach that there are many ways by which men come to God, and that the conditions of the journey profoundly influence one's destiny. The warrior on the battlefield moves by as direct a road as the scholar in his study; the just ruler is as sure of salvation as the wan hermit in his cell. In the Terrestrial Paradise four beau-

[1] *Par.* iii. 88-90.

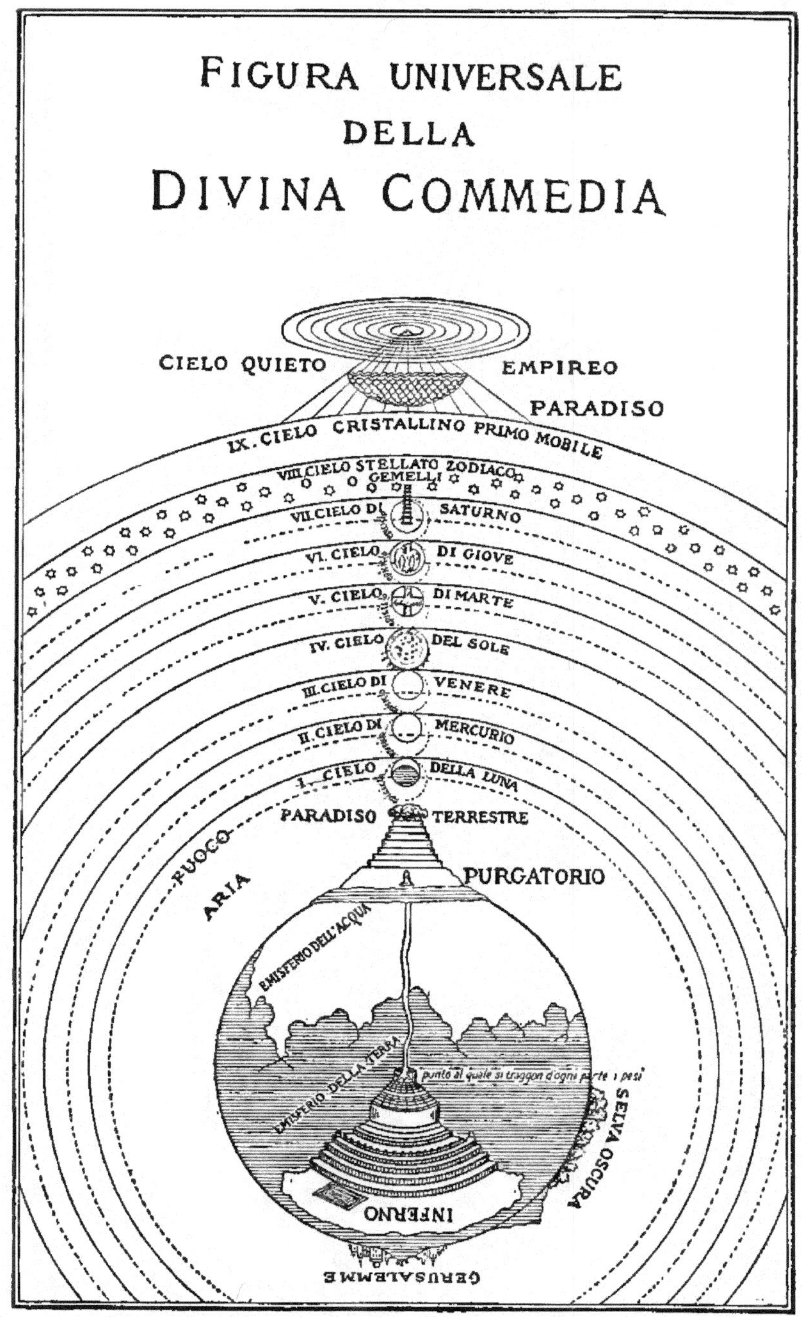

From "La materia della Divina Commedia di Dante Alighieri dichiarata in vi tavole. Dal Duca Michelangelo Caetani di Sermoneta."

tiful ones covered Dante with their arms and led him to Beatrice as she stood by the Griffon, saying: "Here we are nymphs; in heaven we are stars,"[1] symbolizing that the four cardinal virtues bring one into the presence of the truth as it is in Christ. The same teaching is here elaborated. The nymphs are now stars, typical of the virtues which must adorn him who would understand the redemptive and celestial mysteries to be revealed in the eighth and ninth heaven. The way to the ultimate beatitude is along this fourfold road, and the final felicity is shaped and colored by that virtue which is most characteristic. Thus time again projects itself into eternity, and the condition of one's mortal warfare affects his fiual destiny. Each of the four planets stands for one of the cardinal virtues: the Sun for prudence; red Mars for fortitude; the white Jupiter for spotless justice; and Saturn, calm and cold, is typical of temperance or contemplation. The spirits appear in that planet by which they have been most influenced, and whose virtue has been most conspicuous in their lives. They do not dwell there, but have come down to meet Dante that they may instruct him. In the Sun flame forth the spirits of the men of understanding and wisdom, the renowned scholars, and distinguished theologians, whose presence was apparent in that great orb by a lustre more brilliant than its own; in Mars the brave warriors of the faith range themselves into a fiery cross, the symbol by which they conquered; in Jupiter just rulers, moved by a concordant will, even as a single heat comes from many embers, form themselves into a colossal eagle, ensign of em-

[1] *Purg.* xxxi. 106.

pire; in Saturn there shine in ineffable light the clear, radiant spirits of the contemplative, who mount to the Highest up the golden stairway of meditation.

It was clearly in Dante's thought to teach that these four virtues differ in their worth, that when one passes from prudence to fortitude he comes nearer to God, and that the saint rapt in mystic contemplation of divine truth is closer to the ultimate joy than the just ruler upon his throne. This is in perfect harmony with the deep-seated conviction of the times, in this respect so unlike our own, that a cloistered life of ecstatic communion with God is holier than one spent in active benevolence. But this ascending series of virtues involves us in a perplexity. The light of Dante's mind, as Beatrice was the glory of his soul, was St. Thomas Aquinas. He is appropriately placed in the Sun, the sphere of wisdom and truth, ranking thus below Cacciaguida in Mars, and William of Sicily and Rhipeus the Trojan in Jupiter. The most satisfactory explanation is that though justice is a nobler virtue than prudence and the just ruler walks in a diviner way than the profound scholar, yet there are different degrees of glory in the same realm, — and he who shines with the full brightness of the sphere of the Sun may be nearer God, and more filled with the light eternal, than most of those who inhabit a higher circle. That there are various gradations of bliss in the same planet is declared by Piccarda when she says that Constance "glows with all the light of our sphere."

The grand divisions mentioned are marked in the poem by the termination of the earth's shadow, — a long prologue prefacing the ascent to the Sun, — by the ladder of gold leading to the eighth and ninth heavens, and by the essentially different character of the Empyrean.

VI. LIGHT, LIFE, TRUTH.

Not the least proof of Dante's extraordinary creative power is the simplicity of the material which he uses in the construction of this immense spiritual edifice. Three leading ideas only he employs, light, life, and vision of truth. Hallam finds them to be light, music, and motion;[1] but music occupies only a subordinate place, while the growing knowledge of truth is an organic thought. Life is a better word than motion, for by rapidity of movement Dante would symbolize abundant life. With rare artistic skill and spiritual discernment he chose his materials; the religious life is the life with God, and God is light, life, and truth.

No poet has been more keenly sensitive to light in all its manifestations than he. Light itself dissociated from all forms afforded him distinct pleasure, and was to him a rich fountain of poetic suggestiveness. The serene splendor of the stars seems to have been one of the chief consolations in his exiled and passion-swept life. "What!" exclaimed he in his letter declining to return to Florence on ignominious terms, "shall I not everywhere enjoy the light of the sun and of the stars? And may I not seek and contemplate, in every corner of the earth, under the canopy of heaven, consoling and delightful truth?" Light and truth! these are his heaven in this world and in the world to come. Such solace has the shining of the stars been to his

[1] *Literature of Europe*, vol. iv. chap. v.

homesick heart that in gratitude he ends each canticle with the word "stars." Hell is to be shut out from this calm radiance; the beginning of hope and purity is to come "forth to see again the stars;" the symbol of purgatory is the morning and evening light; heaven is to mount from star to star, and its gradations are known by the increasing glory of the light, while the bliss supreme is to fix his eyes on the Fountain of Eternal Light. Dean Church has finely pointed out how significant and beautiful light was to Dante's passionate soul, and how he studied it in all its forms.[1] "Light everywhere, — in the sky and earth and sea; in the star, the flames, the lamp, the gems; broken in the water, reflected from the mirror, transmitted pure through the glass, or colored through the edge of the fractured emerald; dimmed in the mist, the halo, the deep water; streaming through the rent cloud, glowing in the coal, quivering in the lightning, flashing in the topaz and the ruby, veiled behind the pure alabaster, mellowed and clouding itself in the pearl, — light contrasted with shadow, shading off and copying itself in the double rainbow, like voice and echo; light seen within light; light from every source, and in all its shapes illuminates, irradiates, gives glory to the Commedia." Small wonder is it that in his thought heaven is a place of unshadowed, eternal, ever deepening light. The more joyous the spirits are the brighter their splendor, and they glow with a new effulgence as their love manifests itself. Justinian is especially honored by being twined with a double glory.

Motion, indicative of the abundant life Christ promised to give, is also employed to make known the

[1] p. 387.

different degrees of blessedness. According to Aristotle natural motion is either in a right line, in a circle, or mixed. The circular is the perfect form; it alone is continuous, and is that of the Prime Mover. The impulse of motion is love, and the cause of love is vision; therefore the spirits move more or less rapidly in the measure of their inward vision of God. From the Seraphim downward, all the angels, heavens, and ranks of the redeemed are woven in one cosmic dance, and the celerity of their movement is always determined by the clearness of their sight into the nature of the Eternal Light. The mystic dances are Dante's method of expressing joy in the Divine Will, and even Peter Damian, whirling like a millstone on its axis, is not as ridiculous as he seems, for thus only can he express the ardor of his love, and the energy of his exultant life.

But the most commanding idea of all is vision of the truth. It is a somewhat difficult task for us to enter into perfect intellectual sympathy with Dante in his confidence in the power of the mind to know the truth. By a strange paradox the present generation has learned so much, and accumulated such a fabulous wealth of knowledge, that our minds quail in the presence of their riches and distrust their power to know. We delight in the investigation of truth, but lack faith in our ability to know it. The word that is oftenest upon our lips is Life, while the supreme word of the Middle Ages was Truth. The modern feeling is well expressed by Richard Watson Gilder: —

> I know what Life is, have caught sight of Truth:
> My heart is dead within me; a thick pall
> Darkens the midday Sun.[1]

[1] *Five Books of Song*, p. 42.

Dante would have said that the pall and darkness resulted from our dim apprehension of truth. The Middle Ages believed implicitly that man can know, and that perfect happiness consists in perfect knowledge of the Ultimate Reality. The vision of truth stimulates the ardors of the mind, so that love is proportioned to the clearness of sight into the truth. God is the Truth behind all phenomena, the approach to Him is through the truth; in knowing the truth and resting in it the mind has peace; to the beauty of truth the affections of the heart respond; and through the truth divine power comes into the will.

> Well I perceive that never sated is
> Our intellect unless Truth illume it,
> Beyond which nothing true expands itself.
> It rests therein, as a wild beast in his lair,
> When it attains it; and it can attain it;
> If not, then each desire would frustrate be.[1]

There are three writers in the Bible who make religion to consist in a knowledge of God; the author of Deuteronomy, Hosea, and St. John; with them Dante is in accord.

Holding such a noble and scriptural conception of the nature and goal of the spiritual life, Dante naturally traces its development by progressive knowledge of the truth, and makes the glories of heaven to consist in the beauty of truth "enkindled along the stairway of the Eternal palace."

Thus the vision of truth is the structural idea of Paradise. Its glory is the splendor of truth, its progress is the enlarging perception of truth, and its blessedness is the ardent love inflamed by truth. By a poetic conception of peerless beauty Dante measures

[1] *Par.* iv. 124–128.

his ascent, not by conscious motion, but by the radiance on the face of Beatrice. From the very first her glory dazzled his eyes; as they mounted upward she irradiated him with a smile such as would make a man in the fire happy, and finally her beauty became so intolerable that she durst not smile lest his sight be shattered as a bough by the lightning.

He finds that the merits of the redeemed determine the measure of their penetration into truth, and that the love born of sight gives them their sphere of blessedness.

His own power of vision grows stronger as he ascends. At first he beholds the blessed ones as mirrored semblances, then as flames of fire and orbs of light, whose real forms cannot be seen. When he had mounted so high that the vivid light enswathed him and by its own effulgence blinded him, his mind seemed to issue out of itself and was rekindled with a new power of vision. Seeing before him a stream of light like a river, he bathed his eyes in it; then did he look no more through a glass darkly, but face to face. Beatrice — revealed truth — is no longer needed; St. Bernard — type of intuitive insight — takes her place, and Dante reaches the final bliss by gazing with unquenched sight into the Fountain of Light Intellectual full of Love.

God is Light, God is Life, God is Truth; the spiritual life is to know God, and to receive his light, life, and truth. Surely there was no other material than these three elements out of which the divine poet could construct his stately paradise.

CHAPTER VII

INTERPRETATIONS

I

THE CHARACTER, PURPOSE, AND POETIC QUALITIES OF THE DIVINA COMMEDIA

By Dean Church.[1]

The Commedia is a novel and startling apparition in literature. Probably it has been felt by some, who have approached it with the reverence due to a work of such renown, that the world has been generous in placing it so high. It seems so abnormal, so lawless, so reckless of all ordinary proprieties and canons of feeling, taste, and composition. It is rough and abrupt; obscure in phrase and allusion, doubly obscure in purpose. It is a medley of all subjects usually kept distinct: scandal of the day and transcendental science, politics and confessions, coarse satire and angelic joy, private wrongs with the mysteries of the faith, local names and habitations of earth with visions of hell and heaven. It is hard to keep up with the ever-changing current of feeling, to pass as the poet passes, without effort or scruple, from tenderness to ridicule, from hope to bitter scorn or querulous complaint, from high-raised devotion to the calmness of prosaic subtle-

[1] *Dante and Other Essays.* R. W. Church. These extracts are made by the kind permission of Macmillan & Co., London. Although this essay was written in 1850, it has not been surpassed in depth of insight, sweep of thought, or beauty of expression.

ties or grotesque detail. Each separate element and vein of thought has its precedent, but not their amalgamation. Many had written visions of the unseen world, but they had not blended with them their personal fortunes. St. Augustine had taught the soul to contemplate its own history, and had traced its progress from darkness to light;[1] but he had not interwoven with it the history of Italy, and the consummation of all earthly destinies. Satire was no new thing; Juvenal had given it a moral, some of the Provençal poets a political turn; St. Jerome had kindled into it fiercely and bitterly even while expounding the Prophets; but here it streams forth in all its violence, within the precincts of the eternal world, and alternates with the hymns of the blessed. Lucretius had drawn forth the poetry of nature and its laws; Virgil and Livy had unfolded the poetry of the Roman Empire; St. Augustine, the still grander poetry of the history of the City of God; but none had yet ventured to weave into one the three wonderful threads. And yet the scope of the Italian poet, vast and comprehensive as the issue of all things, universal as the government which directs nature and intelligence, forbids him not to stoop to the lowest caitiff he has ever despised, the minutest fact in nature that has ever struck his eye, the merest personal association which hangs pleasantly in his memory. Writing for all time, he scruples not to mix with all that is august and permanent in history and prophecy, incidents the most transient, and names the most obscure; to waste an immortality of shame or praise on those about whom his own generation were to inquire in vain. Scrip-

[1] See *Convito*, i. 2.

ture history runs into profane; Pagan legends teach their lesson side by side with Scripture scenes and miracles; heroes and poets of heathenism, separated from their old classic world, have their place in the world of faith, discourse with Christians of Christian dogmas, and even mingle with the saints; Virgil guides the poet through his fear and his penitence to the gates of Paradise.

This feeling of harsh and extravagant incongruity, of causeless and unpardonable darkness, is perhaps the first impression of many readers of the Commedia. But probably as they read on, there will mingle with this a sense of strange and unusual grandeur, arising not alone from the hardihood of the attempt, and the mystery of the subject, but from the power and the character of the poet. It will strike them that words cut deeper than is their wont; that from that wild, uncongenial imagery, thoughts emerge of singular truth and beauty. Their dissatisfaction will be chequered, even disturbed — for we can often bring ourselves to sacrifice much for the sake of a clear and consistent view — by the appearance, amid much that repels them, of proofs undeniable and accumulating of genius as mighty as it is strange. Their perplexity and disappointment may grow into distinct condemnation, or it may pass into admiration and delight; but no one has ever come to the end of the Commedia without feeling that if it has given him a new view and specimen of the wildness and unaccountable waywardness of the human mind, it has also added, as few other books have, to his knowledge of its feelings, its capabilities, and its grasp, and suggested larger and more serious thoughts, for which he may be grateful, concerning that unseen world of which he is even here a member.

Dante would not have thanked his admirers for becoming apologists. Those in whom the sense of imperfection and strangeness overpower sympathy for grandeur, and enthusiasm for nobleness, and joy in beauty, he certainly would have left to themselves. But neither would he teach any that he was leading them along a smooth and easy road. The Commedia will always be a hard and trying book; nor did the writer much care that it should be otherwise. Much of this is no doubt to be set down to its age; much of its roughness and extravagance, as well as of its beauty — its allegorical spirit, its frame and scenery. The idea of a visionary voyage through the worlds of pain and bliss is no invention of the poet — it was one of the commonest and most familiar mediæval vehicles of censure or warning; and those who love to trace the growth and often strange fortunes of popular ideas, or whose taste leads them to disbelieve in genius, and track the parentage of great inventions to the foolish and obscure, may find abundant materials in the literature of legends.[1] But his own age — the age which received the Commedia with mingled enthusiasm and wonder, and called it the Divine — was as much perplexed as we are, though probably rather pleased thereby than offended. That within a century after its composition, in the most famous cities and universities of Italy, Florence, Venice, Bologna, and Pisa, chairs should have been founded, and illustrious men engaged to lecture on it, is a strange homage to its power, even in that time of quick feeling; but as

[1] *Vide* Ozanam, *Dante*, pp. 535 *sqq.*, Ed. 2de.

strange and great a proof of its obscurity. What is dark and forbidding in it was scarcely more clear to the poet's contemporaries. And he, whose last object was amusement, invites no audience but a patient and confiding one.[1]

The character of the Commedia belongs much more, in its excellence and its imperfections, to the poet himself and the nature of his work, than to his age. That cannot screen his faults; nor can it arrogate to itself, it must be content to share, his glory. His leading idea and line of thought was much more novel then than it is now, and belongs much more to the modern than the mediæval world. The Story of a Life, the poetry of man's journey through the wilderness to his true country, is now in various and very different shapes as hackneyed a form of imagination as an allegory, an epic, a legend of chivalry were in former times. Not, of course, that any time has been without its poetical feelings and ideas on the subject; and never were they deeper and more diversified, more touching and solemn, than in the ages that passed from St. Augustine and St. Gregory to St. Thomas and St. Bonaventura. But a philosophical poem, where they were not merely the coloring, but the subject, an *epos* of the soul, placed for its trial in a fearful and wonderful world, with relations to time and matter, history and nature, good and evil, the beautiful, the intelligible, and the mysterious, sin and grace, the infinite and the eternal, — and having in the company and under the influences of other intelligences, to make its choice, to struggle, to succeed or fail, to gain the light or be lost, — this was a new and unat-

[1] *Par.* ii. 1-16.

tempted theme. It has been often tried since, in faith or doubt, in egotism, in sorrow, in murmuring, in affectation, sometimes in joy — in various forms, in prose and verse, completed or fragmentary, in reality or fiction, in the direct or the shadowed story, in the Pilgrim's Progress, in Rousseau's Confessions, in Wilhelm Meister and Faust, in the Excursion. It is common enough now for the poet, in the faith of human sympathy, and in the sense of the unexhausted vastness of his mysterious subject, to believe that his fellows will not see without interest and profit, glimpses of his own path and fortunes — hear from his lips the disclosure of his chief delights, his warnings, his fears — follow the many-colored changes, the impressions and workings of a character, at once the contrast and the counterpart to their own. But it was a new path then; and he needed to be, and was, a bold man, who first opened it — a path never trod without peril, usually with loss or failure.

And certainly no great man ever made less secret to himself of his own genius. He is at no pains to rein in or to dissemble his consciousness of power, which he has measured without partiality, and feels sure will not fail him. "Fidandomi di me più che di un altro"[1] is a reason which he assigns without reserve. We look with the distrust and hesitation of modern days, yet, in spite of ourselves, not without admiration and regret, at such frank hardihood. It was more common once than now. When the world was young, it was more natural and allowable — it was often seemly and noble. Men knew not their difficulties as we know them, — we, to whom time,

[1] Trusting myself more than any one else. (*Convito*, i. 10.)

which has taught so much wisdom, has brought so many disappointments, — we who have seen how often the powerful have fallen short, and the noble gone astray, and the most admirable missed their perfection. It is becoming in us to distrust ourselves, to be shy if we cannot be modest; it is but a respectful tribute to human weakness and our brethren's failures. But there was a time when great men dared to claim their greatness — not in foolish self-complacency, but in unembarrassed and majestic simplicity, in magnanimity and truth, in the consciousness of a serious and noble purpose, and of strength to fulfill it. Without passion, without elation as without shrinking, the poet surveys his superiority and his high position, as something external to him; he has no doubts about it, and affects none. He would be a coward, if he shut his eyes to what he could do; as much a trifler in displaying reserve as ostentation. Nothing is more striking in the Commedia than the serene and unhesitating confidence with which he announces himself the heir and reviver of the poetic power so long lost to the world, the heir and reviver of it in all its fullness. He doubts not of the judgment of posterity. One has arisen who shall throw into the shade all modern reputations, who shall bequeath to Christendom the glory of that name of Poet, "che più dura e più onora," hitherto the exclusive boast of heathenism, and claim the rare honors of the laurel.

> For now so rarely Poet gathers these,
> Or Cæsar, winning an immortal praise
> (Shame unto man's degraded energies),
> That joy should to the Delphic God arise
> When haply any one aspires to gain
> The high reward of the Peneian prize.
>
> (*Par.* i. 28, 33. Wright.)

He has but to follow his star to be sure of the glorious port:[1] he is the master of language; he can give fame to the dead; no task nor enterprise appalls him, for whom spirits keep watch in heaven, and angels have visited the shades, "tal si partì dal cantar alleluia," who is Virgil's foster-child and familiar friend. Virgil bids him lay aside the last vestige of fear. Virgil is to "crown him king and priest over himself," for a higher venture than heathen poetry had dared; in Virgil's company he takes his place without diffidence, and without vainglory, among the great poets of old — a sister soul.[2]

This sustained magnanimity and lofty self-reliance, which never betrays itself, is one of the main elements in the grandeur of the Commedia. It is an imposing spectacle to see such fearlessness, such freedom, and such success in an untried path, amid unprepared materials and rude instruments, models scanty and only half understood, powers of language still doubtful and suspected, the deepest and strongest thought still confined to unbending forms and the harshest phrase; exact and extensive knowledge, as yet far out of reach; with no help from time, which familiarizes all things, and of which manner, elaboration, judgment, and taste are the gifts and inheritance; to see the poet, trusting to his eye "which saw everything,"[3] and his searching and creative spirit, venture undauntedly into all regions of thought and feeling, to draw thence a picture of the government of the universe.

But such greatness had to endure its price and its counterpoise. Dante was alone, — except in his vision-

[1] Brunetto Latini's Prophecy, *Inf.* 15. [2] *Inf.* 4.
[3] "Dante che tutto vedea." (*Sacchetti*, Nov. 114.)

ary world, solitary and companionless. The blind Greek had his throng of listeners; the blind Englishman his home and the voices of his daughters; Shakespeare had his free associates of the stage; Goethe, his correspondents, a court, and all Germany to applaud. Not so Dante. The friends of his youth are already in the region of spirits, and meet him there, — Casella, Forese; Guido Cavalcanti will soon be with them. In this upper world he thinks and writes as a friendless man — to whom all that he had held dearest was either lost or embittered; he thinks and writes for himself.

And so he is his own law; he owns no tribunal of opinion or standard of taste, except among the great dead. He hears them exhort them to "let the world talk on — to stand like a tower unshaken by the winds."[1] He fears to be "a timid friend to truth," "to lose life among those who shall call this present time antiquity."[2] He belongs to no party. He is his own arbiter of the beautiful and the becoming; his own judge over right and injustice, innocence and guilt. He has no followers to secure, no school to humor, no public to satisfy; nothing to guide him, and nothing to consult, nothing to bind him, nothing to fear, out of himself. In full trust in heart and will, in his sense of truth, in his teeming brain, he gives himself free course. If men have idolized the worthless, and canonized the base, he reverses their award without mercy, and without apology; if they have forgotten the just because he was obscure, he remembers him: if "Monna Berta and Ser Martino," the wimpled and hooded gossips of the day, with their

[1] *Purg.* 5. [2] *Par.* 17.

sage company, have settled it to their own satisfaction that Providence cannot swerve from their general rules, cannot save where they have doomed, or reject where they have approved, — he both fears more and hopes more. Deeply reverent to the judgment of the ages past, reverent to the persons whom they have immortalized for good and even for evil, in his own day he cares for no man's person and no man's judgment. And he shrinks not from the auguries and forecastings of his mind about their career and fate. Men reasoned rapidly in those days on such subjects, and without much scruple; but not with his deliberate and discriminating sternness. The most popular and honored names in Florence, —

> Tegghiaio, Farinata, names of worth,
> And Rusticucci, Mosca, with the rest,
> Who bent their minds to working good on earth,

have yet the damning brand: no reader of the Inferno can have forgotten the shock of that terrible reply to the poet's questionings about their fate: —

> "Mid blacker souls," he said, "they 're doomed to dwell."
> (*Inf.* 6. Wright.)

If he is partial, it is no vulgar partiality: friendship and old affection do not venture to exempt from its fatal doom the sin of his famous master, Brunetto Latini; nobleness and great deeds, a kindred character and common wrongs, are not enough to redeem Farinata; and he who could tell her story bowed to the eternal law, and dared not save Francesca. If he condemns by a severer rule than that of the world, he absolves with fuller faith in the possibilities of grace. Many names of whom history has recorded no good, are marked by him for bliss; yet not without full respect for justice. The penitent of the last hour is saved, but he suffers loss. Manfred's soul is rescued; mercy had accepted his tears, and forgiven his great sins; and the excommunication of his enemy did not bar his salvation: —

> But their fell curses cannot fix our doom,
> Nor stay the Eternal Love from His intent,
> While Hope remaining bears her verdant bloom. (*Purg.* 3.)

Yet his sin, though pardoned, was to keep him for loug years from the perfection of heaven.[1] And with the same independence with which he assigns their fate, he selects his instances, — instances which are to be the types of character and its issues. No man ever owned more unreservedly the fascination of greatness, its sway over the imagination and the heart; no one prized more the grand harmony and sense of fitness which there is, when the great man and the great office are joined in one, and reflect each other's greatness. The famous and great of all ages are gathered in the poet's vision; the great names even of fable, — Geryon and the giants, the Minotaur and Centaurs, and the heroes of Thebes and Troy. But not the great and famous only: this is too narrow, too conventional a sphere; it is not real enough. He felt, what the modern world feels so keenly, that wonderful histories are latent in the inconspicuous paths of life, in the fugitive incidents of the hour, among the persons whose faces we have seen. The Church had from the first been witness to the deep

[1] Charles of Anjou, his Guelf conqueror, is placed above him, in the valley of the kings (*Purg.* 7), " Colui dal maschio naso," — notwithstanding the charges afterwards made against him (*Purg.* 20).

interest of individual life. The rising taste for novels showed that society at large was beginning to be alive to it. And it is this feeling — that behind the veil there may be grades of greatness but nothing insignificant — that led Dante to refuse to restrict himself to the characters of fame. He will associate with them the living men who have stood round him; they are part of the same company with the greatest. That they have interested him, touched him, moved his indignation or pity, struck him as examples of great vicissitude or of a perfect life, have pleased him, loved him, — this is enough why they should live in his poem as they have lived to him. He chooses at will; history, if it has been negligent at the time about those whom he thought worthy of renown, must be content with its loss. He tells their story, or touches them with a word like the most familiar names, according as he pleases. The obscure highway robber, the obscure betrayer of his sister's honor — Rinier da Corneto and Rinier Pazzo, and Caccianimico — are ranked, not according to their obscurity, but according to the greatness of their crimes, with the famous conquerors, and "scourges of God," and seducers of the heroic age, Pyrrhus and Attila, and the great Jason of "royal port, who sheds no tear in his torments."[1] He earns as high praise from Virgil for his curse on the furious wrath of the old frantic Florentine burgher, as if he had cursed the disturber of the world's peace.[2] And so in the realms of joy, among the faithful accomplishers of the highest trusts, kings and teachers of the nations, founders of orders, sainted empresses, appear those whom, though the world had

[1] See the magnificent picture, *Inf.* 18. [2] *Ibid.* 8.

forgotten or misread them, the poet had enshrined in his familiar thoughts, for their sweetness, their gentle goodness, their nobility of soul; the penitent, the nun, the old crusading ancestor, the pilgrim who had deserted the greatness which he had created, the brave logician, who "syllogized unpalatable truths" in the Quartier Latin of Paris.[1]

There is small resemblance in all this — this arbitrary and imperious tone, this range of ideas, feelings, and images, this unshackled freedom, this harsh reality — to the dreamy gentleness of the Vita Nuova, or even the staid argumentation of the more mature Convito. The Vita Nuova is all self-concentration, a brooding, not unpleased, over the varying tides of feeling, which are little influenced by the world without; where every fancy, every sensation, every superstition of the lover is detailed with the most whimsical subtlety. The Commedia, too, has its tenderness, and that more deep, more natural, more true, than the poet had before adapted to the traditionary formulæ of the "Courts of Love," — the eyes of Beatrice are as bright, and the "conquering light of her smile;"[2] they still culminate, but they are not alone, in the poet's heaven. And the professed subject of the Commedia is still Dante's own story and life; he still makes himself the central point. And steeled as he

[1] Cunizza, Piccarda, Cacciaguida, Roméo. (*Par.* 9, 3, 15, 6, 10.)

> Sigieri! dear and everlasting light;
> Who in the Street of Straw as erst he taught,
> Raised by the truths he told, invidious spite (*Par.* 10),

in company with St. Thomas Aquinas, in the sphere of the Sun. Ozanam gives a few particulars of this forgotten professor of the "Rue du Fouarre," pp. 320–323.

[2] *Par.* 18.

is by that high and hard experience of which his poem is the projection and type, — "Ben tetragono ai colpi di ventura," — a stern and brief-spoken man, set on objects, and occupied with a theme, lofty and vast as can occupy man's thoughts, he still lets escape ever and anon some passing avowal of delicate sensitiveness,[1] lingers for a moment on some indulged self-consciousness, some recollection of his once quick and changeful mood — "io che son trasmutabil per tutte guise"[2] — or half playfully alludes to the whispered name of a lady,[3] whose pleasant courtesy has beguiled a few days of exile. But he is no longer spell-bound and entangled in fancies of his own weaving — absorbed in the unprofitable contemplation of his own internal sensations. The man is indeed the same, still a Florentine, still metaphysical, still a lover. He returns to the haunts and images of youth, to take among them his poet's crown; but "with other voice and other garb,"[4] a penitent and a prophet — with larger thoughts, wider sympathies, freer utterance; sterner and fiercer, yet nobler and more genuine in

[1] For instance, his feeling of distress at gazing at the blind, who were not aware of his presence —

To me it seemed a want of courtesy,
Unseen myself, in other's face to peer (*Purg.* 13),

and of shame, at being tempted to listen to a quarrel between two lost spirits: —

Listening I stood intent, with all my mind,
  When unto me the master said, Take heed;
  To quarrel with thee I am much inclined.
When I perceived him speak in angry strain,
  I turned to him with such remorse, I deem
  My mind for aye the impression will retain (*Inf.* 30),

and the burst, —

O noble conscience, upright and refined,
How slight a fault inflicts a bitter sting! (*Purg.* 3. Wright.)

[2] *Par.* 5. [3] *Purg.* 24. [4] *Par.* 25.

his tenderness — as one whom trial has made serious and keen and intolerant of evil, but not skeptical or callous; yet with the impressions and memories of a very different scene from his old day-dreams.

"After that it was the pleasure of the citizens of that fairest and most famous daughter of Rome, Florence, to cast me forth from her most sweet bosom (wherein I had been nourished up to the maturity of my life, and in which, with all peace to her, I long with all my heart to rest my weary soul, and finish the time which is given me), I have passed through almost all the regions to which this language reaches, a wanderer, almost a beggar, displaying, against my will, the stroke of fortune, which is ofttimes unjustly wont to be imputed to the person stricken. Truly, I have been a ship without a sail or helm, carried to divers harbors and gulfs and shores by that parching wind which sad poverty breathes; and I have seemed vile in the eyes of many, who perchance, from some fame, had imagined of me in another form; in the sight of whom not only did my presence become nought, but every work of mine less prized, both what had been and what was to be wrought." (*Convito*, Tr. i. c. 3.)

Thus proved, and thus furnished — thus independent and confident, daring to trust his instinct and genius in what was entirely untried and unusual, he entered on his great poem, to shadow forth, under the figure of his own conversion and purification, not merely how a single soul rises to its perfection, but how this visible world, in all its phases of nature, life, and society, is one with the invisible, which borders on it, actuates, accomplishes, and explains it. It is this vast plan — to take into his scope, not the soul only in its struggles and triumph, but all that the soul finds itself engaged with in its course; the accidents of the hour, and of ages past; the real persons, great and small, apart from and without whom it cannot think or act; the material world, its theatre and home — it is this which gives so many various sides to the Commedia, which makes it so novel and strange. It is not a mere personal history, or a pouring forth of feeling, like the Vita Nuova, though he is himself the mysterious voyager, and he opens without reserve his actual life and his heart; he speaks, indeed, in the first person, yet he is but a character of the drama, and in great part of it with not more of distinct personality than in that paraphrase of the penitential Psalms, in which he has preluded so much of the Commedia. Yet the Commedia is not a pure allegory; it admits and makes use of the allegorical, but the laws of allegory are too narrow for it; the real in it is too impatient of the veil, and breaks through in all its hardness and detail, into what is most shadowy. History is indeed viewed not in its ephemeral look, but under the light of God's final judgments; in its completion, not in its provisional and fragmentary character; viewed therefore but in faith; but its issues, which in this confused scene we ordinarily contemplate in the gross, the poet brings down to detail and individuals; he faces and grasps the tremendous thought that the very men and women whom we see and speak to, are now the real representatives of sin and goodness, the true actors in that scene which is so familiar to us as a picture, — unflinching and terrible heart, he endures to face it in its most harrowing forms. But he wrote not for sport, nor to give poetic pleasure, — he wrote to warn; the seed of the Commedia was sown in tears and reaped in misery, and the consolations which it offers are awful as they are real.

Thus, though he throws into symbol and image what can only be expressed by symbol and image, we can as little forget, in reading him, this real world in which we live, as we can in one of Shakespeare's plays. It is not merely that the poem is crowded with real personages, most of them having the single interest to us of being real. But all that is associated with man's history and existence is interwoven with the main course of thought — all that gives character to life, all that gives it form and feature, even to quaintness, all that occupies the mind, or employs the hand — speculation, science, arts, manufactures, monuments, scenes, customs, proverbs, ceremonies, games, punishments, attitudes of men, habits of living creatures. The wildest and most unearthly imaginations, the most abstruse thoughts take up into and incorporate with themselves the forcible and familiar impressions of our mother earth, and do not refuse the company and aid even of the homeliest.

This is not mere poetic ornament, peculiarly, profusely, or extravagantly employed. It is one of the ways in which his dominant feeling expresses itself — spontaneous and instinctive in each several instance of it, but the kindling and effluence of deliberate thought, and attending on a clear purpose — the feeling of the real and intimate connection between the objects of sight and faith. It is not that he sees in one the simple counterpart and reverse of the other, or sets himself to trace out universally their mutual correspondences; he has too strong a sense of the reality of this familiar life to reduce it merely to a shadow and type of the unseen. What he struggles to express in countless ways, with all the resources of his strange and gigantic power, is, that this world and the next are both equally real, and both one — parts, however different, of one whole. The world to come we know but in "a glass darkly;" man can only think and imagine of it in images, which he knows to be but broken and faint reflections: but this world we know, not in outline and featureless idea, but by name, and face, and shape, by place and person, by the colors and forms which crowd over its surface, the men who people its habitations, the events which mark its moments. Detail fills the sense here, and is the mark of reality. And thus he seeks to keep alive the feeling of what that world is which he connects with heaven and hell; not by abstractions, not much by elaborate and highly finished pictures, but by names, persons, local features, definite images. Widely and keenly has he ranged over and searched into the world — with a largeness of mind which disdained not to mark and treasure up, along with much unheeded beauty, many a characteristic feature of nature, unnoticed because so common. All his pursuits and interests contribute to the impression, which, often instinctively it may be, he strives to produce, of the manifold variety of our life. As a man of society, his memory is full of its usages, formalities, graces, follies, fashions, — of expressive motions, postures, gestures, looks; of music, of handicrafts, of the conversation of friends or associates, — of all that passes, so transient, yet so keenly pleasant or distasteful, between man and man. As a traveler, he recalls continually the names and scenes of the world; as a man of speculation, the secrets of nature, — the phenomena of light, the theory of the planets' motions, the idea and laws of physiology. As a man of learning, he is filled with the thoughts and recollections of ancient fable and history; as a politician, with the thoughts, prognostications, and hopes, of the history of the day; as a moral philosopher he has watched himself, his external sensations and changes, his inward passions, his mental powers, his ideas, his conscience; he has far and wide noted character, discriminated motives, classed good and evil deeds. All that the man of society, of travel, of science, of learning, the politician, the moralist, could gather, is used at will in the great poetic structure; but all converges to the purpose, and is directed by the intense feeling of the theologian, who sees this wonderful and familiar scene melting into and ending in another yet more wonderful, but which will one day be as familiar, — who sees the difficult but sure progress of the manifold remedies of the Divine government to their predestined issue; and, over all, God and His saints.

So comprehensive in interest is the Commedia. Any attempt to explain it, by narrowing that interest to politics, philosophy, the moral life, or theology itself, must prove inadequate. Theology strikes the keynote; but history, natural and metaphysical science, poetry, and art, each in their turn join in the harmony, independent, yet ministering to the whole. If from the poem itself we could be for a single moment in doubt of the reality and dominant place of religion in it, the plain-spoken prose of the Convito would show how he placed "the Divine Science, full of all peace, and allowing no strife of opinions and sophisms, for the excellent certainty of its subject, which is God," in single perfection above all other sciences, "which are, as Solomon speaks, but queens, or concubines, or maidens; but she is the 'Dove,' and the 'perfect one,' —'Dove,' because without stain of strife, 'perfect,' because perfectly she makes us behold the truth, in which our soul stills itself and is at rest." But the same passage[1] shows likewise how he viewed all human knowledge and human interests, as holding their due place in the hierarchy of wisdom, and among the steps of man's perfection. No account of the Commedia will prove sufficient, which does not keep in view, first of all, the high moral purpose and deep spirit of faith with which it was written, and then the wide liberty of materials and means which the poet allowed himself in working out his design.

Doubtless, his writings have a political aspect. The "great Ghibelline poet" is one of Dante's received synonyms; of his strong political opinions, and the importance he attached to them, there can be no doubt. And he meant his poem to be the vehicle of them, and the record to all ages of the folly and selfishness with which he saw men governed.

But the idea of the De Monarchia is no key to the Commedia. The direct or primary purpose of the Commedia is surely its obvious one. It is to stamp a deep impression on the mind, of the issues of good and ill doing here — of the real worlds of pain and joy. To do this forcibly, it is done in detail — of course it can only be done in figure. Punishment, purification, or the fullness of consolation are, as he would think, at

[1] *Convito*, Tr. 2. c. 14, 15.

this very moment, the lot of all the numberless spirits who have ever lived here — spirits still living and sentient as himself: parallel with our life, they too are suffering or are at rest. Without pause or interval, in all its parts simultaneously, this awful scene is going on — the judgments of God are being fulfilled — could we but see it. It exists, it might be seen, at each instant of time, by a soul whose eyes were opened, which was carried through it. And this he imagines. It had been imagined before; it is the working out which is peculiar to him. It is not a barren vision. His subject is, besides the eternal world, the soul which contemplates it; by sight, according to his figures, — in reality, by faith. As he is led on from woe to deeper woe, then through the tempered chastisements and resignation of Purgatory to the beatific vision, he is tracing the course of the soul on earth, realizing sin and weaning itself from it, — of its purification and preparation for its high lot, by converse with the good and wise, by the remedies of grace, by efforts of will and love, perhaps by the dominant guidance of some single pure and holy influence, whether of person, or institution, or thought. Nor will we say but that beyond this earthly probation, he is not also striving to grasp and imagine to himself something of that awful process and training, by which, whether in or out of the flesh, the spirit is made fit to meet its Maker, its Judge, and its Chief Good.

Thus it seems that even in its main design the poem has more than one aspect; it is a picture, a figure, partially a history, perhaps an anticipation. And this is confirmed by what the poet has himself distinctly stated of his ideas of poetic composition.

His view is expressed generally in his philosophical treatise, the Convito; but it is applied directly to the Commedia in a letter which, if in its present form of doubtful authenticity, without any question represents his sentiments, and the substance of which is incorporated in one of the earliest writings on the poem, Boccaccio's commentary. The following is his account of the subject of the poem: —

"For the evidence of what is to be said, it is to be noted, that this work is not of one single meaning only, but may be said to have many meanings (*polysensuum*). For the first meaning is that of the letter, another is that of things signified by the letter; the first of these is called the literal sense, the second, the allegorical or moral. This mode of treating a subject may for clearness' sake be considered in those verses of the psalm, *In exitu Israel*. 'When Israel came out of Egypt, and the house of Jacob from the strange people, Judah was his sanctuary, and Israel his dominion.' For if we look at the *letter* only, there is here signified the going out of the children of Israel in the time of Moses; if at the *allegory*, there is signified our redemption through Christ; if at the *moral* sense, there is signified to us the conversion of the soul from the mourning and misery of sin to the state of grace; if at the *anagogic* sense,[1] there is signified the passing out of the holy soul from the bondage of this corruption to the liberty of everlasting glory. And these mystical meanings, though called by different names, may all be called *allegori-*

[1] *Litera* gesta refert, quid credas *allegoria*
Moralis quid agas, quid speres *anagogia*.
(De Witte's note from Buti).

cal as distinguished from the literal or historical sense. . . . This being considered, it is plain that there ought to be a twofold subject, concerning which the two corresponding meanings may proceed. Therefore we must consider first concerning the subject of this work as it is to be understood literally, then as it is to be considered allegorically. The subject then of the whole work, taken literally only, is the state of souls after death considered in itself. For about this, and on this, the whole work turns. But if the work be taken allegorically its subject is man, as, by his freedom of choice deserving well or ill, he is subject to the justice which rewards and punishes." [1]

The passage in the Convito is to the same effect; but his remarks on the *moral* and *anagogic* meaning may be quoted: —

"The third sense is called *moral;* that it is which readers ought to go on noting carefully in writings, for their own profit and that of their disciples; as in the Gospel it may be noted when Christ went up to the mountain to be transfigured, that of the twelve Apostles he took with him only three; in which morally we may understand, that in the most secret things we ought to have but few companions. The fourth sort of meaning is called *anagogic*, that is, above our sense; and this is when we spiritually interpret a passage, which even in its literal meaning, by means of the things signified, expresses the heavenly things of everlasting glory; as may be seen in that song of the Prophet, which says that in the coming out of the people of Israel from Egypt, Judah was made holy and free; which, although it is mani-

[1] *Vide* pp. 267–269.

festly true according to the letter, is not less true as spiritually understood; that is, that when the soul comes out of sin, it is made holy and free, in its own power.[1]"

The general meaning of the Commedia is clear enough. But it certainly does appear to refuse to be fitted into a connected formal scheme of interpretation. It is not a homogeneous, consistent allegory, like the Pilgrim's Progress and the Fairy Queen. The allegory continually breaks off, shifts its ground, gives place to other elements, or mingles with them — like a stream which suddenly sinks into the earth, and after passing under plains and mountains, reappears in a distant point, and in different scenery. We can, indeed, imagine its strange author commenting on it, and finding or marking out its prosaic substratum, with the cold-blooded precision and scholastic distinctions of the Convito. However, he has not done so. And of the many enigmas which present themselves, either in its structure or separate parts, the key seems hopelessly lost. The early commentators are very ingenious, but very unsatisfactory; they see where we can see, but beyond that they are as full of uncertainty as ourselves. It is in character with that solitary and haughty spirit, while touching universal sympathies, appalling and charming all hearts, to have delighted in his own dark sayings, which had meaning only to himself. It is true that, whether in irony or from that quaint studious care for the appearance of literal truth, which makes him apologize for the wonders which he relates, and confirm them by an oath,

[1] P. 267.

"on the words of his poem,"[1] he provokes and challenges us; bids us admire "doctrine hidden under strange verses;"[2] bids us strain our eyes, for the veil is thin:" —

> Reader! here sharpen to the truth thy sight;
> For thou with care may'st penetrate the veil,
> So finely woven, and of texture slight. (*Purg.* 8.)

But eyes are still strained in conjecture and doubt.

Yet the most certain and detailed commentary, one which should assign the exact reason for every image or allegory, and its place and connection in a general scheme, would add but little to the charm or to the use of the poem. It is not so obscure but that every man's experience who has thought over and felt the mystery of our present life, may supply the commentary, — the more ample, the wider and more various his experience, the deeper and keener his feeling. Details and links of connection may be matter of controversy. Whether the three beasts of the forest mean definitely the vices of the time, or of Florence specially, or of the poet himself — "the wickedness of his heels, compassing him round about" — may still exercise critics and antiquaries; but that they carry with them distinct and special impressions of evil, and that they are the hindrances of man's salvation, is not doubtful. And our knowledge of the key of the allegory, where we possess it, contributes but little to

[1] That truth which bears the semblance of a lie
Should never pass the lips, if possible: —
Though crime be absent, still disgrace is nigh,
But here I needs must speak; and by the rhymes
Reader of this my Comedy, I swear,
So may they live with fame to future times.
(*Inf.* 16. Wright.)

[2] *Inf.* 9.

the effect. We may infer from the Convito[1] that the eyes of Beatrice stand definitely for the *demonstrations*, and her smiles for the *persuasions* of wisdom; but the poetry of the Paradiso is not about demonstrations and persuasions, but about looks and smiles; and the ineffable and holy calm — *serenitatis et æternitatis afflatus* — which pervades it, comes from its sacred truths, and holy persons, and that deep spirit of high-raised yet composed devotion which it requires no interpreter to show us.

Figure and symbol, then, are doubtless the law of composition in the Commedia; but this law discloses itself very variously, and with different degrees of strictness. In its primary and most general form it is palpable, consistent, pervading. There can be no doubt that the poem is meant to be understood figuratively, no doubt of what in general it is meant to shadow forth, no doubt as to the general meaning of its parts, their connection with each other. But in its secondary and subordinate applications, the law works — to our eye at least — irregularly, unequally, and fitfully. There can be no question that Virgil, the poet's guide, represents the purely human element in the training of the soul and of society, as Beatrice does the divine. But neither represents the whole; he does not sum up all appliances of wisdom in Virgil, nor all teachings and influences of grace in Beatrice; these have their separate figures. And both represent successively several distinct forms of their general antitypes. They have various degrees of abstractness, and narrow down, according to that order of things to which they refer and correspond, into the special and

[1] *Convito*, Tr. 3, c. 15.

the personal. In the general economy of the poem, Virgil stands for human wisdom in its widest sense; but he also stands for it in its various shapes, in the different parts. He is the type of human philosophy and science.[1] He is, again, more definitely, that spirit of imagination and poetry, which opens men's eyes to the glory of the visible, and the truth of the invisible; and to Italians, he is a definite embodiment of it, their own great poet, "vates, poeta noster."[2] In the Christian order, he is human wisdom, dimly mindful of its heavenly origin, presaging dimly its return to God, sheltering in heathen times that "vague and unconnected family of religious truths, originally from God, but sojourning without the sanction of miracle or visible home, as pilgrims up and down the world."[3] In the political order, he is the guide of law-givers, wisdom fashioning the impulses and instincts of men into the harmony of society, contriving stability and peace, guarding justice; fit part for the poet to fill, who had sung the origin of Rome, and the justice and peace of Augustus. In the order of individual life, and the progress of the individual soul, he is the human conscience witnessing to duty, its discipline and its hopes, and with yet more certain and fearful presage, to its vindication; the human conscience seeing and acknowledging the law, but unable to confer power to fulfill it — wakened by grace from among the dead, leading the living man up to it, and waiting for its light and strength. But he is more than a figure. To the poet himself, who blends with his high

[1] "O tu ch' onori ogni scienza ed arte" (*Inf.* 4). "Quel savio gentil, che tutto seppe" (*Inf.* 7). "Il mar di tutto 'l senno" (*Inf.* 8).

[2] *De Monarchia.*

[3] Newman's *Arians.*

argument his whole life, Virgil had been the utmost that mind can be to mind, — teacher, quickener and revealer of power, source of thought, exemplar and model, never disappointing, never attained to, observed with "long study and great love:" [1] —

Tu duca, tu signor, e tu maestro. (*Inf.* 2.)

And towards this great master, the poet's whole soul is poured forth in reverence and affection. To Dante he is no figure, but a person — with feelings and weaknesses — overcome by the vexation, kindling into the wrath, carried away by the tenderness, of the moment. He reads his scholar's heart, takes him by the hand in danger, carries him in his arms and in his bosom, "like a son more than a companion," rebukes his unworthy curiosity, kisses him when he shows a noble spirit, asks pardon for his own mistakes. Never were the kind yet severe ways of a master, or the disciple's diffidence and open-heartedness, drawn with greater force, or less effort; and he seems to have been reflecting on his own affection to Virgil, when he makes Statius forget that they were both but shades: —

See now how brightly beaming
Towards thee the fire of my affection springs,
When I forget our airy essence, deeming
Of empty shadows, as substantial things. (*Purg.* 21. Wright.)

And so with the poet's second guide. The great idea which Beatrice figures, though always present, is seldom rendered artificially prominent, and is often entirely hidden beneath the rush of real recollections, and the creations of dramatic power. Abstractions venture and trust themselves among realities, and for

[1] *Inf.* 1.

the time are forgotten. A name, a real person, a historic passage, a lament or denunciation, a tragedy of actual life, a legend of classic times, the fortunes of friends — the story of Francesca or Ugolino, the fate of Buonconte's corpse, the apology of Pier delle Vigne, the epitaph of Madonna Pia, Ulysses's western voyage, the march of Roman history — appear and absorb for themselves all interest: or else it is a philosophical speculation, or a theory of morality, or a case of conscience — not indeed alien from the main subject, yet independent of the allegory, and not translatable into any new meaning — standing on their own ground, worked out each according to its own law; but they do not disturb the main course of the poet's thought, who grasps and paints each detail of human life in its own peculiarity, while he sees in each a significance and interest beyond itself. He does not stop in each case to tell us so, but he makes it felt. The tale ends, the individual disappears, and the great allegory resumes its course. It is like one of those great musical compositions which alone seem capable of adequately expressing, in a limited time, a course of unfolding and change, in an idea, a career, a life, a society, — where one great thought predominates, recurs, gives color and meaning, and forms the unity of the whole, yet passes through many shades and transitions; is at one time definite, at another suggestive and mysterious; incorporating and giving free place and play to airs and melodies even of an alien cast; striking off abruptly from its expected road, but without ever losing itself, without breaking its true continuity, or failing of its completeness.

This then seems to us the end and purpose of the

Commedia, — to produce on the mind a sense of the judgments of God, analogous to that produced by Scripture itself. They are presented to us in the Bible in shapes which address themselves primarily to the heart and conscience, and seek not carefully to explain themselves. They are likened to the "great deep," to the "strong mountains," — vast and awful, but abrupt and incomplete, as the huge, broken, rugged piles and chains of mountains. And we see them through cloud and mist, in shapes only approximating to the true ones. Still they impress us deeply and truly, often the more deeply because unconsciously. A character, an event, a word, isolated and unexplained, stamps its meaning ineffaceably, though ever a matter of question and wonder; it may be dark to the intellect, yet the conscience understands it, often but too well. In such suggestive ways is the Divine government for the most part put before us in the Bible, — ways which do not satisfy the understanding, but which fill us with a sense of reality. And it seems to have been by meditating on them, which he certainly did, much and thoughtfully, and on the infinite variety of similar ways in which the strongest impressions are conveyed to us in ordinary life, by means short of clear and distinct explanation, — by looks, by images, by sounds, by motions, by remote allusion and broken words, — that Dante was led to choose so new and remarkable a mode of conveying to his countrymen his thoughts and feelings and presentiments about the mystery of God's counsel. The Bible teaches us by means of real history, traced so far as is necessary along its real course. The poet expresses his view of the world also in real history, but carried on into figure.

The poetry with which the Christian Church had been instinct from the beginning, converges and is gathered up in the Commedia. The faith had early shown its poetical aspect. It is superfluous to dwell on this, for it is the charge against ancient teaching that it was too large and imaginative. It soon began to try rude essays in sculpture and mosaic: expressed its feeling of nature in verse and prose, rudely also, but often with originality and force; and opened a new vein of poetry in the thoughts, hopes, and aspirations of regenerate man. Modern poetry must go back, for many of its deepest and most powerful sources, to the writings of the Fathers, and their followers of the School. The Church further had a poetry of its own, besides the poetry of literature; it had the poetry of devotion, the Psalter chanted daily, in a new language and a new meaning; and that wonderful body of hymns, to which age after age had contributed its offering, from the Ambrosian hymns to the *Veni, Sancte Spiritus* of a king of France, the *Pange lingua* of Thomas Aquinas, the *Dies irae* and *Stabat Mater* of the two Franciscan brethren, Thomas of Celano, and Jacopone.[1] The elements and fragments of poetry were everywhere in the Church, — in her ideas of life, in her rules and institutions for passing through it, in her preparation for death, in her offices, ceremonial, celebrations, usages, her consecration of domestic, literary, commercial, civic, military, political life, the meanings and ends she had given them, the religious seriousness with which the forms of each were dignified, — in her doctrine and her dogmatic system, her dependence on the unseen world, her Bible. From

[1] Trench, *Sacred Latin Poetry*, 1849.

each and all of these, and from that public feeling which, if it expressed itself but abruptly and incoherently, was quite alive to the poetry which surrounded it, the poet received due impressions of greatness and beauty, of joy and dread. Then the poetry of Christian religion and Christian temper, hitherto dispersed, or manifested in act only, found its full and distinct utterance, not unworthy to rank in grandeur, in music, in sustained strength, with the last noble voices from expiring Heathenism.

But a long interval had passed since then. The Commedia first disclosed to Christian and modern Europe that it was to have a literature of its own, great and admirable, though in its own language and embodying its own ideas. "It was as if, at some of the ancient games, a stranger had appeared upon the plain, and thrown his quoit among the marks of former casts, which tradition had ascribed to the demigods."[1] We are so accustomed to the excellent and varied literature of modern times, so original, so perfect in form and rich in thought, so expressive of all our sentiments, meeting so completely our wants, fulfilling our ideas, that we can scarcely imagine the time when this condition was new, — when society was beholden to a foreign language for the exponents of its highest thoughts and feelings. But so it was when Dante wrote. The great poets, historians, philosophers of his day, the last great works of intellect, belonged to old Rome and the Latin language. So wonderful and prolonged was the fascination of Rome. Men still lived under its influence; believed that the Latin language was the perfect and permanent instrument

[1] Hallam's *Middle Ages*, c. ix. vol. iii. p. 563.

of thought in its highest forms, the only expression of refinement and civilization; and had not conceived the hope that their own dialects could ever rise to such heights of dignity and power. Latin, which had enchased and preserved such precious remains of ancient wisdom, was now shackling the living mind in its efforts. Men imagined that they were still using it naturally on all high themes and solemn business; but though they used it with facility, it was no longer natural; it had lost the elasticity of life, and had become in their hands a stiffened and distorted, though still powerful, instrument. The very use of the word *latino* in the writers of this period, to express what is clear and philosophical in language,[1] while it shows their deep reverence for it, shows how Latin civilization was no longer their own, how it had insensibly become an external and foreign element. But they found it very hard to resign their claim to a share in its glories; with nothing of their own to match against it, they still delighted to speak of it as "our language," or its writers as "our poets," "our historians."[2]

Dante, by the Divina Commedia, was the restorer of seriousness in literature. He was so by the magnitude and pretensions of his work, and by the earnestness of its spirit. He first broke through the prescription which had confined great works to the Latin, and the faithless prejudices which, in the language of society, could see powers fitted for no higher task than that of expressing, in curiously diversified forms, its most ordinary feelings. But he did much more. Lit-

[1] *Par.* 3, 12, 17; *Convito*, p. 108. "A più *Latinamente* vedere la sentenza letterale."

[2] *Vide* the *De Monarchia.*

erature was going astray in its tone, while growing in importance; the Commedia checked it. The Provençal and Italian poetry was, with the exception of some pieces of political satire, almost exclusively amatory, in the most fantastic and affected fashion. In expression, it had not even the merit of being natural; in purpose it was trifling; in the spirit which it encouraged, it was something worse. Doubtless it brought a degree of refinement with it, but it was refinement purchased at a high price, — by intellectual distortion and moral insensibility. But this was not all. The brilliant age of Frederick II., for such it was, was deeply mined by religious unbelief. However strange this charge first sounds against the thirteenth century, no one can look at all closely into its history, at least in Italy, without seeing that the idea of infidelity — not heresy, but infidelity — was quite a familiar one; and that side by side with the theology of Aquinas and Bonaventura, there was working among those who influenced fashion and opinion, among the great men, and the men to whom learning was a profession, a spirit of skepticism and irreligion almost monstrous for its time, which found its countenance in Frederick's refined and enlightened court. The genius of the great doctors might have kept in safety the Latin Schools, but not the free and home thoughts which found utterance in the language of the people, if the solemn beauty of the Italian Commedia had not seized on all minds. It would have been an evil thing for Italian, perhaps for European literature, if the siren tales of the Decameron had been the first to occupy the ear with the charms of a new language.

Dante's all-surveying, all-embracing mind was worthy to open the grand procession of modern poets. He had chosen his subject in a region remote from popular thought — too awful for it, too abstruse. He had accepted frankly the dogmatic limits of the Church, and thrown himself with even enthusiastic faith into her reasonings, at once so bold and so undoubting, her spirit of certainty, and her deep contemplations on the unseen and infinite. And in literature, he had taken as guides and models, above all criticism and all appeal, the classical writers. But with his mind full of the deep and intricate questions of metaphysics and theology, and his poetical taste always owning allegiance to Virgil, Ovid, and Statius, — keen and subtle as a Schoolman, as much an idolater of old heathen art and grandeur as the men of the Renaissance, — his eye is yet as open to the delicacies of character, to the variety of external nature, to the wonders of the physical world — his interest in them as diversified and fresh, his impressions as sharp and distinct, his rendering of them as free and true and forcible, as little weakened or confused by imitation or by conventional words, his language as elastic, and as completely under his command, his choice of poetic materials as unrestricted and original — as if he had been born in days which claim as their own such freedom and such keen discriminative sense of what is real, in feeling and image, as if he had never felt the attractions of a crabbed problem of scholastic logic, or bowed before the mellow grace of the Latins. It may be said, indeed, that the time was not yet come when the classics could be really understood and appreciated; and this is true, perhaps fortunate. But admiring them with a kind of devotion, and showing not seldom that he had caught their spirit, he never *attempts* to copy them. His poetry in form and material is all his own. He asserted the poet's claim to borrow from all science, and from every phase of nature, the associations and images which he wants; and he showed that those images and associations did not lose their poetry by being expressed with the most literal reality.

But let no reader of fastidious taste disturb his temper by the study of Dante. Dante certainly opened that path of freedom and poetic conquest, in which the greatest efforts of modern poetry have followed him — opened it with a magnificence and power which have never been surpassed. But the greatest are but pioneers; they must be content to leave to a posterity which knows more, if it cannot do as much, a keen and even growing sense of their defects. The Commedia is open to all the attacks that can be made on grotesqueness and extravagance. This is partly owing, doubtless, to the time, in itself quaint, quainter to us, by being remote and ill understood; but even then, weaker and less daring writers than Dante do not equally offend or astonish us. So that an image or an expression will render forcibly a thought, there is no strangeness which checks him. Barbarous words are introduced, to express the cries of the demons or the confusion of Babel — even to represent the incomprehensible song of the blessed;[1] inarticulate syllables, to convey the impression of some natural sound, the cry of sorrowful surprise: —

> A sigh profound he drew, by brief intense;
> Forced into "Oh!" (*Purg.* 16),

or the noise of the cracking ice: —

[1] *Par.* 7, 1–3.

For Tambernicchi falling down below,
Or Pietra-pana hurled in ruin there,
Had now e'en cracked its margin with the blow (*Inf.* 32);

even separate letters — to express an image, to spell a name, or as used in some popular proverb.[1] He employs without scruple and often with marvelous force of description, any recollection that occurs to him, however homely, of everyday life, — the old tailor threading his needle with trouble (Inf. 15); the cook's assistant watching over the boiling broth (Inf. 21); the hurried or impatient horse-groom using his curry-comb (Inf. 29); or the common sights of the street or the chamber, — the wet wood sputtering on the hearth: —

Like to a sapling, lighted at one end,
Which at the other hisses with the wind,
And drops of sap doth from the outlet send:
So from the broken twig, both words and blood flow'd forth;
(*Inf.* 13. Wright.)

the paper changing color when about to catch fire: —

Like burning paper, when there glides before
The advancing flame a brown and dingy shade,
Which is not black, and yet is white no more;
(*Inf.* 25. Wright.)

the steaming of the hand when bathed, in winter: —

Fuman come man bagnata il verno: —

or the ways and appearances of animals, — ants meeting on their path: —

On either hand I saw them haste their meeting,
And kiss each one the other — pausing not —
Contented to enjoy so short a greeting.
Thus do the ants among their dingy band,
Face one another — each their neighbor's lot
Haply to scan, and how their fortunes stand;
(*Purg.* 26. Wright.)

[1] *Purg.* 23, 31.

the snail drawing in its horns (Inf. 25); the hog shut out of its sty, and trying to gore with its tusks (Inf. 30); the dogs' misery in summer (Inf. 17); the frogs jumping on to the bank before the water-snake (Inf. 9); or showing their heads above water: —

> As in a trench, frogs at the water side
> Sit squatting, with their noses raised on high,
> The while their feet and all their bulk they hide —
> Thus upon either hand the sinners stood.
> But Barbaricca now approaching nigh,
> Quick they withdrew beneath the boiling flood.
> I saw — and still my heart is thrill'd with fear —
> One spirit linger; as beside a ditch,
> One frog remains, the others disappear. (*Inf.* 22. Wright.)

It must be said that most of these images, though by no means all, occur in the Inferno; and that the poet means to paint sin not merely in the greatness of its ruin and misery, but in characters which all understand, of strangeness, of vileness, of despicableness, blended with diversified and monstrous horror. Even he seems to despair of his power at times: —

> Had I a rhyme so rugged, rough, and hoarse
> As would become the sorrowful abyss,
> O'er which the rocky circles wind their course,
> Then with a more appropriate form I might
> Endow my vast conceptions; wanting this,
> Not without fear I bring myself to write.
> For no light enterprise it is, I deem,
> To represent the lowest depth of all;
> Nor should a childish tongue attempt the theme.
> (*Inf.* 32. Wright.)

Feeling the difference between sins, in their elements and, as far as we see them, their baseness, he treats them variously. His ridicule is apportioned with a purpose. He passes on from the doom of the sins of incontinence — the storm, the frost and hail, the crushing weights — from the flaming minarets of the city of Dis, of the Furies and Proserpine, "Donna dell' eterno pianto," where the unbelievers lie, each in his burning tomb — from the river of boiling blood — the wood with the Harpies — the waste of barren sand with fiery snow, where the violent are punished — to the Malebolge, the manifold circles of Falsehood. And here scorn and ridicule in various degrees, according to the vileness of the fraud, begin to predominate, till they culminate in that grim comedy, with its *dramatis personae* and battle of devils, Draghignazzo, and Graffiacane, and Malacoda, where the peculators and sellers of justice are fished up by the demons from the boiling pitch, but even there overreach and cheat their tormentors, and make them turn their fangs on each other. The diversified forms of falsehood seem to tempt the poet's imagination to cope with its changefulness and inventions, as well as its audacity. The transformations of the wildest dream do not daunt him. His power over language is nowhere more forcibly displayed than in those cantos which describe the punishments of theft, — men passing gradually into serpents, and serpents into men (Inf. 25. 77–78). And when the traitor, who murdered his own kinsman, was still alive, and seemed safe from the infamy which it was the poet's rule to bestow only on the dead, Dante found a way to inflict his vengeance without an anachronism: Branca D'Oria's body, though on earth, is only animated by a fiend, and his spirit has long since fled to the icy prison (Inf. 33).

These are strange experiments in poetry; their strangeness is exaggerated as detached passages; but they are strange enough when they meet us in their place in the context, as parts of a scene, where the mind is strung and overawed by the sustained power with which dreariness, horror, hideous absence of every form of good is kept before the imagination and feelings, in the fearful picture of human sin. But they belong to the poet's system of direct and forcible representation. What his inward eye sees, what he feels, that he means us to see and feel as he does; to make us see and feel is his art. Afterwards we may reflect and meditate, but first we must see, — must see what he saw. Evil and deformity are in the world, as well as good and beauty; the eye cannot escape them, they are about our path, in our heart and memory. He has faced them without shrinking or dissembling, and extorted from them a voice of warning. In all poetry that is written for mere delight, in all poetry which regards but a part or an aspect of nature, they have no place — they disturb and mar; but he had conceived a poetry of the whole, which would be weak or false without them. Yet they stand in his poem as they stand in nature — subordinate and relieved. If the grotesque is allowed to intrude itself, if the horrible and the foul, undisguised and unsoftened, make us shudder and shrink, they are kept in strong check and in due subjection by other poetical influences; and the same power which exhibits them in their naked strength, renders its full grace and glory to beauty — its full force and delicacy to the most evanescent feeling.

Dante's eye was free and open to external nature in a degree new among poets; certainly in a far greater degree than among the Latins, even including Lucretius, whom he probably had never read. We have already spoken of his minute notice of the appearance of living creatures; but his eye was caught by the beautiful as well as by the grotesque.

Light in general is his special and chosen source of poetic beauty. No poet that we know has shown such singular sensibility to its varied appearances — has shown that he felt it in itself the cause of a distinct and peculiar pleasure, delighting the eye apart from form, as music delights the ear apart from words, and capable, like music, of definite character, of endless variety, and infinite meanings. He must have studied and dwelt upon it like music. His mind is charged with its effects and combinations, and they are rendered with a force, a brevity, a precision, a heedlessness and unconsciousness of ornament, an indifference to circumstance and detail; they flash out with a spontaneous readiness, a suitableness and felicity, which show the familiarity and grasp given only by daily observation, daily thought, daily pleasure. Light everywhere, — in the sky and earth and sea, in the star, the flame, the lamp, the gem, — broken in the water, reflected from the mirror, transmitted pure through the glass, or colored through the edge of the fractured emerald; dimmed in the mist, the halo, the deep water; streaming through the rent cloud, glowing in the coal, quivering in the lightning, flashing in the topaz and the ruby, veiled behind the pure alabaster, mellowed and clouding itself in the pearl; light contrasted with shadow, shading off and copying itself in the double rainbow, like voice and echo; light seen within light, as voice discerned within voice, *quando una è ferma, e l' altra va e riede*, — the brighter "nestling" itself in the fainter, the purer set off on the less clear, *come perla in bianca fronte,*— light in the human eye and face, displaying, figuring, and confounded with its expressions; light blended with joy in the eye: —

luce
Come letizia in pupilla viva;

and in the smile: —

Vincendo me col lume d' un sorriso;

joy lending its expression to light: —

Quivi la donna mia vidi si lieta —
Che più lucente se ne fè il pianeta.
E se la *stella si cambiò, e rise,*.
Qual mi fec' io (*Par.* 5); [1]

light from every source, and in all its shapes, illuminates, irradiates, gives its glory to the Commedia. The remembrance of our "serene life" beneath the "fair stars" keeps up continually the gloom of the Inferno. Light, such as we see it and recognize it, the light of morning and evening growing and fading, takes off from the unearthliness of the Purgatorio; peopled as it is by the undying, who, though suffering for sin, can sin no more, it is thus made like our familiar world, made to touch our sympathies as an image of our own purification in the flesh. And when he rises beyond the regions of earthly day, light, simple, unalloyed, unshadowed, eternal, lifts the creations of his thought above all affinity to time and matter;

[1] Entered within the precincts of the light,
I saw my guide's fair countenance possest
With joy so great, the planet glow'd more bright.
And if the very star a smile displayed,
Well might I smile — to change by nature prone,
And varying still with each impression made. (Wright.)

light never fails him, as the expression of the gradations of bliss; never reappears the same, never refuses the new shapes of his invention, never becomes confused or dim, though it is seldom thrown into distinct figure, and still more seldom *colored.* Only once, that we remember, is the thought of color forced on us, — when the bright joy of heaven suffers change and eclipse, and deepens into red at the sacrilege of men.[1]

The real never daunts him. It is his leading principle of poetic composition, to draw out of things the poetry which is latent in them, either essentially, or as they are portions, images, or reflexes of something greater, — not to invest them with a poetical semblance, by means of words which bring with them poetical associations, and have received a general poetical stamp. Dante has few of these indirect charms which flow from the subtle structure and refined graces of language, none of that exquisitely fitted and self-sustained mechanism of choice words of the Greeks, none of that tempered and majestic amplitude of diction which clothes, like the folds of a royal robe, the thoughts of the Latins, none of that abundant play of fancy and sentiment, soft or grand, in which the later Italian poets delighted. Words with him are used sparingly, — never in play, never because they carry with them poetical recollections, never for their own sake; but because they are instruments which will give the deepest, clearest, sharpest stamp of that image which the poet's mind, piercing to the very heart of his subject, or seizing the characteristic feature which to other men's eyes is confused and lost among others accidental and common, draws forth in

[1] *Par.* 27, 28.

severe and living truth. Words will not always bend themselves to his demands on them; they make him often uncouth, abrupt, obscure. But he is too much in earnest to heed uncouthness; and his power over language is too great to allow uncertainty as to what he means to be other than occasional. Nor is he a stranger to the utmost sweetness and melody of language. But it appears, unsought for and unlabored, spontaneous and inevitable obedience of the tongue and pen to the impressions of the mind; as grace and beauty, of themselves, "command and guide the eye" of the painter, who thinks not of his hand but of them. All is in character with the absorbed and serious earnestness which pervades the poem; there is no toying, no ornament, that a man in earnest might not throw into his words, — whether in single images, or in pictures, like that of the Meadow of the Heroes (Inf. 4), or the angel appearing in hell to guide the poet through the burning city (Inf. 9); or in histories, like those of Count Ugolino, or the life of St. Francis (Par. 11); or in the dramatic scenes, like the meeting of the poets Sordello and Virgil (Purg. 6), or that one, unequaled in beauty, where Dante himself, after years of forgetfulness and sin, sees Beatrice in glory, and hears his name, never but once pronounced during the vision, from her lips.[1]

But this, or any other array of scenes and images, might be matched from poets of a far lower order than Dante: and to specimens which might be brought together of his audacity and extravagance, no parallel could be found except among the lowest. We cannot, honestly, plead the barbarism of the time as his ex-

[1] *Purg.* 30, 55.

cuse. That, doubtless, contributed largely to them; but they were the faults of the man. In another age, their form might have been different; yet we cannot believe so much of time, that it would have tamed Dante. Nor can we wish it. It might have made him less great: and his greatness can well bear its own blemishes, and will not less meet its honor among men, because they can detect its due kindred to themselves.

The greatness of his work is not in its details, to be made or marred by them. It is the greatness of a comprehensive and vast conception, sustaining without failure the trial of its long and hazardous execution, and fulfilling at its close the hope and promise of its beginning; like the greatness — which we watch in its course with anxious suspense, and look back upon when it is secured by death, with deep admiration — of a perfect life. Many a surprise, many a difficulty, many a disappointment, many a strange reverse and alternation of feelings, attend the progress of the most patient and admiring reader of the Commedia; as many as attend on one who follows the unfolding of a strong character in life. We are often shocked when we were prepared to admire — repelled, when we came with sympathy; the accustomed key fails at a critical moment — depths are revealed which we cannot sound, mysteries which baffle and confound us. But the check is for a time; the gap and chasm does not dissever. Haste is even an evidence of life, — the brief word, the obscure hint, the unexplained, the unfinished, or even the unachieved, are the marks of human feebleness, but are also among those of human truth. The unity of the whole is unimpaired.

The strength which is working it out, though it may have at times disappointed us, shows no hollowness or exhaustion. The surprise of disappointment is balanced — there is the surprise of unimagined excellence. Powers do more than they promised; and that spontaneous and living energy, without which neither man nor poet can be trusted, and which showed its strength even in its failures, shows it more abundantly in the novelties of success, — by touching sympathies which have never been touched before; by the unconstrained freshness with which he meets the proverbial and familiar; by the freedom with which it adjusts itself to a new position or an altered task; by the completeness, unstudied and instinctive, with which it holds together dissimilar and uncongenial materials, and forces the most intractable, the most unaccustomed to submission, to receive the color of the whole; by its orderly and unmistakable onward march, and its progress, as in height, so in what corresponds to height. It was one and the same man who rose from the despair, the agony, the vivid and vulgar horrors of the Inferno to the sense and imagination of certainty, sinlessness, and joy ineffable, — the same man whose power and whose sympathies failed him not, whether discriminating and enumerating, as if he had gone through them all, the various forms of human suffering, from the dull, gnawing sense of the loss of happiness to the infinite woes of the wrecked and ruined spirit and the coarser pangs of the material flesh; or dwelling on the changeful lights and shades of earnest repentance, in its hard, but not unaided or ungladdened struggle, and on that restoration to liberty and peace which can change even this life into paradise, and reverse the doom which made sorrow our condition, and laughter and joy unnatural and dangerous, the penalty of that first fault, which —

> Chosing a life of sorrow and disgrace
> Instead of virtuous smiles and gladsome sport:
> (*Purg.* 28, 95. Wright.)

or rising finally above mortal experience, to imagine the freedom of the saints and the peace of eternity. In this consists the greatness of his power. It is not necessary to read through the Commedia to see it, — open it where we please, we see that he is on his way, and whither he is going; episode and digression share in the solemnity of the general order.

And his greatness was more than that of power. That reach and play of sympathy ministered to a noble wisdom, which used it thoughtfully and consciously for a purpose to which great poetry had never yet been applied, except in the mouth of prophets. Dante was a stern man, and more than stern, among his fellows. But he has left to those who never saw his face an inheritance the most precious; he has left them that which, reflecting and interpreting their minds, does so, not to amuse, not to bewilder, not to warp, not to turn them in upon themselves in distress or gloom or selfishness; not merely to hold up a mirror to nature; but to make them true and make them hopeful. Dark as are his words of individuals, his thoughts are not dark or one-sided about mankind; his is no cherished and perverse severity — his faith is too large, too real, for such a fault. He did not write only the Inferno. And the Purgatorio and the Paradiso are not an afterthought, a feebler appendix and compensation, conceived when too late, to a finished whole, which has taken up into itself the poet's real mind. Nowhere else in poetry of equal power is there the same balanced view of what man is, and may be ; nowhere so wide a grasp shown of his various capacities, so strong a desire to find a due place and function for all his various dispositions. Where he stands contrasted in his idea of human life with other poets, who have been more powerful exponents of its separate sides, is in his large and truthful comprehensiveness. Fresh from the thought of man's condition as a whole, fresh from the thought of his goodness, his greatness, his power, as well as of his evil, his mind is equally in tune when rejoicing over his restoration, as when contemplating the ruins of his fall. He never lets go the recollection that human life, if it grovels at one end in corruption and sin, and has to pass through the sweat and dust and disfigurement of earthly toil, has throughout compensations, remedies, functions, spheres innumerable of profitable activity, sources inexhaustible of delight and consolation, and at the other end a perfection which cannot be named. No one ever measured the greatness of man in all its forms with so true and yet with so admiring an eye, and with such glowing hope, as he who has also portrayed so awfully man's littleness and vileness. And he went farther, — no one who could understand and do homage to greatness in man, ever drew the line so strongly between greatness and goodness, and so unhesitatingly placed the hero of this world only — placed him in all his magnificence, honored with no timid or dissembling reverence — at the distance of worlds below the place of the lowest saint.

Those who know the Divina Commedia best, will

best know how hard it is to be the interpreter of such a mind; but they will sympathize with the wish to call attention to it. They know, and would wish others also to know, not by hearsay, but by experience, the power of that wonderful poem. They know its austere yet subduing beauty; they know what force there is in its free and earnest and solemn verse, to strengthen, to tranquillize, to console. It is a small thing that it has the secret of Nature and Man; that a few keen words have opened their eyes to new sights in earth, and sea, and sky; have taught them new mysteries of sound; have made them recognize, in distinct image or thought, fugitive feelings, or their unheeded expression, by look, or gesture, or motion; that it has enriched the public and collective memory of society with new instances, never to be lost, of human feeling and fortune; has charmed ear and mind by the music of its stately march, and the variety and completeness of its plan. But, besides this, they know how often its seriousness has put to shame their trifling, its magnanimity their faint-heartedness, its living energy their indolence, its stern and sad grandeur rebuked low thoughts, its thrilling tenderness overcome sullenness and assuaged distress, its strong faith quelled despair and soothed perplexity, its vast grasp imparted the sense of harmony to the view of clashing truths. They know how often they have found, in times of trouble, if not light, at least that deep sense of reality, permanent, though unseen, which is more than light can always give — in the view which it has suggested to them of the judgments and the love of God.

II

THE POETRY OF THE INFERNO

BY ADOLF GASPARY.[1]

DANTE'S poem describes to us a spiritual journey. It passes from place to place, continually changing the scenery and the characters of the drama; one single person always remains, Dante, the traveler himself. In the Commedia the greatest subjectivity rules supreme: the poet himself never leaves the scene of action, he is the hero of the action, the most interesting figure in it, and all that he sees and learns awakens a living echo in his emotional soul. He speaks with the sinners, the penitents, and saints, and in these conversations he paints himself. But for a journey on so grand a scale every conceivable space must needs be limited, even that of the longest poem. An enormous number of persons appears and disappears in this poem. The reader is continually hurried onwards from one to the other: there is little time for each, and a few traits must suffice to sketch his portrait. The great scenes are developed almost casually, or, rather, there is no space for their development, so rapidly does the narrative progress. In this way Dante's Inferno,

[1] *The History of Early Italian Literature to the Death of Dante*, Adolf Gaspary, trans. by Herman Oelsner, M. A., Ph. D. George Bell & Sons, London. The extracts from this valuable book are made through the courteous permission of the translator, Dr. Oelsner.

especially, is a very whirlwind of emotions, passions, and events. If it had not been a Dante that was creating them, the poetical situation would have been destroyed and the figures stifled, the work becoming dry and empty owing to the superabundance of the subject-matter. But Dante possesses the art of drawing his figures even in a limited space. At times they remain sketches, though sketches by a master hand; but frequently the few traits suffice to bring before our mind the entire and complete picture, with all its details. Dante is the great master of poetic expression: with his energetic style, he is able to condense a world of ideas and feelings in a single word, in an image that carries us away and places us in the midst of the situation.

At the very beginning of the Commedia, in the midst of the thorny allegories, the reader is fascinated by the sympathetic figure of Virgil, and by the gentle opening conversation between him and his charge. The fourth canto describes the privileged sojourn of the great heathens in Limbo, and expresses in a most fascinating manner Dante's deep reverence for antiquity, and, at the same time, the consciousness he has of his own merit, when he tells how he was himself introduced by Virgil into the circle of the five great poets as a sixth. He felt that he was destined to revive an art that had been so long lost, and just pride such as this pleases us in the case of a man of genius. The general impression of this situation is vivid, — the noble gathering, all the heroes and sages, and, in their midst, their great admirer and disciple. But the individual figures are not yet clearly distinguished; the poet gives little more than a number of names, rarely adding an epithet or a circumstance that might characterize the man. It is a kind of catalogue, and not even the usual *et cetera* of such enumerations is missing (iv. 145): —

Io non posso ritrar di tutti appieno.

This same method, which is, as it were, an abbreviated form of true poetic exposition, is continued in the following canto. Here the poet has reached the second circle, that of the carnal sinners, who are driven to and fro by a raging tempest. Among them he sees Semiramis, Dido, Cleopatra, Helen, Achilles, Paris, Tristan, *e più di mille.* But these enumerations of Dante's are merely introductory: from the bands of spirits, forming the general background, single ones detach themselves. Among these souls, two that are borne along together by the wind specially attract his attention. They are Francesca of Rimini and her Paolo, who, burning for each other with sinful love, were slain by Gianciotto Malatesta, Lord of Rimini, Francesca's husband, and the brother of Paolo. Dante does not know them, but the pair, united even in the torments of Hell, arouse his sympathy; he would fain speak with them, and obtains his guide's permission. This is one of the passages in which the special character of Dante's poetry is best revealed. Many persons, nowadays, who have heard the famous Francesca da Rimini so much discussed, may perhaps feel somewhat disappointed when they open the book. There are scarcely seventy verses, which are quickly read, and which leave but little impression on the ordinary and superficial reader. A sensitive mind is needed for the appreciation of Dante's condensed poetry. It is to be found in each small detail, in every syllable, — nothing is empty and devoid of meaning, but much remains dumb to him who hurries over the verses.

Acting on Virgil's advice, Dante entreats the two souls by the love that binds them together, and they follow the sympathetic call —

As turtle doves, called onward by desire,
With open and steady wings to the sweet nest
Fly through the air by their volition borne.

This gentle image, taken from the Æneid, but imbued by Dante with a more intimate spirit, serves as a preparation for the moving scene. This very trait of their immediately following the call that is directed to their love, and even more so the first words of the reply, characterize the two figures. Francesca's is a noble and tender soul, and the sympathy shown her by a stranger moves her deeply in her pain. In her gratitude, she would fain pray for him to the King of the Universe; but she is in Hell, and her entreaties are not heard in Heaven. She will at least fulfill his wish by answering him. She tells him who they are, by indicating their native place, and above all by speaking of that which has brought them down there, their unexampled and boundless love. In seven lines is contained the whole history of their feelings. Each *terzina* begins with the word "love;" each one describes to us the growth of its power, and shows us how it arises in the man's heart on beholding the beautiful woman, how it is kindled in the heart of the woman when she sees herself loved, how it becomes their common fate and hurries them to one common doom. When Dante has heard this, he can no longer doubt who the two are, whose destiny has been so powerfully affected by love, and his second question begins with the name Francesca, although she has not told it him. But first he relapses into a deep silence, and bows his head, so that his guide asks him of what he is thinking. The few words he has heard enable him to imagine all the feelings, joys, and sorrows they conceal, and he turns to her again with a deeper interest: —

Thine agonies, Francesca,
Sad and compassionate to weeping make me.
But tell me, at the time of those sweet sighs,
By what and in what manner Love conceded,
That you should know your dubious desires?

Dante puts this question of his in the tenderest manner, for it would be intrusive if prompted by curiosity and not by sympathy. But Francesca at once detects the latter quality, and therefore she will answer, although the recollection gives her pain: —

Farò come colui che piange e dice.[1]

This passage has often been compared with that other one, apparently so similar, at the beginning of Ugolino's narrative (Inf. xxxiii. 4), in order to show the consummate mastery with which Dante was able to depict his various characters, even outwardly, by the sound of the verses. Here in Francesca's speech all is soft and harmonious, in Ugolino's all is rough and hard; in the one all is love, in the other rage and fury. It gives Ugolino pain, as it did Francesca, to speak of the past; but Francesca speaks because she notes Dante's sympathy, Ugolino because he desires to revenge himself on his enemy. Francesca

[1] I will do even as he who weeps and speaks.

scarcely speaks of her enemy, only distantly, and in the most moving manner she alludes to her violent death: Caina awaits him, who killed her and Paolo — that is all. She does not even name him, she does not think of him: she does not hate, but loves. She tells of her love, of her joys, and of the happy time that was happy though sinful. One day they read of Lancelot's love; they were alone and without suspicion. Their eyes met several times, and their cheeks colored, —

But one point only was it that o'ercame us.

The passion is there; but it is still slumbering, concealed in the heart, and on beholding itself, as it were, in a mirror, it recognizes and becomes conscious of itself, and bursts forth suddenly in a mighty flame. When they read how the queen was kissed by Lancelot, Paolo kissed her mouth, all trembling —

That day no farther did we read therein.

While she is speaking these words, the other soul, Paolo, silently accompanies her words with tears. The poet lets her alone speak: for the lament of unhappy love is more touching from the lips of a woman. The short narrative ends with the catastrophe of the passion. Free play is left to the excited imagination, and Dante, a passionate nature, who has experienced the tempests of the heart, is so full of sympathy for them, that he sinks to the ground, "as a dead body falls."

And this scene must be imagined in the surroundings of Hell, in the midst of the darkness and of the raging and howling tempest — a contrast that increases its power. It is the romance of love in its greatest simplicity, but combined with all the emotional elements that make a deep impression on the mind. The dominant feeling, that of boundless love, is expressed in traits that are rapid, but full of significance. By their love are the two spirits conjured, and they come. Their love continues undiminished even in the midst of such agony — "it does not yet desert me," says Francesca — and together they are carried along by the wind, united in punishment, as they were in happiness. Their love was their sin. For him who is condemned, the sin lasts to all eternity, and so their love is eternal. It is their guilt, but there is consolation in it, too —

Questi, che mai da me non fia diviso.[1]

In the sixth canto of the Inferno, among the gluttons who are tortured in the third circle of Hell, Dante meets the Florentine Ciacco, who prophesies to him the sad destiny of his native town. In the seventh canto, the two wanderers are with the avaricious and prodigal in the fourth circle, and here Virgil addresses to Dante the famous lines describing Fortune, an angelic creature like the others, and set by God among men, in order to preserve equality among them, and to let worldly passions pass from one hand to another, as justice demands. In the fifth circle, as they are crossing the Stygian marsh containing the wrathful, in Phlegyas' boat, the meeting with Filippo Argenti takes place. This is narrated with bitter hatred and thirst for vengeance, pointing not merely to moral indignation on the part of the poet, but to personal enmity. In order to enable Dante and Virgil to enter the city

[1] This one, who ne'er from me shall be divided.

of Dis, which occupies the lower portion of Hell from the sixth circle, the "messenger of Heaven" (*del ciel messo*) appears in the ninth canto; this is a poetical creation of great distinction, a figure biblical in its grandeur, introduced from the outset with the sublimest images. The angel is girt with mystery, which is expressed by Virgil's hints at the end of the eighth canto and by the interrupted words at the beginning of the ninth. Virgil does not say who is coming, nor how he is coming, nor who has sent him. All these are circumstances which we do not learn; he who is coming is such a one as will open the gate of the city, it is some one that will bring aid. This mystery excites the imagination, and we remain in suspense; we expect something extraordinary and are not disappointed. Now he comes. His steps are accompanied by a boisterous sound, terrible as the roar of a tempest. The banks of the marsh tremble; before the angel's heavenly purity, before his awe-inspiring majesty, everything flees that is not pure. The damned souls hide themselves like frogs before a snake; the sinner cannot endure the sight of what is heavenly. And he goes onward; the misery and hideousness of the abyss do not affect him, he remains pure and radiant in that darkness, he does not defile himself in that filth. Dante, on seeing him, is seized with an unwonted feeling. He turns to Virgil and would fain speak and question him, but is made by him to keep silence and bow down. This is the time, not for curiosity, but for reverence; one must be silent and devout, humbly receiving the benefit of Diviue grace. When the devils behold the messenger of Heaven, they resist no longer; his staff suffices to open the gates. He reproves the stubborn ones, and turns back without speaking to the poets. This sudden turning back is a movement of incomparable impressiveness. His office is at an end, the gate stands open and he tarries no longer; the things that surround him do not attract his attention, and he turns his back without casting a look, not because he despises those whom he has protected, but because his mind is wholly taken up with other matters. As mysteriously as he came, the messenger of Heaven disappears; but the effect of his presence remains. Before there was excitement, fighting, and threats. He comes, and immediately all opposition is at an end; he goes, and peace reigns supreme, and calmly the two poets enter the flaming city. Each action shows us the greatness of this figure; but the chief effect is produced by the contrast between the purity and majesty on the one hand, and on the other the lowliness and vileness of the place, when he comes, inspiring terror over the turbid waters, traversing the hideous marsh dry-shod, with the movement of his hand keeping the thick air from his countenance, accustomed as it is to the light of the spheres, and then returning full of majesty along the "dirty road." Here we have the appearance of Heaven in the midst of Hell — a situation unparalleled in its sublimity, such as, since the Bible, only Dante's powerful imagination has been able to conceive.

In the tenth canto two powerful scenes are intertwined. Here Dante finds, among the heretics who lie in fiery graves, Farinata degli Uberti, the head of the Ghibellines and a political opponent of his ancestors, who were driven from Florence by him. While they speak together their anger is kindled, and in their rapid dialogue is aroused all the old hatred of the parties that rent asunder the cities of Italy. But while Farinata, after a cutting assertion of the other speaker, is filled with sorrow at the triumph of his enemies and relapses into silence for a time, though his subsequent reply is no less bitter, the shadow of Guido Cavalcanti's father, Cavalcante, rises up. He recognizes Dante, and is surprised not to see his own son with him. Then, as an ambiguous word in the poet's speech has made him believe that his son is dead, he sinks back, overcome by grief: —

Supin ricadde e più non parve fuora,[1]

a verse that depicts in a wonderful manner the emotion of the father, as also the proud and passionate spirit of the great Ghibelline, and his long and silent reflections, during which he has heeded nothing that is going on around him, so that he begins again as though there had been no lapse of time. This period of silence another would have left unoccupied or filled with indifferent matter. Not so Dante: between his own concluding word and the word of Farinata that takes up the dialogue again, he intercalates the whole deep story of fatherly grief. This shows us again the condensed power of Dante's poetry: in this passage of a hundred verses such a variety of emotions assail our mind in turn, that time and calm reflection are essential if we would receive a clear and complete impression of the whole. And yet, if we try to imagine something of less weight, between the two portions of the conversation with Farinata, than the episode of

[1] Supine
He fell again, and forth appeared no more.

Cavalcanti, we shall find that the passage would have lost considerably in effect. The more significant and touching the traits that precede, the more expressive is the impassibility of that magnanimous man, who was occupied only with his own grief, and —

did not his aspect change,
Neither his neck did move, nor bent his side.

The meetings with Pier della Vigna and with Brunetto Latini in the seventh circle, that of the violent, I shall mention only in passing; on the other hand, I shall examine more closely Dante's originality from another point of view. The eighth circle of Hell, that of the deceivers, which consists of ten concentric valleys, spanned by rocky arches in the manner of bridges, was named by the poet *Malebolge* ("Evil Pouches") — a sarcastic expression instead of "sorrowful pits." And these pits are indeed very sorrowful; they are the place for the most odious crimes, the place for mockery and invective. Higher up Dante had, it is true, also been bitter and sarcastic, when he was standing by Farinata, and his political passions and wounded family pride were aroused. In spite of this, however, he remained full of reverence and admiration for that high-souled man, before whom Hell itself appears to sink down when he raises himself from his tomb. But now he no longer feels any reverence: his satire becomes terrible and relentless, being directed against things which he detests most.

The other world, set against this world of ours, generally ends by criticising and satirizing it, as was usual even in the earlier legends; but the true place for the satirical element is the lower regions of Hell. The sins that are punished in the upper circles may be combined with magnanimity and with tenderness of soul. Dante is compelled, by moral conviction, to place in Hell Francesca, Farinata, Cavalcante, Pier della Vigna, and even his fatherly friend Brunetto Latini. But he does not reprove and mock them ; on the contrary, he feels deeply for them in their torments, loves and admires them, and immortalizes their sympathetic figures in the episodes depicted. He does not conceal or excuse their sin ; but this sin is of such a kind that it does not touch their character. Other vices, on the other hand, according to Dante, affect the entire personality of the man, destroy human nature itself, and but rarely leave room for nobler qualities. These sinners are, therefore, detestable beings ; their case must be met not by compassion, but by relentless justice : here mockery and contempt are called for. With these the last two circles are almost entirely filled. We say "almost" advisedly : for even here there is not an utter lack of greatness in all the figures, and we cannot but admire the bold Ulysses, and sympathize with Ugolino, while he fills us with terror. Poetry revolts against the systematic strictness of logic. It is not a religious and philosophical treatise with which we are dealing, and the vivid imagination of the poet, in these portions of the poem as always, traverses the entire gamut of human feelings.

Dante's satirical power is at its height when he encounters Pope Nicholas III. among the simonists (Inf. xix.). The Pope is in a pit in the third *bolgia*, his head stuck in foremost, and his burning soles jutting out. Whilst he painfully moves his legs to and fro in the air, he has to listen to Dante's words of reproof and mockery : —

> Whoe'er thou art, that standest upside down,
> O doleful soul, implanted like a stake . . .

With these expressions of contempt the poet begins his discourse. He then compares him with a murderer, who is buried alive, and who, in order to put off his death for a short while, calls again for the confessor; the murderer is the Pope, and the confessor, Dante. But the bitterest mockery the poet placed in the sinner's own mouth, when he confesses in such a way that his words become a satire against himself: —

> Know that I vested was with the great mantle,

he begins; but scarcely is there time for reverence for the highest dignity on earth to be awakened, when he adds how he defiled it, thus changing the nascent feeling to one of loathing: —

> And truly was I son of the She-bear,
> So eager to advance the cubs, that wealth
> Above, and here myself, I pocketed.

This ironical allusion to the Pope's family name (Orsini), and the play on the word *borsa*, which, in its rapidity, has a sharp point, become all the more effective from the fact that he has to utter the words himself. Nicholas III. was dead in the year of the vision; but two other popes were still alive, whom Dante hated no less, perhaps even more, because they were his political enemies, the opponents or impediments of his political ideal, — Boniface VIII. and Clement V. By means of one of those astounding inventions, so many of which sprang from his fertile mind, he intertwined with this satire against Nicholas a satire against the other two. The simoniacal popes will all come into the same pit, and, coming one after the other, will force each other lower down. In this way it happens that Nicholas is expecting the one and prophesies the other's coming, whereby Dante again has the advantage of placing his sarcasms in another's mouth, thus adding to their power and effect. It is a worthy predecessor of theirs that speaks and foretells their shame. Pope Nicholas hears voices at the edge of the pit, and he immediately thinks that it must be Boniface coming to take his place and to push him down. This eager expectation of the other converts the prophecy into reality, and we already see Pope Boniface VIII., too, head foremost in the pit, moving his flaming soles about in the air. In this way Dante knew how to avenge himself and to deal out punishment, when he considered it just. But after the mockery he rises to a feeling of moral earnestness. It is no longer irony, but genuine pain that rings from his words: "Ah, Constantine! of how much ill was mother . . . ," and this holy wrath pleases his good guide, Virgil, who listens with approval to his disciple's words, and then takes him into his arms, raises him to his breast, and carries him to the top of the next bridge. That is just the reason why Dante's satire is so magnificent, because of the earnestness on which it is based. He is so bold, because he feels himself strong in faith. He does not attack religion and ecclesiastical institutions; on the contrary, he defends the Church against its false shepherds. He reproves the bad popes, but bows reverently before the Papacy, and deeply feels the shame brought on it by Philip the Fair, although the direct sufferer was one whom he placed in Hell.

From satire there naturally develops a comic element, which had its place in the old legends and in the French mysteries, where, after the gradual elimination of the moral intention, it gave birth to farce. With Dante laughter is still essentially an agent for punishment and correction, as in the former visions of Hell. The place for this comic element is the fifth *bolgia*, where the peculators are immersed in a sea of pitch. Here we have the scenes of the shade of the man of Lucca, which the devils are dragging along and throwing into the lake, and of Giampolo of Navarra, who deceives the devils themselves, whereupon they become entangled in a curious brawl and fall into the pitch (Inf. xxi., xxii.). These are humorous descriptions, such as we might expect at that time, rough and primitive in the expressions and images, now and again recalling the infernal kitchen of Fra Giacomino; but they are of a kind to become popular, and, in point of fact, the grotesque figures of the devils, especially, did become popular, — their names, Barbariccia, Libicocco, etc., occurring frequently in later Italian literature.

In the seventh *bolgia* (c. xxv.) occurs the description of the transformation of men into serpents, and serpents into men, which has always been admired as an extraordinary feat of the imagination. And such, indeed, it is. At the same time it appears to me that the effect does not correspond entirely to the means employed. This description is too minute to be fantastic, and the imagination demands greater freedom of treatment in the case of matters that entirely transcend the limits of the natural; being shackled by so many details, it remains inactive and does not really represent the marvel to itself, with the result that the effect produced is grotesque rather than fantastic, as is the case here. I do not mean that even such an effect is wasted; on the contrary, it is well adapted to regions of the comic and grotesque, like the *Malebolge*. All I maintain is that this transformation should not be given out as one of Dante's greatest creations. Farinata on his bed of fire, the celestial messenger traversing the Stygian marsh dry-shod, Pope Nicholas in the infernal *borsa* are splendid creations of Dante's imagination. The eighth *bolgia* (c. xxvi.), again, supplies us with a picture loftier in character, — Ulysses, the immortal type of man's thirst for knowledge, in whose bold voyage of discovery Dante has managed to express all the strange poetry of the sea.

The deeper we descend, the more crude and realistic does the style become: Dante does not hesitate to present to us objects that are ugly, and to call them by their proper name. The sojourn of the forgers in the tenth *bolgia* (c. xxix. *seq.*) is the place of the most loathsome things, of diseases, wounds, and stench, and the poet does not spare his colors; on the contrary, he paints for us, intentionally and with various images, the most disgusting objects. He also describes to us the quarrel between Master Adam of Brescia and the Greek Sinon. They come to blows and hurl vulgar imprecations at each other, so that Virgil is almost angry with the poet for listening: —

For a base wish it is to wish to hear it.

Further on even this ceases; every kind of movement ceases. In the ninth and last circle the very nature of Hell has become ice, and the sinners are frozen in ice. Here treachery is punished, the deepest corruption of the human mind. Against this blackest of sins the heart is closed, for these condemned souls there is naught but cruel hatred. Dante ill-treats them, and ruthlessly treads on them with his feet. Higher up he gave the souls promises of fame, in order to make them speak. But these down here do not wish people in the world to speak of them: they cannot expect glory, but only infamy. Accordingly, they do not wish to speak, and to say who they are; but Dante endeavors to make them do it by force, nay, even by deception. He finds in the ice Bocca degli Abati, who betrayed the Guelfs in the battle of Monteaperti. When he gives no reply to the question as to who he is, the poet's wrath is kindled: he seizes him by the hair, and begins shaking him so that he howls, with his eyes turned down (xxxii. 97). In this trait of savage cruelty towards the sinner, towards the soul abandoned by Divine grace, there is something magnificent in the very barbarism, that shows us Dante as the man of his age, with his pitiless conception of justice. But, none the less, even in the midst of this icy desert, here at the very end of Hell, where every feeling would seem to be dead, appear once again all the poetic elements that we found in such numbers in the upper circles. In the scene of Ugolino the entire poetic character of Dante's Hell is revealed again; it forms, as it were, a final synthesis of this Hell, with all its horrors and emotions. Never was a more terrible spectacle invented by a poet. Here Divine justice has made the injured one himself the instrument for punishing the criminal, and handed the sinner over to the man he has sacrificed, so that the latter may avenge himself; and Ugolino satisfies his boundless wrath by gnawing away the skull of his enemy, the Archbishop Ruggieri. But, on being questioned by Dante, this shade opens its mouth to speak, and tells us its story, — this, too, from motives of revenge; however, it is a story of tender feelings, which, being wounded in bestial fashion, have become the cause of this bestial revenge.

III

THE DIVINA COMMEDIA THE EMBODIMENT OF THE CHRISTIAN IDEA OF A TRIUMPHANT LIFE

By James Russell Lowell.[1]

Let us consider briefly what was the plan of the Divina Commedia and Dante's aim in writing it, which, if not to justify, was at least to illustrate, for warning and example, the ways of God to man. The higher intention of the poem was to set forth the results of sin, or unwisdom, and of virtue, or wisdom, in this life, and consequently in the life to come, which is but the continuation and fulfillment of this. The scene accordingly is the spiritual world, of which we are as truly denizens now as hereafter. The poem is a diary of the human soul in its journey upwards from error through repentance to atonement with God. To make it apprehensible by those whom it was meant to teach, nay, from its very nature as a poem, and not a treatise of abstract morality, it must set forth everything by means of sensible types and images.

> To speak thus is adapted to your mind,
> Since only from the sensible it learns
> What makes it worthy of intellect thereafter.
> On this account the Scripture condescends
> Unto your faculties, and feet and hands
> To God attributes, and means something else.[2]

[1] "Dante," James Russell Lowell. *Among My Books*, vol. ii.; *Literary Essays*, vol. iv. Houghton, Mifflin & Co.

[2] *Par.* iv. 40–45 (Longfellow's version).

Whoever has studied mediæval art in any of its branches need not be told that Dante's age was one that demanded very palpable and even revolting types. As in the old legend, a drop of scalding sweat from the damned soul must shrivel the very skin of those for whom he wrote, to make them wince if not to turn them away from evil-doing. To consider his hell a place of physical torture is to take Circe's herd for real swine. Its mouth yawns not only under Florence, but before the feet of every man everywhere who goeth about to do evil. His hell is a condition of the soul, and he could not find images loathsome enough to express the moral deformity which is wrought by sin on its victims, or his own abhorrence of it. Its inmates meet you in the street every day.

> Hell hath no limits, nor is circumscribed
> In one self place; for where we are is hell,
> And where hell is there we must ever be.[1]

It is our own sensual eye that gives evil the appearance of good, and out of a crooked hag makes a bewitching siren. The reason enlightened by the grace of God sees it as it truly is, full of stench and corruption.[2] It is this office of reason which Dante undertakes to perform, by divine commission, in the Inferno. There can be no doubt that he looked upon himself as invested with the prophetic function, and the Hebrew forerunners, in whose society his soul sought consolation and sustainment, certainly set him no example of observing the conventions of good society in dealing

[1] Marlowe's *Faustus*. "Which way I fly is hell; myself am hell" (*Paradise Lost*, iv. 75). In the same way, *ogni dove in cielo e Paradiso* (*Par.* iii. 88, 89).

[2] *Purg.* xix. 7–33.

with the enemies of God. Indeed, his notions of good society were not altogether those of this world in any generation. He would have defined it as meaning "the peers" of Philosophy, "souls free from wretched and vile delights and from vulgar habits, endowed with genius and memory."[1] Dante himself had precisely this endowment, and in a very surprising degree. His genius enabled him to see and to show what he saw to others; his memory neither forgot nor forgave. Very hateful to his fervid heart and sincere mind would have been the modern theory which deals with sin as involuntary error, and by shifting off the fault to the shoulders of Atavism or those of Society, personified for purposes of excuse, but escaping into impersonality again from the grasp of retribution, weakens that sense of personal responsibility which is the root of self-respect and the safeguard of character. Dante indeed saw clearly enough that the Divine justice did at length overtake Society in the ruin of states caused by the corruption of private, and thence of civic, morals; but a personality so intense as his could not be satisfied with such a tardy and generalized penalty as this. "It is Thou," he says sternly, "who hast done this thing, and Thou, not Society, shalt be damned for it; nay, damned all the worse for this paltry subterfuge. This is not my judgment, but that of universal Nature[2] from before the beginning of the world."[3] Accordingly the highest reason, typified in his guide Virgil, rebukes him for bringing compassion to the judgments of God, and again embraces him and calls

[1] *Convito*, Tr. ii. c. 16.

[2] *La natura universale, cioè Iddio.* (*Convito*, Tr. iii. c. 4.)

[3] *Inf.* iii. 7, 8.

the mother that bore him blessed, when he bids Filippo Argenti begone among the other dogs.[1] This latter case shocks our modern feelings the more rudely for the simple pathos with which Dante makes Argenti answer when asked who he was, "Thou seest I am one that weeps." It is also the one that makes most strongly for the theory of Dante's personal vindictiveness,[2] and it may count for what it is worth. We are not greatly concerned to defend him on that score, for he believed in the righteous use of anger, and that baseness was its legitimate quarry. He did not think the Tweeds and Fisks, the political wire-pullers and convention-packers, of his day merely amusing, and he certainly did think it the duty of an upright and thoroughly trained citizen to speak out severely and unmistakably. He believed firmly, almost fiercely, in a divine order of the universe, a conception whereof had been vouchsafed him, and that whatever and whoever hindered or jostled it, whether willfully or blindly it mattered not, was to be got out of the way at all hazards; because obedience to God's law, and not making things generally comfortable, was the highest duty of man, as it was also his only way to true felicity.

Perhaps it seems little to say that Dante was the first great poet who ever made a poem wholly out of himself, but, rightly looked at, it implies a wonderful

[1] *Inf.* viii. 40.

[2] "I following her (Moral Philosophy) in the work as well as the passion, so far as I could, abominated and disparaged the errors of men, not to the infamy and shame of the erring, but of the errors" (*Convito*, Tr. iv. c. 1). "Wherefore, in my judgment, as he who defames a worthy man ought to be avoided by people and not listened to, so a vile man descended of worthy ancestors ought to be hunted out by all" (*Convito*, Tr. iv. c. 29).

self-reliance and originality in his genius. His is the first keel that ever ventured into the silent sea of human consciousness to find a new world of poetry.

> L' acqua ch' io prendo giammai non si corse.[1]

He discovered that not only the story of some heroic person, but that of any man might be epical; that the way to heaven was not outside the world, but through it. Living at a time when the end of the world was still looked for as imminent,[2] he believed that the second coming of the Lord was to take place on no more conspicuous stage than the soul of man; that his kingdom would be established in the surrendered will. A poem, the precious distillation of such a character and such a life as his through all those sorrowing but undespondent years, must have a meaning in it which few men have meaning enough in themselves wholly to penetrate. That its allegorical form belongs to a past fashion, with which the modern mind has little sympathy, we should no more think of denying than of whitewashing a fresco of Giotto. But we may take it as we may nature, which is also full of double meanings, either as picture or as parable, either for the simple delight of its beauty or as a shadow of the spiritual world. We may take it as we may history, either for its picturesqueness or its moral, either for the variety of its figures or as a witness to that perpetual presence of God in his creation of which Dante was so profoundly sensible. He had seen and suffered much, but it is only to the man who is himself of value that

[1] *Par.* ii. 7. Lucretius makes the same boast: —

> Avia Pieridum peragro loca nullius ante
> Trita solo.

[2] *Convito,* Tr. iv. c. 15.

experience is valuable. He had not looked on man and nature as most of us do, with less interest than into the columns of our daily newspaper. He saw in them the latest authentic news of the God who made them, for he carried everywhere that vision washed clear with tears which detects the meaning under the mask, and, beneath the casual and transitory, the eternal keeping its sleepless watch.

The secret of Dante's power is not far to seek. Whoever can express *himself* with the full force of unconscious sincerity will be found to have uttered something ideal and universal. Dante intended a didactic poem, but the most picturesque of poets could not escape his genius, and his sermon sings and glows and charms in a manner that surprises more at the fiftieth reading than the first, such variety of freshness is in imagination.

There are, no doubt, in the Divina Commedia (regarded merely as poetry) sandy spaces enough both of physics and metaphysics, but with every deduction Dante remains the first of descriptive as well as moral poets. His verse is as various as the feeling it conveys ; now it has the terseness and edge of steel, and now palpitates with iridescent softness like the breast of a dove. In vividness he is without a rival. He drags back by its tangled locks the unwilling head of some petty traitor of an Italian provincial town, lets the fire glare on the sullen face for a moment, and it sears itself into the memory forever. He shows us an angel glowing with that love of God which makes him a star even amid the glory of heaven, and the holy shape keeps lifelong watch in our fantasy constant as a sentinel. He has the skill of conveying impressions indirectly. In the gloom of hell his bodily presence is revealed by his stirring something, on the mount of expiation by casting a shadow. Would he have us feel the brightness of an angel? He makes him whiten afar through the smoke like a dawn,[1] or, walking straight toward the setting sun, he finds his eyes suddenly unable to withstand a greater splendor against which his hand is unavailing to shield him. Even its reflected light, then, is brighter than the direct ray of the sun.[2] And how much more keenly do we feel the parched lips of Master Adam for those rivulets of the Casentino which run down into the Arno, "making their channels cool and soft!" His comparisons are as fresh, as simple, and as directly from nature as those of Homer.[3] Sometimes they show a more subtle observation, as where he compares the stooping of Antæus over him to the leaning tower of Garisenda, to which the clouds, flying in an opposite direction to its inclination, give away their motion.[4] His suggestions of individuality, too, from attitude or speech, as in Farinata, Sordello, or Pia,[5] give in a hint what is worth acres of so-called character-painting. In straightforward pathos — the single and sufficient thrust of

[1] *Purg.* xvi. 142. Here is Milton's "Far off his coming shone."

[2] *Purg.* xv. 7 *et seq.*

[3] See, for example, *Inf.* xvii. 127–132; *Ib.* xxiv. 7–12; *Purg.* ii. 124–129; *Ib.* iii. 79–84; *Ib.* xxvii. 76–81; *Par.* xix. 91–93; *Ib.* xxi. 34–39; *Ib.* xxiii. 1–9.

[4] *Inf.* xxxi. 136–138.

And those thin clouds above, in flakes and bars,
That give away their motion to the stars.
Coleridge, *Dejection, an Ode.*

See also the comparison of the dimness of the faces seen around him in Paradise to "a pearl on a white forehead" (*Par.* iii. 14).

[5] *Inf.* x. 35–41; *Purg.*, vi. 61–66; *Ib.* x. 133.

phrase — he has no competitor. He is too sternly touched to be effusive and tearful: —

Io non piangeva, sì dentro impietrai.[1]

His is always the true coin of speech, —

Sì lucida e sì tonda
Che nel suo conio nulla ci s' inforsa,

and never the highly ornamented promise to pay, token of insolvency.

No doubt it is primarily by his poetic qualities that a poet must be judged, for it is by these, if by anything, that he is to maintain his place in literature. And he must be judged by them absolutely, with reference, that is, to the highest standard, and not relatively to the fashions and opportunities of the age in which he lived. Yet these considerations must fairly enter into our decision of another side of the question, and one that has much to do with the true quality of the man, with his character as distinguished from his talent, and therefore with how much he will influence men as well as delight them. We may reckon up pretty exactly a man's advantages and defects as an artist; these he has in common with others, and they are to be measured by a recognized standard; but there is something in his *genius* that is incalculable. It would be hard to define the causes of the difference of impression made upon us respectively by two such men as Æschylus and Euripides, but we feel profoundly that the latter, though in some respects a better dramatist, was an infinitely lighter weight. Æschylus stirs something in us far deeper than the

[1] For example, Cavalcanti's *Come dicesti egli ebbe?* (*Inf.* x. 67, 68.) Anselmuccio's *Tu guardi sì, padre, che hai?* (*Inf.* xxxiii. 51.)

sources of mere pleasurable excitement. The man behind the verse is far greater than the verse itself, and the impulse he gives to what is deepest and most sacred in us, though we cannot always explain it, is none the less real and lasting. Some men always seem to remain outside their work; others make their individuality felt in every part of it; their very life vibrates in every verse, and we do not wonder that it has "made them lean for many years." The virtue that has gone out of them abides in what they do. The book such a man makes is indeed, as Milton called it, "the precious lifeblood of a master spirit." Theirs is a true immortality, for it is their soul, and not their talent, that survives in their work. Dante's concise forthrightness of phrase, which to that of most other poets is as a stab[1] to a blow with a cudgel, the vigor of his thought, the beauty of his images, the refinement of his conception of spiritual things, are marvelous if we compare him with his age and its best achievement. But it is for his power of inspiring and sustaining, it is because they find in him a spur to noble aims, a secure refuge in that defeat which the present always seems, that they prize Dante who know and love him best. He is not merely a great poet, but an influence, part of the soul's resources in time of trouble. From him she learns that, "married to the truth, she is a mistress, but otherwise a slave shut out of all liberty."[2]

All great poets have their message to deliver us,

[1] To the "bestiality" of certain arguments Dante says, "One would wish to reply, not with words, but with a knife" (*Convito*, Tr. iv. c. 14).

[2] *Convito*, Tr. iv. c. 2.

from something higher than they. We venture on no unworthy comparison between him who reveals to us the beauty of this world's love and the grandeur of this world's passion and him who shows that love of God is the fruit whereof all other loves are but the beautiful and fleeting blossom, that the passions are yet sublimer objects of contemplation, when, subdued by the will, they become patience in suffering and perseverance in the upward path. But we cannot help thinking that if Shakespeare be the most comprehensive intellect, so Dante is the highest spiritual nature that has expressed itself in rhythmical form. Had he merely made us feel how petty the ambitions, sorrows, and vexations of earth appear when looked down on from the heights of our own character and the seclusion of our own genius, or from the region where we commune with God, he had done much: —

> I with my sight returned through one and all
> The sevenfold spheres, and I beheld this globe
> Such that I smiled at its ignoble semblance.[1]

But he has done far more; he has shown us the way by which that country far beyond the stars may be reached, may become the habitual dwelling-place and fortress of our nature, instead of being the object of its vague aspiration in moments of indolence. At the Round Table of King Arthur there was left always one seat empty for him who should accomplish the adventure of the Holy Grail. It was called the perilous seat, because of the dangers he must encounter who would win it. In the company of the epic poets there was a place left for whoever should embody the Christian idea of a triumphant life, outwardly all de-

[1] *Par.* xxii. 132–135; *Ib.* xxvii. 110.

feat, inwardly victorious, who should make us partakers of that cup of sorrow in which all are communicants with Christ. He who should do this would indeed achieve the perilous seat, for he must combine poesy with doctrine in such cunning wise that the one lose not its beauty nor the other its severity, — and Dante has done it. As he takes possession of it we seem to hear the cry he himself heard when Virgil rejoined the company of great singers, —

> All honor to the loftiest of poets!

APPENDIX

APPENDIX

BIBLIOGRAPHY.[1]

I. Italian texts.

Tutte le Opere di Dante Alighieri, nuovamente rivedute nel testo da Dr. E. Moore. (The Oxford Dante.)

La Divina Commedia di Dante Alighieri, riveduta nel testo e commentata da G. A. Scartazzini. (Ulrico Hoepli, Milan.)

In the Temple Classics: Italian text with English prose translations on opposite pages, with maps and notes. 3 vols. Edited by H. Oelsner.

Opere Minori, with annotations and commentaries, by Fraticelli. 3 vols. (vol. i. Canzoniere aud Eclogues ; vol. ii. Vita Nuova, De Monarchia, De Aqua et Terra ; vol. iii. Convivio and Epistles).

II. English translations.

The Divine Comedy of Dante. Longfellow. (Hopghton, Mifflin & Co.)

The Divine Comedy of Dante. Cary. Together with D. G. Rossetti's translation of the New Life. (Crowell & Co.)

The Divine Comedy of Dante. Norton. (Houghton, Mifflin & Co.)

The Divina Commedia and Canzoniere of Dante Alighieri. Translated with notes and studies by Dean Plumptre. 5 vols. (D. C. Heath & Co.)

The New Life. Norton. (Houghton, Mifflin & Co.)

Dante's Eleven Letters. Latham. (Houghton, Mifflin & Co.).

Convivio. K. Hillard. (London.)

De Vulgari Eloquentia, translated with notes. (A. G. F. Howell. London.)

De Monarchia. F. J. Church. (Macmillan.)

[1] Only such important works as are easily accessible are given.

Canzoniere. C. Lyell. (Dante's Lyrical Poems. London.)
Eclogues. Wicksteed and Gardner. (Dante and Giovanni del Virgilio. Constable.)

III. Handbooks and other helps.

Dante. Gardner. Temple Primers. (J. M. Dent.)
A Handbook to Dante. Scartazzini, trans. by Davidson. (Ginn & Co.)
A Dictionary of Proper Names and Notable Matters in the Works of Dante. Toynbee. (Oxford.)
A Shadow of Dante. Rossetti. (Little, Brown & Co.)
The Study of Dante. Symonds. (Macmillan.)
The Treatment of Nature in Dante. Kuhns. (New York and London.)
The Great Poets of Italy. Kuhns. (Houghton, Mifflin & Co.)
The Teachings of Dante. Dinsmore. (Houghton, Mifflin & Co.)
Dante's Ten Heavens. Gardner. (Constable.)
Storia della Letteratura Italiana, Bartoli, vols. v., vi.
The Spiritual Sense of Dante's Divina Commedia. Harris. (Houghton, Mifflin & Co.)
Dante and other Essays. Church. (Macmillan.)
Italian Literature to the Death of Dante. Gaspary. (Bell & Son.)
Dante. Lowell. (Among my Books, vol. ii. Houghton, Mifflin & Co.)
Aquinas Ethicus. Translated by Rickby. (Manresa Press.)

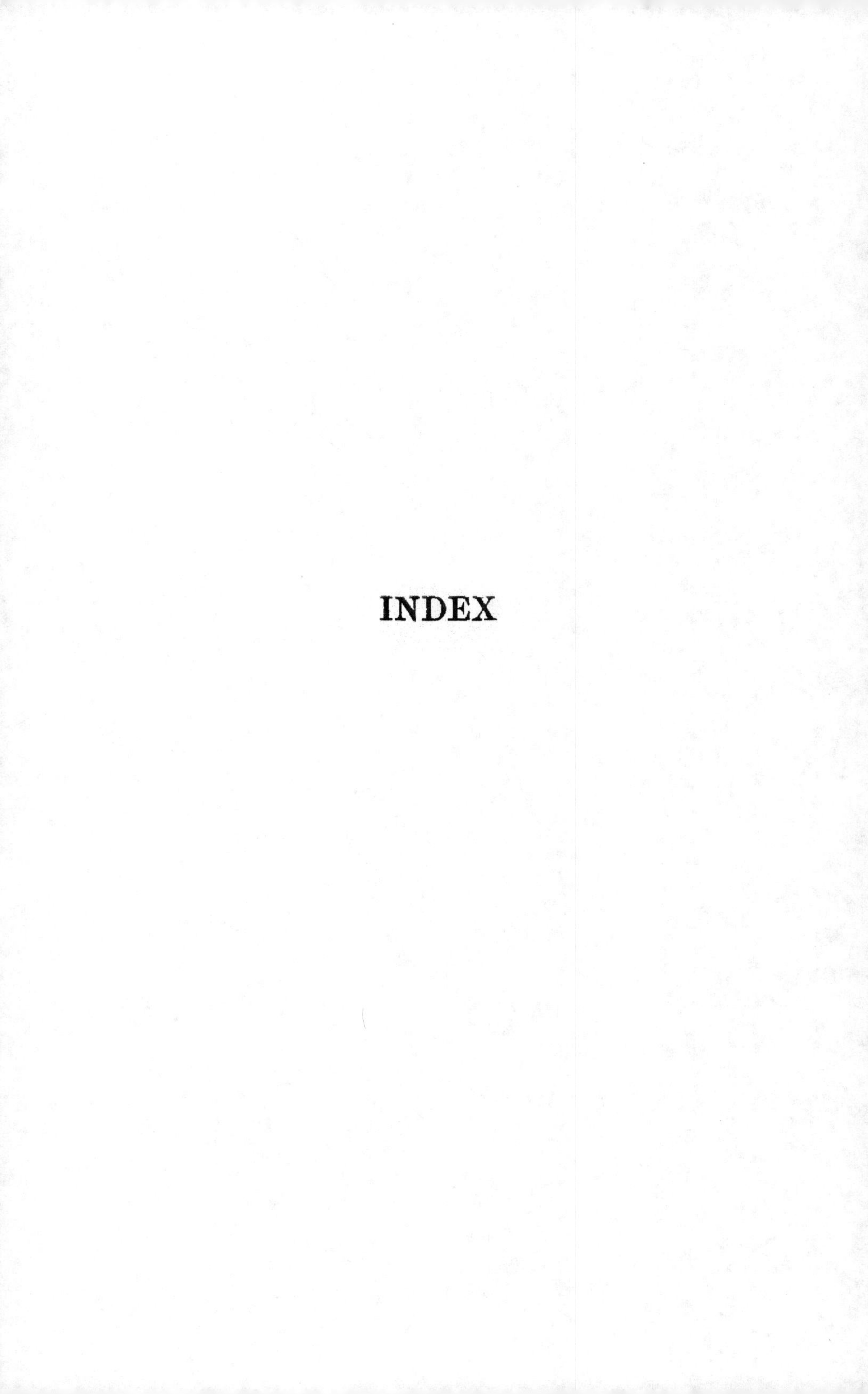

INDEX

INDEX

The Riverside Press
Electrotyped and printed by H. O. Houghton & Co.
Cambridge, Mass., U. S. A.

DANTE TRANSLATIONS

DANTE'S DIVINE COMEDY

PROSE TRANSLATION BY

CHARLES ELIOT NORTON

New and Revised Edition, from new plates

VOL. I. HELL. VOL. II. PURGATORY.
VOL. III. PARADISE

3 vols. crown 8vo, gilt top, $4.50

THIS new edition of Professor Norton's translation of the Divine Comedy gathers up the results of minute revision extending over several years. The translation has undergone many slight changes, which in the aggregate give a closer and more faithful reflection of Dante's meaning and a more rhythmic English version.

In its final form this translation of the masterpiece of Italian literature exemplifies Professor Norton's scrupulous scholarship, his high zeal, and his exquisite sense for language. Professor Norton's experience in his Dante classes has called his attention to the need of various new explanatory notes, which are here added. It is not only a model of accuracy and sympathetic imagination in reflecting a great poet's vision, but is in itself a notable contribution to literature.

DANTE'S NEW LIFE

TRANSLATED BY

CHARLES ELIOT NORTON

Uniform with Professor Norton's Translation of the Divine Comedy

With Notes. 12mo, gilt top, $1.25

MR. NORTON'S version is not only closer to the letter and spirit of the Italian, but also, it seems to us, more melodious than Rossetti's. The New Life is to the Divine Comedy what the Sonnets are to Shakespeare's chief plays; and we can but rejoice that through a translation so excellent a new generation of readers is to become acquainted with Dante's own story of his youth and passion. — *New York Post.*

Reprint Publishing

For People Who Go For Originals.

This book is a facsimile reprint of the original edition. The term refers to the facsimile with an original in size and design exactly matching simulation as photographic or scanned reproduction.

Facsimile editions offer us the chance to join in the library of historical, cultural and scientific history of mankind, and to rediscover.

The books of the facsimile edition may have marks, notations and other marginalia and pages with errors contained in the original volume. These traces of the past refers to the historical journey that has covered the book.

ISBN 978-3-95940-129-6

Facsimile reprint of the original edition

www.reprintpublishing.com

www.ingramcontent.com/pod-product-compliance
Lightning Source LLC
LaVergne TN
LVHW020646110826
845149LV00012B/1934

* 9 7 8 3 9 5 9 4 0 1 2 9 6 *